Flip Lipscomb lives in Derby, England, with his wife, Joan. He enjoys painting, playing guitars, and swimming. He practices Kung-Fu and has been a black belt for over twenty years. A keen interest in the Old West and traveling the western states a few times motivated him to write western novels.

Dedicated to the 393 Lipscombs who fought on both sides in the American Civil War.
And to the memory of Sergeant Alfred B. Peticolas of the 4th Texas Mounted.

For my beautiful wife, Joan.
"Loving her was easier than anything I'll ever do again."
– Kris Kristofferson

Flip Lipscomb

CAST A LONG SHADOW

A JOEL SHELBY WESTERN

AUSTIN MACAULEY PUBLISHERS™

LONDON • CAMBRIDGE • NEW YORK • SHARJAH

Ordering Information:
Quantity sales: special discounts are available on quantity purchases by corporations, associations, and others. For details, contact the publisher at the address below.

Publisher's Cataloging-in-Publication data
Lipscomb, Flip
Cast a Long Shadow: A Joel Shelby Western

ISBN 9781641829175 (Paperback)
ISBN 9781641829182 (Hardback)
ISBN 9781645366317 (ePub e-book)

Library of Congress Control Number: 2019939460

The main category of the book — FICTION / Thrillers / Suspense

www.austinmacauley.com/us

First Published (2019)
Austin Macauley Publishers LLC
40 Wall Street, 28th Floor
New York, NY 10005
USA

mail-usa@austinmacauley.com
+1 (646) 5125767

Chapter 1

Joel Shelby was standing halfway up a Ponderosa Pine, breathing heavily, perched precariously on a slim branch, tightly gripping the narrow trunk with both hands like his life depended on it. Which it probably did. His thick serape and pants were covered in prickly pine needles, which had attached themselves to his clothing as he had quickly scrambled up the tree. His hat, which had fallen off as he had climbed the tree, was snagged on a lower branch just out of reach. He gripped the tree with both arms wrapped around the slender trunk, coughing and wheezing from the quick climb that he had made, but mostly from the cigarette that he had been smoking earlier, which he had nearly swallowed as he fell from his horse.

The cold northerly wind, still blowing a frosty bite in the high country, blew into his face; and every time he opened his mouth to catch his breath, he was left gasping with the chill in his throat. His serape and pants chaps were flapping about in the wind like a two-masted schooner under full sail. He'd known worst days but this one sure took some beating.

I must try and give up the smokes, he thought to himself, spitting tobacco from his mouth. *Although I sure wouldn't say no to one right now.*

He had been on his way from the ranch near San Xavier, up to one of the line shacks in the foothills of the Sierrita Mountains, to tell his friend, Tex, the news of Pat and Charlotte's impending wedding at Tom and Alice's ranch on the Gila river, and that they had both been invited to attend.

Patrick O'Driscoll, the young Irish lad who Joel had met on the trail last year, was going to marry the girl that they had rescued, with the help of Tex and his friend Steve, from the Apache camp on the Salt River, and taken back to the Travis ranch.

Joel had been making his way up through the snow that was still on the ground in the high country in early February, minding his own business and daydreaming in the clear bright late afternoon. He had been thinking about Pat, the young Irish lad, and that it would be good to see him and young Charlotte again, and wondering if he had turned into proper cowboy yet.

He remembered how Pat had followed him from the wagon train, because he wanted to be a cowboy like himself, and how Pat had rescued him from capture in a small town.

Joel tended to let his mind wander as he rode along if he wasn't in too much of a hurry, letting his horse, Clover, travel at its own pace and chewing things over in his mind. It was something which he had developed from spending a lot of time on his own; mostly in the saddle. It helped to pass the time but meant that he wasn't always as alert as he should be when confronted by sudden danger, that was why he always liked to have a dog with him, but it had wandered off somewhere down the trail.

He had just reined in his horse so that he could light a cigarette, shielding his match from the sharp wind, when he had suddenly been startled by a big grizzly bear which he had disturbed. It had been digging up some roots to help fill its empty belly from its recent awakening from its long winter sleep. Joel had just put away his makings and made his way slowly through the trees when a sudden movement, about one hundred yards ahead, made him stop. A flock of birds suddenly took flight, frightened from their perches in the trees by a dark shadow moving below them, and with a loud roar, and a speed that belied its massive bulk, the large hairy beast was closing the gap between them fast. Joel had pulled out his pistol when he first saw the beast approaching and cocked it ready to fire. He had wanted to try and scare it away without having to kill it, but Clover, frightened by the noise of the wild beast, suddenly reared up on its back legs, making his feet slip out of the stirrups. He was deposited on the hard, snowy ground, making him lose his grip and drop his pistol which he had drawn at the first sign of trouble.

Landing heavily on his back, the wind knocked out of him, and not too far from the grizzly which was bearing down on him, Joel quickly struggled to his feet, knowing that his life would depend on his quick thinking. As the gap closed between them, Joel looked over to his pistol which was lying in the snow too far away for him to have any chance of reaching it, and Clover had galloped quickly away from the bear, carrying his rifle and bowie knife in the saddle holsters and his only means of a quick get-away gone.

Joel had quickly gotten to his feet. Well, as quick as a man with bruised ribs, a sore butt, and severely winded could get up. He let out a loud yell, making the grizzly bear suddenly stop in surprise at the noise, and ran for the nearest tree, holding his side with one hand, and managed to scramble a fair way up before the bear arrived at the bottom.

It was surprising how fast a man could move, even with sore ribs, when his life depended on it, Joel thought to himself, as he looked down at the bear, which was looking up at him, and roaring loudly. The bear, standing on its back legs, reached up and tried to bring Joel down, raking the tree with its sharp claws, just a couple of feet below Joel's long legs and dangling boots, as he struggled to get a decent foothold. Hastily scrambling against the trunk with his cowboy boots, he managed to keep just out of reach of the bear which was snapping some of the small lower branches off in its fury.

Joel wedged his shoulders between a narrow fork in the trunk, breathing heavily, his sore ribs aching, and looked down at the bear which was looking up at him with its mouth wide open and saliva dripping from its tongue and teeth, eager for him to be its next meal.

Joel's young dog, Ben, who had been off down the trail trying to dig up a gopher that he had chased out of its hole, suddenly came running up, attracted by the commotion, barking furiously when it saw the grizzly bear at the base of the tree that Joel had taken refuge up.

Joel had only had the dog for a few months, and it was not yet fully matured, but it was fast and vicious and always up for a fight. It had come from the same mother as his old dog, Snake, who had been killed by the Apaches the previous year on the Salt River Canyon. It was probably fathered by the same wild Coyote as Snake had been, as the ranch bitch tended to wander off into the hills every so often and come back in pup.

Back at the ranch old Stumpy, the cook, had been told by the ranch foreman, Briggs, to put the latest litter of pups in a sack and toss them in the river, but he had saved one for Joel to replace Snake after he had lost him, thinking it would take his mind off his loss.

Ben was a good hunting dog, brave and fearless, but not yet up to old Snake's standard of fighting. It had a lot less savvy than his old dog, and Joel needed a lot more time with it to train it properly to prevent it dashing headlong into trouble that it couldn't always get out of on its own.

Joel hadn't wanted to bring Ben along on the trip up to the line shack, as it hadn't been out this far before with him, as it lacked discipline, but old Stumpy had encouraged him to take the dog with him, saying that the journey would do it some good and be company for him, so he had reluctantly agreed and let it follow him from the ranch.

"Keep back, Ben, you damn fool," yelled Joel, seeing what the dog's intentions were, as it headed in the direction of the grizzly bear. "Don't mess with that big bastard, it's too much for you. You'll get yourself killed if you tangle with that beast."

Ignoring Joel's command, the dog kept barking and growling, moving slowly towards the bear, its hackles rising and teeth bared. The bear turned to face Ben, as it heard its threating racket, and as it moved away from the tree and looked down at the dog, Ben fearlessly launched itself in the air towards the big grizzly's throat. The dog landed with its front legs on the bear's large chest and fastened its teeth into the shaggy fur at its neck, trying to find its throat, as its back legs struggled for a better grip.

As Joel watched the dog's bravery, unable to give it any help, he remembered the last time he had encountered a bear. It was a few years ago and his old dog, Snake, had tried to defend him by attacking the bear, a smaller black bear, and the dog had got a good mauling for his courage. Joel had to shoot the bear to save his dog from the one-sided fight, but this time he was unarmed and perched up a tree and could only look on in impotent desperation as his dog took a firmer grip on the bear's neck, tightly fastening its jaws in its thick fur.

The bear, surprised at the ferocity of the small creature that had attacked it, angrily grabbed the dog's head with both of its massive paws and pulled it violently away from its neck, with a large clump of fur and skin coming away in the dog's teeth, making it roar in pain and fury. With the dog still growling, as the bear held its head in a tight grip, the grizzly shook it fiercely and, still holding it by its head with both paws, hit it hard against the tree that Joel was perched in, breaking its back and ribs, making it squeal in pain.

Joel heard the sickening sound of breaking bones as the bear smashed his dog into the tree again and winced at the thought of poor Ben's suffering, as it let out another sharp yelp of pain. The bear, tiring of the dog as it suddenly went limp in its clutches, hurled it away into the undergrowth and Joel could hear its whimpering as it hit the ground and lay there dying. Its breath came out in short quick gasps, and the cold air made it rise-up in small frosty white clouds above its pathetic crumpled form.

Joel had watched his dog's one-sided fight from the relative safety of the tree, and he knew that now it had finished with Ben, then the bear would turn its attention back to him, and start to climb the tree, when it realized it couldn't reach him from the ground. He tried to think of a way he could get back to his horse, Clover, which had stopped running a safe distance away from the danger, her breath condensing in the cold mountain air, as she stood nervously watching the Grizzly, ready to run if it came in her direction.

It was no good shouting for help from Tex, Joel thought, as the line shack was still a couple of miles away, and he would be sitting inside warming himself by the stove, oblivious to his friend's plight. He remembered what his old grandpappy had said to him when he had once caught him stuck up a tree, when he was a young lad, unable to get down and begging for him to help him down.

"Never start something that you can't finish, boy, and never climb up a tree that you can't get down on your own," he had told him and the old timer had then left him to get down, without his help, as he had struggled at the top of a lofty pine tree. But then the old timer had never been chased by a grizzly bear and had to seek safe refuge up one.

The sound of the bear starting to climb up the tree trunk broke into his reverie, and he tried to climb up higher, scrambling frantically as one of his spurs became embedded in a branch, as the bear clawed at his leather chaps, one of the bear's big claws tearing a jagged hole clean through to his pants, catching him just below the knee, and making him cry out in pain as he felt something scrape his bone.

Even in the chill of the high-country, Joel was sweating as he gripped the tree trunk a little tighter, and he could feel his leg starting to bleed. The sweat ran down his back, beneath his, shirt, and gathered at his waist, around the small of his back, before disappearing, like a small mountain stream, between the cheeks of his backside. It made him feel a mite damp and more than a little foolish. It wasn't fear, no he wasn't afraid, he told himself, but it was the closest damn thing to it. He calmed himself down and took a few noisy quick breaths, making him feel worse, as he tried to climb higher, his spur still stuck in the tree.

He remembered his old grandpappy telling him that in a moment of danger or fear the biggest mistake was hesitation so, regaining his composure, he pulled the spur free with a quick kick of his boot. He had an idea now that his head had cleared. The spurs had saved him once before, he remembered, in a much worse situation on the Salt River, when he had been captured by the Apaches. He reached down to unbuckle the strap holding the spur to his left boot, keeping well out of the bear's grasping claws as it roared at him, not far below. It wouldn't take the grizzly long to reach him, as it snapped the small branches which were impeding its noisy progress.

As he pulled the spur free from his boot, the bear, which had climbed a bit higher, started to reach up, trying to claw at his legs again. Joel caught a strong smell of coffee emanating from the bear's fur, as it tried to reach him, but thought nothing of it. He dangled the spur by its leather strap as the bear reached up for him and, pulling his legs up out of the way, he let it drop into the bear's outstretched, grasping paw. He had considered dropping the spur into the wide, gaping mouth of the grizzly but thought better of it as, with his present bad luck, the bear would have probably closed its mouth as he let go of it.

The bear seized the shiny spur as it landed in its large paw, closing its claws tightly around it, making the sharp pointed silver rowels embed themselves deeply in the soft fleshy pads on its palm. The sudden pain made the bear roar wildly, and it lost its grip on the tree as it tried to get away from the cause of its injury and fell the short distance to the ground, landing in a heavy undignified heap on its rear end, the sharp spur still firmly embedded in its paw.

The grizzly stood up on the ground, howling in pain and roaring madly, blood running from its injured paw and, ignoring Joel, it shook the spur free from its wound, making it jingle as it bounced off a nearby tree and landed in the snowy ground. The bear, now free from the cause of its pain, gave a mighty roar, shook itself, and ran off through the trees on all fours, ignoring Joel, and leaving a trail of bloody paw prints in the patches of snow to mark its progress.

Making sure that the beast had gone and wasn't lurking in wait for him, Joel climbed slowly, and painfully, down from the tree, pausing to retrieve his hat from a lower branch. As he leaned over to reach it, the flimsy branch he was standing on snapped and he lost his grip and fell from the tree, his face scraping down the trunk as he tried to stop his fall. Joel was deposited in a heap on the snowy ground, at the foot of the tree, landing in the same spot which the bear had recently vacated, his hat landing at the side of him.

He lay there for a while—his breath coming in short pants, his side still aching from the fall from his horse, and his leg throbbing from the damage the bear had inflicted on him—before deciding to get up and move on.

As he sat there, Joel picked up a clump of the bear's fur from the ground, which must have been pulled off as it lost its grip on the tree. He could smell the faint aroma of coffee on it, which he thought he had smelt earlier, as he held it closer to his nose. He shrugged, slightly puzzled, and tossed the clump of hair away.

Cursing profoundly to himself, Joel examined the deep scratches on his hands and face, caused by the fall out of the tree, picking bits of bark and pine needles from his lacerated chin. His serape hadn't fared too well either, as it had been torn in two or three places on the journey to the ground, and he could see fresh blood on his leather chaps from where the grizzly had nearly grabbed his leg. Dusting himself down, he hobbled over and retrieved his pistol, which was lying in the thin snow on the ground, and picked up his blood-stained spur from where the bear had tossed it in its mad dash to get away. Joel cleaned the spur with some snow, wiping the damp rowels on his serape, and strapped it back on his boot.

His spurs were sometimes awkward to walk in, and he had to make sure he didn't injure his horse, with the sharp rowels, when riding, but he was thankful that he wore them as they had been useful to him, more than once in the past, and he never traveled far without first strapping them on his boots. He was glad that he had called in at Billy-Bob Cannon's hardware store in Tucson before coming up to find Tex, as he had left one spur with Billy-Bob to be repaired and matched with another one, and had only remembered to pick them up at the last moment, before he left.

Billy-Bob had made a good job of matching the missing spur that he had lost on the Salt River Canyon, and although it had cost him all the money that he had, Joel thought that it had been well worth it when Billy-Bob gave them to him, as they looked like new, the rowels shining and jingling when he spun them round.

Joel went over to where his dog, Ben, lay and knelt beside him but could see that the poor mutt had died, so with a sigh he scraped a shallow grave out in the soft, top layer of the ground with a broken branch and placed him gently in his final resting place. He then covered him over with some larger branches, kicking the soil over the top, and placed some leaves, bracken and a few small stones over it, and stood up, carefully looking around for any more signs of trouble. He didn't have time to give the dog a proper burial and knew that the predators would find him later, but he had no other option than to leave him where he had died.

Joel examined the claw marks on his leg, but they were mainly superficial, with just one nasty gash that was deeper and still bleeding but would, hopefully, soon stop. His chaps and pants were torn in three or four places. The scratches on his face stung him a little, but he wiped the blood off his cheek with his bandanna, which he moistened in the snow, then he wrapped the bandanna around the leg wound, poking it through the hole in his pants.

He stood quietly amongst the trees, for a short while, listening for any sound of the bear returning, but he could only hear a faint roar in the distance of what must have been the wounded, angry grizzly disappearing through the trees. It had left a clear, and bloody, trail in the patchy snow, and Joel was relieved to see that it had not gone in the direction that he would be traveling up to the line shack.

Getting out the makings, Joel rolled himself a cigarette, his hands still shaking from his narrow escape with the bear, cussing as he spilled some of his precious tobacco on the ground. He leaned up against the tree as he lit his smoke, coughing and spluttering and taking long puffs to calm his shattered nerves, holding his pistol in one hand, ready for any more trouble, while he savored the soothing effect of the tobacco as he inhaled. Every time he coughed, it made his ribs ache, but he thought that they were only bruised and not broken.

Treading his cigarette butt in the ground as he finished his smoke, Joel quickly dusted the pine needles from his clothing, holstered his gun, and whistled his horse, Clover, which was quietly eating some fresh shoots of grass. Clover pricked up her ears at the sound of Joel's whistle, looked around and sniffed the air, and deciding that there were no signs of danger trotted over to Joel, who mounted her with a slow deliberation. The movement causing him to feel all his fresh aches and pains as he eased himself painfully into the saddle.

"Good girl," he said, patting Clover's neck to reassure her, as it wasn't the horse's fault that he had fallen off. Gripping the reins in one hand, he moved up the hill towards the line shack, holding his other hand near his pistol and looking around warily for any signs of the grizzly, or its mate if it had one. He didn't want to be caught out a second time so kept alert as he slowly weaved his way through the trees and undergrowth. The sky was beginning to turn a dark red and deep purple, the color of the fresh bruise that had appeared on the side of his face, and he wanted to get to the relative safety of the line shack before evening and the darkness came down, and it became too difficult and dangerous to travel. He needed to catch up with his old friend, Tex, and get some hot food inside him.

Tex had been up in the line shack for nearly a month with one of the other cowboys for company, a young lad of about 18 years old named William Brand. Young Billy, as the other cowboys called him, liked to be with Tex and never tired of hearing the Indian fighter's tales, and Tex never tired of telling them to Young Billy. Joel thought that by the time that he arrived, Young Billy must have heard most of Tex's stories more than once and probably believed them all. He caught sight of the shack up the hill, looking forward to seeing his old friend again and getting out of the chilly evening, and having a change of clothes and tending his aches and pains.

Joel holstered his pistol as he neared the line shack and gripped the reins with both hands, urging his horse forward with his knees.

Chapter 2

As Joel neared the line shack, he could see the smoke belching out of the old tin flue pipe from the stove inside and a flickering light showing in the small dirty window, from what must have been an oil lamp, and he anticipated the hot coffee and bacon when he got inside there. His serape was covered in a thin coating of frost, as was his hat which glistened from the reflected light from the window. He had brought along some provisions tied behind his saddle held securely by his cantle strings: some coffee, beans, and bacon. And the bacon was probably what the grizzly bear had caught a scent of when it had spooked Joel's horse.

Joel had also brought a small jar of corn liquor, which he knew Tex would appreciate, and he could hear it sloshing about in one of his saddlebags. He had already opened the jar earlier to take a good swallow of the fiery brew, after the bear had run away, to chase away the jitters from his time up the tree.

He reined in near the shack, shouting a greeting and, as he dismounted, the door opened and a familiar figure stood framed in the doorway, smiling, rubbing his stubbly chin with one hand, and holding a pistol in the other one.

"Well, if it ain't Joel Shelby," Tex said as he stood there in just a thin shirt and pants, chewing on a piece of beef jerky, as he grinned at Joel.

"Come on in and shake the chill of you, pardner." He looked up at Joel as the light from the open door shone on him. "You look like you've met some trouble on the way up here, the state that you are in, my friend."

Smiling, Joel went to his saddlebag and brought out the liquor jar, handed it to Tex, and followed him inside with the provisions and nodded to Young Billy who was standing near the stove warming his backside.

"Get away from that stove, Young Billy," Tex yelled to the young cowboy. "You'll have your pants on fire. Go outside and unsaddle Joel's horse, and put it with the others, and give it some feed," he added, playfully cuffing Young Billy around his head with his hat to help him on his way.

As Young Billy went outside and closed the door, Joel took of his frosty serape and put it near the stove to warm, and as the heat dried it out, it made the steam rise from the torn garment. He sat by the stove, rolled a smoke, and looked around at the small, sparse cabin. He had spent some time in one himself, a couple of years before, with Tex and his old trail buddy, Steve, and there wasn't much room in them, with just two bunks, a small table, two chairs, and the stove. They were mainly for two men and if a third was there, then the floor was a bed for the unfortunate cowboy who arrived last.

Tex uncorked the jug of liquor and took a long swallow and, with a gasp of satisfaction, replaced the stopper and wiped his mouth with the back of his hand.

"That sure hits the spot. I'm glad that you brought it, but what brings you all the way up here, Joel?" asked Tex, putting the liquor jar down on the table behind him and pulling up a chair next to Joel near the stove. "We figured on heading back down ourselves in a few days anyway, so there was no need for you to come and get us."

"Well," said Joel, enjoying the warmth from the stove as he smoked. "I heard from Tom Travis, up on the Gila river. He told me that young Pat and Charlotte are getting married in about a week or two, and they would both like us to be there."

"That sounds good to me," said Tex, picking up the liquor jar again. "As long as there'll be plenty of booze available, I'll be there." He paused taking a slug from the jar. "But I suppose it means I gotta have a bath, shave, and put on some clean duds for the festivities."

"Well you've got to look your best for the young couple, Tex. They don't want an old saddle tramp turning up at their wedding."

"I suppose not," replied Tex, spitting on the hot stove, his whiskey laced saliva sizzling as it landed and danced along the top of the stove like tiny whirling dervishes, and ran down the side of the hot metal, leaving a dirty brown stain in the dust that had gathered on the black surface. "And I ain't that old," he added, with a smile.

"I see you're still smoking them damn coffin nails then, Joel," Tex said coughing as the small cabin began to cloud up from the smoke emanating from Joel's cigarette. "They'll be the death of you yet."

"Well, a fella has got to have some pleasures in life," Joel said, taking another puff on his cigarette. "You like the booze more than most," he added, looking at the liquor jar back in Tex's hand.

"Well," said Tex, "between too much booze and just enough, there's a happy medium that suits me just fine." He replaced the stopper on the jug and wiped his mouth again with the back of his hand, a broad grin on his face.

Joel was happy to see his friend smiling again. Tex had taken the untimely death of his old friend, Steve, at the hands of the old Scalp-hunter, Sheep's Head, very badly. Even though he had shot Steve's killer himself, it hadn't helped him get over the loss. He missed the friendly banter and his dependability in a tight spot, knowing that together they could always get their way out of trouble. He had suffered bouts of black moods, sometimes taking his anger out on Young Billy, but he always apologized to the young cowboy later. His left leg had been giving him some pain lately, due to the cold weather in the high country, a legacy from when he had been thrown by a wild stallion that he had been trying to ride, and he suffered with toothache every now and then. The liquor seemed to have taken the toothache away, and he felt better for it.

The outside door opened and Young Billy came in stamping his feet and blowing on his hands, as he headed for the warmth of the stove, joining in the coughing with Tex, as he walked into the cloud of cigarette smoke. Joel thanked him for looking after his horse and made room for the young cowboy next to him, on the small bench, and Tex handed him the liquor jar.

"Here, Young Billy, have a drink of this, boy; it'll shake the chill off you and help clear all that cigarette smoke from out of your lungs. But don't drink too much, boy."

Young Billy took the jar from Tex, removed the stopper, and took a long swallow and started coughing and choking on the fiery brew, sending the contents of his mouth all over the stove in a fine spray. The flammable liquid started to catch fire on the hot surface, and Joel and Tex beat out the flames with their hats. As the steam and smoke cleared, from the result of Young Billy's choking, and the flames, Joel and Tex both sat there laughing as the young cowboy wiped his mouth in silence, turning a bright shade of red.

Recovering, Young Billy took another swallow from the jar but only a small one this time, letting the powerful brew ease gently around his mouth before swallowing it.

"Take it easy with that liquor, Young Billy. It's strong stuff and you'll end up burning the shack down at this rate," said Tex. "You need to grow a few more hairs on your chin before you take to the drink. Anyways don't waste anymore." He took the jar from Young Billy, before the lad could have another drink, and placed it on the small table out of reach.

"I reckon it'll put hairs on your chest, boy, but we don't want to get you drunk," laughed Joel as he undid the ties on his chaps, exposing the blood on his pants and the gashes in his leg showing through the torn garment, which were still bleeding.

"What the devil have you been up to now?" said Tex, looking down at Joel's leg as he took off his chaps. "And what have you done to your face? You look like you've been in one of those civil war battles or done a few rounds with one of those Galveston prize-fighters."

"It was a damn grizzly bear that I met up with on the way here," said Joel, examining the wounds on his leg between the tears in his pants. "It's a good job that I had my spurs on though," he added, telling Tex and Young Billy about his tangle with the grizzly. "But the damn critter killed my dawg, Ben. That's the second dawg that I've had die on me, damn it. But I wish that I'd still got my old dawg, Snake, he would have seen that bear off, no problem."

"I'm sorry to hear about the dog Joel. You sure have had some bad luck with dogs. About as much luck as I have with women. Old Snake was a damn good dog though. He got you out of many a tight spot, except that one on the Salt River."

Joel nodded to Tex, remembering how his faithful dog, Snake, had been killed by the apaches, and how he had only escaped in a heavy rainstorm and with a lot of luck on his side.

"Well I'm just gonna have to manage without one from now on. I'm finished with dawgs."

Tex nodded his head in agreement. "Well that bear you tangled with is probably the same one that tried to get at our horses a couple of nights ago. And it tore up our last sack of ground coffee that someone had left out the back of the shack," Tex said, looking over, accusingly, at Young Billy, who was busy filling the stove with wood. "When we chased it off, it was covered in the damn stuff."

Joel suddenly remembered the smell of coffee on the bear's fur and nodded in agreement.

"It must have been the same bear, Tex. I wondered why the damn critter smelt of coffee."

Joel finished his tale with Young Billy listening intently to every word, hoping that he would get to have some exiting adventures like Joel and Tex when he was older. Especially like Tex, who Young Billy thought must have been the best Indian fighter in the Southwest. Most of Tex's tales usually included his old friend, Steve Hurst, as they had spent a lot of time together in the past, fighting Indians. Young Billy had known Steve for a short time before he went with Tex to find Joel on the Salt River and met his untimely end at Painted Rocks. Young Billy never heard Tex's remarks about him leaving the sack of coffee outside for the bear to mess up, but if he had he would have kept quiet about it.

"I had to drive the bear off with my rifle," said Tex, recalling the grizzly that had tried to get at the horses. "I scared the damn brute, but I don't think I hit it. I reckon it'll be back again if it's hungry. I'll sure be glad to get back down from this wilderness and get some decent conversation," he added, looking over at Young Billy, who was still digesting Joel's tale about his run in with the grizzly bear. "It's all one way with Young Billy here. I get more stimulation and intelligent conversation when I'm out back feeding the horses. And this damn cold weather isn't good for my bad leg." He rubbed his left leg with his hand.

"Well, we'll head back to the ranch in the morning," said Joel to Tex. "That is if you'll be sober enough come sunrise," he added, watching Tex pick up the jar again for another drink.

"Well I can't wait to get back to the ranch for some home comforts," Tex said, pausing with jug near his mouth, about to take another swallow.

Joel laughed. "Don't you mean the comforts of Jeanie Eagle Feather Shaw's whore house in Tucson?" he said.

"That's right my friend," said Tex. "The comfort of 'Donna the Slut's' warm bed is top of my list when we get back."

"Why do you call her that?" said Joel, wincing at the way Tex spoke about the woman. "It ain't very nice to call her a slut. I thought that you were fond of her."

Tex shrugged his shoulders. "Well, she ain't never complained when I call it her," he replied, laughing. "I am fond of her. If I could only get her to leave that whorehouse, I'd make an honest woman of her."

Joel knew that Tex had a passion for Donna and would do anything for her. His friend visited Jeanie Eagle feather's establishment every time he was in Tucson, and Donna was the only girl that he would pay for.

Young Billy sat quietly listening, wide eyed, to the conversation between the two cowboys. He would often pass the whorehouse when he was in town but had never dared to venture inside. Some of the younger girls, who worked there, used to wave to Young Billy when he wandered by, and a few had tried to entice him in, but he would only quicken his pace when they called his name, their laughter ringing in his ears as he turned bright red.

"I can't get her to leave that damn whorehouse," said Tex. "And Jeanie Eagle Feather doesn't want her to go because she's the best-looking girl that she's got, and I sure don't want to get on the wrong side of that woman."

"That's true," laughed Joel. "I hear that she's part Kickapoo Indian, and they are a mean bunch of savages."

"You ain't wrong there, Joel. Why I remember a few years back, just before you came to the ranch, when old One-Eared Leroy Creed tried to climb out of the back window at the whorehouse. He had given one of the girls a beating when she threatened to tell Jeanie Eagle Feather that he hadn't got enough money to pay her."

Tex paused while he moved back from the heat of the fire. "Well, Jeanie Eagle Feather heard the ruckus and caught old One-Eared Leroy halfway out of the window. He took a swing at Jeanie, as she grabbed him by his pants, which he hadn't put back on properly in his rush to leave. She was too damn fast for him, and he came back to the ranch minus his left ear and part of his cheek all bloody. She threatened to take off his other ear if he didn't come back with the money that he owed her."

"So that's how he got the name 'One-Eared Leroy,'" said Joel, laughing.

"Yep! Jeanie Eagle Feather sure is fast with that sharp skinning knife of hers. I heard she fed old Leroy's ear to her two cats after she had sliced and fried it. He went back a few days later, full of apologies, with half of the money that he owed her, promising to give her the rest after his next pay day."

"Didn't One-Eared Leroy get trampled in a stampede up on the Brazos last year?" said Joel.

"That's right, Joel. He was stone deaf in what remained of his left ear, after Jeanie Eagle Feather had carved it off. He used to lie on his good ear so that he couldn't hear the other cowboys snoring, and he never heard the shout of Stampede." Tex paused with a smile, looking at Young Billy's intense gaze as he took in every word.

"We were all mounted and rode clear, but One-Eared Leroy was still asleep in his bedroll, poor sod. We found what was left of him later, trampled into the ground. Why he was flatter than a witches' tit when we went and picked him up to bury him."

Young Billy laughed uncontrollably at Tex's last remark. Tex smiled at the young cowboy and turned back to Joel. "When Jeanie Eagle Feather heard about One-Eared Leroy's unfortunate accident, she laughed, then she complained about the money that she was still owed."

"Well," said Joel. "Getting back to Pat and Charlotte's wedding, we've also got to call and see Father Francesco at the Mission in San Xavier and ask him if he will come with us to marry them."

Young Billy rustled up a meal with the fresh bacon and beans that Joel had brought with him, and Tex eventually put down the liquor jar and made some fresh coffee from the sack in Joel's saddlebag.

"I'll be fine now we've got some decent coffee again," he said holding the coffee sack to his nose and smelling the strong aroma emanating from it.

* * * * * *

"Here, Young Billy," said Joel, pulling a small bag from the bottom of his gunny sack, which he had brought some of the provisions in. "Old Stumpy made these especially for you."

He handed the bag to Young Billy, who quickly opened it and took out a cookie and bit onto it.

"He's put plenty of molasses in them 'cause he knows what a sweet tooth you have," Joel said, smiling at Young Billy, who was happily eating the cookie.

Young Billy thanked Joel, spitting crumbs out as he spoke, and walked away not wanting to share them, but not before Tex had gripped the wrist that held the bag of goodies and took two for himself.

"Don't be greedy now, Young Billy," said Tex, crunching on the sweet cookie. "You're supposed to share things with your pardners. Didn't I let you have a drink of my liquor earlier?"

Young Billy nodded in agreement, still crunching on the cookie, and reluctantly offered the cookie bag to Joel, who declined.

"No, thanks, Young Billy, I had a couple of those on the way up here yesterday. You enjoy them, boy."

After the meal, Tex lit the spare oil lamp and went outside to check on the horses, accompanied by Joel. The horses were kept in an open sided lean-to that had been erected against the back of the line cabin, with a rickety fence, made of trimmed tree branches tied together, around it. The shingle roof kept most of the rain and snow off the horses, but the wind blew through the open sides forcing the horses to huddle together at the rear, where Tex had tied an old oilskin, from the roof beam as a makeshift shelter from the elements.

"I see you're still riding Clover, Joel," Tex said as Joel brushed his mare down with some loose straw.

"She's a damn good cow pony Tex," answered Joel. "I'm sure glad we got her back from the apaches, last year."

"Yep," said Tex, remembering the shootout, and feeling his ear where an apache bullet had sliced of the lobe. He never did find that gold earring that the bullet had removed. They both laughed when Joel reminded Tex about the way that he and Steve had both shot the apache chief from his horse, as he rode at them with a spear in his hand.

"I still reckon I hit him first," chuckled Tex, suddenly lost in thought for his old friend.

After they had made sure that the horses were fed and watered, Tex picked up a long length of rope, which was lying on the ground, and attached one end to one of the timber posts that was holding up the lean-to roof and looped it around the other posts above the fence, about three or four feet above the ground. He then tied the other end of the rope to a short length of rope which was poking through a small hole in the cabin wall.

"What the hell are you up to?" enquired Joel, looking puzzled at Tex's finished handiwork, and examining the rope that came through the cabin wall.

"It's an early warning trap that I thought of after the grizzly came last time and nearly got in amongst the horses," said Tex, making sure that the rope was secure. "I've done it every night since it last came, and I reckon the critter could be back tonight now that you've gone and got it riled. The rope should warn us if the varmint tries to get at the horses again in the night. Come on inside and I'll show you what I mean."

Tex stood back a pace, looking pleased with what he had done, dropped a timber rail across the opening to the lean-to, and they both went back inside the cabin and closed the door to keep out the cold. Joel stood and looked at Tex, trying to figure out what his friend was going to do next.

Tex took the rope which went through the wall and gently pulled it tight, removing the slack, and tied the end to an old saddle that he had placed on the small table which he had placed near the cabin wall.

"If that damn grizzly comes, it'll get tangled up in the rope outside and then it should pull the saddle off the table and wake us all up," said Tex, placing a couple of tin cups on top of the saddle for added effect. "Well, that's if the damn thing works," he said, more to himself than the other two.

"Now, just you be mighty careful that you don't knock the damn things over in the night," he added, looking knowingly over at Young Billy, who nodded back at him, still munching on a cookie. Young Billy had seen Tex carry out this ritual before and doubted that it would work.

"Well, if the grizzly comes back, I hope this contraption of yours works," said Joel, laughing, as he placed his bedding on the floor, well away from the table with the saddle perched on the edge of it, and rolled his last smoke of the day. He borrowed a needle and thread from Tex and set about making a few repairs to his torn serape. When he had finished, he examined his needlework, which wasn't the neatest of jobs, and Tex laughed when he saw the results. It needed a woman's touch here, and Joel remembered, with a sigh, how the young Irish girl, Caitlin, had neatly mended his torn shirt when he had visited the immigrants' camp last year. He shrugged his shoulders at the memory and looked down at his sewing. It would have to do. He still had the garter which Caitlin had given to him when he had left her. It was now washed and neatly folded in his saddlebag.

Tex picked up his playing cards, a well-worn, dog-eared pack that he always carried with him.

"Fancy a game, Joel, before we get bedded down for the night," he said, shuffling the pack. "I'm fed up with trying to teach Young Billy here the finer points of poker."

"No thanks, Tex, I'm not much good at poker either. Save it for when you get back to town, then you can try and beat Billy-Bob Cannon. He's always up for a game."

"That no good cheat," laughed Tex, "I can beat him if he ain't using his own marked deck."

Joel nodded at Tex's comment then unbuckled his gun belt and put it nearby along with his rifle. He then removed his spurs and boots and tossed his cigarette butt into an old bucket near the stove. He took out a clean pair of pants from his saddlebag and changed into them and rolled up the torn and bloody pair to be disposed of in the morning.

He kept most of his clothes on, in case they were disturbed in the night, but removed his thick winter shirt and lay back, as Tex doused the oil lamp. Just the glow from the stove, which Young Billy had filled up with wood, cast flickering shadows around the small shack as it crackled and burned, keeping the three of them nice and warm. The only other noises were the whistles of the wind, as it found its way through the myriad cracks in the old log walls of the line shack, and Young Billy loudly crunching on one of the cookies, as he lay on the bunk above Tex.

"You can quit that damn crunching, Young Billy," shouted Tex in the darkness, poking the young cowboy with his hand. "Or I'm gonna climb up there and take that bag of goodies off you."

It all went quiet as Young Billy put away the small bag under his bedding and quietly munched the remains of the cookie in his mouth, enjoying the taste of molasses, but nearly choking on the crumbs as he tried to swallow. He stifled a cough and took a drink of water from his canteen, hoping that he hadn't disturbed Tex with his coughing. He had been on the wrong end of the Indian fighter's anger before, when he had been in one of his bad moods, but smiled to himself as he lay back on his bunk with both hands behind his head. He was looking forward to getting back to the ranch and enjoying some of old Stumpy's wholesome cooked food. He didn't like to tell Tex, who had done most of the cooking while they had been staying in the line shack, but the food that he had prepared had never been that appetizing. He savored the remains of the cookie in his mouth, sucking the crumbs in silence, enjoying the sweet taste as the warmth of the stove, along with the effects of the liquor he had drank earlier, lulled him to sleep.

Chapter 3

In his dreams, Joel was back on the bank of the Salt River, re-living his incarceration at the hands of the apaches and the severe storm that he had endured, one terrible night the year before, when he suddenly heard a loud clattering noise and was immediately wide awake, and wondering what the hell had woken him up. The stove had nearly burnt itself out so it was dark in the shack when Tex, who was also awake, struck a match and lit the oil lamp.

The sudden light made Joel aware of what had brought him out of his deep sleep, as he could see the saddle lying on the floor, with the tin cups nearby, which must have made the racket that had woken him. One of the tin cups was still slowly spinning on the floor, coming to a halt as it reached the saddle. He could see the saddle moving jerkily across the floor, like a young calf on the end of a lasso, as something in the lean-to, on the other side of the wall, must have been caught up in the rope that Tex had tied around the fence, where the horses were corralled.

A muffled roar and the sound of frightened horses could be heard outside the cabin.

"Yee-ha!" yelled Tex, with a wide grin on his face. "I told you it would work. Didn't I?" He picked up his rifle and looked over at Joel. "Let's go and get the bastard, Joel, before it gets at the horses."

Tex had already pulled his boots on and was making for the door with his rifle in his hand, as Joel quickly followed behind with Young Billy bringing up the rear, also clutching a rifle and stifling a yawn as he followed the two cowboys. He was struggling to keep his pants up as he went, his suspenders dangling behind him, as he followed the two men out the door.

It was a clear moonlit night, and very cold, as Tex and Joel went cautiously around to the back of the line shack. They could both feel the chill as neither of them had put on a warm coat in their rush to get outside. Joel had put his boots on but hadn't time to put on a shirt. He only had his thick winter 'long johns' and pants on and the cold air bit into him like a sharp knife. Their breaths were condensing in small clouds, as if they were both smoking one of Joel's stogies, as they hurried to get to the source of the noise still coming from the direction of the lean-to, at the rear of the shack.

Rounding the corner of the line shack, they were confronted by a large grizzly bear, which had smashed down part of the flimsy fence as it tried to get at the horses and was tangled up in the rope that Tex had rigged up. The three horses were crowded together in the far back corner trying to keep well away from the fearsome beast which was roaring angrily at them, which they could all smell and hear, and making frightening whinnying noises and stamping their hooves in blind panic, making the bear even angrier.

Tex put the oil lamp down on the ground. He could see well enough in the clear, bright, starry, moonlit night and cocked his rifle and fired into the air, hoping to frighten the grizzly away from the horses. The shot made the bear suddenly stop. It shook off the rope that was around its arm and the massive beast turned to look where the noise had come from, its teeth glinting in the moonlight, saliva running from its open mouth. It was clearly hungry, and the smell of the horses had brought it down from its lair in search of an easy meal.

Suddenly, Young Billy appeared out of the gloom and rushed forward past Joel and Tex, his rifle clutched firmly in his hand, towards the bear, which had shaken itself free from the tangled rope and was roaring loudly at the men. This was his chance for some glory, the young cowboy thought to himself. He wanted to be like Tex and Joel, and some of the older hands, and tell stories of his adventures. Sure, he was scared, but he wasn't going to let it show to the other two.

"Get back, boy," yelled Joel, seeing what Young Billy's intentions were. "Don't be a darned fool, you'll get yourself killed."

Joel cocked his rifle, but he couldn't get a clear shot of the grizzly with Young Billy in his line of fire.

As Young Billy approached the bear, he raised his rifle to shoot it but froze as the large, hairy beast looked down at him, dwarfing the young lad. As it stood on its back legs looking down at him with a puzzled look on its face, as if it were thinking that here was an easier option for a meal than the horses, it let out another loud roar. Before Joel had a chance to shout another warning, the grizzly took a couple of steps towards Young Billy, as he was about to fire his rifle with his hands shaking in panic and fear, and swiped at him with one of its large hairy paws. The blow caught Young Billy a glancing blow on his shoulder, sending him flying backwards with a scream, the rifle falling from his hands as he hit the ground hard.

The huge bear bent down towards Young Billy, intending to finish him off, when Joel and Tex both fired at the beast, both shots hitting it in the chest, stopping it in its tracks. As the grizzly bear roared and stretched to its full height, both large paws clutching at its chest, where the sudden pain had come, the two cowboys both fired again, this time hitting it in its head. The bear staggered back a couple of steps, holding its face, stopped for a second, and tottered forward again towards Young Billy, who was lying on the ground.

As Joel and Tex were about to fire again, the bear suddenly fell forward, mortally wounded, landing in a heap at the side of Young Billy. The bear's heavy weight sent bits of snow and pine needles everywhere as it hit the ground. Some of it landed on Young Billy, who was lying and holding his shoulder, sobbing quietly to himself, both with embarrassment and pain, as the bear nearly fell on top of him.

As Joel and Tex carefully approached the bear, both levelling their rifles ready to shoot again if it moved, its face turned to one side looking straight at Young Billy. It let out a strange snort from its nostrils, its last breath blowing out hot air in a small cloud towards the frightened young cowboy, and it died, one great hairy arm resting across Young Billy's lower leg.

"Well, I'll be damned. Will you look at this," said Joel as he knelt to remove the bear's heavy paw from Young Billy's leg, who was still too frightened to move. "I reckon it's the same bear which I ran into yesterday," he added, lifting its paw to show the still, bloody marks where it had grabbed his spur the day before. "And look at its neck," he said, pointing at a large patch of missing fur below the bear's jaw, its raw, red flesh showing through. "My dog, Ben, did that when he tried to help me."

"It sure is a big bastard," said Tex, looking down at the grizzly, its body still steaming from its exertions before it had died. "And you can still smell the coffee on its fur, so it must be the same critter that came the other night." Then, turning to Young Billy, who had stopped crying but was clutching his damaged arm, which was pouring with blood, and moaning softly to himself, he added. "What the hell was that stupid play for? You, young fool, you could have got yourself killed."

He stopped berating the young lad when he realized that he had passed out cold. With a smile, he bent over, moved the bear's paw from his leg, and helped Joel to carry him back inside the shack.

Once inside, they laid Young Billy on the floor and examined his wounds, cutting his shirt off to get a better look and delicately removing the pieces of torn cloth from his shirt that were embedded in his shoulder. There were three deep wounds running down his right shoulder all the way down to his elbow, which must have been caused by the bear's sharp claws, and Joel cleaned them up with some water and a clean bandanna. When he had finished, the best he could, the wounds were still bleeding, so Tex brought a needle and thread from his saddle bag and proceeded to sew up the deep gashes, but not before he had poured a little of his precious whiskey over the wounds.

"I think I'd better sew the boy up," said Tex, laughing. "I saw the state of your needlework when you mended your serape last night, so I don't think Young Billy would thank you if you did the same to his arm."

"Sure, you get on with it, Tex. It needs a delicate woman's touch."

Joel donned his shirt and serape while Tex attended to Young Billy. He was feeling the cold after being outside, so he stoked up the stove with a few small logs and stuffed his discarded pants inside to help the fire burn.

"It's a good job he's still out cold," said Tex, ignoring Joel's last remark about his needlework. "Cos, I reckon it must hurt the lad really bad, he's cut pretty deep."

"He sure looks in a sorry state," nodded Joel in agreement, looking down at the small figure of Young Billy Brand. "Why he ain't no taller than the summer corn, but as my old grandpappy used to say, 'heroes come in all shapes and sizes.'"

"That's true," Tex said as he finished threading the needle. "It'll make a man of him, 'cause what don't kill you will only make you stronger." Joel nodded in agreement, wishing that he had thought of that himself. Tex poured some more of the corn liquor on the open wounds again before completely stitching them up.

"Seems like a damn good waste of booze to me, but it should help clean the wounds," he said, taking a long swig of the strong liquor himself and handing the jar to Joel who also took a good swallow to warm himself up after being outdoors in the early morning chill.

"I reckon Young Billy has gone and peed in his pants with all the excitement," said Tex, looking at the wet stain slowly spreading in Young Billy's crotch.

"Well, he was lucky not to have been killed. I nearly filled my pants when I saw the size of that bastard grizzly back in the woods yesterday," answered Joel. "I don't mind admitting that it scared the hell out of me when it tried to get me out of that tree. I think I'd have done more than pee my pants if it had managed to grab me."

As Tex finished his needlework, Young Billy started to come around and, looking down at his shoulder with all the fresh stitches in it, he started to panic and breathe heavily, blowing out of his mouth in short, sharp gasps.

"Cut that out, Young Billy, you're going to be alright," said Tex, putting away his needle and thread and wrapping a piece of clean shirt that he had torn up, around the boy's shoulder as a bandage. He then fashioned a sling around Young Billy's arm, with the rest of the shirt, not telling him that he had used the young cowboy's own spare shirt from his saddlebag.

"You sound like an old man with the wet farts," said Joel, handing the boy the liquor jar and helping him sit up. "Here, have a drink of this. It'll calm you down. But don't have too much now. Remember what happened last time."

"I did alright out there, didn't I?" gasped Young Billy as he swallowed the liquor and handed the jar back to Joel, coughing and spluttering as the strong brew hit the back of his throat. He looked up at the two men standing over him and wiped his mouth with his good hand, as he smiled and waited for assurance from them.

"You did fine, boy," said Tex, smiling. "More than a bit damn risky mind, but now you'll have a lot to tell the others back at the ranch."

Young Billy sat up smiling at the thought, but as he did, he noticed the damp stain in his pants.

"Don't you worry now, Young Billy," laughed Joel, noticing the young cowboy's embarrassment. "We shan't tell 'em back at the ranch that you went and peed your pants."

"Well, I wasn't frightened out there," said Young Billy, trying to steer the conversation away from the unfortunate accident in his pants.

"Sure, you were, Billy," said Tex. "We all were. Show me a man that ain't frightened in a situation like that, and I'll show you a damn liar."

Joel nodded in agreement, and Young Billy felt all the better for Tex's reassurance.

Tex finished bandaging the arm and shoulder, helped Young Billy to get up off the floor and sat him down on a chair, and fetched him a clean pair of pants from his small pile of spare duds.

"Put these clean pants and underwear on, Young Billy, before you start to smell like the inside of a cheap whorehouse," Tex said, handing them to him. "But I'm afraid I had to use your other shirt as a bandage."

Young Billy looked down at the bandage and recognized his own shirt, as Joel helped him off with his pants, the movement making him wince from the pain in his shoulder.

Tex and Joel went outside to see to the horses and to have a look at the dead grizzly bear. As they went out of the door, Young Billy looked down at his blood-stained bandage and puffed his chest out a little. Not too much though, because the movement made his shoulder hurt again. But he felt more than a bit proud of himself and he couldn't wait to show the cowboys back at the ranch, especially the younger ones, his 'red badge of courage' and tell them how he had fought and killed the big grizzly bear 'single-handed.' He pulled off his pants with his good hand, shrugged out of his underwear, and stood up and warmed his damp private parts in front of the, now warm, stove.

"Now you stay put there 'til we get back, Young Billy," said Joel as he and Tex went out of the door, closing it behind them. "I think that you've had enough excitement for one day, and there isn't even proper daylight yet." He and Tex both began to laugh at the sight of Young Billy standing their half-naked, as they closed the door.

Chapter 4

Outside it was starting to get light, and it wasn't too far away from sunup, as the dawn chased away the gloom, so Tex doused the lamp, which they had left on the ground, and went around to the lean-to at the rear. Joel and Tex calmed the horses down, speaking softly to them and gave them some feed and water, replacing the part of the fence which the bear had trampled down in its effort to get at them.

"We'd better move this dead bear away from here," said Joel, looking down at the beast's large body. "The horses can smell it, and it will soon attract other varmints. I'll get my knife from the cabin, and we'll take some prime cuts off it first to take back to old Stumpy. The boys will enjoy some bear steaks for a change."

"That's a damn good idea, Joel, but we can use my knife," said Tex, pulling his sharp knife from his boot. He spat on both hands and proceeded to cut off one of the bear's large paws.

"What are you going to do with that?" queried Joel as Tex hacked through the bear's thick wrist bone.

"This should make a good trophy for Young Billy and make the others believe him when he gives them all the bullshit back at the ranch." He snapped off the bone at the wrist and dipped the bloody end into the dusty ground to dry up the blood on it.

"As long as he doesn't bullshit too much, like you," said Joel, laughing as he went back inside for his hat.

"That wasn't me, that was old Steve who did all the bullshitting," Tex chuckled, remembering his friend again, who had been killed last year at Painted Rocks, and giving a sigh and a nod of his head to acknowledge him.

After they had partly butchered the bear, cutting off some choice pieces—which they took back in the shack and wrapped in an old bed sheet—Tex laid the severed, bloody paw by the side of Young Billy, who was sleeping off his earlier escapade with the bear and the corn liquor which he had drank, snoring loudly.

"You can still smell coffee on that bear's paw," laughed Tex.

They both smiled at the sleeping boy and then went back outside and tied ropes around the dead bear's legs and proceeded to drag the carcass a good distance down the hill, through the woods, and away from the shack. They had intended using one of the horses to pull the bear away, but they had all shied away from the bloody remains and wouldn't go anywhere near it, so Joel and Tex had to do it the hard way and drag it themselves. Luckily, the going was down a long, gradual slope, but it was still hard work, as they seemed to get snagged on every small bush or thicket on the way down, and the bear was heavier than they thought, leaving them both panting and sweating as they paused for breath.

They could already hear the howling of wolves, or coyotes, not too far away in the woods, circling around them, when they both decided that they had pulled the bear far enough away from the line shack. They untied the ropes from the bear's legs and coiled them up.

Joel looked back to where they had dragged the bear down the hill and saw the trail of blood and gore that they had left, and the furtive shapes of wolves following the fresh tracks.

"I think that maybe we made a big mistake dragging the bear this far down here," he said to Tex, pointing at the wolf pack closing in on them. "Those damn wolves are following the scent, and I've forgotten to buckle on my gun belt, and I left my big knife back in the shack." Joel put his hand on his hip where his pistol should have been and silently cursed.

"Me too, I left mine behind while we were busy cutting up the bear, along with our rifles as well," said Tex, pulling his knife from his boot. "This is all that we've got to fight off the damn varmints with then."

They both stood watching as the wolves came nearer, with two of them eating some of the bears innards that had fell onto the ground, as it was dragged along, and at least five more were edging slowly towards them. As the wolves got closer, they were more confidant, probably realizing that the two men were no match for their pack, and they started growling, ready to attack. They were more interested in two live prey than one dead bear.

The nearest wolf, a big alpha male, who was obviously the leader of the pack, approached Tex, its muzzle wrinkling back, teeth bared, and growling deeply from its throat. Tex quickly spat on both of his hands and rubbed them together; a habit he always did before preparing for a hard task, or when he was about to draw his pistol. His old partner, Steve, always used to joke about his habit whenever he had seen him doing it.

Suddenly, the big wolf lunged for Tex, who raised his arm defensively and fell backwards with a shout, rolling on the ground with the animal as it tried to reach his throat. Joel started to go to the aid of his friend, who was still struggling with the wolf, cussing and shouting, as he kept it at arm's length, but another wolf broke from the pack and leapt at him. As the wolf jumped at him, Joel side-stepped and punched it with a sideways motion with both hands clasped together, on the side of its head, knocking it backwards and sending it yelping into the bushes.

Joel quickly turned back to Tex, who was just getting to his feet, having used his knife to kill the large wolf, which was lying near him on the ground, its fresh blood staining the frosty woodland glade. Both men quickly stepped back a few paces and moved away, as the rest of the pack leapt on their dead leader, tearing it to pieces, giving the two men a brief respite as they both backed away from the feeding frenzy. Tex retrieved his hat from the ground and backed away, shaking the dirt from it as he put it back on his head, his knife thrust out in front of him ready for another attack.

"As my old grandpappy would say, 'It looks like we are stuck between a rock and a hard place,'" said Joel, readying himself for another attack by the wolves. Tex gave his friend a mean look and wiped some of the wolf's blood from his chin with his sleeve.

"We ain't got time for that old fart's homespun philosophy, right now, damn it," he grunted, holding the bloodstained knife in front of him, as the wolves approached, and pointed it at them. "Just get ready for the bastards and save the smart-assed comments for later when we're back in the cabin. That's if we manage to get back to the cabin in one piece."

Joel quickly looked around him and picked up a piece of rock to defend himself with and stood near Tex, wishing that he had strapped his spurs on before he had come out of the line shack. They would have made a useful weapon against the wolf pack, he thought. He stood ready as he looked at Tex. "I'm sure glad we left Young Billy back up there, safe in the cabin. That boy has had enough excitement for one day."

Tex spit on his hands again and grunted in agreement. "Let's hope he has the sense to bury what's left of us after this is all over," he sighed. "Seems like I'm always fighting my way out of trouble when I'm with you," he said, looking over at Joel with a smile and giving him a reassuring nod. "But I suppose it beats being back at the ranch, riding herd, and listening to old Briggs moaning at us."

"Well, as my old grandpappy used to say, 'It's not the years in your life, but the life in your years that count.'"

"Will you give it a bloody rest, damn it," Tex said as he edged closer to Joel, standing shoulder to shoulder with him, as they both watched the wolves finish off their dead leader.

"I wish that I'd brought my makings with me," Joel said, more to himself than to Tex. "I sure could do with a smoke right now." He swapped the rock into his other hand, feeling the weight of it, and wondered if he should throw it at the wolves or keep it to use as a weapon.

"And I could sure use a drink of that corn liquor right now," muttered Tex, readying himself for the next attack. "I ain't never going to see 'Donna the Slut' again the way things are panning out. Come on you bastards," he yelled at the wolf pack. "Let's get this over with."

As the wolves finished ripping up the dead wolf, they began to move forward, readying themselves to attack, growling and snarling. Their fangs covered in their leader's blood, eyes glinting in the early morning light as they circled the two men. They were starving from a winter with very little to eat, and the meagre few morsels they had taken from their dead leader had done little to satisfy their hunger.

Suddenly, as the pack closed in on the two men, a shot rang out, and a bullet hit a tree near the wolf pack, chipping a lump of bark from it, and stopping them in their tracks as they prepared to attack. The wolves quickly recovered from the gunshot and moved towards Joel and Tex once more, just as another shot sounded, above the growling and snarling of the wolf pack. Whoever was shooting must have improved their aim, as one of the wolves was hit and fell to the ground with a piercing howl. Two of the younger, submissive wolves dropped their heads in fear, tails between their legs, and skulked away from the direction of the gunshot, glancing behind them as they went behind a tree. The rest of wolves panicked as another bullet hit and wounded one of them, and they all turned and fled away from the unseen shooter, disappearing through the trees, yelping and howling. The wounded animal limped and struggled to catch up with the others, as they left their dead companion behind.

Joel and Tex both smiled at each other, mainly with relief, but in surprise, as a figure emerged from behind a tree, and they both realized it was Young Billy Brand, as he stepped into the half light of the orange glow of a new dawn breaking, holding a smoking rifle in one hand. His bandaged shoulder was stained with fresh blood, where the stiches had come apart from his exertions. He was obviously in some pain but had a wide smile on his face, as he approached Joel and Tex.

"I thought I told you to stay in the shack and rest, Young Billy," said Joel, with a stern look on his face, as he tossed the rock out of his hand.

"Well, when I woke up, I could hear the wolves howling from back up in the line shack and wondered where you both were, so I thought that I'd better come and rescue you," said Young Billy with a grin on his face wide enough to make his ears wiggle.

"Rescue us!" Tex said with a laugh. "We were managing fine on our own, Young Billy. Why, me and Joel were just about to finish off the varmints before you turned up." He paused to spit out some soil that had caught in his in mouth when he had rolled on the ground with the wolf that had attacked him. "But thanks for the help, anyway, Young Billy."

"We ain't going to live this down, Tex, being rescued by a young sprig like Billy," said Joel, clapping the young cowboy on his back, and making him wince from his recent wound.

Tex bent over the dead wolf which Young Billy had shot and with a quick swipe of his sharp knife he cut off its bushy tail. "Here you are, boy," he said, handing the wolf's tail to Young Billy. "Something else for your trophy collection." He paused as Young Billy took the tail from him. "And thanks for what you did, boy, I reckon you'll be man enough now for a visit to Jeanie Eagle Feather's establishment, the next time we get to Tucson."

Young Billy laughed, slightly embarrassed by Tex's praise and his comments about the whorehouse and happily accepted the wolf's tail and examined it closely.

"I thought that you were a goner when that big wolf leapt on you, Tex," Joel said as Young Billy stood inspecting his prize.

"It'd take more than one of those varmints to see me off," said Tex, feeling the fresh scratches on his face from the wolf's claws. "Damn it! I always seem to get my face damaged. Last time it was my ear." He felt his torn ear, which was injured in a fight with the apaches the year before. His other ear wasn't too good either, which was why he had let his hair grow over them. "I don't want end up looking like old One-Eared Leroy."

Joel took the rifle off Young Billy, who was still busy stroking the wolfs tail, and they all quickly headed back to the line shack, keeping a look out for any more predators and looking forward to a good breakfast of fresh bear steaks before going back to the ranch. The first signs of the dawn fully breaking made Joel feel hungry after the mornings experiences, first with the grizzly bear and then with the wolves, so he quickened his pace back up the hill to the line shack.

"Come on, Tex. You never were that pretty anyways," Joel said, looking back at his friend, as he dabbed at the scratches with his bandanna. Tex laughed as he hurried to catch up with the other two, and he turned to Young Billy.

"I hope you ain't left that cabin door wide open? Young Billy. Or you won't look that pretty yourself, if you've let any wild critters get in there and get to our bear steaks."

"Erm, I don't think I did, Tex," stammered Young Billy as he quickly ran past the other two cowboys back to the shack to check for himself, with Joel and Tex laughing like a couple of young school boys, as he ran, clutching the wolf's tail in one hand.

Young Billy wasn't too sure about leaving the door open, as he had come out of the shack in a rush when he had been woken up by the wolves howling, and it was with more than a little relief, as he approached the shack that he found the door closed and the latch down. He turned back to Tex and, grinning, put a thumb in the air, as he opened the door and went inside the shack.

Back in the shack, Tex stoked up the fire, and Joel got out the large frying pan, lined it with grease, and proceeded to fry some thick, juicy, bear steaks for them all, while Tex put the coffee pot on to boil. They both looked around at Young Billy, who was taking a swig from the liquor jar, and both laughed as the tension left them both. Young Billy looked up at the two cowboys, wondering what they were both laughing at, and quickly put the stopper back on the jar and set it down on the table, thinking that maybe he shouldn't drink any more of Tex's liquor.

Tex took off the bandage from Young Billy's wound, which had started bleeding again, and looked at the stitches that had come apart. He ripped up another piece of Young Billy's shirt and re-dressed the wound.

"I reckon that's best left 'til we get back to the ranch, Young Billy," he said, tying up the makeshift bandage with a piece of buckskin and putting the sling back around his shoulder. "We'll let old Stumpy take a look at it." He looked over at Joel with a sly grin. "Perhaps, old Stumpy will have to take your arm off if it gets any worse."

Young Billy sat down, feeling sorry for himself, as Joel put a plate of fried bear steak in front of him.

"Cheer up, Young Billy. You'll live," he said, picking up a knife and cutting the meat into small pieces for him. "There, I've cut it up for you, just like your ma used to. Now eat it all up like a good boy, and we might let you have one of those cookies after."

Tex placed a cup of hot coffee down next to Young Billy's plate, and watched him eating the food with one hand, and winked at Joel. He resisted the temptation to have more fun at the young cowboy's expense and sat down himself to eat his breakfast. They were all feeling mighty hungry after their early morning's exertions.

Chapter 5

After a good hearty breakfast, they all tidied up the shack, Young Billy helping the best that he could with his injury. They put out the fire, closed the door, shuttered the small window, and saddled up, helping Young Billy to mount his horse. They didn't bother to lock the door to the line shack, just wrapping a short length of rope around the hasp, to keep it shut, as it might be needed by another cowboy looking for a place of safety for the night. They left most of the coffee, just taking enough for the journey, a goatskin of freshwater, and some logs for the stove.

Young Billy looked, and felt, a lot better after his breakfast, and with a clean pair of pants, and Joel's cleanest, dirty shirt on, he was ready for the trip back to the ranch to show off his trophies and tell everyone about his run in with the wild animals. He had wrapped the bear's paw and the wolf's tail in his slicker and securely tied it to his cantle strings behind his saddle.

"You're a proper mountain man now, Young Billy," Joel said as they rode down to the lower slopes. "I reckon we should call you Wild Billy from now on."

They were all in good spirits while heading back, especially Young Billy, who thought that maybe he had proved himself to the two older cowboys at last.

"We had better let old Stumpy take a look at that wound when we get back, just in case that old mangy bear had rabies," said Tex, over his shoulder, as he led the others down through the trees, trying to keep a straight face as he winked at Joel.

They passed the spot where Joel had encountered the grizzly bear, the day before, and he pointed out the tree where he had sought refuge and fought off the bear. He looked over at the small grave where he had buried his dog, Ben, and noticed that it had already been disturbed. The pile of leaves and bracken had been dug up, and he could see where something had been dragged along in the frosty ground, which was marked with a few paw prints, probably wolves or coyotes.

Not wanting to linger near the place any further, Joel urged his horse into a trot to catch up with Tex and Young Billy. The sun was coming up, and it felt a lot warmer once they had left the high ridge, and the snow line was behind them. He smiled to himself, as he saw Young Billy reach into his coat and pull out one of his cookies and take a bite. The boy had soon recovered from his run-in with the grizzly bear.

Back on the lower grass land, the three of them spent the rest of the day rounding up the cattle which had scattered for miles on the plains. There were about 60 of them, scattered in small groups, and they found four of the cows with young calves, which looked no more than a couple of weeks old. Another cow was standing forlornly in the sage brush, bellowing, and when they approached it, they could see that it was standing over a dead calf, which must have been killed by a predator in the night. The cow was standing protectively over its dead offspring and was reluctant to leave it. Joel moved it away with the help of his horse, which was well used to cutting out cattle.

They also rescued a young heifer, which was lame and must have lost its mother. Tex roped the heifer and slung it over the front of his saddle to take back to the ranch. Young Billy wasn't a lot of help, rounding up the cattle, with his wounded shoulder hampering his movements. Joel told him that he was about as much use as a one-legged turkey at a thanksgiving meal, but he was able to herd them on once Joel and Tex had bunched them into a small herd.

They made camp before nightfall by a stream, letting the cattle get a drink and settle down for the evening. Joel got a fire going, and Tex rustled up some grub. After the meal, Joel took first watch riding herd, although the cattle didn't look like they would wander far, it was always best to make sure that they weren't attacked by any marauding predators. If they were spooked by something in the darkness, cattle could run for miles before they were exhausted. Joel slowly circled the herd, playing his harmonica to reassure them. He was feeling tired himself after the long day, and he didn't realize he had fallen asleep in the saddle until Tex shook him awake and offered him a cup of hot coffee that he had brought over from the campfire. He reached up and handed the drink to Joel.

"Get this down you, pardner, you look all in. Get back to the fire, I'll take over riding herd. I reckon those critters are plumb fed up with that noise you've been making with that harp of yours by now."

As Joel dismounted and headed for his bedroll, taking a sip or two of coffee, Tex shouted after him. "Anyways, you'll be lucky if you can sleep while Young Billy is snoring."

****** *

It was late evening the next day when the three of them arrived back at the ranch near San Xavier, herding the cattle before them, and they were met by Briggs, the ranch foreman, who wasn't very happy to see Young Billy with his bandaged arm, which was still oozing blood under his shirt.

"What's Young Billy been up to now?" growled Briggs at Joel and Tex. "If there's any trouble to be found then you can bet that you two are in the middle of it." He turned to Tex, still looking angry. "I never should have let him go up to the line shack with you, Tex. How did he get in that condition?"

After Joel explained about the grizzly attack, Briggs calmed down a little and sent for old Stumpy, the ranch cook, who took care of the cooking chores and most of the shaving and haircuts for the cowhands, he also attended to a lot of the minor injuries that happened around the ranch, including pulling out the odd bad tooth when required.

Old Stumpy came running out of the bunkhouse half-asleep and not too pleased to be disturbed from his slumbers, as he had been preparing for the following day's breakfast and had not long been in his bunk, where he had been snoring like an old pig in its sty. He came ambling over, out of breath, carrying a large, flickering oil lamp and nodded sourly at Joel and Tex. Then he saw Young Billy standing, holding his wounded arm. He took one look at the young lad's blood-soaked shirt and quickly hustled him into the ranch kitchen.

Once inside the kitchen, Stumpy sat Young Billy down and removed his shirt and threw the soiled and dirty garment out of the open door just as Joel and Tex were entering. Joel caught the shirt in mid-air and looked at Stumpy. "Hey Stumpy, that's my goddamn best shirt that you're throwing about."

"Well," laughed Stumpy, regaining some of his humor, showing the odd tooth in his mouth. "I wouldn't brag about that. If that's your best shirt, I sure wouldn't like to see the worst one."

"You can damn well wash it for me later, Stumpy, 'cause I've got a wedding to go to soon, and I'll need to look my best."

Stumpy mumbled something unintelligible, his unlit pipe clenched firmly between the few teeth that were still in his mouth, and went back to Young Billy's injury. He removed the dirty bandages and re-stitched the wounds, where they had come apart, making Young Billy wince with the pain, as he poked him in the arm with the needle in parts that didn't need stitching. His eyesight wasn't as good as it used to be, and he hunched over Young Billy, squinting with his rheumy eyes, to enable him to focus properly.

While he was working on the arm, he had to listen to Young Billy's tales of his fight with the grizzly bear, which had sure got a lot bigger, and his rescue of Joel and Tex from the wolves, whose numbers were a lot more, and promised to take a look at his trophies the next morning.

Young Billy had soon stopped talking when he saw the size of the old cook's darning needle, which he brought out from a large sewing box, after he had removed the loose stitches from his arm. The cook sterilized the needle in some boiling water and, when it had cooled down, threaded it with some strong twine that he used for wrapping around joints of beef. Old Stumpy had to give Young Billy a shot of whiskey to calm him down, after Tex had told him of his recent liking for it.

"He's taken to the booze like a new-born calf to its mother's teat," he said, handing the jug to Stumpy. "But go easy with it, the boy's still growing. He ain't started shaving properly yet."

Joel and Tex, with help from some of the other hands, managed to get all the cattle into the stock pens for the night. They would be looked over in the morning and then let out to pasture. One of the older cowboys took the lame calf into the barn to nurse it. If its leg healed, then he would put it with the cow that had lost its calf, back up in the hills, and hope that it would take to it like it was its own. If it didn't recover, then it would end up in Old Stumpy's larder.

Old Stumpy was delighted when Joel gave him the cuts of prime bear meat, and he went and stashed them away in his larder, promising a treat for the cowhands at breakfast the next morning.

* * * * * *

The next day, Joel told Briggs, the ranch foreman, that he and Tex would be heading off for the wedding at the Travis ranch straight after breakfast. Briggs was not too pleased about losing two of his top hands, once again, even for a short time, as many of the younger cowboys had heeded the call and gone off to fight in the war, which was still raging further to the north and east. Most of the hands that were left were older men who weren't interested in going to war, a lot of them had done their share of fighting against the Indians, or down in Mexico, when they were younger. The rest of the hands were made up of a few young boys and three wounded men who had returned from the fighting and helped with the chores around the stables and stock pens.

Young Billy had proudly gone around the cowboys after breakfast, especially the more impressionable, younger ones, showing them his wounded arm and displaying his trophies. He held the large bear's paw in one hand, and the wolf's tail in the other, while they all listened intently about his fight with the huge grizzly bear and his heroic rescue of Joel and Tex from the pack of wolves. He left out the parts where he had fainted and wet his pants, looking over at Joel and Tex, who were both standing nearby, smiling, and hoping that they wouldn't mention them and spoil it all for him. He also omitted to tell them that Joel and Tex had actually killed the bear and that he had passed out when the bear clawed his shoulder.

"Young Billy sure tell a good story," said Joel to Tex, laughing as he rolled himself a smoke, as they both listened. "He could put you to shame one day with his tall tales. I reckon all that time with you up in the line shack hasn't been wasted on him."

Joel and Tex both left after breakfast, packing some clean duds for the wedding, and said their farewells to the other cowboys who were still around the ranch house. Young Billy came to see them off, still clutching the large paw that Tex had cut off the grizzly, which was starting to smell a mite rancid, but he still delighted in carrying it about.

"You take care now, Young Billy Brand," Joel said to the young cowboy as he and Tex mounted up, ready to make trail.

"Yep," agreed Tex, raising his hat to the young lad. "And thanks again for what you did back there in the hills. We owe you big time for that, Young Billy. And keep away from Jeanie Eagle Feather's whorehouse the next time you get to town. I don't want you spoiling the merchandise."

Young Billy grinned his wide smile and waved the two men off, feeling good after Tex's few kind words, except for the remarks about the whorehouse. He respected the Indian fighter and was pleased that he had been treated more like an equal.

"I could sure do with a good shave before the wedding." Tex said, stroking the black curly growth on his chin, as they rode along at a leisurely pace.

"You can always borrow the razor that Charlotte took from that bastard, Shreeve Moor, when we get to Tom's ranch," said Joel, rubbing at the bristle on his own chin.

Chapter 6

On the way to Tucson, Joel and Tex called at the Spanish Mission in San Xavier. It was a small Mission with less than a dozen monks living there and had been founded by the Spanish many years ago when they had traveled through the land, conquering all before them and spreading their Christian religion. A few small adobe dwellings had sprung up around the mission, inhabited by poor Mexican families, and a few down at heel local Indians, who all relied on the goodwill of the Friars for their livelihood.

The friars kept sheep, chickens, goats, and a couple of milk cows. The cows had been donated by the ranch, where Joel worked, along with an old bull. They also grew maize and wheat on the land, which was barely suitable for crops when the dry season was long. In good years, when the weather had been kind and the rain had soaked the land, they also grew grapes to make wine with. They also had a few donkeys and mules which they used for carrying goods from town, when they could afford to purchase things, although the locals in Tucson were always ready to help out and donate food and clothing for the Mission. The townsfolk all liked to keep a foothold in the Lord's house, especially the older folks, who had less time in the land of the living and hoped that their donations were a down payment for an easy passage into the hereafter.

Father Francesco, the Abbot in charge, came out to greet Joel and Tex, when he saw them approaching, shaking their hands firmly and offering them a drink of cool water from the well. Joel thanked the Abbot, who he had met before, and took a drink from the ladle which he offered him, but Tex declined.

"Perhaps, your friend would prefer a cool glass of our wine instead of water," Father Francesco said, looking over at Tex and smiling benevolently. "It was good year for the grape, last year, and we have a plentiful supply of wine in our store."

"Now you're talking my language, Father Abbot," said Tex, smiling, as he followed Father Francesco into the shade of the small adobe building next to the church. "I could sure drink a couple of drops of your wine."

You could drink more than a couple of drops, Joel thought to himself as he followed the Abbot and Tex into the wine store.

Standing in the shade, while Tex enjoyed a flask of wine that Father Francesco had given to him, Joel asked the Abbot if he would like to travel with them to the Gila River to perform a wedding ceremony at Tom Travis' ranch. The Abbot considered it for a moment then said that he was sorry, but he couldn't go with them, as he was far too busy with his work helping the poor people in the village and couldn't spare the time away from his flock. However, he said, they were welcome to take one of the other monks with them and their old friar, Father Benedicto, would be only too pleased to accompany them and perform the wedding ceremony.

The old friar came out to meet them after Father Francesco had sent one of the other monks to find him and tell him that he would be traveling with the two cowboys. The old friar came out of the living quarters, where he had been disturbed in his siesta, rubbing the sleep from his eyes and walking in a slow shuffle towards them. He looked rather frail, as he approached them, and must have been in his late sixties. He bowed reverently to the Father Abbott and nodded to Joel and Tex, waiting patiently for the Abbott to speak.

"This is Father Benedicto, my sons," the Abbott said, introducing the old monk to them. "His name means 'Blessed,' but we all call him Father Benito." He spoke in Spanish to the old monk, explaining that he would be going with the two cowboys to perform a wedding ceremony.

The small, stocky, old friar came over to them, walking with the aid of a stout cane, shaped like a shepherd crook, and smiled and bowed to Joel and Tex. The two men smiled back at him, Tex saying something to him in Spanish, and Joel turned to Father Francesco as the old friar went back to his room to collect his few belongings for the journey.

"Will he be strong enough for the journey, Father?" he said quietly, not wanting to offend the old friar. "He sure doesn't look very healthy to me, and it's a long ride up to the ranch on the Gila River. Maybe we should take someone along who is a mite younger and healthier."

"Don't worry, my son, you must not be fooled by appearances. He has the stamina of a young oxen, and he may well surprise you on your journey," answered Father Francesco. "He has been with us for a long time, and it will do him good to get away from the monastic life for a short time and step out into the real world. He has spent far too long in sleep and prayer these last few years, and the change may well revitalize him. I could let you take one of the younger, less experienced monks, but I think that you will find that Father Benito will be an asset to you on your journey and not a burden. He will not fail you; he has led a varied and diverse life before taking the holy vows."

"That's fine, Father, we'll take him then. We'll take good care of him and bring him back to you in one piece."

The Father Abbott smiled, more to himself than at Joel.

Father Benito quickly returned, carrying a small bundle with him that he tied to the rope which held the old, ragged blanket that was draped across the old mule's back, his means of transport for the journey. There wasn't even the comfort of a saddle for Father Benito to sit on.

They thanked Father Francesco for allowing them to take the old Friar, and Joel gave him some money to help the poor and needy, which he had collected from the other ranch-hands before leaving. In return, Father Francesco gave Joel two small jugs of wine. "Take this for the young couple who are to be married with our blessing." He made the sign of the cross to Joel and Tex and had a last word with Father Benito.

Joel thanked him again and put the wine in one of his saddlebags, and the two cowboys mounted up and both rode off, with Father Benito frantically trying to keep up with them on his small mule. He had a large straw sombrero perched on his bald head to keep off the sun, which was beginning to get a little warmer as the days grew longer. He urged his mule on, shouting encouragement to the beast in Spanish, his robes flapping about in the breeze—like a single-masted schooner under full sail—as the other monks stood in the shade of the mission building and watched them depart, waving and shouting encouragement to Father Benito.

Tex looked back at old Father Benito and turned to Joel.

"I can understand a little Spanish, Joel, and I reckon that Father Benito was swearing at his old mule back there."

"Well, I'm sure that God will forgive him," laughed Joel, glancing back at the old friar, who smiled back at him, sweat running down his face, as he tried to hurry the old mule onward. "I sure hope that we've done the right thing bringing him along, and that old mule is mighty slow. I reckon I could walk a darn sight faster."

Hearing the wine jugs clinking in Joel's saddlebag, Tex smiled and turned to Joel.

"That was kind of the Father Abbot to give us some more wine. It sure tasted good back at the Mission."

"You heard Father Francesco, Tex. That wine is a present for Patrick and Charlotte, so don't even think about it," said Joel.

Tex scratched at his bristly chin, as they rode slowly along, waiting for Father Benito to catch up with them. "Well, maybe they don't like wine," he said. "Anyways, the Abbot gave us two bottles, so I'm sure they won't miss one of them."

"No, Tex, forget it, you can have plenty of booze when we get to the wedding, not before. I want you getting there nice and sober."

"Yeah! Alright. I just thought that it might help with this damn toothache that's been giving me some trouble lately." Tex rubbed the side of his chin, trying to elicit some sympathy from Joel.

"Well, you should have let old Stumpy have a look at it before we left the ranch. He'd have probably pulled it out for you."

Tex winced at Joel's remark and pulled out his liquor jar and took a long drink of the firewater, letting it swill around his gums before he swallowed it. He spat some of the liquor out of his mouth, some of it spattering his horse's ear, and replaced the jar in his saddlebag.

"I wouldn't let old Stumpy near my mouth," Tex said, looking around to see if Father Benito was catching up with them. "The old timer needs a pair of spectacles. Did you see the way he re-stitched Young Billy's shoulder? He kept poking the needle in the wrong place. No wonder Young Billy was complaining. He looked like he'd got on the wrong side of a porcupine, with all the holes in his flesh."

Tex said something in Spanish to the old Friar which made him try to get the old mule to go at a faster pace, but it just kept plodding along at the same rate.

The journey from the Mission to Tucson wasn't very far, but it took a while to get there, as Joel and Tex had to keep stopping to help Father Benito move his stubborn old mule along. The more the old Friar hit it with his stick the less it wanted to carry on, and it was only by one of the cowboys riding in front of it and enticing it along with some carrots, that Father Benito had brought with him for the mule, that they were able to make any progress at all.

Chapter 7

Arriving in Tucson, Joel and Tex went into the hardware store, leaving Father Benito sitting outside on his mule. As they went in to the store, Joel looked back at the old friar, who had removed his hat and was mopping his sweaty forehead and tonsure with a large bandanna that he had pulled out of his voluminous robes.

"We've got to get the friar a better mount, or we ain't never going to the wedding on time, the speed that he travels on that old mule," he said to Tex as he struck a match on the store counter and lit a stogie. Tex nodded in agreement, as he followed Joel into the hardware store.

"By the time we get to Tom's place, I reckon Father Benito will be able to baptize their first born, the pace that mule travels."

Billy-Bob Cannon, the proprietor, looked up with a smile as the two men walked in. He was always pleased to see them both, especially if it meant making a good profit. He quickly pulled a cloth from his apron pocket and wiped the mark that Joel had made on his counter with his match. His wife, Julie, had polished the counter tops earlier, and he didn't want her to see the mess that Joel had done to her handiwork.

Billy-Bob inhaled the smoke from Joel's stogie, the smell making him want to go and get one of his own smokes from his secret stash, but his wife was in the store, so he suppressed the craving and sucked on a boiled sweet that he had in his apron pocket.

"Howdy boys," said Billy-Bob. "What can I do for you two cowboys on this fine day?"

"I came for that marker plate that you were making for me, for Steve's grave," said Tex. "I hope it's ready 'cause I already paid you for it last year."

"Yep, it's ready, Tex," said Billy-Bob, walking a little stiffly out to the back of the store to his workroom. His bad leg played up these fresh, chill mornings. He soon returned with the plate, wrapped in a cloth, placed it on the counter, and unwrapped it for Tex to examine.

"That sure looks fine to me," Tex said, picking up the shiny brass plate and holding it at arm's length, to see it better. He breathed on the plate, over the words that were etched deeply into it, and gave it a polish with his shirtsleeve. "Old Steve sure will like this. Thanks a lot, Billy-Bob, I sure appreciate the work that you've put into it."

Billy-Bob knew how close Tex and Steve had been, and he could see that Tex was moved on seeing his dead friend's name on the plate. He was nearly tempted to give Tex the money back that he had paid him to carry out the work, but the sudden moment of compassion quickly passed, and he suppressed the thought before he lost a profit. With a mental shrug of his shoulders, Billy-Bob re-wrapped the plate, neatly tied it up with some string, and handed it back to Tex.

"Who's the old fella sitting out there on the mule?" Billy-Bob said, looking at Father Benito through the store window. "I saw you both ride in with him and thought that he didn't look like one of the usual cut-throats that you both usually hang around with."

Ignoring the last remark, Joel inhaled on his stogie, took it out of his mouth, and blew a perfect smoke ring at the storekeeper, watching it slowly dissipate as it reached him. Billy-Bob wafted the smoke away, as Tex told him that they were heading up to the Gila River, to Tom Travis' ranch, for a wedding, and the old Friar was going to conduct the ceremony.

The retired Texas Ranger leaned closer to the two cowboys, placing the back of his hand to his face, and whispered, conspiratorially, through the side of his mouth, not wanting his wife, Julie, to hear him. "Don't you forget now, boys," he said quietly. He paused for a second and looked over to his wife, who was filling one of the shelves, too far away to catch the softly spoken words of his well-used mantra. "If you ever need an experienced man with a gun on one of your expeditions, then I'm your man."

He brushed his mustache with his finger and thumb and winked at them both.

"Sure, Billy-Bob," Joel said. "We'll bear that in mind, but we're only going to a wedding, not shoot-out."

They thanked Billy-Bob and headed for the door, both saying goodbye to Julie Cannon, who waved to them.

As they both went out of the store, Joel's spurs jingling as he walked, Billy-Bob shouted after them. "Now don't forget what I said boys," he said, tapping the side of his nose with his forefinger and giving them another sly wink.

Billy-Bob's wife, Julie, stopped filling the shelf and looked over at her husband, hearing perfectly everything he had said to Joel and Tex. She knew that her husband hankered after his old life, chasing outlaws on the border country, and caught his eye and sighed, and turned back to what she had been doing. Julie was dressed primly in a long sleeved, baggy, shapeless blouse, buttoned up to her neck, and a skirt reaching down to the floor. It was a far cry from when Billy-Bob had first met her in the local saloon, when she had been dealing poker, and she had been dressed in a low-cut blouse, and a split skirt showing her shapely, stocking clad legs; a style of dress that the customers used to call 'low and behold.'

She too sometimes hankered after her old life but never mentioned it to her husband, as she was now content with her present life with him and their twin girls, Chloe and Molly.

Billy-Bob smiled at Julie, as she went back to her shelf stacking. He too was happy with his lot, but there was still that itch that needed to be scratched, a need for a bit of excitement in his humdrum life, running the store. His hand felt the belt buckle below his apron, and he sighed. He was proud of his old belt buckle with the Texas Rangers insignia engraved on it, as it was presented to him by the legendary Texas Ranger, Captain Rip Ford.

After leaving Billy-Bob's store, Joel and Tex took Father Benito over to the stables and—after some hard bargaining with the proprietor and more than a few threats from Tex—they managed to trade his little old mule for a horse, and for a few extra dollars, he let them have an old saddle and reins. The horse looked like its best days were way behind it, but it would get the old friar up to Tom's ranch a lot quicker than the mule, and the saddle would give him some extra comfort.

Father Benito thanked Joel and Tex for their kindness, blessing them both with the sign of the cross. He placed all his gear in the saddlebags and, with some help from Tex, mounted his new horse, which was a lot taller than the old mule, and tried out his new steed around the stable yard at the rear. He liked the feel of a saddle after sitting on the old mule's blanket, and being on a horse brought back distant memories of a time long past, making him sit upright in the saddle, reins in one hand and holding his staff in the other.

"Will you look at the old duffer, Joel," Tex said, laughing at how Father Benito rode the horse. "He looks like a regular cavalry officer the way he sits that horse, and he holds his staff like it was a sword."

They both stood watching Father Benito, as he handled the horse like he had been born to it, laughing as the old Friar raised his staff above his head, with both hands, and steered the horse with his knees as it circled the small corral. He was soon tired, and Joel and Tex helped him down from the horse and helped him to tether it up with their own mounts.

"You rode that horse pretty good, Father," said Joel, clapping him on his back and making the dust rise from his well-worn robes. "I don't think it's the first time that you've rode a horse like that."

Father Benito just looked up at Joel and smiled at him, as they walked into the street.

Before they left Tucson, Joel and Tex looked in on Marshall Tucker, at the jail house, to enquire about the albino, Shreeve Moor, and the other prisoner. They were both still behind bars in one of the small cells at the rear, and 'The Butcher' Moor, visibly flinched when he saw the two cowboys standing on the other side of the cell door looking at him. He backed away to the far wall, his shifty eyes darting about, and a tic appeared in one of his eyes as he recognized the two men, remembering how they had captured him at Painted Rocks. His bottom lip had swollen up, brought on by the nervous complaint that he suffered from.

"He looks like one of those cut-throat trout with that swollen lip," said Joel, to Tex. They both laughed at the albino as they approached the bars of his cell.

"Keep away from me, you bastards," yelled Shreeve Moor, his gaunt features looking even paler in the far dark corner of the cell, where he had retreated to. "When I get out of here, I'm gonna take your god-damn ears off. Both of you," he shouted in his squeaky voice, his word fading as Tex leaned towards the bars, giving him one of his hard looks.

"He's already threatened to do that to old Snowy, one of our deputies," said the Marshall, standing behind the two cowboys, as Joel blew the smoke from his stogie through the bars at Shreeve Moor. Snowy, standing at the side of the Marshall, nodded his agreement, as he watched in amusement as the smoke from Joel's cigar gathered around the albino's face and lingered in the few strands of pure white hair that remained on his pock marked scalp.

"Don't you forget what we did to that old bastard Sheep's Head, you sniveling little toad," said Joel, staring through the bars at the albino, his cigar butt clenched firmly between his teeth. Without another word, Joel and Tex turned and walked back into the Marshall's office, as the weasel faced albino, Shreeve Moor, started to have a coughing fit, brought on by Joel's cigar smoke that still hovered in an acrid cloud in the confined space of the small cell.

As the adjoining door closed behind them, they could hear Shreeve Moor still coughing and yelling threats at them. "I'll get both of you bastards when I get out of here. I'll make you both pay. Just you wait and see," he shouted, between coughs, his voice muffled by the thick wooden door, as Snowy closed it behind them.

"I'll bet that albino ain't got many friends, the way that he carries on," said Tex, laughing.

"The Circuit Judge should be around in a week or two," said the Marshall, putting his rifle back on the gun rack. He didn't like to take risks when he was around Shreeve Moor. "Then he can have a fair trial, and after that we'll hang the bastard. And I sure won't be sorry to see the back of him. We've had him here long enough."

"Well, we should, hopefully, be back from the wedding before he has his neck stretched," said Joel, thanking the Marshall as they headed for the front door. "We wouldn't want to miss him doing the 'Wichita Two Step' at the end of a noose."

"Yep," agreed Tex. "We sure don't want to miss that neck-tie party."

They both walked out on to the street, where Father Benito now sat in the shade of the overhang, where he had dismounted, waiting patiently for the two cowboys, puffing away on his old clay pipe, as he said a few prayers, one hand holding his rosary beads as he fingered them. He looked up from his silent litany, as he heard Joel's spurs jingling, and he finished his devotions, putting his rosary back into his robes, and slowly got to his feet. He knocked the ash from his pipe and placed the still smoldering pipe inside his robes.

"I should save some of your prayers for that albino back in the jail," Tex said to Father Benito. "I reckon that, pretty soon, he's going to need all the help he can get from the Almighty."

The old friar smiled at Tex, not sure what the Indian Fighter meant by his remark, as he patted at his robe where a spark from his pipe had nearly set it on fire. A closer inspection of Father Benito's baggy robes would have shown quite a few scorch marks on the brown material, which had appeared over the years. Testament to his habit of putting his pipe away before properly putting it out.

Father Benito followed the two men, as they untied their horses from the hitching rail. He hoisted his robes up and struggled to mount his newly purchased steed. It was a lot higher than the old mule that he was used to riding, and it looked a long way down to the ground when he was sitting nervously in the saddle, holding the reins, with his sandaled feet in the stirrups, but it was preferable to the old mule.

As they mounted up, Tex looked across the street at the whorehouse, where Jeanie Eagle Feather Shaw, the proprietor, was standing outside the entrance, puffing away on her pipe, as she leaned against a timber post. She waved her old felt hat to Tex, who raised his chin to her and smiled.

Jeanie Eagle Feather liked Tex, who was one of her regular customers when he was in town, although he only called to see 'Donna the Slut' and never went with any of her other girls. She had yet to see Joel Shelby in her establishment and hoped that Tex would one day persuade the young, good-looking cowboy to enjoy the delights of one of her girls.

"You ain't got time to go calling over there, Tex," smiled Joel as he saw Jeanie Eagle Feather waving at his friend. "Save it 'til we get back from the wedding."

"I know that, Joel. I was just looking to see if 'Donna the Slut' was around. I don't like to pass through town without letting my favorite girl know that I'm around."

'Donna the Slut' was one of the best-looking girls in the whorehouse, and Tex always made a point of seeing her and was always trying to persuade her to give up the work but hadn't yet persuaded her to retire. She once said that she might settle down if he gave up his peripatetic ways and stayed around Tucson, but he never knew what the word meant. He hadn't had much schooling and was too proud to ask her to explain, in case it was an insult, so he had let the matter drop.

Just before Tex turned away, 'Donna the Slut' came out and stood in the doorway, next to Jeanie Eagle Feather, and on seeing Tex, she waved at him and blew him a kiss. Tex grinned, happy now that he had seen her before leaving town, and took off his hat and waved it at her.

"She sure is one pretty girl, is my Donna," Tex sighed as he turned his horse up the street. "I must get her to marry me one day."

Joel smiled at his friend and turned to the old friar. "Come on, Father Benito, let's make trail. We got a fair way to go before sunset," he said, turning his horse to follow Tex, as he reached in to his pocket to bring out a match to light his cigar stub, which he still had in his mouth. He took a pull on the stogie and, with a nod to Tex, urged his horse into a slow trot along the street. Father Benito quickly tried to make his steed keep up with the two cowboys, giving it a light tap on its rump with his staff.

Billy-Bob Cannon stood in the open doorway of his hardware store and raised his hand to the three riders as they passed. He was smoking a cigarette that he had sneaked out of the jar in his kitchen after his wife, Julie, had disappeared into the back room. The two cowboys waved back at Bill-Bob, as he flicked his cigarette butt into the street and went back into the store, quickly popping another boiled sweet into his mouth to remove the tobacco smell from his breath.

Chapter 8

The main street was nearly deserted as the three men rode out of town, just a few old timers lounging in the shade of the porch outside the saloon. Most of the younger men had gone to fight on the side of the Confederate States, thinking that they were going to have an easy time of it, and General Sibley had taken his men, along with the new recruits, to fight the Union army up towards New Mexico Territory. He wanted to capture Fort Craig from the Union troops occupying it, and give him a clear route up the Rio Grande.

The temporary recruiting office at the end of the street was now deserted. All that remained was a Confederate flag flapping in the wind on a flagpole above the entrance, and a faded, weather-beaten note on the door, partly torn, urging all able-bodied men to enlist for the cause.

"I reckon this damn war is going to leave a lot of widows behind, before long," Tex said, with a shrug, as they passed the recruiting office. Joel nodded in agreement. "This war is going to cast a mighty long shadow over the country before it's over, Tex."

"You never said a truer word," agreed Tex. "Did you think that up yourself, or is that one of your old grandpappy's daft sayings?"

"No, it's all mine," laughed Joel, taking a drag of his cigar stub.

"Well you're getting to sound more like the old coot every day."

"Well I did spend a lot of time with my old grandpappy. He brought me up when my folks died, and he never got tired of telling me things. I reckon that a lot of it has rubbed off onto me."

Just as they were passing the deserted recruiting office, their progress was suddenly blocked by two men, armed with rifles, who came from around the corner of the building and stood in front of their horses, one of the men holding his hand up to make them stop. As Joel and Tex reined in their horses, two more men—both armed with rifles like the first two—came up behind them. Father Benito's horse, bringing up the rear, nearly collided with Joel's horse, as he tried to make it stop.

"Step down off those horse, boys, nice and easy. We'd like a word with you," said one of the men, who Joel recognized as Mason Carter. Mason had a small place a few miles out of town, and two of his sons had gone off to fight in the war, and he had just received word that his oldest boy, Tyrone, had been killed in a battle up north. The other three men had also got sons who had recently joined the army and had rode off with General Sibley.

"What the devil do you want with us, Mason?" asked Joel as he and Tex carefully dismounted under the watchful gaze of the four, armed men, both keeping their hands well away from their side arms.

"We want to know why you two haven't enlisted yet. Especially you, Joel Shelby. You're young enough and fit enough to go and fight like our boys. Are you both yeller?" said Mason Carter, levelling his rifle at Joel, as Tex was covered by the other man. The other two came up behind Joel and Tex, ignoring the old friar, who posed no threat to them and brushed past him as he sat on his horse

"No, we ain't yeller, Carter, and we're sorry for your loss. Your boy, Tyrone, was a fine young lad, but it's no concern of ours, and we are in a hurry, so step aside and let us be on our way," said Tex, staring angrily at the four men who surrounded them. He was itching to draw his pistol, and he spit on his hands in readiness but knew that he probably wouldn't beat the four rifles that were aimed at him and Joel, cocked and ready to fire.

Joel tossed his cigar butt into the dusty road and stood ready; his right hand near his holstered pistol. He had seen Tex spit on his hands and knew that it meant he was ready for action but hoped that he wouldn't be too reckless with the odds stacked against them.

Father Benito had managed to dismount after a struggle with his stirrups. Sandals weren't the best of footwear for riding a horse, and he nearly fell of as his foot became trapped between the stirrup and his sandal, making one of the men laugh. Dusting himself down, he walked slowly up to the stand-off in the street, leaning on his staff.

"*Señores,*" he said, trying to make himself heard above the raised voices. "Please, let us through, we mean you no harm to you, and we have a long way to travel."

"You can keep out of this, you, old fart," said one of the men, looking arrogantly over his shoulder at the brown-robed friar, and turning his back on him disdainfully, but not before he had spat on the ground at the feet of Father Benito. "This is none of your damn business, old timer. Just be careful you don't trip over that stick that you're carrying."

As the man with the rifle turned away from Father Benito, to face Joel and Tex, he suddenly felt his neck trapped in something hard and was pulled violently backwards. Choking, he dropped his rifle as he struggled desperately to free himself, his fingers clutching at the thing at his throat. Father Benito had moved up quickly behind the man, gripping his staff in both hands, as he hooked the curved end of it around the man's throat, jerking him off balance.

The man fell backwards with a shout, as the friar, moving quickly for an old man, leapt over him, catching him with a heavy blow to the ear with the other end of his staff as he passed.

Landing in a crouch, in front of the injured man, Father Benito then hit Mason Carter on his arm with a hard downward stroke, making him drop his rifle. He then followed swiftly with a sharp rap to the bridge of the Mason Carter's nose, sending him staggering backwards with blood pouring from his large nose, which was clearly broken. Then—with an agility belying his years and the use of old muscle memory and a swift forward fluidity of motion—Father Benito poked the end of his stout staff into the groin one of Mason Carter's henchmen who was about to level his rifle at him. Father Benito hit him hard in his testicles and with a loud shriek, the man fell forward—his eyes bulging and filling with tears from the pain in his family jewels—and he hit the ground hard, taking the impact with his face.

Joel and Tex stood open mouthed, both transfixed with astonishment, as if spectators in a strange dance. The old friar paused for a moment and stood still in the middle of the fracas, in a ready stance, his staff held firmly in both hands above his head, legs slightly apart as he gazed about him, ready to spring into further action at the first sign of any more trouble from the men. The three men that he had laid out were all lying groaning in the middle of the dusty street.

Recovering quickly from the sudden surprise, the whole of the fight had taken less than a minute, Joel hit the remaining rifleman in the face, as he stood watching the way that his friends had been so easily dispatched, knocking him backwards to the ground. Tex drew his pistol and covered the four men, as they all tried to struggle to their feet. They all wondered what the hell had hit them, and how many had they been up against, as they stared at the old friar in amazement, who was, by now standing, smiling benevolently at the men and feeling in his robe to make sure that his old clay pipe hadn't been damaged with all his physical exercise. He looked down at Mason Carter, as the injured man struggled to his feet, holding his bleeding and battered nose, as he tried to stem the flow of blood, his arm swollen from the blow from Father Benito's staff.

"I am truly sorry for the loss of your son, *señor*," said the old friar, helping Mason Carter to get up from the ground. "In a time of peace, a son buries his father, but in a time of war, a father must bury his son. I shall pray for his soul and your redemption." He turned his back on the hapless man and walked slowly back to his horse, all the energy drained from him.

"On your way now, Carter," Tex said, with a smile, pointing his pistol at the four beaten men. "And take your friends with you, unless you want to have some more of Father Benito's rough justice."

The man that Father Benito had hit first backed away from him, holding his bruised throat and gasping furiously for breath, as he croaked something unintelligible. Blood was running down his neck from a cut behind his ear.

Billy-Bob Cannon came running up the street, as the four men shuffled away, embarrassed by the beating that Father Benito had meted out to them. Mason Carter was still holding his bloody nose in both hands, and one of his friends clutched at his balls, as they all scuttled away, leaving their rifles on the ground where they had dropped them.

"I saw all that," said Billy-Bob Cannon, catching his breath from his run up the street, a freshly lit cigarette held firmly between his lips.

"That sure was something that the old friar did to Mason Carter and his friends."

"It sure was, Billy-Bob. It looks like we may not need your help after all, now that we've got the fighting monk with us," said Tex, clapping Father Benito on his back and sending a cloud of dust in the air from his well-worn robes.

"Don't say that, Tex," said Billy-Bob, turning around and starting to head back to his store, feeling more than a little put out by Tex's remarks.

"Don't worry, Billy-Bob. We may yet need the help of an old Texas Ranger," Joel said as he saw the dejected look on the shopkeeper's face and tried to lift his spirits. "So keep that gun of yours ready, just in case. And take these rifles back to your store for Carter and his cronies to collect later, when they have all recovered from their embarrassment."

Billy-Bob picked up the four rifles and carried them back to his store, hoping that Joel would keep his word and let him ride with him one day. But if he did, would his wife, Julie, let him go? He thought to himself.

Joel and Tex helped the old friar to get back on his horse, as he seemed to have regressed back into his old self after all the earlier excitement, and they both mounted up themselves, glad to be on their way again.

"Let's make trail before we run into any more trouble, Tex," Joel said, smiling at Father Benito, as he urged his horse forward.

"Sure thing," agreed Tex. "It seems like we are always needing help these days. First with Young Billy Brand, up in the hills, and now Father Benito here. I reckon that we must be getting old or slow."

Chapter 9

Making camp by a stream, later that evening, Father Benito once again showed his worth. First making a campfire, then disappearing into the undergrowth and returning a few minutes later, clutching a dead jackrabbit by its ears, which was still twitching. Borrowing Tex's sharp knife, he expertly skinned and gutted it then proceeded to roast it over the campfire, using a sharp, pointed stick pushed through the unfortunate animal's body. He also fried some beans from the small food sack that he carried with him, stirring them in Joel's small frying pan, making the cowboy's mouths water in anticipation of the meal. Father Benito had brought the beans with him from the Mission. He had filled his sack from a large pot where they had been soaking in water for days, and they were now soft enough to fry.

When the meal was ready, Father Benito divided it amongst the three of them on metal plates and set them down on a blanket near the campfire. He quickly scolded Joel and Tex, as they were about to tuck in to the meal, for not letting him offer up a prayer before they ate. Sheepishly, Joel and Tex both looked at each other and both removed their hats and bowed their heads in mock reverence, both stifling a grin, as the friar put his hands together and said grace.

After what seemed like a long time to the hungry cowboys, but was perhaps less than a minute, Father Benito finished his prayer and nodded for them both to proceed with their meal. But they both held back, letting the friar start eating first, not wanting to offend him again. He smiled at them both, as he chewed on a piece of well-cooked rabbit meat.

"Don't let your food go cold, my amigos, there is a time for prayers and a time for eating, and I am feeling very hungry after this morning's light exercise back in town."

Laughing, Joel and Tex didn't need telling twice, and they both tucked in to the meal with a relish, enjoying the friar's culinary skills.

With the meal finished, Father Benito took the dirty plates and pans to a nearby stream and washed them, drying them on the hem of his robe, which wasn't the cleanest part of his clothing. He then stowed them away in one of the saddlebags.

Finishing his chores, Father Benito then sat by the fire, opposite Joel and Tex, and pulled out his small clay pipe from beneath his robes along with a small tobacco pouch, filled his pipe, and lit it with a burning twig from the fire.

"Damn it," cussed Tex, moving away from the cloud of smoke that both Joel and the old friar were creating as Joel lit a cigarette. "I always seem to be sitting in a cloud of smoke when I'm around you, Joel. I'm off to water my horse."

He wandered off into the gloom and could be heard having a pee and muttering to himself about the qualities of Donna 'The Slut,' and how he wished that he had brought her along with him. "I'm gonna make an honest woman of her one day."

Tex came back and sat once again by the fire, but away from the other two. He lay back on his blanket, head resting on his saddle, gazing up at the evening stars, lost in his own thoughts. Breaking the silence— as the two men smoked—Tex suddenly sat up, leant over, and spoke to Father Benito.

"What was all that fancy stuff about, that you did with your staff, Father? When you laid into Mason Carter and his friends, back in town."

"Well, my son," said the friar with a smile, taking a puff of his pipe and making Tex lean back away from his smoke. "One of those men spat and swore at me, and also, they were threatening you and Señor Shelby. I could not stand by and let them harm you both." He paused for a moment, picking a small piece of rabbit meat from his teeth. "I haven't known you for very long, but you have both been extremely kind and patient to an old man like me. I am a man of God and try to avoid violence, but Jesus took a stick to the moneylenders and traders and drove them out of the Temple for being blasphemous. So I was only following tradition when I came to your aid."

66

"Yes, Father, and we are very grateful," said Joel, joining in the conversation, as he threw his cigarette butt into the fire and warmed his hands against the flames. "But what my friend here meant was, how the hell did you learn to fight like that with your stick? And all that jumping about that you did. I've never seen anything like that before." He paused and poured himself a cup of coffee and took a drink. "And please excuse my language, Father. I've been too long in this ruffian's company." He pointed with his thumb at Tex.

Father Benito took another long draw on his pipe, savored the smoke for a second or two, then blew it out in a small blue-colored cloud over the flames of the campfire. Tex dropped back on his blanket to avoid the smoke that blew his way in the light breeze, as Father Benito began to speak again. He took a drink of water from his canteen, thinking about the two jugs of wine that were in Joel's saddlebags, and listened to the old friar.

"I was not always a man of God, my sons. I was, for a long time, in the service of the Mexican army as a cavalry officer, before I was called to serve the Lord. I became very proficient with the sword and the fighting staff, and sad to say, fought many duels and was in a few battles in Mexico, in my younger days. Some of them, sadly, against your own countrymen."

He paused, and with a sigh and a shrug of his shoulders, carried on speaking. "I am not proud of my past and spend a lot of time asking the Lord for forgiveness for my past sins. I was not unlike you two hombres when I was younger, always ready for trouble and never walking away from a fight." He paused and looked at Joel and Tex with a smile. "I do not mean that maliciously, my amigos, so please do not be offended by what I say."

"We ain't offended, Father," laughed Tex, with Joel nodding in agreement.

Father Benito relit his pipe and spoke again. "I have seen too much killing and now seek solace in prayer and helping the poor, but the old ways are still with me as you saw back in town. And as you cowboys must know." He paused, looking at their pistols in their holsters. "You can only avoid conflict by being ready for it, so I still try to practice with my staff when the weather is dry and the stiffness in my old knees and back is not too painful. But now, I am a soldier of God."

Rising from the fire, Father Benito tapped the ashes from his pipe and placed it, still smoking beside his blanket. He then took his bible from his bag and walked slowly into the darkness, away from the campfire, carrying his trusty staff. "And now, my amigos, I go to pray for forgiveness before turning in for the night. *Via con Dios, amigos.*"

"And God go with you too, Father," said Tex. He was just about to tell the old friar to be careful, out in the dark on his own, but then thought how foolish it may sound after the way that he had performed back in Tucson. Joel and Tex nodded to the old friar and both shrugged their shoulders to each other, as he walked slowly away, stick in one hand and bible in the other.

"That's one helluva man there, Joel," Tex said, looking at Father Benito's robed figure, as he disappeared into the gloom, away from the light of the campfire. "Back in Tucson, when I saw him ride his horse for the first time, at the back of the stables, I figured there was something different about the old fella."

"You ain't wrong there, Tex. As my old grandpappy would say, 'never judge a book by its cover.'"

Father Benito returned to the campfire about an hour later, just when Joel and Tex were beginning to worry about his safety and go and look for him. He was softly humming to himself, and when he sat down on his blanket the two men noticed a small, fresh cut on his forehead, the blood glistening from the reflection of the flickering fire. He dabbed at the wound with a bandanna, as Joel leaned over to question him, but before he could say something Tex tapped him on his arm.

"I should leave it, Joel," he said quietly. "Whatever he's been up to I think we're probably better off not knowing. If he wants us to know, then the old fella will tell us."

Father Benito laid his staff and bible by his pipe, pulled his hood over his head, and curled up on his blanket. He was peacefully snoring in no time at all. Joel and Tex silently chuckled and both lay back against their saddles, hats pulled over their eyes, and joined the old friar in sleep.

Joel and Tex woke up the next morning to the smell of bacon frying and hot coffee steaming in the pot. They both sat up and stretched themselves as Father Benito came over to them with some food. "Buenos Dias, amigos," he said, smiling, as he dished out the breakfast on to plates. "I hope you are both hungry, after your sleep, my sons? I have already eaten, but I didn't want to disturb you while you both slept."

They both took the plates from the old friar, but this time, remembering to let him say grace before tucking in, and they sat patiently waiting for him to finish. As the two men were eating their bacon and beans, Father Benito made them some pancakes in the frying pan and served them out to the hungry cowboys, who were both waiting in hungry anticipation, as they smelled the delicious aroma. The old Friar looked at Joel and Tex in bewilderment as they both sat with the warm plates of pancakes on their knees, looking up at him.

"What are you waiting for, my amigos? Don't you like pancakes?"

"We sure do, Father, but we didn't want to eat before you said your prayer," said Joel, sitting with his fork in his hand, poised above his plate.

Father Benito laughed. "I only thank the Lord once before a meal. Not before every mouthful. Please, Señores, eat up before the food goes cold."

Joel and Tex didn't need telling twice, and they both ate the pancakes like it was the Last Supper. The pancakes tasted of cinnamon, which Father Benito had sprinkled into the mix, and he brought out a small jar of honey from his bag, which he liberally pored over them.

"This honey is from the bees at our small Mission," he said, replacing the lid back on his small honey pot and licking his sticky fingers.

"We'll be mighty sorry to say goodbye to you, Father, after the wedding," said Tex, between mouthfuls, as they both finished off their pancakes. "These pancakes sure are delicious."

"Amen to that," added Joel, licking honey from his mustache and wiping his chin with his bandanna to remove the warm sticky crumbs from his stubble. "Father Francesco never said a truer word when he said that we might be pleasantly surprised by Father Benito on the journey. If they ever get rid of old Stumpy, back at the ranch, then he can take his place as the cook."

"That's if the boys like saying their prayers before every meal," laughed Tex, putting down his empty plate.

Father Benito smiled and collected the dirty plates and pans and carried them down to the stream to wash them, returning after a short while with a tin cup filled with water. With a small brush, which he moistened with water, he poked in the cold ashes at the edge of the campfire and he proceeded to clean his teeth.

"Now that's a damn good idea," Joel said, copying the friar, as he licked his forefinger and poked it into the ashes. He rubbed his ash-laded finger on his teeth and started to cough, as he swallowed some of the wet, gritty paste, quickly spitting it out as it caught in the back of his throat, and rinsing his mouth out with water from his canteen.

Father Benito smiled benevolently at Joel, watching him spit out the ash, as he rinsed his own mouth out with water, displaying a mouth full of, well kept, pearly white teeth.

"*Ser fiel a los dietes, de mis hijos, o van a ser falso a usted,*" he said, to Joel, with his usual smile.

"What did he say, Tex? You understand some Spanish," Joel said, turning to Tex.

"Be true to your teeth, my sons, or they will be false to you," said Tex, roughly translating the old friar's words. Joel laughed, with Tex joining in. "I sure wish that my old grandpappy had said that; I must remember it," said Joel, rolling his first smoke of the day.

Tex rubbed at his jaw and groaned. "Those pancakes were good, but they sure brought on my damn toothache again. It must have been that honey. Too damn sweet."

Father Benito saw that Tex was in some pain and asked him, in Spanish, what the problem was. Tex told him that he was suffering from toothache, as he took a drink of whiskey from his jar. The old friar nodded and went over to fetch his small pack from his saddle and came back and rummaged through it.

He brought out a small piece of ginger root, leant over and removed Tex's knife from his boot, and cut it in half. He then proceeded to crush the ginger in the hollow of a small boulder and added some salt and a few herbs from his bag and made a paste by adding a few drops of water to the mix.

Tex and Joel sat and watched as Father Benito rolled the paste between his hands. He looked at Joel and smiled.

"Put this in your mouth, my friend. Place it against the tooth and leave it for a while. Do not swallow it."

"I'll try anything." Tex said, taking the paste from Father Benito and wedging it between his gum and tooth and lying back on his saddle. "But I can't see this stuff doing any good."

Joel laughed at the sight of Tex, lying on the ground with a mouthful of paste, making him look like a Pack Rat with its mouth full of food, as he wandered off towards the trees to heed the call of nature, his chosen position amongst the thicket marked by a cloud of cigarette smoking filtering up through the shrubbery.

As Tex and Father Benito were breaking camp and saddling up their horses, they heard a cry from the bushes, in the direction where Joel had been having a pee. Picking up his rifle Tex rushed over, followed by Father Benito, and he nearly ran over the prostrate figure of Joel, who was trying to get up from the ground.

"What did you yell for, Joel? I thought you had been bushwhacked," said Tex, spitting the paste from his mouth.

Joel got to his feet and looked down at what he had stumbled in to. "That wasn't there when I went for a pee yesterday," he said. "I was heading back when I fell over it." He pointed down at a small mound of earth and leaves and kicked at it with his boot exposing the rear legs of an animal.

"It looks like some sort of grave," Tex said, squatting down for a closer look, as Joel removed some more earth. "It's a dead Bobcat," he said. "And I don't reckon it's been dead too long."

As the two men examined the dead wild-cat, Father Benito came over, out of breath from trying to keep up with Tex. He looked down at the bobcat and spoke, in an embarrassed voice, to Joel and Tex.

"Let me explain, Señores. Last night, while I was out here at prayer, I must have disturbed this animal. As I stood up, I heard a growl and looked up at this tree here. It was very dark, I could not see a thing but felt a sharp pain as it struck my forehead with its claws. I struck out with my staff and, luckily, hit it before it could attack me. The blow must have killed it, breaking the beast's neck, so I covered the poor thing up with some loose soil and said a prayer over it before returning. I am sorry that I had to kill it."

"No need to be sorry," said Tex. "Bobcats are vicious little bastards." He took of his hat as an apology for cussing in the presence of the old padre. "They might be small but this one could have killed you in the dark; they are nocturnal animals and can see to hunt when its pitch black." He kicked some soil over the dead bobcat and walked back with Joel, to their camp, with the old monk following behind them.

"I don't think that there was any luck involved when the old timer hit that Bobcat," Joel said, relighting his cigarette. "It might have been damn dark, but he knew where it was, and he hit it right behind its ear. One hit and a killer blow."

"You're not wrong there, Joel. We could have done with the old boy's help, when those wolves attacked us, back up near the line shack. We wouldn't have had to rely on Young Billy Brand's help."

As Joel and Tex finished saddling their horses, Tex looked over to Joel, as he felt inside his mouth with a finger.

"You know," he said, removing his finger, smiling, "I reckon that medicine that Father Benito made me did the business with my toothache. I had a swollen gum and it seems to have gone down, and the toothache's gone." He looked over to Father Benito, who was trying to mount his horse, and shouted something in Spanish to him, pointing at his mouth. "Gracias, Father," he added, as the old friar struggled to get his sandaled feet into the stirrups.

After finishing packing away all the gear and putting the campfire out, the two cowboys usually peed on the fire to douse it, but in deference to Father Benito they kicked some soil over the embers, they mounted up, followed by the old Friar. He rode behind, his lips moving in silent prayer, as he held on tightly to the reins of his tall horse.

"I sure hope the old friar ain't praying to save your soul," Joel said to Tex, twisting around in the saddle and looking back at Father Benito. "The old boy will be at it from now 'til Thanksgiving before he gets an answer from the Almighty."

Tex laughed as he rode along, still licking honey and cinnamon from his stubble. "I feel damn good after that breakfast, Joel, especially now my mouth ain't sore. I can't wait to get back to Tucson and see my Donna again. I'm missing her already."

"Well, I reckon that Jeanie Eagle Feather will be missing your contributions at her whorehouse while you're away, Tex," said Joel, spurring on his horse.

Chapter 10

Arriving at Tom and Alice's ranch, towards noon, on the third day, the three men were met by Pat and Charlotte, who had seen them coming down the trail and rode out to meet them. Pat, the big Irish lad, was all smiles as he as welcomed the two cowboys, giving them both a bear hug when they had dismounted.

"Top of the morning to you both, me boyos," he said as Joel pulled away from his strong grip. It's good to see you both again. I'm glad that you could both come to our wedding."

Tex had insisted on stopping at the hill where Steve was buried, to have a few quiet words with his old friend. He removed the brass plaque from the sheet that he had wrapped it in and placed it carefully on the grave, against the wooden cross.

"You'll like this, Steve, old friend," he said wistfully, kneeling down and picking a few stray weeds that had grown on the grave, since he was last there, and tossing them away. His vision became blurred as his eyes filled up with sudden tears, and he wiped them away with the back of his hand.

"I'll fix it on properly, with some nails, later, but you can have a chance to look at it before I do."

He stood up, replacing his hat that he had respectfully removed, sniffing his nose to clear away the snot. He didn't want the others to see how sad he was. After all, he used to fight Indians, and he had lost more than a few friends in battle over the years. But he had known Steve Hurst a long time, and they had been like brothers together.

Tex suddenly realized that Charlotte was standing next to him. She put her hand on his arm and smiled up at him. "I'm sure he'll like that, Tex," she said, ignoring the dewdrop that had formed on the end of his nose and looking at the shiny brass plaque on the grave. "It looks mighty pretty." She had seen Tex shed a tear, as his hard veneer had momentarily slipped, but pretended that she hadn't noticed.

"Don't let him hear you say that, Charlotte," said Tex, recovering his composure, as he looked down at the attractive young girl. "Old Steve didn't do pretty."

"Oh, I'm sorry, Tex, I didn't mean pretty," she giggled, happy to see the Indian Fighter again, as he stooped down and kissed her on the cheek. "I meant neat and tidy."

"That's more like it, Charlotte. He liked things to be neat and tidy."

Joel introduced Pat and Charlotte to Father Benito, who bowed gracefully to them, and said that he would be happy to marry them both, and he placed his hand on each of their shoulders and gave them his blessing. The friar then paused to say a few words over Steve's grave and also the grave of the young runaway slave girl, who had been killed by Confederate deserters the year before.

After the brief pause at the graves, they all followed Pat and Charlotte down to the ranch house, where Tom and his family were waiting to meet them. Alice welcomed Joel and Tex warmly and gave Tex a special hug. She hadn't forgotten how he had saved her and her daughter, Sarah, from the old scalp hunter, Sheep's Head, last year and was forever grateful to him. Alice was carrying baby Rose—the little orphaned black girl—who Joel, Tom, and her boys had saved, the year before, down by the river. Her daughter, Sarah, was clutching at her skirt, gazing up at all the visitors.

Joel introduced Father Benito to them all, and he shook hands with everyone, bowing respectfully to each of them. Tom was glad to see the two cowboys again, and he led them both into the shade of the front porch with Father Benito, while Alice and Charlotte went inside to fetch some cool lemonade that she had made that morning. Tex would have preferred a drop of the hard stuff, but it felt impolite to mention it, so he accepted the lemonade gracefully.

Tom offered Joel one of his stogies, which the cowboy gratefully accepted, and he lit it happily, drawing in a lungful of smoke. The old friar declined one of Tom's cigars, instead getting out his old clay pipe from beneath his robes, filling it and lighting it. Tex moved away from the smokers, making coughing noises to show his annoyance.

After finishing his glass of lemonade, Father Benito put out his pipe and stood up. He asked Tom if he could rest for a while, after the long Journey, as he was feeling very tired from sitting on a horse for the last few days. Tom offered to get Alice to make him up a bed in the house, but the old monk wouldn't have any of it, saying that he would be happy to sleep in one of the barns or stables, on some straw.

"If a stable was good enough for Jesus to be born in, then I am more than happy to rest my humble bones in a barn," he said in his quiet Mexican accent, standing up and waving away Tom's protestations. Picking up his staff, and his bible, he slowly walked away, with young Ike, who was showing him the way, carrying his small bag for him.

When he was well out of earshot, Tom turned to Joel and Tex with a worried look on his face. "Is the father well?" he asked them, shaking his head. "He sure don't look in the best of condition to me. He looks plumb tuckered out. I don't want to sound ungrateful, and I'm pleased that you managed to bring a man of the cloth to marry Pat and Charlotte, but I thought that you would bring a younger man with you. I hope that he will be alright for the wedding tomorrow."

"He's fine," said Joel, winking knowingly to Tex, as his friend laughed. "He's just a mite worn out from the ride out here. He's not been on a proper horse for a long time, and the mule that he started out on was too darn slow. We'd never have got here in time, so we traded it for that horse that he came on."

Joel then told Tom and the others about the run in with Mason Carter and his bullying friends, back in Tucson, and the way that Father Benito had knocked three of the men to the ground, in the wink of an eye, before he and Tex had time to make a move. Tex joined in, elaborating about the incident, while Tom and his sons listened intently at the tale.

"You mean to tell me that the old monk went and larruped three grown men with that stick of his?" Tom said, amazed.

"He sure did," said Tex. "He put me and Joel to shame the way that that he dealt with them. They'd got the drop on us both, but they never even got a chance to fire a shot, before Father Benito was amongst them like a wild thing."

"And the way that he moved," agreed Joel. "It was like watching a dancer, as he leapt over them. But when he had finished, and it was all over, he seemed to go back to his slow, old self again."

"Well I'll be damned," laughed Tom. "If that don't beat all."

Turning to three of his sons, who were equally amazed at the unbelievable feats of the old friar, he said. "I told you boys before that the Lord works in mysterious ways. Didn't I?"

They all nodded in agreement, discussing what they had heard amongst themselves, and retelling the tale to their brother, Ike, on his return from the barn.

"He also cured my toothache with some potion that he mixed up for me," said Tex, rubbing his jaw and feeling that the swelling hadn't returned.

Sitting on the porch, Tom asked Joel and Tex if they knew how the war was going.

"We've been trying to avoid getting involved," said Joel. "But it's getting harder to keep out of it. It's all anyone talks about back in town. Most of the young boys around Tucson have enlisted. That's what the ruckus in town was about. One of the men had lost his son in the war and wanted to know why we hadn't enlisted."

Tom nodded. "It sure is hard to keep away from it. My boys are itching to go and enlist, but their Ma won't let 'em go. And I don't want them to go and fight either. We had a Confederate troop come by last month, to buy some cattle, and they were asking when the young 'uns were going to enlist. I said that I needed them on the ranch, but it's getting harder to keep them from going."

"Let's hope it will be over soon," Tex said. "You wouldn't even know that there was a war, this far south. Unless you went into town and heard the latest news."

"That's true," said Joel. "Look at the aggravation we got back in Tucson. If you ain't enlisted they call you yeller. From what we heard, the South ain't as well equipped as the North."

"Do you remember that troop of Confederate soldiers who stopped by here last year, Joel? They were after those murdering deserters," said Tom.

"Yep, I remember them," agreed Joel. "They were mostly young men who had never been in a fight before. Except for their sergeant. Now he looked like he could handle himself. I believe his name was Peticolas." He paused deep in thought. "Sergeant Alfred B Peticolas, as I recall. I remember giving him some tobacco 'cause he had run out of the makings. I wonder how they are getting on with the war."

"He was a nice fella," said Tom. "I think he was from Texas; you might have known him, Tex? But let's try and forget about the war for a while and think about this forthcoming wedding," Tom said, reaching under the porch and bringing out a jug of liquor, which he handed to a grateful looking Tex.

"That's a damn good idea," agreed Joel, getting out his makings and rolling a cigarette. He lit his smoke and sat back, lost in thought for a moment, thinking about Sergeant Peticolas and his Texas volunteers. *I hope Sergeant Peticolas is managing to avoid getting shot,* he thought to himself. He looked down at the grubby old pouch containing his tobacco, cigarette papers, and a few matches. *And I hope that he's looking after my best tobacco pouch. My old grandpappy gave it me, but I don't suppose I'll see that again.*

He put the makings back in his vest pocket, took another drag of his cigarette, and shrugged his shoulders. Just lately, he had been thinking about the war, and whether he should enlist; and the run in with Mason Carter, back in Tucson, had brought it to the front of his mind. He hadn't discussed it with anyone, especially Tex, as he couldn't make his mind up which side was in the right, and the idea of friend fighting friend and brother against brother stopped him from going to war. He decided to forget about the war, for the moment, and look forward to the impending wedding of Pat and Charlotte instead.

A long way to the east of Tom Travis' ranch on the Gila River, Brigadier General Henry Hopkins Sibley's 3,000 strong rebel force—consisting of Mew Mexicans, Utah Mormons, and Colorado miners, along with Captain George Hampton's 4th Texas Mounted—were moving up the Rio Grande, attacking union forts along the river.

The young Texan conscripts had been organized into an able fighting force by Sergeant Peticolas and proved their worth in a few skirmishes against the enemy without the loss of a single man from Company C.

Sibley's force first clashed with Colonel Edward R Canby's union forces on February 21st, 1862, near Fort Craig, about 100 miles south of Albuquerque, in what is known as the Battle of Valverde. The Confederates won, forcing Canby's forces to withdraw to the safety of the fort, but half of the Confederate supplies were destroyed in the battle. Flush with victory, Sibley moved northward towards Albuquerque.

During a brief rest from the heat of battle, Sergeant Peticolas sat with his men, finishing a cold meal of pork belly and bread washed down with water from his canteen. He would have preferred a drink of something a mite stronger but had finished his small supply of whiskey a week ago, so he made do with the brackish water from a small stream.

He got out his makings, rolled himself a smoke, looked at the hand-tooled buckskin tobacco pouch, and smiled as he remembered the young cowboy who had kindly given it to him last year on the Gila River.

I wonder whether he has enlisted yet, he thought to himself. *I think his name was Joel.* He paused in thought. *Joel Shelby, that was his name, and he wore shiny spurs on his boots. I sure would like to return the favor someday. Still, I don't reckon we'll meet again.*

Sergeant Peticolas shrugged his shoulders, stood up, stretched his tall, six-foot four-inch frame, tossed his cigarette stub on the ground, and stomped on it with his boot. He looked at the young men who all looked up at him as he walked towards them, holding his rifle in one hand, and thinking that most of them appeared far too young to be in the army. Maybe they were, he thought, but they all were growing up fast now that they had been under fire.

Sergeant Peticolas was from Richmond Virginia but had been practicing law in Victoria, Texas when the war had begun, so he had enlisted in the 4th Texas mounted, and with his natural flair for leadership, was soon promoted to Sergeant.

"Come on, lad's, we'd better see if the captain has finished his meeting with the other officers' and find out what his orders are," he said, rousing the young men around him.

They all started to gather their equipment together, and as Sergeant Peticolas reached them, he dropped the tobacco pouch from his stiff fingers and, cussing, bent down to retrieve it. As he picked up the makings, a shot rang out and a musket ball, meant for the back of his head, flew over him and hit the young private who was just getting up from his blanket on the damp ground. Private Sean Felan, a young Irish immigrant, who had enlisted in Texas, with a few of his own countrymen, fell back dying from a fatal wound to his neck.

Sergeant Peticolas quickly turned around and dropped to one knee as another shot ploughed a furrow in the dirt a few feet away from him. He saw the puff of smoke from halfway up a tree about 200 yards away, cocked his rifle, and quickly fired two shots at where he thought the sniper was perched. A distant yell and the sight of a dark blue uniform marked the fall of the enemy sniper, as he fell from the tree.

Another shot rang out from the direction of the distant trees, and a puff of smoke rose, marking the location, as another Union sniper tried to get the range of Sergeant Peticolas' troop. Two young privates jumped up as a musket ball hit the canteen of water that was lying on the ground between them.

The two young conscripts had enlisted when General Sibley had marched through the land, near their homes in Arizona, drums and bugles played loudly, keeping time to the pace of the foot soldiers.

Ross and Jamie were cousins, who lived on adjoining homesteads, and were always out hunting together, shooting birds and small animals to help feed their families. They had heard about the war and were eager to enlist on the side of the Confederacy but were told by their parents that they were too young. Jamie was 16 and his cousin, Ross, was a couple of years older. On the day that General Sibley and his men rode by, Ross and Jamie had been sitting in a nearby field of maize, examining a pair of rabbits that they had shot and arguing about which one of them was the best shot, when they had heard the marching of soldiers and the sound of horse's hooves.

They had both looked up at the column of dust kicked up by the soldiers' progress and stood up to see who was passing by as the bugles sounded again. Realizing that it was a large band of soldiers, off to fight in the war, they had both looked at each other, nodded, and without a backward glance raced through the tall maize, clutching their rifles, in one hand, and a dead rabbit in the other, to catch up with Sibley's men. They had enlisted that evening and were put in the charge of Sergeant Peticolas, who swore them in and gave them both a confederate cap to wear. Uniforms were in short supply and it wasn't until their first skirmish with the union army that they were able to take their pick of the uniforms from the soldiers who had been killed or badly wounded.

Ross Phillips looked down at the canteen that had been hit by the musket ball, as the water trickled out of the hole, like fresh blood from a wound, and laughed.

"That could have been one of us," he said to his cousin, Jamie. "Let's see if we can get that varmint."

Jamie Heald jumped up, clutching his rifle. They had both been issued with the latest repeating rifles, to replace their outdated firearms, when Sergeant Peticolas had learnt that they were handy with a rifle.

"I'm right with you, cousin," said Jamie, his freckled face frowning as he squinted in the distance to see where the shot had come from, the sun shining in his eyes.

Another shot rang out, hitting one of the other privates in his arm, as Ross and Jamie both took aim and fired at the same time. Everyone stopped for a moment and looked at the trees, waiting to see if the cousins had hit the sniper, as there was a sudden crashing of broken branches and another blue uniformed body fell to the ground. Ross and Jamie let out a yell, as the other men cheered and congratulated them, and then both began arguing about which one of them had hit the sniper first.

Alfred Peticolas laughed and walked back to where he had left his sketchbook on the ground and tucked it inside his coat. He had been busy detailing scenes of the previous day's action before he had eaten. He always liked to keep a diary of the day's events, along with pencil drawings of scenes of battle, as a reminder of the carnage of war.

He returned to his men and picked up the fancy tobacco pouch, silently thanking the Almighty for making him drop it.

"Come on, lads," he said, bending over the body of the unfortunate Irish Private. "Let's bury the poor sod and get back to the business of the war." He walked over to Ross and Jamie, who were both still arguing the merits of their own shooting skills. "Well done, lads. That was a fine bit of marksmanship." He paused as he looked back at the trees. "Nearly as good as mine," he added. "I'll make soldiers out of you both before this war is over."

Ross clapped a hand on his cousin's back and laughed, pleased with the Sergeant's praise. He brushed the lock of long hair off his face and replaced his cap. "I think he likes us, Jamie," he said as his cousin kicked at the canteen, which had emptied of water, soaking into the dry ground.

* * * * * *

Back at Tom's ranch, Joel finished his cigarette, shook the thoughts of war from his head, and turned to Tom Travis.

"How is Pat here, shaping up as a cowboy?" he asked.

"He's getting better at sitting on a horse without falling off," said Tom, laughing at Pat, as the young Irishman blushed slightly. "But he'd look more like a cowboy if he ditched that old cloth cap of his," he added as his sons joined in the laughter.

"And if we could only understand what he was saying," said Daniel, ducking out the way as Pat took off his cap to hit him with.

"If it hadn't been for me leaving my old cap where you could find it, last year at Painted Rocks, you might never have found me and Charlotte. So I'll not be getting rid of it just yet, me boyos. And, anyway, it reminds me of the old country."

"Well, he ain't wearing that old cap tomorrow for his wedding, that's for sure," said Tom.

Father Benito joined them all later after he had enjoyed a good rest. He was looking a lot livelier than he had been when he had first arrived and was happy to sit and discuss the forthcoming nuptials with Pat and Charlotte. Although with Pat's thick Irish brogue and his own Mexican accent, there was a certain lack of communication between the two of them, and it took Joel and Tex to act as translators before much progress could be made.

Tom's four sons sat listening to the discussion, doubled up with laughter at the puzzled looks on Pat and Father Benito's faces, as they both struggled to understand each other. And it wasn't until they all received withering looks from their pa that they eventually calmed down.

Charlotte joined in the conversation, as she was able to put her opinions over a lot easier, as she understood Pat's accent a lot better than the others and didn't have too many problems with Father Benito's Spanish, as she had learnt a lot of the language from her time spent as a prisoner of the apaches. The Indians spoke Spanish, which they had learnt from the Mexicans, and Charlotte had managed to become quite fluent.

Joel hadn't seen Charlotte for over six months, and he was struck by the changes in her appearance. Since he had rescued her from the apaches, with the help of Steve and Tex, she had put on a few pounds, which made her look more mature. Less like a young girl and more like a young woman, and she was even prettier than before. She had also lost the sullen, haunted look that three years of captivity had left her with, after she had first been freed, and was now happy and smiling, more talkative, and a lot more confident. She had learned to trust people a lot more, but she still liked to keep Pat close by her side.

Pat too had matured since their last meeting, losing a lot of the extra fat that he had been carrying, since his easy-going life with the settlers on the wagon train. He had put on a lot of muscle now that he was doing the work of a cowboy, but he was still a big strapping lad. The ranch life had been good to him, and the outdoor work had made his reddish complexion even redder. He had a lot more freckles below his mass of red, curly hair; Charlotte had threatened, more than once, to trim his unruly locks before they were wed.

Father Benito was sitting, holding the little girl, Rose, on his lap, and she was playing with his rosary, sucking on the beads and gurgling happily, as he softly sang to her in Spanish.

Chapter 11

The evening meal was a noisy affair with everyone seated around the large kitchen table. Father Benito said a prayer before eating. Tex had warned them all beforehand that he liked to say grace, and they were all prepared and waiting for him, with Tom pleased that the old friar had brought some religion back in to his household.

Joel told them that Shreeve Moor was still in jail in Tucson, awaiting his impending trial, and Tex told them all about the run in with grizzly bear and the wolves, leaving out the part that Young Billy Brand had played in saving them from the wolves.

Pat smiled at Alice as she placed a steaming jug of boiling water on the table in front of him.

"You are a saint, Alice, to be sure," he said, proceeding to pour some of the hot water into a tin cup, which held a metal strainer with some leaves inside it.

"What the hell have you got there, boy?" Tex said, looking at Pat, as he added some milk to the brew, stirring it with the end of his fork, and taking a satisfying drink. He exhaled with the pleasure of it, licking his lips, and smiling.

"It's tea, me old pal," he said, looking around at the others. "I kept telling Joel that I didn't like his strong coffee and preferred a cup of tea. Well, Alice finally took pity on me and managed to buy me some tea from a passing trader."

"Tea!" said Joel, trying to hide a smile. "You'll never be a cowboy drinking that stuff. I remember sampling it back with your Irish friends, on the wagon train, and it tasted like ant's pee. And look at him! He even puts milk in his tea. You won't get milk in your tea when you are out herding cattle."

"Ah! Me boyo, after a couple of cups of the old brew, I'm ready for anything that the day will throw at me. And I can always milk one of the cows," said Pat, taking another drink of tea, as the others laughed. He suddenly jumped up and took Charlotte in an Irish dance, which they had both obviously been practicing together.

"Anyway, I hope that bloody Albino gets what's coming to him," Pat said, breaking off from his jig and remembering how 'The Butcher' had insulted Charlotte, after they had captured him last year.

"Let's have no more talk of killing," said Alice angrily. "And no more swearing in front of the friar," she added, looking at Pat, who was looking suitably contrite, "We've got a wedding in the morning, and Charlotte and I have still got a lot of preparing to do before this evening. So it's early to bed for everyone, and I've got to make sure that you boys have all got clean shirts for the big day tomorrow."

"That's right," said Tom. "I want you boys all on your best behavior tomorrow, 'cause we've got visitors coming for the wedding. Your ma's cousin, Kyle, and his wife and son will be here, and we've also got Lukas Bergman and his family coming over from their spread down the river. They are bringing along a couple of their young hired hands with them who are friends with you boys. No doubt they shall be wanting to show you how good they are with the horses that we're going to break in later, after the wedding."

"I'll be looking forward to that myself, after the wedding, to be sure," said Pat, looking over at his bride to be for reassurance. "I'll show you cowboys how good I am on a horse."

"You save your energy, Pat," Tex said, winking at Charlotte and making her blush. "You'll be too busy with other matters after you're wed."

"I sure hope the Bergman's don't bring Brigitte with them," said Jake, looking over to his Pa.

"Let's hope not," agreed his twin brother, Ike.

The Bergman's, Lukas; and his wife, Heike, were German immigrants who lived in a small ranch about 20 miles west of Tom's place down the river. They had two sons, Felix and Klaus, who they had brought over from the old country when they were small boys. The two boys were quite friendly with Tom and Alice's four sons. The

Bergman's also had a daughter named Brigitte, a plump girl of about 17 years old, who the Bergman's were always trying to marry off to one of Tom's sons. None of the boys fancied the chubby girl, who always followed them around whenever she visited with her family.

"The last time that I saw old Lukas, he told me that young Brigitte had been sent to a place back east to help turn her into a proper lady," said Tom. "But you never know, she may well be back home now," he added with a look at his sons.

"I sure hope not, Pa," moaned young Daniel. "You know how she follows us all about, putting her fat arms around us, and trying to give one of us a kiss." He shuddered at the thought.

"Yeah, and I'll bet that she'll have those stupid pig-tails in her hair, and they'll have dressed her in one of those old-fashioned German dresses that are always a size too small for her," agreed Jake, throwing his hands in the air.

"Oh, come now, boys," Alice said, laughing at her son's unflattering comments. "She's a lovely girl, and it's about time that one of you found someone nice to settle down with. I was only 16 when I married your pa, and you could do far worse than young Brigitte."

The boys all groaned in unison, making heaving noises like they were about to be sick, all of them remembering the big, chunky young girl with the chubby face and blond pig-tails.

The other guests that were invited to the wedding were Alice's cousin, Kyle, and his family. Kyle was a surly individual, who controlled his wife and young son, mainly with his tongue but occasionally with his hands. He resented Tom and the success that he had made of his ranch, as his small spread was going downhill fast, due to the lack of work that he had put into the place.

Tom didn't like the man very much and hadn't wanted to invite him to the wedding, but when they had visited last Christmas, to take advantage of the Travis hospitality, Pat and Charlotte had inadvertently mentioned the impending nuptials to them. Kyle had jumped at the chance of a free meal and drinks and had all but invited himself and his family before Tom could say anything. And as Kyle was Alice's only relative in the area, he could hardly refuse them.

Kyle and his wife, Lisa, had a young son, Clovis, a gangly youth of 14, who was nearly as tall as his father. He was filling out, and it wouldn't be too long before the boy would be standing up to his bullying pa.

"I'll need to borrow that razor, Charlotte. If you still have it," Tex said, changing the subject and rubbing the dark growth on his face, making a rasping noise on the stubble with his finger and thumb. "I'll need to look my best for your wedding."

"I sure have," said Charlotte, opening one of the cupboard drawers and producing the cut-throat razor which she had taken from the albino, Shreeve Moor. "It's still nice and sharp. I'll give you a shave myself in the morning. And you sure will need to look your best 'cause you're going to give me away at the wedding."

Tex nearly choked on his coffee. "Give you away!" he spluttered. "Why me?"

"Because Steve saved our lives, last year, and sadly he can't be here. So you're the next best thing, Tex. I've discussed it with Tom, and he agrees."

"The next best thing?" said Tex, pausing to think about Charlotte's comment about him being 'the next best thing' and not sure if he was getting a compliment or not. "I'm not sure whether that's a statement of praise or disapproval, young lady. But OK, I'll do it," he said somewhat reluctantly. "But only 'cause you asked me nicely," he added, winking at Charlotte.

"You can shave me as well," said Joel. "And trim my sideburns and mustache. I'll need to look good for the wedding too."

"That's right, me boyo. I forgot to tell you, Joel," said Pat, jumping up and grabbing Joel by the hand. "If it hadn't been for you, I would never have met Charlotte and all these lovely people here. So you can be my best man tomorrow and stand at my side, me old mate."

"Alright, Pat," Joel said, looking over at Tex and shrugging his shoulders. "But if me and Tex had known about all this before we came, we probably wouldn't have turned up. There was no mention of this in the letter that Tom sent to me. I'm not even sure what a best man is. If it doesn't mean long speeches, then I'll do it. I don't do long speeches."

Tom laughed. "The main reason that you have a best man is to make the bridegroom look even better than he actually is."

"He ain't going to look any better if I'm standing next to him," said Joel, smiling at Pat.

"Well, you'll all have be to up mighty early, 'cause we've got a lot to do in the morning," said Alice. "We don't want you boys under our feet in here while me and Charlotte are getting ourselves ready."

After all the wedding plans were agreed, Father Benito bid everyone goodnight and retired to the barn to say his prayers and have an early night. He wanted to make sure his fading robes were clean enough for the wedding, so after borrowing some soap from Alice, he stood in his undergarments, in the barn, and washed them out in a bucket of clean water. He wrung them out and then hung his damp robes over the back of one of the stalls to dry and knelt down to pray.

The rest of the men took their drinks outside, and Joel and Tom had themselves a smoke, as a large, full moon rose in the clear sky, casting a silvery light on the ranch house and yard, giving a surreal look to the starlit Arizona evening, which for the middle of February, made for a pleasant evening, although there was still a chill in the air.

After Alice and Charlotte had washed the dishes, they both came outside and ushered Pat off to the barn, to join Father Benito, for his last night as a single man. Charlotte gave him a lingering kiss, and he went off with some shouts, and lewd remarks following him, from the Travis boys, as he carried his blanket and oil lamp with him.

Entering the gloom of the barn, Pat saw Father Benito at prayer, kneeling in his underwear, by the light of a candle, which was sending flickering shadows across the timber walls. Pat removed his cap and knelt down, with the old Friar, remembering his good Catholic upbringing, and joined him in the prayers.

Me mammy would be proud of me now, he thought to himself. "I sure wish that she could see me now. Although she would think it strange to see an old priest in his underwear praying with me. But she would have loved Charlotte as a daughter-in-law."

Father Benito turned and smiled at Pat, when he realized that he was praying with him, and asked him if he would like him to listen to his Confession and receive the Holy Sacrament before the wedding. Pat agreed and knelt before the old friar, as he listened to his list of sins, which wasn't too long, and Father Benito got out his small container of wine and bread and performed the ceremony in the surreal atmosphere of the gloomy barn with just three unconcerned horses, which had been put in the barn because the stable was full, in the stalls next to them, as the only witnesses to the proceedings.

Pat thanked Father Benito, and they both turned in for the night, putting their blankets on a bed of hay. Pat had doused his lamp, and Father Benito blew out his candle but not before he lit his pipe from the flame.

Pat lay for a while in the darkness, feeling more than a little righteous after his confession, thinking of Charlotte and his married life before him, with her. He would care for her, he thought, as he watched the glow from the old friar's clay pipe and smelled the tobacco smoke. He would, hopefully, help her to forget the three years of hardship that she had endured as a prisoner of the apaches.

Eventually, Father Benito finished his smoke and emptied the remains into a bucket, which was half filled with water, that he had placed there earlier in case he was caught short in the night and bid Pat goodnight. He was soon fast asleep, and Pat lay there listening to him snoring away in the darkness, as he himself drifted into an untroubled sleep. Not even the scurrying of the mice along the walls, or the occasional snorting of the horses disturbing his peaceful slumber.

Joel and Tex bedded down in the barn later. They crept silently in, trying not to disturb Pat and Father Benito. Joel had removed his spurs before he left the porch, and all they could hear was loud snoring coming from the old friar and the occasional drip, drip of water from Father Benito's freshly washed garments. Pat opened one eye on hearing the two cowboys enter the barn, smiled at them, and went back to sleep.

Joel and Tex bedded down on some hay, enjoying the soft bedding as they were both used to sleeping outdoors on the hard ground.

Chapter 12

Everyone was up bright and early next morning, eating a hearty breakfast around the large kitchen table. Everyone, that is, except Pat, who was told by Alice to stop out on the porch, and his breakfast would be brought out to him. She had ushered him out of the kitchen when he had come in from the barn and tried to enter the ranch house kitchen.

"It's bad luck to see the bride on the day of the wedding before she joins you in front of the alter," Alice said. "Now you can stop outside and eat." She handed him a plate of bacon and eggs and pushed him forcefully out of the door. "I'll bring out your wedding suit later, when you've had a good wash."

Pat did as he was told and sat out on the porch and ate his breakfast and was soon joined by the four Travis boys. As he finished his meal, little Sarah came out of the ranch house, carefully carrying Pat's wedding suit in her arms with a crisp white shirt and necktie, which she placed on one of the porch chairs for him.

"Ma says that you've got to go and wash at the water pump," Sarah said, handing Pat a thick bar of soap and a towel from the top of the clothes. "And she said don't forget to wash your hair and behind your ears," she added, remembering what her ma had told her.

This last remark brought howls of laughter from the Travis boys, as he took the soap and towel from the little girl. Pat thanked Sarah, gave her his empty breakfast plate, and smiled at her. "Now you ignore these idiot brothers of yours, my girl, and go and get yourself ready for the wedding," he said to her. "Why if I hadn't got to go and tidy meself up, then I would be taking them all around the back of the barn and giving them a good Irish thrashing."

Sarah smiled at Pat and went back inside, promising to bring out his clean boots later, picking up his cap from the porch seat as she went.

"Ma says I've got to take this from you," she giggled. She had her hair all wrapped in small pieces of different colored cloth, which her ma had put in before she had gone to bed last night. It was to make her hair look even curlier for the wedding, and the colored ribbons shook like blossoms in the wind as she happily skipped back indoors, humming to herself.

Pat thanked her again and wandered over to the water pump to carry out his ablutions. He was feeling more than a little nervous, now that the wedding day had arrived, but he wasn't going to let the Travis boys see it. He forced a smile and flicked the towel at one of the Travis boys, catching young Jake on his backside with a resounding crack, making him jump in the air with a shriek. Pat ran off, feeling better for the friendly exchange, as the other three boys laughed at their brother's misfortune.

To calm his nerves, Pat took off his shirt and worked the handle to the water pump, and as the cold water cascaded out of the pipe, into the trough, he plunged his head into the deep water and held it there for a while, emerging gasping for breath. After repeating it twice more and soaping himself down, he felt clean, invigorated, and ready for whatever the day would bring him.

As he was finishing washing himself, Pat heard a yell from the porch and, looking up, with soap on his face, he saw what could only be the Bergman family, who were coming down the hill.

Lukas and Heike Bergman sat in their buggy, flanked by their two sons and three of their young cowhands, on horseback. They must have set out well before sunup to get to the wedding so early.

Ike, Jake, Dan, and Zack Travis all stood up ready to go out and meet them, whooping and hollering as they went, their noise bringing Tom and Alice out of the ranch house to see what all the ruckus was about. Suddenly, Ike stopped halfway down the steps and let out a loud groan. He had the best eyesight amongst his brothers and could see that Lukas and Heike were not alone in their buggy. Another person was sitting wedged between them, in the shade of the buggy's low canopy, their face hidden from view under a large bonnet.

"Well, I'll be damned," groaned Ike, holding his right hand above his eyes to see more clearly. "I reckon that they gone and brought that big Brigitte along with them."

"Oh, no!" Zack exclaimed, standing alongside his brother, looking to see if he was fooling with them and finding out that he wasn't and clapping his hand to his head in exasperation.

Lukas and Heike Bergman were coming slowly down the trail in their old-fashioned buggy with an old, black, well-repaired, sun shade above them, pulled by two of their big, black plough horses. From a distance, it looked as if they were in their Sunday best attire, both sitting bolt upright with stern expressions on their faces. The Bergman's weren't known for their humor, and they rarely laughed even when they were in a good mood.

Lukas had an eye patch over his left eye, which made him look even more severe. He claimed that he had lost the eye in a mining accident, back in Germany, but it was rumored that his wife, Heike, had clawed his eye out on finding him in bed with a young Fraulein, when she had returned home early, one afternoon, from her work at the local abattoir. There was no talk of the damage his wife had inflicted on the young German girl, but by the size of her large frame, which was considerably larger than her husbands, it must have been very harsh. They had left Germany in a hurry and emigrated to America, leaving a house and all their belongings behind, just taking what they could carry, giving fuel to the rumor that Mrs. Bergman had exacted a severe revenge on the girl, and all of them leaving before she was apprehended by the authorities.

Sitting wedged tightly in the middle, as most of the buggy's seating space was taken up by the two older and larger Bergman's, was a young female with a large bonnet on her head, hiding most of her face, who could have only been the Bergman's only daughter, Brigitte.

Tom's four sons stood watching in silence as the gate was opened by one of the Bergman's cowhands, and the buggy pulled into the yard and stopped in front of them. Tom came down the porch steps to greet the visitors with a wave of his hand.

"Give Mrs. Bergman and Brigitte some help down from the buggy, boys," Tom said, smiling to himself, as he ushered his sons towards the buggy, each of them holding back to let the others get there first.

Ike and Jake helped Mrs. Bergman alight from the buggy, both offering an arm for her to lean on. She was a hulking brute of a woman, and her considerable weight made the buggy shake as she struggled to get down from it, leaning heavily on the two Travis boys and making them both stagger under the hefty burden.

Joel and Tex were watching the arrival of the Bergman's from a safe distance, back on the porch, and Tex elbowed his friend in the ribs at the sight of Mrs. Bergman's descent from the buggy.

"I'll bet your old grandpappy never had a saying for a moment like this," he said quietly.

"Well if he did, then he sure never told me," Joel whispered, stifling a laugh.

"I think I'll go and ask Charlotte to give me that shave while everyone is busy with these folk," said Tex as he turned and went indoors.

"I think I'll come and join you," said Joel, treading on his cigarette butt and following Tex inside the ranch house, chuckling to himself. "I reckon this wedding is going to be a barrel of laughs."

As Mrs. Bergman reached the ground, supported by Ike and Jake, and her husband got out of the buggy from the other side, the small carriage went visibly upwards with a groan from its rusty metal springs, leaving their daughter aboard. Tom went forward to welcome Lukas Bergman and shake him by the hand, as Mrs. Bergman came around the buggy to meet him, leaving Dan and Zach to, reluctantly, help Brigitte down.

"*Guten morgen*, Tom," said Lukas, in his thick German accent, vigorously shaking Tom's hand. "It is good to see you on this fine morning, my good friend." His face nearly broke into a smile but then thought better of it.

"It's good of you all to come to the wedding, Lukas," said Tom as he turned to Mrs. Bergman and kissed her on the cheek, as she turned it towards him, as if daring him to ignore her whiskery face. As he lightly kissed her on the cheek, he couldn't help thinking that she smelled like a pile of musty old hymn books, bringing back memories of his childhood spent at Sunday school. He smiled at Mrs. Bergman, as he withdrew from kissing her cheek, feeling one of her stray hairs on his bottom lip and quickly removing it with his finger and thumb as she turned away from him. Looking at the offending whisker, Tom couldn't help thinking that it reminded him of a watch spring, as he brushed it away on his pants.

As Brigitte rose to get out of the buggy seat, her bonnet brushed against the low canopy, knocking it back from her head, letting it fall, loosely tied, around the back of her neck and exposing her face to Dan and Zack, who were both standing looking up at her. There was an audible gasp from the two boys, as they saw Brigitte, who they hadn't seen for over a year. She started to step down to the dusty yard with a smile on her face and a look of self-belief in the twinkle in her eyes.

It was certainly Brigitte Bergman, no doubt about it. She had the same features, but she looked different. Gone was the puppy fat that used to make her wobble when she walked, and her once chubby features were now slim and chiseled. Her hair was done up in the modern style from the east, and she wore a smart dress that accentuated her shapely figure, making her look taller.

Brigitte smiled at Dan and Zack, with a confidence that she never had before, and offered a gloved hand to them both, as they stood looking up at her, their mouths wide open, their chins just about dropping into the dusty yard. Young Dan dashed forward and took the proffered gloved hand lightly in his own.

"Why, Miss Brigitte," he stammered, amazed at the difference in her. "It sure is a pleasure to see you."

"It's good to see you again, Daniel. You too Zachariah," she said as his brother came rushing forward. "I'm really looking forward to the wedding today."

"You're looking mighty pretty this morning, Brigitte," Zack said, taking his hat off and bowing slightly towards her. "In fact, you never looked prettier."

"Why thank you, Zack, that's very kind of you." She paused to wipe her brow with a silk handkerchief that she had removed from her sleeve. "I sure would appreciate a cool drink after that long buggy ride," Brigitte said, looking at the two Travis boys coquettishly, as she stood and adjusted her bonnet.

"I'll get it," said Dan, dashing up the porch steps in front of his twin brother; to the amusement of his ma, who had come out to greet the visitors and was herself marveling at the change in the young Bergman girl. She stepped to one side as Dan dashed past her, hoping to get in Brigitte's good books by getting her a cold drink.

"Sorry, Ma," he said as he swept past his mother, beating his brother to the door.

Brigitte turned back to the buggy and waved her arm at someone who had been hidden by her and her parents, sitting behind them in the small bucket seat.

"Let me introduce you to my new friend, Mrs. Monks," said Brigitte, as the newcomer alighted from the buggy. "Mrs. Joan Monks."

Everyone turned to look at the young woman, as she stepped down. A beautiful young lady, who looked to be in her early thirties, who caught her long dress on something as she reached the ground and accidently exposed too much of one of her shapely legs. Adjusting her clothing and dusting herself down, she went and stood with Brigitte Bergman and looked around at the others.

Joan Monks was elegantly beautiful, with long, wavy, auburn hair, a lovely smile, which showed her perfect teeth, and her shapely figure was enhanced by the tight fit of her dress, which drew attention the curvy bosoms straining beneath it. She had a light tanned complexion and the large hat she wore accentuated her Latin looks.

Brigitte was getting all the attention from the Travis boys, although the young men noticed how pretty she was, Mrs. Monks looked far too old for them, so Tom went over and introduced himself to her.

Alice went over to join her husband, who was also talking to Lukas and Heike, and greeted them both warmly, and asked them to join her and Tom on the porch for a cool drink. Lukas Bergman introduced Brigitte's friend to the Travis's.

"This is our Brigitte's new friend, Mrs. Monks," he said with a smile. "They met back east at Brigitte's college. Sadly, Mrs. Monks' husband, a ship's captain, was lost at sea last year, so she decided to travel back with Brigitte and find a teaching position nearby. She will be staying with us for the present." He paused for a moment, holding his hat in both hands. "I hope you will not be offended that we brought her to the wedding, but we didn't want to leave her alone in this wild country."

Alice went and grasped Mrs. Monks by the hand. "Of course, she is welcome here. We are very pleased to meet you Mrs. Monks. I shall show you around our place later."

"Please, call me Joan," she said, smiling warmly. "Only my students call me Mrs. Monks."

Alice linked arms with the beautiful newcomer and led her onto the porch.

The Bergman's sons and their three cowhands were trying to engage the other Travis boys in conversation, but they were hovering around young Brigitte, like a pack of hungry wolves circling their prey.

Mrs. Bergman smiled at Alice and Tom, the expression making one of her warts disappear into the folds of her cheeks, like a gopher down its hole. She looked down at little Rose, who was being held in Alice's arms and without any expression of disapproval or malicious comment, she swept the little girl into her arms and kissed her on the forehead, making her giggle with delight. "What a beautiful girl you have," Heike said to Alice, handing back the child. Alice explained to Mrs. Bergman how Rose had been found down by the river last fall and all about the death of her mother, killed by deserters, causing Heike Bergman to shake her head in sadness as she followed Alice to the porch.

Tom introduced Joel and Tex to the Bergman's, who had both come out of the house, clean shaven and smelling of soap, Joel with two fresh cuts on his chin. They were both dressed in their best duds, sporting shiny, polished boots; Joel wearing his usual spurs, which were jingling as he walked. They had both left their pistols and gun belts in their saddle bags. Tex had even removed the long, wicked looking, skinning knife from his boot, and they both felt a little naked and vulnerable without side arms but realized the impropriety of being armed for the wedding ceremony, especially Tex as he would be giving the bride away.

Joel and Tex were then introduced to Joan Monks, and she greeted them both warmly, reserving a special smile for Joel, who blushed with embarrassment at the look that she gave him. Tex nudged Joel in his back and walked away with a smile on his face, leaving them both to get to know each other.

Damn! Tex thought to himself. *I sure wish that I had brought 'Donna the Slut' along to this wedding. I'm sure that she would have fit in with these good folk.*

"It's a good day for the wedding," said Lukas Bergman as he sat drinking a glass of cool lemonade. "The days are starting to get warmer and longer now." He put down his glass and took out his handkerchief, turning away from the others who had gathered on the porch, and slightly raised his eye patch to remove the sweat and dust that had accumulated during the dusty ride. He was more than a little self-conscious about his missing eye, and, if asked, would explain in some detail about the mining accident that, he claimed, had caused it. Although most folk liked to believe the other story, that was common knowledge in the Territory, due to an influx of German immigrants in the area, some of them from the Bergman's hometown in Germany.

To rid himself of the attention that he had made with his eye patch, Lukas turned to look at Tom's boys, who were all still giving his daughter their undivided attention, and spoke to Tom.

"It looks like there could well be another wedding soon, Mr. Travis, if our Brigitte takes a fancy to one of your sons."

"It sure looks that way," Tom said, laughing and looking at Alice, who was laughing herself at her son's antics. "They are all running around her faster than a clutch of nervous chickens in a henhouse being chased by a fox."

More like flies on a dog turd, as my old grand pappy would say, thought Joel, listening to the conversation, as he stood behind Lukas and Tom, and glancing over at Joan Monks, who was sipping her cold lemonade. She seemed to know that Joel was looking at her, even though he tried not to make it too obvious, and looked up at him with a confident smile and winked.

Joel, seeing Joan's playful gesture, started to cough and choke on the cigarette that he was smoking and reached for the jug that Tex was holding and took a good swallow.

"She has turned into a fine young lady," said Alice to Lukas, above the noise of Joel's coughing. "I'll bet that you are both proud of her."

Lukas and Heike both nodded in agreement, smiling proudly.

"Looks like that young lady has got her eye on you, Joel," Tex said, quietly whispering in Joel's ear. "It's about time that you went and found yourself a good woman."

"Don't be foolish, Tex. What would she see in a cowboy like me? Anyways, I heard her say that she's still trying to get over the loss of her husband." He sighed and turned to Tex. "Still I gotta say she's one hell of good looking woman."

"Well, don't hang back my friend. I don't reckon that she'll be without another man for too long. Don't let the grass grow under your feet."

Father Benito came walking over from the barn, assisted by his sturdy staff, and accompanied by Pat, who was looking clean and smart in his wedding suit. Pat still felt more like a lumbering oaf, even in his finery, but Alice smiled her approval at him, which gave him some confidence, but he could still feel his face reddening up from his discomfort.

"Why, Patrick, you certainly look the dashing bridegroom this morning," she said to him.

"Thank you, Alice, but I don't feel very dashing to be sure. I feel more like a young Dublin boy off to Sunday School in his brother's hand me downs," he answered, tugging at the too tight shirt collar at his neck.

"Now, leave that shirt collar alone," Alice said, adjusting his necktie, which he had pulled loose, and trying to button the suit up. She gave up, realizing that the suit borrowed from one her boys, wasn't meant to fit a big beefy lad like Pat. "You'll get it all dirty before we've even started," she added, flicking imaginary dust from the suit with a cloth. "And give me that old cap. I took it off you once," Alice took the offending headgear from him, putting it into her apron pocket, then pulled a hairbrush out and smoothed his unkempt locks into some semblance of tidiness. "I told Sarah, earlier, to take that cap away from you, but you must have retrieved it."

As they were all standing in the yard, talking, Alice's cousin, Kyle, with his wife and son, came riding in. They were, all three, perched on an old buggy, pulled by a single old plough horse that looked like it was heading for the knackers' yard.

Seeing them arrive, Alice turned to her husband. "Now do try and be nice to them, Tom. You know that he's my only kin," she said quietly.

"I ain't got nothing against Lisa and young Clovis, Alice. In fact, I feel sorry for them both," he replied softly. "It's that no good cousin of yours that I can't abide. But I shall keep my feelings to myself, on this happy wedding day, so don't you worry now."

Tom gently squeezed his wife's hand as Kyle and his family climbed down off the buggy and approached them, forcing a smile to his face as he held out his hand to welcome Kyle.

"It's good to see you, Tom," said Kyle. "Thanks for inviting us to the wedding."

"Sure thing," grunted Tom as he shook Kyle's hand, feeling the softness in the man's fingers and the lack of calluses on his palm. Alice's cousin hadn't done a decent day's work for quite a while. Alice hugged her cousin, Kyle, and warmly greeted his wife, Lisa, introducing them to the rest of the gathering, as the Travis boys made young Clovis welcome.

Alice and Tom introduced Kyle and his family to Joel and Tex, and then presented the Bergman's to them. Kyle couldn't take his eyes off Joan Monks, and he only let go of her hand after his wife, Lisa, had pulled him away, none too gently.

Joel saw how infatuated Kyle was by the beauty of Joan and thought to himself that maybe Tex was right, and he shouldn't let a woman like that get away.

Chapter 13

Once all the guests were assembled and the newcomers had rested from their journey, Tom took Father Benito to one side and had a quiet word with him. He then rounded up everyone, and they all went over to the area at the side of the barn that had been set out with benches and a makeshift altar for the wedding.

It was a fine morning for the wedding; there was still a bite in the air from the snow high up in the mountains, but it was going to be a bright sunny day as, once again, the days began to give out their first few breaths of warm spring air and close the door on winter. The women wore shawls over their best dresses to keep off the chill, until the day warmed up.

Joel took a seat at the front with Pat, as he had been asked to act as the lad's best man, although he hadn't the faintest idea of what his duties were. He sat with the nervous Irish lad, wishing that he could pull out a stogie from his pocket and have a well-earned smoke, and occasionally glancing around to look at Joan Monks, who saw him looking and smiled provocatively back at him.

Tom and his sons sat on the bench behind Pat and Joel with the Bergman's seated directly behind them and Brigitte's friend Joan beside her. The Travis boys spending most of the time looking round at Brigitte, trying to catch her eye. She smiled to herself and ignored the smiling and lecherous looks from the boys, knowing that now she had the upper hand when it came to matters of romance.

Alice sat at the rear with her cousin, Kyle. His wife, Lisa, was keeping the little girl, Rose, occupied while Alice kept Sarah in check. Sarah was all dressed up in her bridesmaid's outfit, raring to get on with it, and if her ma was to let go of her before the bride arrived then she would be all messed up in no time at all.

Lukas Bergman sat with his old accordion on his lap, and he kept glancing around him to see if the bride was ready. His wife kept scowling at him, her face like an old, upturned, well-worn, leather saddlebag. She didn't like him playing his accordion and thought he played it badly, but he was determined to defy her and play it. After all, he had managed to bring it with him from Germany, much to the displeasure of his wife, and he would probably be made to suffer for his disobedience later, when they returned home. *But, what the hell*, he thought as he rubbed at his eye patch, bringing back pleasant memories of a young German girl, dressed in pig-tails and nothing much else, back in the old country. He would enjoy a glass of Schnapps later with Tom, as he had brought a couple of jars of it with him, hidden in the buggy below the seat. It was rare that Lukas had an opportunity to enjoy himself, and he was determined to make the most of it today.

Lukas was beginning to fidget on the hard, wooden bench when he heard a movement behind him and, turning around, he saw that the bride had arrived. He quickly squeezed some air into the accordions bellows and, placing his hands into the worn leather straps, began to coax a tune out of the old instrument.

Charlotte walked slowly past him on the arm of the smiling but slightly embarrassed Tex, with little Sarah walking proudly behind them with a smile on her face wide enough to nearly touch both of her ears. Sarah's hair was hanging down in bright, curly ringlets, and she was dressed in a frock that had taken Alice, with the help of Charlotte, a long time to make. Charlotte was carrying a small bunch of early spring flowers, which Alice had managed to gather that morning—some Bluebonnets and red and yellow desert blooms—all tied neatly in a strip of white lace.

The tune that Lukas began to play, an old German melody, made the rest of the small group look around at the bride to be, and even Heike Bergman nodded her approval at her husband's choice, and the way that he played. She gave Lukas her best smile and what was supposed to be a wink, but instead, it gave her face the look of a collapsed trifle and made him think that she must be pleased with him and that maybe he was in for a treat later in the evening. But then, he thought, maybe that was an aspiration too far. He carried on playing until Charlotte and Tex reached Pat and Joel at the front of the seated gathering, and Father Benito nodded to him to cease his playing. Lukas placed the accordion beneath the bench, at his feet, and sat back, as his wife and daughter both smiled at him benevolently.

Joel nodded to Tex as he arrived with Charlotte on his arm. The two cowboys were both bareheaded, as they had been told not to wear their hats, and Tex's hair had been plastered down with water, and it still looked damp. Joel too had tried hard to tame his unruly locks, without much success, but his usually straggly mustache looked neatly trimmed.

Charlotte handed her bunch of flowers to the, still smiling, Sarah, who happily took them and waved them vigorously at her ma and pa, making them both laugh as petals flew in the air, landing in the laps of those in the front seats.

The service was a short and simple affair, which Father Benito conducted in his broken English, with the occasional Spanish and Latin phrases thrown in, to make up for his lack of understanding of the language. Coming from a good Irish, Catholic upbringing, Pat understood most of the Latin, as the priests at the orphanage had made him learn it with a daily beating to help him remember it. It was the rest of the service that he struggled to understand.

Joel passed the ring over to Pat, for him to place on Charlotte's finger. It was Alice's mother's old wedding ring, which she had given to Charlotte for a wedding present. Standing behind Pat and Charlotte, Joel remembered his time spent with the settlers, where he had first met Pat and the beautiful Irish girl, Caitlin, and he wondered if he would ever see her again. He made a mental note to ask Pat, after the service, if he knew where the settlers were headed for, as he absently picked at a bit of dried blood on his chin, from Charlottes handiwork with the razor, making it bleed again. He noticed how Pat and Charlotte gazed adoringly at each other and could see that they were both very much in love, as he recalled his short time with Caitlin and regretted not taking advantage of the situation, but the memory of his time with her was beginning to fade, as he thought of the attractive young woman sitting a few feet behind him.

Father Benito blessed the bride and groom and said that they were now man and wife and told Pat that he could kiss the bride. Pat stood there puzzled, not quite understanding the old friar, until Charlotte grabbed him around his neck and pulled him down towards her. He soon understood and, lifting his new bride off her feet, with both large hands around her waist, he planted a long lingering kiss on her mouth, with the noisy cheering and clapping sounding behind them.

The small group of wedding guests gathered around the bride and groom, Joel and Tex shaking the happy looking Pat by the hand. Tom's boys and the Bergman's sons, along with their young cowhands, all queued up to give Charlotte a kiss, each of them lingering for far too long when it was their turn, having to be pulled away by the next eager lad in the line.

"Come on now, boys. That's quite enough of that," shouted Tom, as the situation looked like getting out of hand, with Pat getting a bit frustrated at all the attention that his new bride was getting.

The Travis boys moved away, laughing, leaving Charlotte all flustered, and turned their attention to Brigitte, who was busy talking to Alice, telling her all about her trip to Pennsylvania and the young ladies college that she had attended.

"Look out, Brigitte, here come my sons," Alice said to Brigitte. "No doubt they'll all be wanting a dance with you soon. You will have to tell me, later, all about the latest fashions from back east."

"I shall do that, Mrs. Travis," Brigitte said, her eyes twinkling as she smiled at the four Travis boys, as they surrounded her. Alice moved away, carrying the little girl, Rose, and with Sarah leading her over to the table that was laden with food, which she had covered over with some spare cotton sheets to keep away the insects and dust. She poured Sarah a glass of lemon drink, while she waited for the others to join her at the tables, removing her apron and wiping her hands on it, as Sarah quietly raised a corner of the sheet covering the food and poked her finger into something wet and juicy looking. Alice laughed as the little girl sucked her finger and pulled a face, spitting out the taste of vinegar, and quickly taking a drink of lemonade to get rid of the sour taste in her mouth.

"That'll teach you not to poke your fingers into places that you shouldn't, young lady," laughed Alice as Sarah stamped her feet and walked off in a huff.

Charlotte and Pat joined Alice and took their seats at the head of the table for the wedding breakfast, both looking extremely happy, but Pat was trying to undo the, too tight, button on his shirt collar before he was overcome with the choking sensation he felt. Alice, seeing his predicament, quickly went over and deftly removed his necktie and unbuttoned his shirt collar, much to his relief, and handed him a glass of lemonade to calm him down.

"Is that better, Pat? You can have nice a cup of tea later," said Alice as Pat took a couple of swift gulps of the cool drink. Turning to Charlotte, Alice said, "You'll have to get him some larger shirts, Mrs. O'Driscoll, now that you are married."

Charlotte laughed, both at her new husband's predicament and her new surname.

"Gosh Alice, I never realized until today that I would be Mrs. Charlotte O'Driscoll. Pat had never told me his surname before. It's got a lovely sound to it." She repeated the name to herself, smiling happily.

"Well," said Pat, recovering from nearly passing out. "I never knew that your last name was Anderson, until Father Benito said it back there."

They both took their seats at the head of the table, waiting for the others to come and sit down. Joel was talking to Tom, both enjoying a stogie, while Father Benito and Lukas Bergman were both smoking their pipes, having swapped tobacco with each other. They both had their heads together in earnest conversation, as they carried on with the game of checkers that they had set up earlier. Sitting in the shade, they made strange companions, one a friendly old Mexican, Catholic monk, and the other a serious German, Lutheran Protestant, but they both seemed to hit it off together, and Lukas was even wearing a smile, as he listened to Father Benito.

They left their board game, to be carried on later, and followed the others to take their seats at the long table for the wedding breakfast.

After Alice had got everyone seated, she and Tom brought the hot food from the kitchen and distributed it on the table, alongside the platters of cold food that were already set out. Then, with the help of the boys, Tom brought some jugs of home-made lemonade, beer and corn liquor, and shared them out between the guests.

Joel had warned the others of Father Benito's need to say a prayer before eating, so everyone sat there, respectfully and patiently, while he blessed the meal. While everyone bowed their heads in reverence, the Travis boys winked at the Bergman boys, two of them stifling a laugh, until their pa saw them and scowled over his clasped hands.

Alice's cousin, Kyle, sat with his wife and son, looking at the sumptuous spread laid out before him, waiting hungrily for Father Benito to finish saying grace. He hadn't seen so much good food in a long time and thought that, perhaps, he should make more effort in the future to provide for his family. He kept glancing over to Brigitte's friend, Joan, with a lascivious look on his face, but she ignored his stares, keeping her attention on the handsome cowboy further along the table.

The wedding breakfast went well with everyone enjoying the food and drink, and the newlyweds, Pat and Charlotte, the center of attention, with all the guests toasting their happiness, and Tom making a long speech, as Tex had refused to stand up in front of the small gathering and say a few words. He said that he didn't mind escorting Charlotte, but he drew the line at speech making. He had never been one for too much conversation and, in the past, had always let his old pardner, Steve, do most of the talking when they had ridden together.

Joel was forced stand up and say something. He took off his hat, took a long draw of his stogie, and stood there nervously looking at the small gathering, feeling everyone's eyes upon him. He picked up his glass and quickly drank the contents, wiped his mouth with the back of his hand, and smiled.

"That's better, folks," he said, refilling his glass, as the others laughed, and raised it in the air. "I ain't as educated as Tom, so don't expect me to come out with big words and long phrases. The only learning I got was from my old grandpappy, and I don't reckon he would have had too much to say on the subject of marriage." He paused and looked down at Tex, who closed his eyes at the mention of Joel's Grandpappy, hoping that his friend wouldn't come out with one of his sayings.

Joel took a big breath and carried on. But I'd just like to say just one thing to Pat." He turned to the young Irish lad, who was grinning up at him. "As my old grandpappy used to say, 'A man is incomplete until he's married, then he's finished.'" As everyone laughed, except Tex, he took another pull on his stogie, and raised his glass again. "To the bride and groom," he said. He swallowed his drink and sat down, glad it was all over.

Pat leaned over and shook Joel's hand, stood up and toasted the bride, and thanked everyone for attending with a special mention for Joel for befriending him and teaching him to be a cowboy.

"If I hadn't met me old mate, Joel, then I would never have met Charlotte, and I wouldn't have been standing here the happiest man in the world," Pat said, looking adoringly at his bride and raising his glass again. He also told everyone to raise their glasses in memory of Steve Hurst, Tex's old friend, who had saved the couple's life, last year, at the cost of his own. They made a toast to Steve, in memory of his bravery, Tex even taking off his hat—which he had put back on his head after the wedding—as a sign of respect for his old friend.

Joel and Tex sat together, drinking after all the speechmaking, both feeling a little uncomfortable in their best duds. They weren't used to these sort of gatherings, especially weddings, preferring the company of cowboys and frontiersmen.

"This has sure put me off getting married, Joel," Tex said, rubbing his fingers on his smoothly shaven chin. "I don't like all these big shindigs and all this dressing up."

"Yep, I know what you mean, my old friend. I think that's why my old grandpappy never married my grandma. He was a confirmed bachelor until the day he died," replied Joel. "Weren't you once married to an Indian squaw?" he added, pulling out another stogie from his vest pocket.

"No, we were never wed. I just traded her for three horses and two rifles, to one of the Comanche chiefs, although I suppose we were married in their traditions. She was a good woman though, Joel, but she died a few years back. The only woman I would consider getting married to would be 'Donna the Slut.' Now that's my kind of woman. But it would only be a small affair."

"I sometimes used to think the same way about that Irish girl, Caitlin, who I met last year. But I don't reckon that ever I'll see her again," Joel

106

sighed, lost for a moment in thought. Then he looked over to Brigitte's friend, Joan, who saw him looking at her and raised her glass to him, and all thoughts of the Irish girl had gone.

The other center of attention was Brigitte Bergman, but that was only from her new admirers, the four Travis boys, who had all managed to sit opposite her on the long table. In fact, the eldest Travis boy, Daniel, was directly opposite her, and he seemed to be getting all of Brigitte's attention, much to the annoyance of his three brothers, especially the twins, Ike and Jake, who were both trying to get her attention. Young Zach, though, was seated directly opposite Mrs. Bergman, who kept treating him to one of her stern looks, commonly known as 'The Shriveller' by her family, every time he looked in her direction. Zack looked away from her, smiling to himself, as he thought that Mrs. Bergman, with her fat body, looked like she was perched behind a pile of cushions. And her hairstyle reminded him of the Knave of Hearts on a pack of playing cards.

Before everyone left the table, Alice brought a bowl of water and placed it in front of Father Benito and fetched little Rose, so that he could baptize her. The old friar had gladly agreed to do this when Alice had asked him the evening before. Father Benito added some holy water to the bowl from a small flask that he carried with him and conducted the short ceremony, with little Rose crying and the Bergman's acting as godparents—a duty they had been only too pleased to perform when Alice had asked them earlier.

After the meal and the christening, and all the plates had been taken away, Alice brought out her fiddle and was accompanied by Lukas Bergman, on his accordion. Joel joined in on his mouth organ, a replacement for the harp that he had lost on the Salt River, and Pat led his new bride in a dance. Tom politely asked Mrs. Bergman to dance, and his sons pushed and jostled each other to be the first one to dance with Brigitte. Daniel managed to be the victor, grinning smugly at his younger brothers as he took a tight grip around Brigitte's waist. Young Zach shrugged his shoulders and went and helped himself to a tot of the corn liquor, while his pa was busy dancing with Mrs. Berman, but the twins both went around the back of the barn, in a rage, arguing with each other about why Brigitte should favor one of them more than the other.

Ike and Jake both came back, a short while later, with their shirts ripped and their pants covered in dirt. Both were showing the beginnings of a black eye apiece, and each had a bloody nose, but they were both laughing, and had their arms around each other, the best of friends again. It would take a lot more than a pretty girl to break the close bond that was between them. Tom glanced at them both, knowing that they had been fighting; there weren't many days when the twins didn't fall out over something, but they soon made it up. Tom gave them both a small glass of beer to calm them down, and they guzzled it down in a couple of gulps, both burping and laughing.

Not used to drinking beer, Ike and Jake handed the empty glasses back to their pa, and still laughing, they joined in the dancing, linking arms and whirling around. As the music stopped, they both fell to the ground and lay on their backs laughing.

With a lot of encouragement from Tex, Joel plucked up courage to ask Joan Monks for a dance.

"I sure would be honored if you would dance with me, Miss Joan," he said, looking down at her, as she sat drinking a glass of wine from the supply that he and Tex had brought back from the Mission at San Xavier. "Although I must warn you that I ain't much of a dancer, I was brought up by my old grandpappy, and he never taught me to dance."

Joan put her glass down, stood up, and placed her hat on the seat beside it. "That's not a problem, Joel," she said, taking his hand and leading him onto the small dance area. "It's only a waltz, I'm sure that you can do that without treading on my feet with your cowboy boots. And please, call me Joan, there's no need to be so formal." She smiled up at him, as he held her hand and placed the other on her waist.

The other dancers made room for them both, as they started to dance. Tom was still in the clutches of Heike Bergman, one of the boys was pulling Brigitte around, and Kyle was dancing with his wife.

Pat and Charlotte had sat down, as the new bridegroom was all hot and bothered from his exertions and the too tight shirt he was wearing. Pat went and got a drink of wine for himself, and his wife and sat down and removed his coat. Taking a welcome drink, he noticed Joel dancing with Joan Monks and laughed. "That's it, me boyo," he yelled, raising his glass as Joel turned to look at him. Joel stumbled as his attention was drawn away from looking down at his feet, nearly tripping over Joan. Pat roared with laughter at Joel's efforts, nearly spilling his wine. "Go for it, Joel. Show them that a cowboy can dance," he shouted.

Thankfully, for Joel, the music stopped as Lukas Bergman put down his accordion and picked up his drink. Joan smiled up at Joel, who was looking more than a little embarrassed by his efforts at dancing.

"You did fine, Joel, except for that last bit, when you fell over your feet. Now let's sit down, and you can tell me all about yourself." She clasped his cheeks and kissed him on his mouth. She then led him over to a bale of straw where they sat down together; Joel looked at the others who were all looking slyly at them both.

Joan laughed at the big cowboy's apparent discomfort at being the center of attention.

"You can smoke if you like, Joel, if it makes you feel better," she said smiling at him and reaching into his vest pocket and pulling out a slightly crumpled stogie. She placed it into his open mouth and sat back on the bale with a twinkle in her eye. He lit his cigar and relaxed a little, unused to the attentions of a beautiful woman. He told Joan a little about himself, but after a few tales of roping steers and riding herd, she excused herself to get acquainted with the newlyweds, Pat and Charlotte.

"You really are a lovely man. Joel," said Joan, kissing him on his forehead as she stood up. "But I really must meet the bride and groom. We shall talk again later, before I leave with the Bergman's." She smiled at him, and he watched her as she walked away, thinking that she even looked good from the rear.

As Joan left Joel, sitting there finishing his stogie, Tex wandered over holding a glass in his hand. "This is sure fine booze that we brought from the monastery," he said, sitting down in the seat that Joan Monks had just vacated. He looked at Joel with a big grin on his face. "You seem to be getting along fine with that pretty lady, Joel. Could this be the end of your bachelor days?"

"Hell now, Tex, I've only just met the woman. But she sure is mighty pretty. I'd like to see her again, but we've got to get back to the ranch after the wedding and make sure that Father Benito gets back to the mission in one piece."

Tex laughed. "Don't use Father Benito as an excuse, Joel, you know the old friar can take care of himself better than we can. I reckon you're just frightened of being tied down."

"Well, I ain't ready yet for all that marrying business, Tex. Look at all the palaver that Pat and Charlotte have been through today. And Pat don't look so happy now that he's tied down. As my old grandpappy once said, 'Don't go poking your finger in a hornet's nest unless you're ready to be stung,' and he was a confirmed bachelor all his life. Never did marry my grandma."

"The old fool was right when he said that. Joel. But you could do worse than Joan, I reckon she's got the hots for you."

"I know, Tex, but she's going back with the Bergman's later. But I know where they live, so I reckon I'll mosey on over there sometime."

"Well, just make sure that you do, Joel. You don't want some other cowboy putting a brand on her," Tex said, emptying the contents of his glass of wine and doing a loud belch. "I can't wait to get back to Tucson and see my Donna."

"Sure, Tex," said Joel, reaching into his vest pocket for his makings. "I'll make a note of your fine words of wisdom."

Chapter 14

After the dance, everyone went and changed out of their wedding finery, all except the Bergman's, Joan, and their young cow-hands, who hadn't brought a change of clothes. The men went over to the corrals, to try and ride the unbroken horses that Tom and the boys had rounded up over the last week. Joel, Tex, and Tom declined, preferring to watch the competition between Tom's sons and the Bergman's boys, along with the young cowboys who had traveled with the Bergman's. Alice's cousin, Kyle, sat on the corral fence with his son, watching the bronco busting with a mixture of envy and interest. He loved horses, as did his son, Clovis, but had never been able to afford a decent mount of his own.

The bronco busting was a vigorous affair, with Charlotte stopping Pat from taking any further part in it, after he had been thrown twice. She wanted him in one piece, later, for their wedding night and made him watch the rest of the competition from the fence, with much jeering and lewd remarks from the other lads.

Young Daniel also left the horse breaking early after getting the 'come on' from Brigitte, and they both rode off in Tom's buggy, heading for the river bank, with much ribald commentary from the rest of the bronco riders, ringing in their ears.

Father Benito and Lukas Bergman resumed their game of checkers on the porch, both re-lighting their pipes, and enjoying a drink of Schnapps from the jar that Lukas had retrieved from his buggy. The old friar enjoyed the taste of schnapps. He thought that it was a lot different from the cheap corn liquor and the Mission wine that he was used to, and it didn't take too much encouragement for him to have another glass, or two.

Joel sidled up to Joan, who was standing at the corral, and put an arm around her waist. She looked up at him and smiled. "Aren't you going to help break in the horses, Joel?"

"No, ma'am, I'll leave it to the others. I prefer to stand and watch with you."

Joan tapped him on the hand that was around her waist. "Don't call me ma'am, Joel. It makes me sound like an old lady."

Joel tightened his grip on her and smiled. "You sure don't look like no old lady to me." He paused and added. "Joan."

They stood and watched the horse breaking for a while, Joel laughing when one of the Berman's young cowboys was thrown off a frisky young stallion. Joan looked concerned, as the young man limped away.

"I hope he's alright, Joel. He looks like he's hurt his leg."

"The boy will be fine, Joan," said Joel, smiling at Joan's concern for the cowboy. "Me, Tex, and Steve have had a lot worse than that at Rodeos. I remember once when Tex got rolled on by a bull that he had been riding. It threw him off its back and then rolled over him. He just got up and dusted himself down. Once he'd had a drink of whiskey, he got right back on that young bull and rode it into the ground. Although he's suffered a bit with a stiff leg ever since."

"Well, it looks very dangerous to me," Joan said, watching the young cowboy being helped out of the corral.

The horses had all been broken and removed from the corral, back to the pasture, and there was much snorting and kicking as the Travis twins herded a young bull into the area. All the young cowboys wanted to try out their roping and riding skills on the frisky young beast, as it rushed around, butting the fence posts with its sharp horns.

Distracted by the commotion, at the corral, Father Benito and Lukas set aside their game of checkers and wandered over to look at the young bull. Little Sarah Travis climbed to the top of the corral fence, laughing and shouting, and perched precariously on the top rail, wanting to get a good view of her brother's efforts with the bull. The corral gate was closed and the bull was left on its own while it got used to its surroundings. It rushed around the corral, kicking up the dust, as the young cowboys argued amongst themselves about which one of them would have first chance at it.

Suddenly, the young bull stopped in the middle of the corral, looking wildly around for something to charge at, as little Sarah leaned over to get a better look at it. She suddenly lost her grip on the fence rail that she was perched on, and with a scream, landed on her hands and knees in the dust. Panicking and disorientated, she crawled further into the middle of the corral closer to the bull, which turned towards her, distracted by her yelling. The bull looked at the helpless little girl, who was by now sobbing loudly, and pawed at the ground, ready to charge.

Everyone watched, transfixed with the sudden shock of what was happening, as the bull charged at Sarah. Suddenly, there was a movement as Alice's cousin, Kyle, leapt over the fence, ran to the stricken Sarah, swept her up in his arms, and held her tightly to his chest. Ignoring the charging bull, Kyle turned and took a few quick steps back towards the fence. But realizing that he wasn't going to make it, with the bull closing on him, he hurled Sarah over the fence at the astonished men on the other side.

As Joel caught Sarah in his outstretched arms, Kyle stumbled and fell into the path of the charging bull. His fall probably saved him from being pierced by the bull's horns, as it caught up with him and trampled over him. Kyle felt his left leg crack as the bull ran over him, and he lay on the ground, in pain, as it stopped and turned back towards him, ready to charge him again.

The angry beast suddenly felt a hard rap on its rump, and it turned to see who was tormenting it. Standing there was Father Benito, his staff clasped firmly in both hands, ready to strike the bull again. He had seen Sarah fall into the corral and Kyle's heroic rescue attempt, and realizing that the man was in trouble had leapt over the fence, brandishing his trusty staff.

The bull made a sudden lunge at Father Benito, but the old friar was too quick for it and side stepped, poking it in its ear with his staff and backed away, trying to lure it away from the injured Kyle. The bull then tried to butt the friar; but with the skill of a matador, he moved quickly out of reach, rapping it on its head with his staff, as it passed within a few inches of him.

While Father Benito was distracting the bull and luring it further away from the injured man, Kyle was carried out of the gate by Lukas

Bergman and two of Tom's sons and taken into the ranch house to be examined by Alice and Lisa.

Meanwhile, Tex had entered the corral, twirling a lariat above his head. Picking the right moment, he managed to rope the bull by its back legs, sending it tumbling to the ground, and tied the loose end to one of the stout gateposts. He then led Father Benito out of the corral gate, as the bull thrashed about trying to get up. Tom Travis, holding little Sarah in his arms, who by now had calmed down from her lucky escape, went over to the old friar and shook him by the hand.

"You were great in there, Father Benito," he said, laughing, more in relief than in anything else. "Great, but very foolish. It was a miracle that the bull didn't hurt you, but you were too darn quick for it. Joel and Tex told me how you stood up against those men back in Tucson. I never quite believed it all, but I sure do now."

Father Benito smiled at Tom and patted Sarah on her head. "It was nothing, *señor*. I worked with the bulls many times, when I was a young man, back in Mexico. We used to perfect our skills with the fighting staff with them. It was good practice for when we were in battle."

Joel and Tex came over to join in the praise, both smiling at each other, as if in some private joke, with a look of 'well, we told you' on their faces. Lukas Bergman handed Father Benito his bottle of schnapps. "You look like you could do with a drink of this, my friend. You were *wunderbar*. That was very heroic."

Father Benito took a long drink and handed the bottle back to Lukas. "No, my amigos," he said to the men gathered around him. "The real hero was that hombre Kyle." He looked at Tom. "It was a very brave thing that he did when he went into the corral, unarmed, and faced the bull to save your little girl. We must go and see how badly injured he is."

"You're right, Father," said Tom. "I must go and see how he is and thank him for what he did. He saved my little Sarah, and I shall always be indebted to him for that. I know I haven't always liked the man, and he has always been a mite work shy, preferring to scrounge rather than work for a living. But I've seen a different side to him today, and he's probably had more bad luck than most, so I shall be more tolerant with him from now on."

While some of the young cowboys untied the bull, and took it back to join its herd, the men went into the ranch house to see how much damage it had done to Kyle. He was lying on Alice and Tom's bed with his wife, Lisa, and Alice looking at his swollen and twisted leg. Pat and Charlotte were there also feeling a little upset that their wedding day had ended with an accident.

Father Benito knelt at the side of the bed and examined the man's injured leg.

"I am afraid it is broken, Señor," Father Benito said, looking at Kyle, who was clearly in pain and wincing as the old friar felt his leg. "It is a clean break, below the knee, and I can set it for you if you will allow me. I have had a lot of experience mending bones, and treating wounds back at the Mission and back in my old country."

Kyle nodded to Father Benito. "Go ahead, Father." He tried to smile through the pain. "I ain't in no fit state to argue with you anyways."

The old friar produced his little bag, which he had brought with him, and laid out a few items from it on the small bedside table.

"Give the Father some space now," said Tom, ushering everybody out of the bedroom, except for Kyle's wife, Lisa, and Alice. Young Clovis went out of the room, not wanting to see what his father would have to suffer while his leg was being set. Joel paused and handed Kyle a whiskey jar that he had taken from Tex, who willingly accepted it. "Here you are, pardner. Get some of this inside you. It should help dull the pain."

As Joel closed the door behind him, Pat looked at him and gave a shrug. "I'm sure glad that you're not setting his leg," he said with a smile. "I still remember when you put all that dirty mud all over my broken arm last year. What a mess you made of me, boyo."

"Yes, but it did the job, didn't it?" answered Joel as he went out on to the porch, pulling a stogie from his pocket and striking a match on the doorframe.

Just then, the bedroom door opened and Alice and Lisa came out, Alice put a pan of water on the stove and handed Lisa a clean white sheet from the cupboard, which she proceeded to tear into strips. Alice turned to Pat, who was about to follow Joel, and the other men, outside. "Pat, will you go and fetch a bucket of damp clay from down by the stream, please. Father Benito wants to pack it around Kyle's leg, when he has re-set it. And bring a handful of clean straw from the stable."

"Well! I don't believe it," said Pat, picking up a bucket and taking it outside. Joel laughed as he heard the exchange between Alice and Pat. "Now, didn't I tell you that my old grandpappy's remedies worked," he said as Pat walked past him, nodding his head from side to side.

Pat walked down to the stream with the pail, muttering to himself in his Irish brogue, and laughing loudly. Charlotte caught up with him and clasped his hand, laughing too, as she listened to her new husband's tale about the time that Joel had set his broken arm, last year—a story that she had heard, more than a few times before, but it still made her laugh.

It didn't take long for Father Benito to set Kyle's broken leg, and he was soon fast asleep with the empty whiskey jar still clutched in his hand.

Before sunset, the Bergman's left for home after waiting for Daniel and Brigitte's return in the buggy. Lukas Berman was a little angry that their daughter had gone off with Daniel Travis unchaperoned, and also that they would be late getting back to their own place before sunset, but his wife was smiling at her daughter when she returned, hoping that, at last, she had found someone to marry, and she looked over to Alice who was also looking happy with the blossoming romance. Daniel helped Brigitte up into the Bergman's buggy and whispered in her ear, as she sat between her parents, promising to ride over and see her very soon. He looked a mite sad as she went away, wedged tightly between her parents.

Joel helped Joan Monks up into the rumble seat at the back of the buggy, and once she was seated, he leaned in and gave her a lingering kiss. She held him tightly for a while, then pulled back, removed her silk scarf and tied it loosely around his neck.

"There, that should remind you to come and call on me, when you're not too busy roping steers."

Joel whispered something in her ear and stepped back with a big grin.

Alice went and stood by Daniel and put her arm on his shoulder, as he stood there looking crestfallen, as he waved goodbye to Brigitte. "Is there something you ought to be telling me, Son," she said, looking up at her eldest boy, and smiling.

"Erm! No, Ma. I don't reckon there is," stammered Dan, starting to go red around his neck. His ears turning bright pink.

"Well, when there is, don't forget that I asked," she added as her son waved to the receding buggy. She smiled up at Joel, as she turned to walk back to the ranch-house, and tapped him playfully on his rear. "You too, Joel. It's about time that you settled down."

With all the festivities over, Pat and Charlotte went into the ranch house for an early night, with Pat receiving a few knowing winks and nudges from Tom's boys. Tom had been busy through the winter, extending the ranch house, with the help of Pat and the boys. They had constructed two extra bedrooms, one for Pat and Charlotte, although they had never used it before the wedding. And a separate room for Sarah and little Rose, as Tom and Alice wanted some privacy of their own at last. Charlotte had used the new bedroom herself, all winter, as Tom and Alice wouldn't allow Pat to share it with her until after the wedding, so he had to bunk with the Travis boys, who were glad to see him go, as much as he was to leave. He too was looking forward to a peaceful night alone with Charlotte, away from the snoring, farting, and belching, and the occasional fight that seemed to be a nightly occurrence in the large bedroom, especially with the twins.

Although that wasn't the main reason that Pat was eager to get Charlotte alone, as he held his new bride's hand tightly in anticipation as they made their way indoors, both shaking grains of rice from their hair that had been thrown over them as they were married. Alice whispered something in Charlotte's ear, before they went into the bedroom, and she giggled shyly at her as she followed Pat and closed the door behind them.

Tom went into the bedroom where Kyle was recovering, accompanied by Lisa and Clovis. Kyle was sitting up, wide awake, but looking very tired, a combination of the pain from his leg and the contents of Tex's whiskey jug, which he had quickly hidden under the pillow when he heard the door opening.

"How are yah doing, Kyle?" Tom said, shaking him by the hand, as Alice came in with little Sarah. She had wanted to come and thank her uncle Kyle for saving her from the bull.

"That was a fine thing you did, Kyle. You saved our little girl from getting injured, or worse," Tom added as Sarah skipped over to the bed and planted a big kiss on Kyle's forehead. He blushed as Sarah returned to her ma, looking self-consciously at his wife and son, as they both looked proudly at him. He had never seen them looking at him that way before, and it was a new experience which he could get used to.

"That's alright, Tom. I couldn't let that bull trample her down, so I had to do something to help her. Anyway, I can't take up your bed any longer, so help me to get up."

Kyle tried to get out of the bed, but Alice put a hand on his shoulder. "Now you stop right there, Kyle, and rest. You and Alice can have our bed tonight. Can't they Tom?"

Tom nodded in agreement as Alice spoke again. "And Clovis can bunk down in Sarah's bedroom. She won't mind."

Tom and Alice went out of the bedroom and left Kyle alone with his family. They would be sleeping in their large pantry tonight.

Chapter 15

Joel and Tex sat out on the porch, with Tom and Father Benito, enjoying the evening as the days grew longer, and finishing a jug of corn liquor. Tex had found another jug of the hard stuff after Joel had given his last one to Kyle, and was drinking most of the contents himself, as the others enjoyed a smoke. Father Benito held the jar of schnapps tightly in his hand, which Lukas Bergman had given to him as a parting gift, promising that when they next met, perhaps, at Brigitte's wedding, then he would share another jar with him.

"We'll be heading back to the ranch, come the morning," Joel said. "We had better get old Father Benito back to the Mission in San Xavier, all in one piece, before he gets too much of a liking for all the wrong things," he added, looking over at the old friar, who was sharing the jug of corn liquor with Tex, as he had already finished his jar of schnapps.

"Yep," agreed Tex. "But I reckon the old fella can take care of himself. Why he's even a damn fine bullfighter now."

Father Benito took a long drink from the jug, wiped his mouth with his sleeve, and smiled at the others as he passed the liquor jug back to Tex. He looked like he was more than a little tipsy, as he sat back, closed his eyes, and puffed away on his old clay pipe as he perched on the porch steps. "Ole!" he shouted, waving his straw hat in the air.

"I don't reckon that he'll be up too early in the morning, the state that he's in," Tom said, looking at Father Benito, and smiling. "But he sure is one hell of a man."

"Yes, but we should have kept him well away from corn liquor, and especially that jar of German grog that Lukas Bergman gave to him," agreed Joel.

"You're damn right there, Joel. It looks like he's drunk all of it," said Tex, tipping the jug up and watching the few drops trickle out onto the dusty boards of the porch. He put the jug down and, with the help of Joel, carried Father Benito safely back to the barn and laid him down on his bedding. Before they left him to sleep the booze off, Joel took the pipe from his mouth and placed it on the ground, first making sure it wasn't still lit. He didn't want to spoil the old friar's clothing after he had gone to so much trouble washing and mending it the night before

Joel and Tex crept quietly out of the barn, trying to close the door behind them without too much noise, so as not to disturb Father Benito. All they could hear from the darkness was Father Benito muttering in his sleep, in Spanish. As Joel gently dropped the latch into the door keep, he turned to Tex with a smile.

"It sounded to me like Father Benito was praying to himself, in his sleep."

"I can understand Spanish, Joel, and it didn't sound like the old boy was praying to me. The state that he's in we'll be lucky to get away from here before noon, tomorrow. He's going to need a few strong cups of coffee inside him before he'll be fit to mount a horse, let alone ride it for any distance."

"Well, I don't reckon he gets much chance to let his hair down back at the monastery, and with all the things that he's been up to, just lately, the old fella deserves to have some fun."

"Yep, you're right," said Tex. "Let's go and see if we've got any of that wine left, before we turn in."

Father Benito was up and about well before sunrise the next morning. He had risen early from his bed of hay, making sure that he didn't disturb Joel and Tex, who were both snoring soundly, up in the hayloft. He said his prayers, carried out his ablutions at the water trough, and walked into the ranch kitchen just as Alice was about to prepare breakfast for everyone. She looked at the old friar in surprise. Tom had told her last night about the amount of drink that he had consumed, and how Joel and Tex had helped him to the barn and put him to bed.

"*Buenos Dias, señora,*" said Father Benito, smiling at Alice as he entered the kitchen, holding a few fresh eggs in his upturned straw sombrero. "I took the liberty of collecting some of your eggs for breakfast, as I thought that you would like to try some of my pancakes.

I made some of them for *señors* Joel and Tex on the journey from Tucson, and they seemed to like them very much."

He placed the eggs in a bowl that Alice gave him and brought out a small jar of honey and a bag of cinnamon from out of his robes.

"That's very kind of you, Father," Alice said, smiling at Father Benito. "I'll get the bacon and corn bread and we'll prepare breakfast together." She looked at the old friar, who smiled at her. "How are you feeling, Father, after all the wedding festivities," she said tactfully. Trying not to mention the fact that he had been very drunk last night.

"I feel wonderful, *señora*. It is a long time since I enjoyed myself so much. It was a lovely wedding, but I cannot wait to return to the Mission at San Xavier, and my life of prayer and devotion to the Lord."

Joel and Tex came in from the barn, where they had been bunking down. They could smell the bacon frying, but both were feeling the effects of the booze that they had drunk the night before, after putting Father Benito to bed. Especially Tex, who had finished off the jug of corn liquor with Father Benito and had staggered off to bed down in the hay next to him. They had both dipped their heads in the water trough to shake off their hangovers and entered the kitchen, wiping their faces with their bandannas, as they were met with the sight of Father Benito looking as fresh as the early morning dew, and as chirpy as a day-old chicken.

"Well blow me down," said Tex, holding his sore head and looking at Father Benito, as he turned to greet them both, holding his bowl with the pancake mixture in and stirring it vigorously. "It feels like I've got a herd of Buffalo stampeding through my head and that stirring ain't helping it. You look like all that you drank last night was strong coffee, and I reckon you drank more booze than me and Joel put together."

"*Buenos Dias, señors*. How are you both on this fine morning? I am making some pancakes for your *desayuno*. I remember that you both enjoyed them before."

"Sit yourselves down, you two. You look as bad as Tom does. I'll pour you both a strong cup of coffee," Alice said as the pantry door opened, and her bleary-eyed husband came slowly into the kitchen, and took his place at the table, forcing a smile at Joel and Tex. He looked at Father Benito in the same incredulous manner that Joel and Tex had.

Tom and Alice had both bunked down on the floor of the large pantry, sleeping on an old mattress, because they had given up their own bed to Kyle and Lisa.

As Alice poured the three men a cup of coffee each, and dished them up some bacon and beans, the four Travis boys entered the kitchen. The twins sat down, both sporting a black eye apiece, laughing and joking between themselves. Zach sat down yawning, and Daniel came in with a smug expression on his face, and as he passed Alice, he kissed her on the cheek.

"Morning, Ma," said Dan as Alice nearly dropped a plate in surprise. It wasn't often that she got a kiss from one of her sons.

"You look mighty happy this morning, Son. Do I smell romance in the air?"

Young Daniel sat quietly down and busied himself with his plate of bacon and beans, while his brothers began to tease him.

"Be quiet you three. It's good that your brother has found a nice young girl to court, and young Brigitte is a fine catch for any boy," said Alice.

"It sure is, Son," Tom said, waking up a bit after a drink of coffee and patting his eldest boy on his back. "That Brigitte has sure turned into a real beauty. She doesn't take after her ma and pa one little bit. I reckon they both must have been hiding behind the door when the good Lord handed out good looks, especially Mrs. Bergman. Now, don't you let her get away, Son, 'cause I reckon there's three more around this table who would like to take your place."

Daniel puffed out his chest and looked around at his brothers, feeling all the better for the kind words from his pa.

"And what about you, Joel?" Alice said, turning around with the frying pan in her hand. "You seemed to have taken a liking for the Bergman's friend, Joan. She's a fine-looking woman, Joel, and I reckon that she likes you too." She nodded at the silk scarf that Joel had tied around his neck under his bandanna.

Joel blushed and nearly choked on a mouthful of beans, as the others looked at him.

"You're not wrong there, Alice. She sure is a beautiful woman, and I would like to see her again. But I ain't rushing into anything that I might regret. As my old grandpappy used to say, 'Don't always take the fast road, sometimes it's better to enjoy the long, easy way around.'"

Tex let out a loud groan and carried on eating.

Father Benito finished his pancake mix and quickly poured it on the hot griddle. He looked around and caught Dan's eye, as he saw him busy eating and raised a finger up to the ceiling, as the others put down their plates and patiently waited for the old friar's blessing to eat. Dan looked at the others, put his fork down, and bent his head in supplication, still chewing a mouthful of bacon. Father Benito said a short prayer before he laid a plate, filled with pancakes, in the center of the breakfast table.

Pat and Charlotte were the last to enter the kitchen, and they both took their places at the table, wearing a look of satisfaction and contentment on their faces.

"Top of the morning to you all," said Pat, smiling. "And what a fine morning it is, to be sure," he added, kissing his new wife on her cheek and making her blush.

As they all finished breakfast, Tom sat back and wiped the honey from his mouth with the back of his hand.

"Those pancakes were the best that I've ever had in a long time," said Tom, looking across the table at Father Benito. "If you ever want to leave the mission and come and cook for us, then let me know," he added, as he quickly ducked to avoid a damp cloth that Alice had playfully thrown at him.

"Sorry, Tom, but I reckon we'd better get him back to the mission before the other friars miss his cooking," said Joel, sliding his chair back from the table, and heading for the door, as he pulled out his makings. "We've enjoyed seeing you folks again, especially Pat and Charlotte, but we'll be making trail after I'd had me a smoke."

Tex licked the honey from his fingers, wiped pancake crumbs from his lips, and followed Joel out of the door to get his horse saddled up for the long ride back.

"We'll ride back with you, part of the way," Pat said, looking at Charlotte, who nodded her approval.

"That's a good idea. I reckon I'll ride with you as well," said Tom. "I'll go and see how Kyle is getting on first."

Kyle hobbled out on to the porch, with the aid of a wooden crutch that one of the boys had found under a bed, one arm over his wife's shoulder for support. It had been used before by young Ike, when he had been wounded in his leg the year before.

"You look a lot better this morning, Kyle. How's the leg?" asked Tom, helping Kyle to sit down.

"It's feeling a lot better, thanks, Tom. I don't know what Father Benito did to it but, whatever it was seems have made the swelling go down."

"Well you rest up here a while. I'm going to ride back with Joel and Tex as far as the high mesa. I'll be back some time tomorrow, and we'll sort out a few things when I return." The old animosity towards Alice's cousin had mostly left Tom after the brave rescue of Sarah in the path of the bull. "I'll get the twins to ride over to your place to make sure your livestock is alright."

Tom knew that Kyle didn't have much in the way of livestock—a couple of old milk cows and a few goats and chickens—but he felt the need to help him out. "They can also cut out a few young calves from my herd and take them back for you. I'll get them to make sure that one of them is a bull calf."

"That's mighty kind of you, Tom," said Kyle, looking a little embarrassed. He held his wife's hand. "You and Alice have taken a lot of hassle from me in the past, and I've deserved all the things you've said to me, but I can't thank you enough for all the help you're giving me."

"That's fine, Kyle," Alice said. And we've got a young mare that I'm sure Clovis would like to have. He can take it back when you are well enough to travel." She looked over to her husband, who smiled and nodded in agreement.

Father Benito came out of the ranch house to prepare for the journey back, and Kyle called him over to thank him for his help. He looked at Kyle's leg and examined the dried mud and straw that he had daubed around the break. He looked up at Lisa and smiled.

"It looks fine, Señora, but keep this moist. Don't let the clay dry and come off. Leave it on for a week and then try and see a proper doctor. My skills are very limited when it comes to medical matters."

Chapter 16

Joel and Tex said their goodbyes to Alice and Sarah and three of the boys. Young Zack had been allowed to join his pa, as they rode back with the newlyweds and Father Benito riding with them.

Riding up the hill, they passed Steve Hurst's grave and Tex took off his hat and saluted his old friend. Father Benito raised his hand in a blessing, and Tom promised that he would fix the brass plate that Tex had brought back from Tucson that he had left leaning against the wooden cross.

******

The journey from the ranch was mostly uneventful. Joel had been talking to Pat, as they rode along together, asking him about the settlers who he had been with when they had first met. He wanted to know where they had been heading for and also trying to get as much information about the Irish girl, Caitlin, who he still had some feelings for. Pat hadn't been too sure of where the settler's destination was, he had been happy just going along with them, but thought that they had mentioned north west, possibly Oregon.

Joel told Pat that, perhaps, he might try and forget about Caitlin, as finding her could be difficult and anyway, he thought that he had strong feelings for Joan Monks and would like to see her again in the summer when he had got some more time away from the ranch. Pat said that he would be happy to help him locate her, once he had settled in to married life with Charlotte.

"I ain't going to drag you away from that pretty new wife of yours Pat. I think that you've both had too many risky experiences just lately, and Charlotte looks a lot happier since we rescued her from those apaches last year."

"We shall see, me boyo. I'm not chained to the kitchen sink just yet," said Pat. He abruptly finished his conversation with Joel, as Charlotte moved her horse closer to the two men after hearing her name mentioned.

* * * * * *

It wasn't until the late afternoon, when they had stopped to make a fire to heat up the coffee pot and have some of Alice's cold meatloaf and apple pie, that events took a sudden unexpected turn. Pat and Charlotte were going to spend the night under the stars with the others, before returning to the ranch with Tom and Zack, and they were all enjoying the remains of the day out in the wilderness. Joel and Tom were having a smoke by the fire, and Tex was trying out his Spanish on Father Benito.

Pat and Charlotte had gone for a walk to the top of a nearby hill, accompanied by Zack, to look at the view from the top, when suddenly Pat came rushing back to the camp, out of breath, and pointing towards the south.

"We can see a rider in the distance, Joel, so I thought that I'd better warn you," said Pat, catching his breath, as he reached for the small telescope that he kept in his saddlebag, and pulling out his rifle in case of trouble. He had become a lot more cautious in the short time that he had lived in the West. The young Dublin boy had been replaced by a young cowboy, still a mite green, but a lot surer of himself now.

Joel and Tex quickly followed Pat up the slope, and they both looked into the distance, in the direction that Charlotte was pointing.

"It's a white man," said Charlotte whose eyesight was better than the others. "He's coming up from the south, and he looks in one hell of a hurry."

"I wonder who it is, and where he is heading?" said Joel, squinting his eyes to get a better focus.

The rider suddenly slowed down and turned his horse towards their camp. He must have seen the smoke from their campfire as he spurred his horse in their direction, kicking up dust from the dry ground. Joel looked through the spyglass that Pat handed to him, focused it on the rider, and let out a low whistle.

"Why that sure looks like Young Billy Brand kicking up the dust. What the hell is he doing out here all on his lonesome and so far from the ranch?"

He handed the spyglass to Tex who focused it on the rider and nodded in agreement.

"Yep, that's Young Billy alright. I'd recognize that horse anywhere, and he looks to be in an all fired hurry to get somewhere. Perhaps, the lad has gone and got himself lost."

"That wouldn't surprise me at all," agreed Joel.

As Young Billy approached, Tex and Joel waved their hats at him, and the young cowboy's face lit up as he realized it was his friends from the ranch. He reined in near the campfire and dismounted, his horse looking tired and sweaty. Flecks of foam were gathered around the metal bit in the horse's mouth and steam rose from its flanks. Young Billy looked worn out from his long ride but, like a good cowboy, the first thing that he did was think about his tired horse. He quickly unsaddled it, removed the blanket from its back, and let it run free down to the small creek. Joel and Tex smiled at each other at the way that Young Billy had looked after his horse as it drank its fill from the stream and then rolled in the long grass to remove the sweat from its body. Young Billy came over to them, still grinning.

"I'm sure glad that I found you both," he said, removing his bandanna and wiping the dust and sweat from his face. "I could sure use a drop, or two, of that corn liquor of yours after my long ride to find you. I've been in the saddle for hours heading for the Gila River, and if I hadn't seen the smoke from your campfire I'd have rode right past you."

"Well you found us now, boy. But you're out of luck with the liquor. I know that you've developed a taste for it recently, but between me and that old friar over there, it's all gone. You'll have to make do with a strong cup of coffee instead," said Tex. "Now sit down and take the load off, and tell us what you're so, all fired, excited about."

Young Billy dropped wearily down onto his saddle, which he had put down near the campfire, and gratefully accepted a mug of coffee from Charlotte, who handed it to him with a smile.

"How's the shoulder, Young Billy?" enquired Joel, noticing the bandage that was on his wound from his encounter with the grizzly bear. It was covered in dust, but a few drops of dried blood were showing through the dressing that old Stumpy had put on, back at the ranch.

"It's fine, thanks, Joel," said Young Billy, looking up at the others who had gathered round to hear why he had come looking for Joel and Tex. "Did they tell you that I got this wound fighting a grizzly bear?" he said, his words coming out in a rush of excitement, as he rubbed his bandaged arm.

"And did they tell you about how I saved them from a pack of wolves?" he added as he started to undo the cantle strings at the back of his saddle to remove the wolf's tail.

"Another time, Young Billy," said Tex, before he could show off his prize to the rest of them. "I'm sure that you ain't come all this way just to tell these good folks all about your exploits and show them that smelly wolf's tail. Now calm down and tell us why you came looking for me and Joel, before I lose my patience with you, boy."

"It's a wonder that you ain't still carrying that mangy bear's paw around with, Young Billy," Joel said.

"No. Old Stumpy took it off me and fed it to the pigs. He said it was getting a mite smelly."

Young Billy took another drink from his mug of coffee and took a bite from the piece of apple pie that Charlotte had given him, and sat back on his saddle. He seemed to have lost some of his normal ebullience, as he began to tell them the reason for his long ride to find them.

"Well," said Young Billy, "I was in Tucson a couple of days ago. I went in town with old Hootie Swenson and..."

"Hootie Swenson," exclaimed Joel, butting in. "What the hell did you go in town with him for?"

"I was heading for Doc Sherman's place in town. Gus Briggs said I should get my arm looked at properly by the doctor, and he didn't want me to travel on my own." Young Billy paused as he collected his thoughts and took another drink of coffee. "Hootie said that he would ride with me, as he was hoping to meet an old friend of his in Tucson."

"Hootie's alright as long as he stays sober," said Tex. "He's a good man to have on your side when there's a fight going on. But he's usually the one who starts it. He's a big strong fella. You don't want to shake hands with him 'cause he's got a grip like the bite of an angry mule."

"You ain't wrong there," agreed Joel.

"That's part of what I'm trying to tell you both," Young Billy said. "If you give me a chance I'll tell you why I'm here." He stood up agitated and walked around, looking at Joel and Tex, and began to speak again.

"That Albino, Shreeve Moor, bust out of jail this morning. Well a gang of no good outlaws got him out." He carried on as he saw that everyone was now listening to him intently. Everyone, that is, except Father Benito, who was still sitting by the fire, smoking his pipe and fingering his rosary beads and trying to understand what all the conversation was about. Well, no doubt they would tell him who the young stranger was, when everything had calmed down, he thought to himself as he puffed way, his lips moving in silent prayer.

"There was a lot of shooting," said Young Billy. "The Marshall was wounded, and his two deputies were killed. They shot two men down in the street, as they rode off. I think one of them was Mason Carter. Someone said that Jeanie Eagle Feather, you know her Tex. Well, she killed one of the outlaws with a knife, and I think that one of her girls was shot in the arm."

On hearing that, Tex grabbed Young Billy by his arm, making him wince. "Which girl was it? Young Billy. Which one got shot?"

"I think someone said it was the one called Donna. You know her Tex. The pretty girl."

Tex looked shocked at the news, as Young Billy carried on with his story.

"Billy Bob Cannon came out of his store and shot one of them off his horse. He sure done good. He stood outside his store while bullets were flying all around and killed one of them with his first shot with my pistol. After it was all over, he told me to go and find you and Tex, as I'd got a fast horse and most of the town's horses had been run off by the jail breakers. He drew a map of where you had gone, but if I hadn't seen your camp fire, I reckon I'd have ridden straight past."

Charlotte's hand went to her mouth as she took in the gravity of it all, and she looked over at Pat, as he jumped up with a look of anger on his face.

"Well, what are we waiting for, Joel? Let's get after the buggers. Come on, we've got to catch that Albino before he gets away, or comes looking for us," he shouted, all red in the face with worry, as he remembered the last time he had seen Shreeve Moor. He clenched one of his large fists and slammed it into the palm of his other hand.

"Now, hold on there, Pat," said Joel, holding up his hand to calm the young lad down. "Let Young Billy finish telling us what happened, and then we'll decide what we're going to do."

Young Billy sat back down on his saddle, still feeling tired from the long ride, and carried on telling Joel and the others about the jail break in Tucson. He began with his visit to town with Hootie Swenson, in the early evening, the day before. And, on finding that Doc Sherman was out of town and wouldn't be able to look at his wound, how they had both gone into the saloon for some liquid refreshment, which turned out to be a big mistake.

Chapter 17

A couple of days ago, Young Billy Brand had come into town, with Hootie Swenson, to visit the doctors and get his wound attended to. He wondered if he had done the right thing, allowing Hootie to accompany him, and hoped that he wouldn't regret it, but he wasn't going to fall out with the big man, and the ranch foreman had sanctioned the Swede to go with him.

Hootie Swenson was a giant of a man, about six feet five inches tall and built like an ox. He was probably over 60 years old, but nobody knew his exact age and he never told anybody. In his younger days, Hootie had fought down in Mexico, done some trapping and buffalo hunting, and was a crack shot with his old long barreled hunting rifle. He had fought with Sam Houston's men at the battle of San Jacinto, back in 1836, and often told how he had helped beat the Mexican army, led by Santa Anna. Although the battle had only lasted less than an hour, Hootie had been in the thick of the fighting and was wounded twice. He was later personally commended for his bravery by General Sam Houston.

When Colonel Davy Crocket had led his Tennessee Volunteers down to the Alamo to help Colonel Travis in his defense of the mission against the invading Mexican army, a young Hootie Swenson had ridden with him, intending to help fight the Mexicans. However, Hootie had been left behind at the house of Joshua Peters in the north of the Republic of Texas, with raging toothache and a mouth swollen with a large abscess, and a couple of rotten back teeth. A local dentist had to be sent for to extract the bad teeth, drain the abscess, and put a few stitches in his gums. Hootie was at the Peter's house for over three weeks, unable to eat properly and running a fever, while recovering from

131

the dentist's painful surgical procedure to his gums. He was looked after by the Peter's family before he was well enough to travel.

He received the news of the fall of the Alamo Mission and the deaths of all the defenders, when he was about to set out to catch up with Crocket and his men, and it was with a mixture of regret and relief in equal measures that he had joined up with General Sam Houston's forces and helped to stop the Mexican army at San Jacinto.

Hootie now spent most of his time helping out at the ranch, where Joel worked, but would disappear every now and then, sometimes for a couple of months, usually hunting and trapping beaver with an old backwoodsman friend of his.

Everybody called him Hootie, friend and foe alike, as nobody knew his real first name; it was probably something Swedish and totally unpronounceable. He was good at imitating animals and making birdcalls and could lure a duck or quail within range of his long rifle, but his specialty was howl hoots and that was probably how he had got the name Hootie.

Young Billy had been pleased that Hootie had wanted to go to town with him, as he liked the big man and felt safe in his company, and he thought that Hootie's stories about his early life were nearly as good as the ones that Tex had frequently told him. Hootie was also a good listener and liked to hear about Young Billy's exaggerated story of his fight with the grizzly bear and wolves and always laughed at the amusing parts. He sat astride his large horse, as they rode into town and laughed heartily in all the right places, as he puffed away on his pipe.

Young Billy thought that Hootie was the friendliest and easiest going man that he had ever met, as they rode together, and couldn't understand why Gus Briggs had taken him to one side, before they had left, and told him to keep Hootie away from the saloon. He soon realized his mistake, as on finding that Doc Sherman was out of town, they had ended up in the saloon, mainly for something to eat and a drink of ale.

After a few beers, Hootie had progressed on to the whiskey bottle, and the usually peaceful, laid back individual, who never liked to cause offence and never usually took offence, became a different man when the booze took a hold of him.

When four cowboys from a neighboring ranch wandered into the saloon, that was the start of all the trouble. The only other patrons of the saloon were three gamblers, sitting in the far corner, who were involved in a game of poker and were oblivious to everything but their gambling.

The four cowboys went to the bar and ordered a couple of bottles of whiskey and stood drinking for a while, participating in small talk and smoking, but when they looked around the room and saw Hootie with Young Billy, they started taunting the big man. They laughed at his buckskin clothing and the large sombrero on his head, but Hootie ignored them and carried on, quietly, drinking.

It was only when they started making bird noises and hooting like an owl that Hootie began to get angry. The cowboys had met Hootie before and knew that the big man was easy going and would never look for a fight, but they had never seen him drunk. They started to dance around the table where Hootie and Young Billy were sitting, jeering, and shouting at Hootie, ignoring Young Billy's pleas to leave them alone.

Young Billy sat there, as nervous as a long-tailed raccoon in a room full of rocking chairs, as the men, full of cheap whiskey and high spirits, pushed and jostled them both. He had his pistol in his belt but was too shaky to make a move for it, and he didn't want to be the one to start a gunfight.

The barman was telling the cowboys to calm down and get back to the bar, and the three gamblers looked up from their game, disturbed by the ruckus, when one of the cowboys accidently stumbled into Hootie's chair, knocking his whiskey glass out of his hand. Hootie's mood changed when the precious contents of his glass went all over his buckskin shirt and, with a roar, the big man stood up and clamped a large hand around the offender's throat, lifting him a good three feet off the floor.

"You spilled my drink, you bastard," Hootie shouted, spittle from his mouth spraying the cowboy in the face, as he held him close to him. The man struggled, with his feet off the ground, choking from the strong grip of Hootie's large hand, as his three friends stopped their dancing and shouting. "And for that you're gonna pay, mister," he added, in his thick Swedish accent, as he slurred his words.

As his victim struggled in his grip, two of the other men drew their pistols ready to shoot Hootie down and free their friend. Hootie, even in his inebriated condition, saw what the other two cowboys were going to do and hurled the struggling cowboy at them, knocking all three of them into one of the tables, which broke under their combined weight,

Young Billy stood up and backed away from the fracas, not wanting to be part of it, and holding his bandaged arm, as Hootie slammed a huge fist into the face of the last man standing, who had been preparing to draw his own gun, laying him out on the saloon floor alongside his companions.

"Ta det din javel," Hootie yelled, waving his huge fists in the air, as he reverted to his native Swedish. *"Ga upp och kampa mig ni fegisar,"* he added, spittle running down the corners of his mouth, as he stood defiantly before them. Realizing that the cowboys wouldn't understand him, he repeated his last sentence in broken English. "Get up and fight me, you cowards."

As three of the cowboys struggled to their feet, two of them picked up their pistols and fired them in the air, more to keep Hootie away than hit him. Ignoring the gunfire, Hootie let out a loud owl hoot and yelled at them. "Remember the Alamo," he shouted and waded in, fists flying, and in a few seconds, the three men were groaning in a heap, on the saloon floor, lying amongst the debris of broken chairs and tables, next to their unconscious friend.

Hootie bent down and picked up his hat with one hand, and the whiskey bottle with the other, from the debris on the floor. Surprisingly, the whiskey bottle was still in one piece, so Hootie took a long drink from it as the barman came up behind him with a large pick-axe handle, which he kept behind the bar in case of trouble, and hit him on the back of his head. Hootie staggered forward a couple of steps, then turned around, one hand feeling the bloody lump that was already forming behind his ear, and looked at the barman with a soulful expression on his face. "What the hell did you do that for?" he said, looking at the blood on his fingers, his hand reaching down for his pistol.

As the barman backed away from the angry looking Hootie, Marshall Tucker entered the saloon, alerted by the gunfire. He was accompanied by one of his deputies, Jim Slade, and they both had their pistols pointed at Hootie and Young Billy, as they took in the situation before them.

"You can give me that gun, big fella," the Marshall said as his deputy covered Young Billy. He took Hootie's pistol from his holster and moved back from him. Marshall Tucker wasn't a small man, but he felt intimidated standing too close to the big Swede.

"We don't want this to end in bloodshed, 'cause Doc Sherman's out of town," said Marshall Tucker. "And there ain't nobody around else here who can patch folk up. Come on now, Hootie, you're going to cool off in the jailhouse,"

Hootie looked at the Marshall, as he rubbed at his head wound, and meekly stood looking at the lawman, as he took a final drink from the whiskey bottle and handed it to the barman, who quietly took it from the big man.

"You too, young fella," said the Marshall, turning to Young Billy, and pointing his pistol at him. "You'll be sharing a cell with your friend here. Now hand over your pistol."

"It's alright, Marshall," the barman said, recovering from the ruckus. "The lad wasn't involved in any of this. It was just the big man here." He added, looking at Hootie, who was standing there, big shoulders drooping, blood running down the back of his neck and soaking the back of his bandanna. "He's the one who beat up on these cowboys and caused all this damage."

The Marshall looked at Young Billy. "Alright, young fella, you can stay put."

The three gamblers went back to their poker game as Marshall Tucker, and his deputy, led Hootie off to the jailhouse, "We'd better see what we can do with that head of yours, big fella," he said, pushing Hootie before him and silently pursing his lips at the sight of Hootie's injury. "And then you can cool down in the cells. It's getting a mite crowded in there, but I reckon we can find room for you. I'll have to put Shreeve Moor in with the other prisoner for the night 'cause I reckon that you're too big to share a cell with anybody else."

"I'm sorry about all this trouble, Young Billy," Hootie said, remorsefully, as he was taken out of the saloon. "I didn't look for no trouble, you know that. It was those cowboys who started it all."

"Don't worry Hootie. I'll stop in town 'til morning, and wait until they let you out of the jail. Just don't get into any more fights," Young Billy said, picking up Hootie's long rifle from the saloon floor where it had fallen during the fight.

As the two lawmen disappeared through the saloon doors with Hootie, Young Billy dug into his pocket and brought out four silver dollars, which he had brought with him to pay for the doctor to treat his shoulder wound, and handed it to the barman. "I hope this will pay for some of the damage my friend caused," he said. "You can get the rest of what you are owed from those four." He pointed over to the cowboys who were still lying on the floor amongst the damaged furniture. "They started it all. You know they did. It's them that should be in the Jail, not Hootie."

As he was about to leave, Young Billy caught sight of Hootie's old pipe on the dusty floor and picked it up. He put his hat back on and walked out of the saloon door, just in time to see Hootie disappear into the Jail, with the Marshall and his deputy herding him along.

As Young Billy stood on the boardwalk, in the gathering darkness of the evening, wondering what to do next, Billy-Bob Cannon came walking up the street towards him.

"Hey, Young Billy," said Billy-Bob, recognizing the young cowboy as he reached him. "What's going on? I heard gunfire in the saloon and thought that I saw the Marshall taking Hootie Swenson into his office."

"Hootie's been locked up for the night, Mr. Cannon," said Young Billy. "He got into a fight in the saloon with four cowboys."

"Well, if there were only four, I'll bet that Hootie got the better of them."

"He sure did, Mr. Cannon. You should have seen how he beat them all up." Young Billy paused as he looked up the dark street. "I reckon that I'd better hang around town 'til morning and wait for Hootie, when he gets out, but I ain't got nowhere to stay. I'm a bit short of money, as I gave the barman my last few dollars to pay for the damage."

"Well I reckon that you'd better come with me then, lad, and tell me all about it. You can bunk down in my storeroom, and I'm sure that Mrs. Cannon will rustle up some supper for you," Billy-Bob said, taking pity on the young cowboy.

"Thanks, Mr. Cannon, that's mighty kind of you, sir."

"Think nothing of it, Young Billy, and you can call me Billy-Bob, not Mr. or sir. I ain't your pa or your teacher. Now go and get your horses and bring them round to the back of my store. We'll tie them up and find some feed for them."

"OK, Billy-Bob," said Young Billy as he went and untied his and Hootie's horses and followed the storekeeper. He was glad that he had somewhere to rest his head after the trouble in the saloon. He had heard a lot about Billy-Bob Cannon and his days as a Texas Ranger and was looking forward to hearing a few of his stories, especially about his time with Rip Ford, the famous Ranger Captain, who he had rode with along the border country.

Young Billy stood with Billy-Bob, at the rear of his store, while he lit a cigarette and stood in the darkness smoking it, as they tied up the two horses. They both unsaddled the horses, and Billy-Bob gave them some hay and stomped on his cigarette butt. He stood there, for a moment, blowing out his smoky breath and popped a boiled sweet into his mouth and placed a finger on the side of his nose and winked at Young Billy.

"Not a word now, Young Billy, about my smoking habit. Mrs. Cannon doesn't abide me smoking."

"Yes, sir, Billy-Bob. My lips are sealed."

"Come on inside then, and I'll introduce you to my family. But pay no mind to my daughters. They don't get to meet many young cowboys like yourself, but don't go taking no liberties with them, or you'll answer to me."

Young Billy smiled nervously at Billy-Bob and followed him into his place. He had seen Billy-Bob's twin daughters before and thought that they were both very pretty but didn't want to get on the wrong side of their pa.

Billy-Bob's wife, Julie, prepared a meal for Young Billy with her twin daughters both sitting, staring at him while he ate. They had both taken a shine to the young cowboy and were trying to get his attention, but their scrutiny made him feel like a prize pony in a show ring, as he tried to eat his food without making a fool of himself.

Chapter 18

Early the next morning, just after sunup, Young Billy Brand was woken up by Billy-Bob, who handed him a steaming mug of hot coffee. He had been fast asleep in the small storeroom at the rear of the hardware store, stretched out on some old empty canvas sacks. Young Billy had been sleeping off the beer from the night before, so he wouldn't have seen Chloe and Molly, Billy-Bob's twin daughters, peeking around the door about ten minutes earlier, to take a look at the handsome young cowboy as he slept. They were both giggling as their pa came along with a mug of coffee and shooed them both away.

"Get out of here you two and leave the lad alone," Billy-Bob said to the girls, trying to hide the smile on his face.

"Oh, Pa, we only want to talk to him. He's so good looking," said Molly

"Well, I saw him first," Chloe said, glaring at her sister, as they both jostled each other for a better look at Young Billy through the half open door.

"I shan't tell you again. If you don't give Young Billy some peace and quiet, I'm gonna go get your ma," said Billy-Bob as he entered the storeroom. The two girls scuttled away back to the kitchen, quietly arguing with each other. They didn't see many handsome young cowboys in town, usually older cowboys and gamblers who came into their pa's hardware store, and Young Billy Brand wasn't much older than they were.

Young Billy could hear the twins arguing as they went away, and he sat up and yawned and stretched and took the mug of coffee from Billy-Bob. He knew that Molly and Chloe had taken a fancy to him and enjoyed the attention that they both gave him, but he was a mite wary of the craggy ex Texas Ranger and didn't want to get on his bad side.

"Mrs. Cannon will rustle us up some breakfast in a while, Young Billy. But first, I'm going out the front of the store and have me a quiet smoke. But don't you go telling Mrs. Cannon what I'm up to now, will you, Young Billy? She thinks I've finished with the cigarettes."

"No, sir. I mean no I won't Billy-Bob," stammered Young Billy. The storekeeper had a stern look on his craggy face, and Young Billy didn't want to upset the man.

Billy-Bob's wife, Julie, heard the conversation between her husband and Young Billy, from the adjacent kitchen, as the walls were only thin boarding. She smiled to herself because she knew that Billy-Bob still smoked but pretended that she didn't know. She knew where he kept his 'secret stash' of tobacco and paper and could sometimes smell cigarette smoke on his breath and clothing, even when he sucked on a boiled sweet to mask the smell. She shrugged her shoulders. At least, it meant that he didn't smoke as many when she was around him.

Young Billy pulled his boots on and followed Billy-Bob through the store to the front door. He hadn't bothered to undress and had slept with his clothes on, just buckling on his gun-belt as he got up. He went after Billy-Bob, clutching the still hot mug of coffee, as the storekeeper retrieved a smoke from his hidden stash in the dresser and stood in the open doorway, looking down the empty street, and struck a match.

Billy-Bob moved to one side of the shop door to allow Young Billy to join him on the boardwalk, as he enjoyed his first smoke of the day.

Young Billy looked up towards the end of the street and saw Marshall Tucker come out of the saloon and walk slowly over to the jail, carrying his rifle in one hand and tucking his shirt into his pants with the other. The Marshall had a room above the saloon, for which the townsfolk contributed towards, as part of his lawman's salary.

It was a clear early morning, the sun starting to break above the far mountains, and most of the town's people were still abed as the Marshall walked across the street, absent-mindedly scratching at his butt.

I reckon that damn bed has got fleas in it, he thought to himself, as his fingers found the source of the itch on his plump cheeks. *I gotta tell that saloonkeeper to change them damn bed sheets, or I'll have to have a bath more regularly. Damn it, I already had one bath last month, and we're only just into spring.*

He paused for a moment, deep in thought, thinking that perhaps it was the Mexican woman, Conchita, who helped out in the saloon kitchen, who had given him the itches. She had been sharing his bed lately and wasn't the cleanest of women, but she sure was pretty. Marshall Tucker shrugged his shoulders and carried on towards his office.

A man's gotta have a few pleasures in life, he thought. *But I must get her to have a good wash before she warms my bed again.*

There was no one in the quiet town, except four strangers tying their horses to a hitching rail further up the street, and three other men slowly riding into town from the opposite end of the street, two of them leading rider-less horses with their saddles and bridles on. The three riders reined in when they saw the Marshall coming out of the saloon, waiting for him to get off the street and into his office.

The men were all hard and mean looking, their eyes darting furtively around, taking in everything around them, as they assembled in the empty street. They all wore long dust coats, concealing rifles that they carried beneath them, and their hats were pulled well down their foreheads, hiding their faces from any curious onlookers. One of the strangers finished tying up his horse to the hitching rail and struck a match on the timber post, as he lit a cigarette, keeping a wary eye on the Marshall as he approached the jail house. He raised a gloved hand to the four other men down to street in a pre-arranged signal, as he smoked and went into a furtive conversation with his colleagues.

Young Billy never gave the strangers a second thought, as he watched Marshall Tucker enter the jail. He was still feeling tired from last evenings excitement in the saloon, and the beer he had consumed, and he leaned lazily against the door jamb, drinking his coffee, as Billy-Bob squatted on his heels and smoked his cigarette with his eyes closed.

Marshall Tucker never paid the men much attention either, as he was too intent on scratching his backside and hurrying to check on the prisoners before he went back to the saloon for his breakfast, as his empty stomach was already rumbling. He wanted to get Hootie Swenson out of the cells, as the barman at the saloon had already explained to him about trouble the evening before, and how the four cowboys had started all the ruckus by baiting Hootie. Marshall Tucker knew that Hootie wasn't a troublemaker but trouble always seemed to head his way, and a night in the cells would sober up the big man. He hoped that Hootie's head wound hadn't turned bad, as the barkeep had really opened up a nasty injury behind the man's ear.

As Marshall Tucker pushed open the door and walked into his front office, still scratching his butt, his deputy, Jim Slade, jumped up out of the easy chair that he had been snoozing in and picked up his cup of coffee from the desk. It had gone cold while he had been asleep, so he put it down on the small table against the wall and nodded, blearily to the Marshal, as he vacated his chair.

"Is everything alright, Jim?" said the Marshall, as Snowy, the older deputy came through the doors that led to the cells at the rear. "Are the prisoners keeping quiet?"

"I think that Hootie Swenson kept the albino and his cellmate awake for most of the night," replied Jim.

"Well, let's get him outa there. He should have sobered up by now."

Jim Slade reached for the bunch of keys and followed Marshall Tucker through the door leading to the cells, and as soon as Shreeve Moor saw them, he began ranting and shouting at them both.

"Will you get that big drunken bum out of here, Marshall?" yelled the albino, his bottom lip swelling with the stress. "The bastard has been hooting like an owl for most of the night. And when he wasn't hooting, he was snoring louder than a pig in its sty."

"Who the hell are you calling a drunken bum?" Hootie said, standing up from the small bunk that had hardly supported his large frame in the night, and casting a big shadow across Shreeve Moor and most of his cell. The albino backed away to the far corner, as Hootie glared at him menacingly, and stepped closer to the bars dividing the two cells. His cellmate ignored the exchange of words and lay on his bunk with his hat over his eyes.

"And don't call me a pig, you albino bastard, or I will come in there and have you for breakfast. But I don't reckon there's enough meat on your scrawny carcass to satisfy my appetite, and I might end up with a bad case of the shits if I bit into you."

"Come on now, Hootie, you're outa here," said Marshall Tucker, unlocking the door to the big man's cell. "Go pick up your pistol from the front office and clear off. The barman over at the saloon ain't gonna press charges for the damage. He got those four cowboys to pay up, after they had all recovered from the larruping that you gave them. And they admitted to starting all the trouble so be on your way."

"What about some breakfast, Marshall? I'm mighty hungry," said Hootie as he followed Jim Slade into the front office, with a last look at the nervous Shreeve Moor. "I'm so hungry I reckon I could eat the soles off my boots."

"Breakfast! This ain't no fancy hotel, so don't test my patience, Hootie, or I'll put you back in that cell. The only prisoners who get fed here are those two back there, who are waiting for the judge to come and try them."

"OK, Marshall, keep your hair on. You can't blame a fella for asking," said Hootie, with a smile, holstering his gun and putting his large sombrero on his head, as he opened the door to the street. He blinked his eyes in the early morning daylight, on leaving the relative shade of the Marshall's office, and looked down the street and spotted Young Billy standing in the doorway to the hardware store with Billy-Bob Cannon. He waved to Young Billy, as the lad recognized him and waved back.

Hootie ambled slowly down the street, feeling at the lump on the back of his head which Snowy, the deputy, had bandaged for him before putting him in the cell for the night. Touching the wound made him wince with pain, and he tried to remember how he had got it. *Perhaps Young Billy would know*, he thought. He would ask him later, after he had satisfied his hunger. Snowy had cleaned the wound and stitched it with a needle and thread that he had found in the Marshall's cupboard, making him wince with the pain.

Hootie couldn't remember much about the fracas in the saloon either. *I must have drunk too much,* he thought. But Young Billy would, no doubt fill in the blanks for him.

"I'm sure sorry about all the trouble last night, Young Billy," Hootie said, looking suitably contrite, as he reached the hardware store and nodded to Billy-Bob Cannon, as he recognized him. "You'll have to tell me what I got up to 'cause I don't remember much about it."

"That's alright, Hootie. It sure livened the evening up," said Young Billy, glad to see the big Swede. He handed Hootie his pipe, who thanked him and dug out his baccy pouch and filled up the bowl ready for a well-earned smoke. He squatted down on the boardwalk outside the store, still feeling the effects of the previous night's booze, and his head still throbbing from the barkeep's pickaxe handle, and pulled his hat down over his eyes. The early morning sun made his eyes hurt, as he slumped against the shop front, keeping the back of his injured head away from the woodwork.

Billy-Bob handed Hootie some matches, as he turned to go back inside the store to inform his wife that there would be an extra guest for breakfast, when suddenly, from down the street, all hell broke loose. Loud gunfire and muffled shouting came from inside the Marshall's office.

If the Marshall had taken a bit more notice of the strangers across the street, and less interest in his itchy rear end and his impending breakfast, he would have probably recognized some of them from the wanted posters that adorned his office walls. They were a mean looking bunch, and it was only because of the early hour and his lack of sleep that they didn't arouse any undue curiosity in him.

There were the Coffey brothers, Waylon and Jeb, both wanted for cattle rustling and attempted bank robbery. They were from up north but had moved down south to get away from the war and the law that was after them. Riding with them was Troy Collis, known as 'The Smiling Assassin.' He was middle aged and slightly over-weight, with a permanent goofy grin, although, there wasn't any humor to be seen in his cold staring eyes. He didn't take orders from anyone, had a nihilistic attitude to everyone and everything, and had only joined the others for the pleasant anticipation of killing someone. Collis was wanted for killing three unarmed men who happened to stare at him for too long, so he had been hiding in the Badlands down on the border until he had been asked to join the others.

The other rider with them was a lanky, pock-marked, young individual who went by the name of Gopher Spriggs. He had ridden with the Coffey brothers before and the promise of easy picking from the bank in Tucson sounded like a good time to the farm boy, so he had ridden in with his pa, Keefer Spriggs.

Amongst the other three men, with the spare horses, were Skeeter Hancock and Elvira Jones, a pair of mean looking bushwhackers from the border country, who had once ridden with Henri LeClere, 'The Buffalo Man,' a few years back. Luckily for them both, they hadn't been with the old scalp hunter when he had been killed in a shoot-out the year before. They had ridden with Shreeve Moor in the past, with his gang of Comancheros, and although they didn't always like his methods and the savagery that he meted out to his victims, they always enjoyed the ill-gotten gains that he shared out.

The last man in the group was a weedy looking individual named Randy Moor, Shreeve Moor's younger brother. He was even skinnier than his brother, and his face looked like someone's reflection in the back of a large soup spoon. His thin pointed elbows and knees protruded through his shirt and pants like knots in an old dried twig.

He was of limited intelligence and had the mental capacity as shallow as a worm's grave, and his brain was as sharp as a damp sponge, but he had somehow managed to get the others to help him break out his brother from the Tucson jail, as he had heard that Marshall Tucker had recently sent for the circuit judge to try him for murder. Randy Moor knew that his brother would probably hang for his crimes, and he found it difficult to function without his brother's influence and leadership, so in desperation, he had called in a few favors from some of Shreeve Moor's old outlaw accomplices, with promises of some easy, rich pickings at the bank in Tucson, after they had got his brother out of jail.

He had recently been released from prison in Yuma, where he had spent a year, for stealing the contents of the church poor box, after being quickly apprehended as he sat at the back of the church, counting the small piles of coins and giggling to himself with childish delight at the candy he could buy with his ill-gotten gains.

As Hootie Swenson ambled up the street, head down, and rubbing his head wound, Troy Collis, who without any agreement from the rest had assumed control of the gang, nodded to the others and walked purposely over to the Marshall's office, followed by four of them.

The Coffey brothers stayed in the street, with Gopher Spriggs, to keep a lookout for any trouble, and they both pulled out their rifles from beneath their long dust coats, watching Hootie as he headed for the store, not seeing him as much of a threat to them. Gopher Spriggs lounged against the hitching rail, trying to look nonchalant and carefree but with beads of nervous perspiration running down his forehead and into his eyes. With a nervous grin at the Coffey brothers, he wiped his eyes with the back of his gloved hand, and let his mind wander to other things to stop himself shaking.

Chapter 19

As the door to his office suddenly burst open, Marshall Tucker looked up from the conversation that he was having with old Snowy, as he prepared his shaving tackle to remove the two-day stubble from his face. He thought that, maybe, Hootie Swenson had returned for a free breakfast, and he turned to give him a piece of his mind, as a rifle barrel was pushed into his face, and he saw a group of armed strangers crowd into the small office, and the door closed behind them.

"No sudden moves, Marshall, or I might be tempted to shoot you," said Troy Collis with the usual goofy grin on his pudgy face. "Skeeter, get those cell keys hanging on the wall behind the old timer there." He pointed behind Snowy, at a large bunch of keys on a metal ring, all the while watching Marshall Tucker in case he went for his pistol in the holster on his hip.

As Skeeter Hancock picked up the keys from the wall, the door leading to the cells opened and Jim Slade came into the front office, carrying two empty coffee mugs from the prisoners. In an instant, the deputy weighed up the situation, dropped the mugs, and foolishly reached for his pistol, as Elvira Jones, who was standing near the door, clubbed him on his head with his rifle. With a shout, the deputy fell to the floor, blood running from his head, as Randy Moor, full of bravado, stepped up to Jim Slade, who was trying to get up, pulled out his pistol and pumped three bullets into him and looked around at the others with a stupid, smug grin on his face.

"I got him," crowed Randy Moor, proudly puffing up his scrawny chest and dancing around the unfortunate deputy, waving his arms in the air like a demented circus clown. "Did you see that?" he said, ripping the deputy's badge from his shirt and waving it in the air.

"You dumb-assed fool," yelled Troy Collis. "You'll wake up the whole damn town with that racket. I told you before we came in here that there was to be no shooting unless there was no other option. And there was no need to shoot the deputy after Elvira had dealt with him."

"Who are you calling a dumb-assed fool?" said Randy Moor, backing away from the angry looking Collis and nearly tripping over the dead deputy. "My brother don't like folk calling me names. I'll tell him what you called me."

Troy Collis walked purposefully towards Randy Moor, as he shrank away from him, and turned to Elvira Jones. "Keep the Marshall and the old timer covered, Elvira. And take the Marshall's pistol from him. We've got to move fast now that this idiot has warned everyone." He turned back to Randy Moor, the smile had gone, and he had a face like bad weather.

"Don't give me any more of that horse shit, Moor. I've only come along for the profit, and maybe some killing, so let's get on with it and get your brother out of here, before you're the next one to be shot. I reckon that you've alerted the whole town with all that shooting, so get outa my way before I lose my temper."

Collis pushed Randy Moor to one side, as he took the cell keys from Skeeter Hancock, who was grinning at the sniveling Randy Moor—a wad of tobacco making a bulge in his left cheek, distorting his face and giving him the appearance of a packrat—and went through the doors leading to the cells.

As they approached the cells, Shreeve Moor and his cellmate, Clem Johnson, were both standing at the bars, having been alerted by the gunfire and shouting.

"Hey Randy. Is that you, boy?" shouted Shreeve Moor, as he saw his brother enter the rear part of the jail. Recognizing Troy Collis, he let out a yell. "Troy old buddy, it's good to see you too. Hurry up and get me out of here, the bastards are planning to put me on trial as soon as the judge turns up, and then they'll hang me."

Collis fiddled with the few keys on the ring and, after a couple of attempts, he unlocked the cell door and swung it open.

"Come on, Shreeve," Collis said. "We'd better hurry. This idiot brother of yours has made enough noise to bring the rest of the town in here."

Randy Moor gave a silly grin as his brother came out of the cell but said nothing to him. He didn't want his older sibling to take sides with Troy Collis.

"Tell me about it later, Randy," said the albino, giving his brother a severe look, as he turned and picked up his hat from the bed. "Come on, Clem," he said, grinning at his cellmate. "We're free now. Let's get the hell outa here."

Clem Johnson didn't need to be told twice. He quickly grabbed his hat and followed Shreeve Moor out of the cell and into the front office. Elvira Jones looked up as the others came into the office, momentarily distracted, and Marshall Tucker made a grab for his rifle, trying to wrench it from the outlaw's grip. As the Marshall tried to stand up, still holding one end of Elvira's rifle, Troy Collis shot him in his shoulder, making him let go, and he slumped back into his chair, holding his shoulder with blood seeping through his fingers.

Snowy, the old deputy, backed away as Shreeve Moor saw him and moved towards him. 'The Butcher' hadn't forgotten that the deputy had once struck him through the bars of his cell, with his rifle butt, and wanted to settle the score before he left the jailhouse.

As he reached the frightened deputy, he saw the shaving bowl, with the shaving brush next to it, on the Marshall's desk, which had been prepared just before the outlaws had entered. What caught Shreeve Moor's eye was the cut-throat razor next to the shaving bowl. Its freshly sharpened edge glinting in the early morning sun, as it shone through the dusty widow. With an evil looking grin, Shreeve Moor's hand was a blur as the razor suddenly appeared in his hand, a few inches from Snowy's white whiskered throat.

"It's payback time, you old bastard," leered 'The Butcher' as he swiftly swiped the sharp razor across the whimpering deputy's Adams Apple. He stood back as Snowy let out a gurgling noise, blood spurting from his throat, as he fell to the floor. Even before the old man had landed on the floor, Shreeve Moor bent over him and, with surgical precision, removed both his ears with the razor. He stood up, and with a yell, proudly displayed his grisly trophies to the others.

"Here's a nice pair of ears to start off my collection again," cackled Shreeve Moor as he stuffed the bloody ears in his pocket, and wiped the razor on the dead man's shirt. "That'll teach the old fart to mess with me." He folded the razor and put it in his other pocket.

"You Moor brothers are crazier than a sack full of Raccoons," laughed Troy Collis as he broke open the rifle box on the office wall and took the guns and ammunition and distributed them amongst the others. He then followed them out of the office front door, into the street, but not before pointing his pistol at Marshall Tucker, who was still slumped in his chair, bleeding profusely from his shoulder wound.

"Just you stay there, Marshall, and keep quiet," said Collis with his toothy, menacing grin. "Or you'll be joining those two in Boot Hill." He looked down at the two bodies on the floor, both with a fresh pool of blood surrounding them, soaking into the dusty floorboards, and went out of the door, slamming it shut behind him.

* * * * * *

Marshall Tucker breathed a sigh of relief, as Troy Collis left, glad that the outlaw had let him live. He sat there, too weary to move, hoping that someone would soon come to help him, trying not to look at his two dead deputies. Especially old Snowy, with his ears removed, and the large gaping wound at his throat, his once white beard soaked with his own blood. He struggled unsteadily to his feet, leaning against the nearest wall with his good shoulder, the effort making beads of sweat break out on his forehead, as the pain nearly made him return to the relative comfort of his chair.

Damn it, he thought to himself. *I'm getting too old for this sort of life.*

He pulled off his bandanna and pushed it under his shirt over the still bleeding bullet wound, closing his eyes as a wave of nausea swept over him. He wasn't yet 50 years old, but the grey, thinning hair on his head and the lines on his weather-beaten face were testament to the life that Milo Tucker had lived on the frontier. He had been a lawman for over

20 years, first in Abilene as Deputy Sherriff, and for the last six years as Marshall of Tucson. This was the fourth time that he had been shot, and he carried the scars in his back and leg from his previous encounters with law breakers and bushwhackers.

Milo had come down to Tucson with his wife, who had suffered with Tuberculosis, hoping that the dry Arizona climate would help prolong her life. She had begun to feel a lot better and lost her cough, as the local air agreed with her but, by some unfortunate quirk of fate, she had been killed crossing the street when a bunch of drunken cowboys had stampeded some cattle through the town. Since then, Milo Tucker had dedicated his life to upholding the law and enjoying the favors of the lovely Conchita.

Leaning against the wall, Marshall Tucker pulled out a small, faded, tintype photograph of his wife from his vest pocket and smiled fondly at it, and the memory that it gave him, and made a renewed effort to get to the office door. He reached for a jug of water from his desk, took a swallow, and opened the front door, but not before he pulled out his spare pistol, from his desk drawer, as he went. Maybe he could still catch those killers before they got clean away.

"I'm still the Marshall here," he said out loud, taking a last look at his two deputies, lying dead on the office floor, and struggling out onto the street, where gunfire had started up.

Chapter 20

Out on the main street, the citizens of Tucson were waking up to the sound of gunfire as Shreeve Moor and Clem Johnson were freed from the jail house. Troy Collis and Elvira Jones fired their pistols in the air to deter any nosy, or foolhardy, citizens. The Coffey brothers were minding the horses, with Gopher Spriggs, as the others came running out, just as a man came out of the livery stables brandishing a shotgun, and discharged one of the barrels in their direction. It was Mason Carter, who had been checking on his horse for an early ride back to his place out of town, when he heard the gunshots from the jail. Realizing that there must be a problem at the jail, he had pulled out his loaded shotgun from his saddlebag, stepped out of the door, and fired at the men.

Mason was still battered and bruised from his run in with Father Benito the week before. His arm was swollen, and his nose looked like a squashed tomato, and he was sporting a black eye. He had quickly fired from the hip, and because of his injuries, his aim wasn't good. But he managed to hit Jeb Coffey in his arm, making him drop his rifle. As he prepared to fire the other barrel, this time taking better aim, Jeb's brother Waylon shot Mason Carter in his chest, and before he hit the ground, Waylon put another bullet in him for good measure.

This time Mason Carter's luck had finally run out, as he fell heavily on his face, taking most of the fall on his already broken nose, and hitting the ground with a muffled cry. As his vision began to fade, his last thoughts were what a crap time he'd had just lately.

He lay on the ground, where he had bit the dust, literally, bits of gravel and dirt in his mouth, and he thought to himself. *First, I hear about my boy being killed in the war, then I get beaten up by an old monk, and now this. Still, at least, my busted nose doesn't seem to hurt me anymore.*

As the gunfire all around him begins to fade into the distance, he spits out a small pebble from his mouth, wishing that he had gone straight home to his wife, instead of staying over at Jeanie Eagle Feather's whorehouse all night to enjoy the ladies. With a last sigh and a mental shrug of his shoulders, Mason Carter died.

"Are you hit bad, Jeb?" Waylon Coffey said, to his brother, reaching down to pick up his sibling's fallen rifle.

"Nah! The bastard only winged me, Bro. But you got him. Thanks." He took the rifle from his brother and mounted up. Most of the buckshot was embedded in his thick dust coat, just a few managing to penetrate the thick material and lodge in his forearm. "I've been stung worse by hornets in the past. Let's get the hell outa here before anybody else gets trigger happy."

As he spoke, bullets began to fly from out of windows, and doorways in nearby buildings, and the brothers wheeled their horses around and followed Shreeve Moor and his brother, who were both trying to urge their horses into a gallop, intent on getting out of town in a hurry. The rest of the gang followed closely behind, bullets flying everywhere as they rode off. The outlaws began firing their guns at the buildings, shooting indiscriminately, mainly to give themselves cover, and keep anybody away from the windows, as they made their getaway.

A thin film of dust kicked up by the horses settled on Mason Carter's lifeless body, as the Coffey brothers rode away, and Gopher Spriggs, who had already mounted with them, saw a young, pretty girl across the street and paused. He was nearly 18 years old, a gangly, cross-eyed youth, with a face covered in holes from the smallpox, from when he was younger. He had ridden with his pa, Keefer Spriggs, who was an old associate of Troy Collis, with a promise of easy pickings at the Tucson bank, after they had carried out the jail break.

Gopher had never been very successful with girls, so on seeing the young girl across the street, everything else was pushed to the back of his mind—what there was of his mind. His brain was about as sharp as a damp sponge, and he was unable to think clearly at the best of times, so all thoughts of a quick getaway disappeared. He had never seen such beauty in a girl and had never been fortunate enough to have had any girl, so ignoring all else, he spurred his horse across the street.

* * * * * *

In the whorehouse, next to the saloon, known by the grand title of 'Jeanie Shaw's House for Young Ladies,' the proprietor, Jeanie Eagle Feather Shaw was up early, sitting in her backroom parlor. She always rose early, while the town's menfolk and her girls were all abed, giving her chance to reflect on the previous day's work and happily count her takings. She sat with a smile on her face, and a small clay pipe clenched between her teeth, puffing merrily away, as she placed the silver dollars into small piles. Her two cats, Mickey and Manny, were rubbing themselves around her feet and purring loudly, as she stroked them both in turn. She mouthed a curse on finding a couple of dud silver dollars in the pile, startling the cats as she tossed them into the nearby spittoon.

"The swindling bastards," she muttered. "I must tell the girls to check the money more carefully, in future, or I'll take it out of their wages."

Jeanie Eagle Feather was a short, thickset woman, in her late sixties with white hair cropped short, a shawl draped around her shoulders, and a small felt hat perched on the back of her head with an eagle's feather protruding from the hat band. She was wearing a pair of baggy pants that failed to reach all the way down to her moccasin clad feet. Her spectacles were perched on the end of her nose, as she counted her takings. Over the last few years, her eyesight had deteriorated so badly that it was only after Billy-Bob Cannon had taken pity on her and brought her a pair of spectacles back from one of his trips back east, had she managed to see properly to do her book-keeping.

Jeanie Eagle Feather was part Kickapoo Indian, and she still had a lot of the natural beauty for which men had admired her for in her younger days. Her father had been a fur trapper, who had lived with the tribe for a few years and had taken her mother for his squaw in exchange for one of his horses loaded with beaver pelts.

The girls all called her Miss Jeanie, but the clients had to call her Mrs. Shaw, and woe betide them if they misbehaved in her establishment. Usually, a raised voice by her would keep the men in line, sending them scuttling away from her wrath, but if that wasn't enough, she wasn't averse to using her fists, as more than one customer would testify to. She had come down from the tribal lands to get away from Kickapoo's, who had treated her like an outcast, because of her white blood, and had settled in Tucson with a mule skinner named Fennimore Shaw, who had married her to make an honest woman of her, but mainly because she could control a team of horses better than most men.

Fennimore had treated her badly, or tried to, and they had only been married a couple of months when he had been found in the livery stable, lying on his back with a pitchfork between his legs, sticking out of his family jewels, and his throat cut. Most of the townsfolk suspected Jeanie Eagle Feather, because they had seen how Fennimore had treated her, but mainly because her distinctive tobacco pouch, made from the hairy scrotum of an old bull Buffalo had been found next to her dead husband's body.

The Marshall, who had been one of the first on the scene, and had never liked the mule skinner, had quickly removed the tobacco pouch and returned it to Jeanie Eagle Feather and nothing more had been said about the matter.

After she had buried Fennimore, Jeanie Eagle Feather had discovered his stash of silver dollars amongst his meagre possessions and had opened the whorehouse. She had brought in some girls from back east, to the delight of the local cowboys, but to the dismay of the married town's women, when their husbands began frequenting the establishment.

Jeanie Eagle Feather never indulged in any of fornication with the clients, except every now and then, when she fancied one of the men and was feeling a mite randy. She kept herself busy running the place and her main form of exercise, these days, was some friendly arm wrestling with the men, when they were waiting for a girl to be available. This was something she had learned from the Kickapoo Indians, as they liked to indulge in various forms of wrestling, and she found that she had a natural talent for it. She had beaten most of the men, except the big Swede, Hootie Swenson, who had proved too strong for her, even when he was drunk.

Jeanie Eagle Feather had nearly finished arranging the previous night's takings into neat piles, when the sudden shouting and gunfire outside made her jump, knocking the orderly stacks of coins off table, and sending her two cats scuttling out of the parlor. With a curse, Jeanie Eagle Feather headed through the parlor, towards the front door, to see what all the noise was about and also to give the miscreants a good telling off for disturbing her at such an early hour.

As she neared the door to the street, Jeanie Eagle Feather heard a scream from outside. One of her girls, a young orphan named Matilda, who she had recently taken in, was standing on the boardwalk too frightened to move. Matilda had got out of her bed early to do some of her chores, knowing it would please Miss Jeanie if she was seen to be busy.

Men were coming out of the jail, firing their guns indiscriminately, to keep everyone off the street, as Jeanie Eagle Feather stepped out onto the boardwalk in front of her establishment. She saw Mason Carter lying dead in the middle of the street and nodded her head from side to side, thinking to herself. *I told the damn fool last night to get off home to his wife, after he had spent an hour with two of my girls, but he wouldn't listen. Damn it, he was one of my best clients. I sure will miss his weekly contributions.*

She took another puff on her pipe and started to turn away, to get off the street and take young Matilda with her, out of danger, as Gopher Spriggs, who had been the first to mount his horse, looked across the street and saw the young girl standing transfixed with fear. The young halfwit outlaw spurred his horse forward, intending to grab the girl and carry her off with him. He sure liked the look of her and liked the idea of getting something from the town besides breaking Shreeve Moor out of the jail. This looked like a far easier option to Gopher.

As Gopher neared the whorehouse, Matilda let out a scream, which was nearly drowned amidst all the noise in the street, making Jeanie Eagle Feather turn back just in time to see the outlaw approaching fast. Seeing what Gopher Spriggs intended to do, she pushed her spectacles back from the front of her nose, quickly pulled out a knife from beneath her shawl, and with a practiced accuracy, hurled it at the fast approaching rider. The knife hit the unfortunate man in his neck, just below his large Adam's apple. Sending him flying backwards off his horse into the street, and he was dead before he hit the ground. His rider-less horse galloped off up the street, trying to get away from all the commotion, and, free of its rider, it soon cleared the busy street without being hit by any stray bullets.

As the bullets flew all around them, one stray shattering the small glass panel above her front door, Jeanie Eagle Feather turned to Matilda, who was still standing frozen with fear.

"Get inside, Matilda. You, silly girl," she yelled at the young girl, who was suddenly startled out of her trance by Jeanie Eagle Feather's loud voice. "You're gonna get yourself killed if you stay out here much longer. Go on now, shoo, girl."

"Alright, Miss Jeanie," said Matilda in a frightened, croaky voice, which could hardly be heard above the gun fire, as she was stirred into action by the way that Jeanie Eagle Feather had dispatched the young outlaw. She started to go indoors but collided with some of the other girls who had been woken from their sleep by the gunfire, as they stood in the doorway.

'Donna the Slut,' seeing that Matilda was hesitating and in danger of catching a stray bullet, went out, and ignoring her own safety, grabbed her by the arm. She pushed Matilda roughly through the open doorway to get her out of harm's way, and as she turned to follow her, a bullet hit her in the shoulder, and with a shout, she stumbled, nearly falling backwards onto the boardwalk. One of the other girls, seeing her plight, pulled Donna to safety into the front parlor.

Ignoring the bullets flying all around her, some too close for comfort as one stray took a piece out of her old felt hat, making it fall from her head, Jeanie Eagle Feather calmly walked over to the unfortunate Gopher Spriggs, who was lying sprawled in the street. She bent over him and retrieved her knife from his throat, wiped the blood-soaked blade on his coat, and, catching sight of a small leather bag attached to his belt, she paused and cut the leather thong which held it. Taking a quick puff from her pipe, she shook the small pouch in her hand, listening to the coins jingling inside. She smiled to herself, as she took her pipe from her mouth and spit out some tobacco juice, most of it landing in Gopher Spriggs' left ear, replaced her pipe in her mouth, and casually walked back into her establishment, picking up her old felt hat as she went.

"This should help pay for my broken window, and then some," she said, more to herself than to the girls, as she pocketed the small money pouch. She walked back inside 'Jeanie Shaw's House for Young Ladies,' her girls all moving away from the door to let her enter. One of the older girls began to clap and the others joined in. They had all seen how she had saved Molly from the outlaw's clutches and were rightly proud of her.

Jeanie Eagle Feather smiled to herself. "Now come on, girls, don't stand about gawping, there's work to be done. Get away from the windows and doors and one of you fetch a broom and clear up this mess." She took her old clay pipe from out of her mouth, which had gone out, "And one of you go and get my whiskey bottle. I'm spitting damn feathers," she added, searching for a match to re-light her pipe with.

Jeanie Eagle Feather considered fetching her old buffalo rifle to join in the gunfight outside, as she always did enjoy a good scrap, but she thought that maybe she had had enough excitement for one morning. Instead, she sat down in the nearest chair, the gunfire still echoing through the door, and removed her hat, and looked at the bullet hole in the brim, poking her finger through it.

"That was mighty close," she said, as she was handed her whiskey bottle. "Mighty close indeed. Damn it, I always did like my old felt hat," she added, laughing out loud as she realized the unintentional pun that she had made. She took a long swallow from the bottle and sighed with pleasure as the brew hit the back of her throat. She took another long drink and sat back with a sigh and thought to herself. *That sure was one hell of a morning. Old Fennimore would have enjoyed that gunfight.* She re-lit her pipe, took a long pull, and blew out the smoke. Picking up the bottle again, she poured herself a glass of whiskey and raised it in salute. "Here's to you, Fennimore, you old bastard, wherever you are," she said out loud, laughing to herself, as she sat back in her chair with a smile. "I think I'll wander over to Boot Hill, later, and piss on the old sod's grave."

* * * * * *

Chapter 21

Marshall Tucker came out of his office as the outlaws were mounting up. He saw Mason Carter lying in the street, and he fired his pistol towards the group of killers, not taking proper aim, just hoping to hit one of them, as his hand shook with the pain of his shoulder wound. Somebody appeared at one of the upstairs windows of the saloon, just a shadow behind the curtain, and began firing a rifle at the horsemen as they began to return fire, their horses bucking and wheeling about in the confusion. Most of the shots missed their intended targets, hitting the wooden sides of the buildings.

Some of the townsmen had come out on the street to see what all the commotion was about, some of them armed, but they all went scuttling back indoors as bullets flew past them, breaking a few windows. One of the men was hit, but it was only a flesh wound, as they all disappeared indoors. But an old timer, slower than the rest, took a stray bullet in his back, sending him staggering into the man in front of him, as he felt the bullet crunch through one of his ribs and enter his lung. He was pulled through an open doorway by two men, but they saw that there wasn't much they could for him, so they both ran for cover as another bullet ricocheted off the door hinge next to them.

As he fought to control his horse, Elvira Jones was hit twice by the unknown rifleman in the upstairs saloon window, and his horse went down in a hail of bullets, throwing him down into the street. He staggered to his feet, clutching his stomach, blood pouring between his fingers, as Jeb Coffey, who had been about to follow his brother to safety, saw Elvira get shot and turned his horse, reached down, and helped him to mount up behind him.

Jeb Coffey quickly rode off with his badly wounded friend, holding tightly to his waist, managing to get clear of the shooting, as he followed his brother down the street. He could feel Elvira's blood soaking the back of his dust coat and knew that he must be badly wounded, as he had seen that he had also been hit in the shoulder. "Hang on to me, Elvira. I'll get you outa here," yelled Jeb Coffey, digging his spurs into his overburdened horse, as a bullet tore through his long dust coat and grazed his horses back.

"Thanks, Jeb, I owe you," whispered Elvira as he clung to Jeb Coffey, his words lost in all the noise and confusion.

As Clem Johnson mounted one of the spare horses, he got shot in the arm from the shooter in the upstairs window. Keeping low in the saddle to make himself less of a target, he urged the horse forward as bullets missed him by inches, making him wish that maybe he should have stopped in the safety of his cell and waited for the circuit judge to arrive. A stray bullet grazed the flank of his horse making it quicken its pace as he caught up with the Moor brothers, who were both yelling wildly as they rode out of town, firing their pistols at the nearby buildings.

Meanwhile on the north end of town, in the deserted cattle pens, waited Keefer Spriggs. He had been told to wait there and keep watch in case anybody headed for town who might give them trouble, and to raise the alarm by firing his rifle three times. He had with him a young, half-breed Comanche named Farlowe Rainwater, who sat cross-legged in the shade poking at a scorpion, with his sharp knife, which he had dug out of its hole under a rock.

Keefer was just rolling himself a smoke when the sudden gunfire from in the town startled him, making him spill his makings on the ground.

"Damn it!" he shouted to Farlow. "Sounds like there's trouble back in town. We'd better go and see if they need our help." He dusted the remains of the tobacco from his hands and mounted up, unsheathing his rifle, as he spurred his horse down the road into Tucson.

"I sure hope young Gopher is alright," he muttered to himself as Farlow Rainwater put his knife away, picked up his rifle and leapt onto his pony, and followed Keefer. "I shouldn't have brought the boy along with me; his mind tends to wander at times. His ma will kill me if I let anything happen to him."

Keefer arrived in the main street with bullets flying all around him, his horse bucking and wheeling, at the gunfire, as he reined in to take stock of the situation. He saw the Coffey brothers riding out of the south end of town, and then his eyes focused on one of the bodies lying in the main street, and he realized it was his son Gopher. He let out a moan of despair on seeing that his only son was maybe wounded or dead, as his own horse was hit by two or three bullets, sending him falling to the ground, losing his rifle as he fell.

Keefer struggled to his feet, trying to get his pistol out from beneath his long dust coat, one of his boot heels caught up in the long tail of it, where one of his spurs had torn a hole. Cussing as he freed his pistol, Keefer was hit in the shoulder from a rifle bullet, sending him spinning around as he fired wildly in the air, as he felt another bullet enter his back. Another bullet, this time from Marshall Tucker's pistol, went up through Keefer Spriggs' jaw and he hit the ground, with blood bubbling from his mouth as he tried to shout for his son.

Keefer Spriggs tried to look around for his boy, as he lay dying in the street, but his body wouldn't respond to his commands, and his head felt too heavy to move, with the side of his jaw in tatters. A crushing, all consuming, weight of grief and despair swept over him for the loss of his son. He tried to call his boy's name again, but his words were lost in a rush of blood and spittle, and with a tear in his eye, the noise of the shooting all around him faded slowly away, as he died.

Farlowe Rainwater, surprised by the ferocity of the gunfire and seeing Keefer Spriggs shot down, decided to get out of town the way that he had come in. He wheeled his pony around, knees gripping its flanks, as he steered it to the side of the street away from the gunfire. With a canter, he took his pony onto the boardwalk, under the overhang of the buildings, and as he passed the bank, a salvo of bullets hit him and his pony, sending them both crashing through the large plate glass, front window. Both horse and rider were dead as they landed in the bank, bleeding heavily from the bullets and shards of glass that had penetrated them.

He was the only one of the gang to get inside the bank, that they had intended to rob, but the irony of it was lost on the young Comanche.

Troy Collis and Skeeter Hancock were the last to leave town, and as Collis drew level with Billy-Bob Cannon's hardware store, he slowed down on seeing two men outside, thinking that they were going to try and stop them getting away. He pulled out his pistol ready to fire. His blood was up, and he wanted to kill someone. When the red mist came over Collis, his urge to kill had to be satisfied. He was angry that he had missed robbing the bank through Randy Moor's stupidity back in the jail, but he would make up for it by taking these two strangers down. His mouth opened in an evil smile, showing his buckteeth, as he levelled his gun at the two men.

Hootie Swenson was still sitting outside the hardware store, his hat pulled down over his eyes, and taking the occasional puff on his pipe, when the jail break had begun. Still recovering from too much booze, the night before, and the pain in his head from the barman's pickaxe handle, it took him a while to realize what was happening. As he heard the gunfire down the street and the riders heading his way, he raised his head, the sudden movement making his throbbing head even worse, so he closed his eyes to shut it all out.

Young Billy Brand stood near Hootie, leaning against a door jamb, still holding the cup of coffee that Billy-Bob had given to him earlier. The tin cup had kept his drink warm, and he was taking a sip when the horsemen came up the street. Most of them went quickly by, but one of the last riders reined up and pulled his pistol out, just as Hootie pulled his hat back down and went back into his stupor.

As Billy-Bob returned from the kitchen to see what all the shooting was about, Troy Collis fired his gun at Young Billy, but his aim went wide as his horse reared up, and the shot went through the open door of the hardware store. There was a loud scream from inside as the bullet went into the wall just above Julie Cannon's head, and Billy-Bob, who was unarmed, reached the door as Troy Collis steadied his horse to take another shot.

Billy-Bob quickly weighed up the odds and saw that Hootie was incapable, due to his hangover, and Young Billy was frozen to the spot, he quickly reached down and pulled out the young cowboy's pistol from his holster, cocked it, and shot Troy Collis in the head, just as Collis was preparing to fire again.

Troy Collis fell backwards off his horse, as his own pistol fired harmlessly in the air, and he was dead before he hit the ground, and the 'Smiling Assassin' was smiling no more as the dust cleared. Skeeter Hancock took one look at Billy-Bob Cannon, seeming to recognize him from a long way back, as he watched Collis fall off his horse, and he dug his spurs into his own horse and rode off at a gallop, bending over his horse's neck to make himself less of a target.

Hootie got slowly to his feet as Julie Cannon came to the door, making the air turn blue with her swearing and cussing. "Where's that bastard who nearly killed me?" she shouted, ranting and raving. She was using words that she thought she had long forgotten, but had been tucked away in some dark recess of her mind, only now surfacing with the shock of how close she had been to getting a bullet in her head

Hootie Swenson turned and looked at Julie Cannon with more than a little respect and smiled at her. "I ain't heard that sort of language since I was up on the Brazos with a gang of greasy mule skinners," he laughed, turning to Billy-Bob, who had lowered the still smoking pistol.

"Well, Hootie," he said, laughing. "You can take the woman out of the saloon, but you can't take the saloon out of the woman."

He quickly moved to one side, as Julie aimed a playful slap at him, as Hootie and Young Billy joined in the laughter.

As the dust settled from the retreating outlaws, Billy-Bob Cannon walked over to where Troy Collis lay in the middle of the street, accompanied by Hootie and Young Billy. Collis lay with his one sightless eye staring up at the sky, no doubt contemplating the folly of stopping off at Billy-Bob Cannon's hardware store. The other eye was a bloody mess where Billy-Bob's bullet had entered and ended up in his skull.

"That was mighty good shooting, Mr. Cannon. You got him right in the eye," said Young Billy, looking down at the dead gunman, whose mouth was wide open, showing his buckteeth.

"It wasn't that good Young Billy, I was aiming between his eyes. I should have put my spectacles on, but I hadn't time to get them out. My eyes ain't what they were these days."

He shrugged and absent-mindedly rubbed the small scar below his left eye where Doc Sherman had once performed a small, but painful, operation on him and handed Young Billy his pistol back with a smile and a wink. "And I've told you before, its Billy-Bob not Mr. Cannon," he added.

Billy-Bob turned and led Julie back inside the store, heading off their two daughters, Chloe and Molly, who had both come out to see what all the ruckus was about, but mainly they had wanted to catch sight of Young Billy Brand again. Billy-Bob didn't want his daughters to see the body of the dead outlaw, who he had just shot. They had only known him as a peaceful shopkeeper, and not the fearless Texas Ranger that he had once been. The twins both grabbed Young Billy by an arm apiece and led him back into the store, making his face turn a light shade of red with all the attention that he was getting. He hoped that Billy-Bob didn't think he was leading his daughters astray, as they both held him tightly, as he had just witnessed the speed and accuracy of the man's shooting and didn't want to get on his bad side.

Hootie Swenson, now fully alert, picked up his long rifle and stepped off the boardwalk onto the street. His hangover had mostly gone, but the back of his head still hurt like hell. He wished that he could remember how he had got the wound, but the happenings of the evening before were still too mixed up in his head. He stood over the dead outlaw and cocked his rifle, glancing up the street in the direction the fleeing outlaws had taken, in case any of them were still around.

He saw that they had all gone and looked the other way, back towards the jail, and saw Marshall Tucker raise his hand in his direction. Hootie waved back, bent down, picked up the dead outlaw's discarded pistol, tucked it into his belt, and walked back into Billy-Bob's store, the thought of a good breakfast foremost on his mind.

******

Marshall Tucker was still leaning against the outside wall of his office, bleeding heavily from his wound. He had seen Shreeve Moor and his gang ride off and had smiled with satisfaction when he had seen Troy Collis get shot and Billy-Bob Cannon standing outside his hardware store with the still smoking gun in his hand. He was sure that he had hit one of the gunmen, but it may well have been one of the two men who had taken position in the livery stable, and had been shooting at the outlaws. There was also the unknown rifleman in the upstairs saloon window, who had been firing at the jail-breakers. He could see that the person was still there and raised his pistol in salute, as he wondered who it could be. Suddenly, a head appeared at the window—with shoulder length hair, and Milo recognized the seductive smile and the hair, as black as a raven's wing—and knew that it was Conchita, his bed warmer. He smiled up at her, thinking that maybe he could put up with a few flea bites in his bed, after all. Her smile faded as she saw that Milo was wounded, and she quickly came down to help him, and with the help of one of the other men, led the Marshall over to the doctor's small office to get him treated. Doc Sherman had returned in the early hours of the morning, and he had heard the gunfire and was preparing his surgery for the casualties that he knew would be wanting medical attention.

As the gunfire outside became less intense, Jeanie Eagle Feather's two cats came back from where they had been hiding and settled themselves, once more, under her small desk, wanting her attention. She ignored them and attended to Donna's shoulder wound. The bullet had passed clean through her shoulder, missing the bone, and not making too much damage on the way out, just leaving her with a painful reminder of the eventful day.

Jeanie Eagle Feather gave Donna a glass of whiskey and dripped some of it out of the bottle onto the wound to sterilize it, just a small amount as she didn't want to waste her precious liquor on the girl. She then proceeded to dress the wound with some bandages that she always kept for these sorts of emergencies.

"Well, Donna," she said. "That was mighty brave of you. Brave but damn foolish—" She paused while she tied a knot in the bandage. "But I hope it won't stop you from working tonight?"

"No, Miss Jeanie," said Donna, finishing the drink before her employer could change her mind. "I'll be fine. I'm just glad that Tex wasn't here to see this."

Looking at Donna, sitting there, looking tired and a little upset from the shooting, Jeanie Eagle Feather reconsidered her last statement, as a small amount of compassion crept into her.

"You go to your room girl and lie down for the rest of the day. You look plumb tuckered out, so you've no need to work tonight."

She helped Donna to her feet and steered her towards the stairs leading to the bedrooms and nodded to one of the other girls to help her.

"You won't get paid for tonight, though, Donna," added Jeanie Eagle Feather, as Donna ascended the stairs. "I'm not made of money. I can't afford to pay you when you ain't working."

"No, Miss Jeanie," said Donna, smiling through the pain as she went up to her bedroom. The girl who was helping her looked at Donna and raised her eyes to the sky in silent disapproval.

As the gunfire ended, Jeanie Eagle Feather went to the front door of her establishment. "Come on, girls," she ordered. "We'd better go and see if anybody needs our help out here." She planted her red felt hat firmly back on her head and walked onto the street, all her girls following dutifully behind.

Some of the other men carried out the bodies of the two deputies and took them over to the undertakers, along with the unfortunate Mason Carter, who had been gunned down outside the livery stables, and the old timer who should have kept himself indoors. The bodies of Troy Collis, Keefer, Gopher Spriggs, and the Comanche boy, Farlow Rainwater, were also taken to the undertakers where they would be put on display in open coffins outside his funeral parlor for any interested people to look at. The citizens would pose for photographs, with the bodies, taken by the town's newspaper editor, and their contributions would help pay for the undertaker's fees. The dead horses were dragged behind a wagon and dumped well out of town for the vultures and other predators to feed on.

******

As soon as Julie Cannon had calmed down, she fed Hootie and Young Billy a hearty breakfast, while Billy-Bob went and saddled up the young cowboy's horse after feeding it. He wanted Young Billy to ride out and find Joel and Tex and tell them what had happened and that their old adversary, Shreeve Moor, had been broken out of the jail, and the Marshall had been wounded and his two deputies killed. He tied up

Troy Collis' horse to the hitching rail at the front of his store, meaning to unsaddle it later.

With the two deputies killed and the Marshall incapacitated, there wasn't much law in town, and nobody to organize a posse to try and catch the killers, so Billy-Bob hoped that Joel and Tex would help get some men together. Billy-Bob also hoped that he would be included in the posse if his wife, Julie, allowed it, as he felt that he now had some unfinished business with the outlaws, and shooting down the gunman, Troy Collis, had reignited the fire that had not yet been fully extinguished in him.

Billy-Bob sketched a rough map on the back of an old delivery note for Young Billy to follow. He had traveled up the Gila River a few years ago and could remember the quickest way to the Travis ranch. After going over the route with Young Billy a couple of times, just to make sure that the young lad had understood, he sent him on his way, with Chloe and Molly both planting a kiss on his cheeks.

"I'll wait here in town for you, Young Billy, 'til you get back," Hootie said as Young Billy mounted up. "I'm still waiting for my old friend to meet me here."

"Well, keep out of the saloon, Hootie. I don't want to come back and find you in the jailhouse again," replied Young Billy as he rode away.

"Don't you worry about me, I'll keep off the booze."

"And I'll make sure that he does, Young Billy," yelled Billy-Bob as Young Billy urged his horse into a gallop. "Now, don't you go tiring your horse out too quickly. You've got a long way to go, so take it easy, boy."

Young Billy eased his horse into a trot and turned to wave at the small group, the twin girls giggling with delight, thinking that the young cowboy had turned for a last look at them both. He turned back, smiling to himself.

Those two girls are mighty pretty, he thought. *But I couldn't choose which one I liked best, and I sure don't want to get on the wrong side of Billy-Bob.*

He rode out of town, trying to remember the route that Billy-Bob had told him and hoping that he had still got the storekeeper's map in his pocket. He had never been given this much responsibility before in his life. *Still,* he thought, *didn't I save Joel and Tex from a pack of wolves?* He smiled to himself again has he rode on.

Chapter 22

About 20 miles south of town, after a fast ride, the outlaws turned off the trail and rode into a rocky gully where, once they had dismounted, four Indians appeared from behind some large boulders. They were all armed with the latest repeating rifles, but each of them also had a bow slung across their shoulder with a quiver of arrows tied around their waist with buckskin.

Randy Moor shouted them over and, on seeing that Shreeve Moor was with him, they all let out a whoop. The four Indians were renegade Comanche's, who had ridden with 'The Butcher' in the past and were in awe of his prowess with his cut-throat razor. They called him 'Little Man with A Fast Knife,' a name Shreeve Moor wasn't too happy about, mostly because of the 'Little Man' part, but he knew that it gave him some sort of legendary status with the Comanche's, so he put up with it.

Randy Moor had asked the Indians to join him as he needed their tracking skills, and they had quickly agreed when they knew that they would be helping 'Little Man with A Fast Knife' to escape. They had kept out of town, as the appearance of four Indians would arouse too much suspicion if they had been seen, so they had sat around drinking the cheap whiskey that Randy Moor had provided them with. Shreeve Moor nodded to the Comanche's as they gathered around him, and he pulled out the cut-throat razor from his pocket and waved it in the air along with the ears of the deputy, bringing more excited shouts from the savages.

As Skeeter Hancock came galloping into the gully, Shreeve Moor looked behind him down the trail.

"Where's Troy Collis, Skeeter?" he said. "I thought that he was with you."

"They got him, Shreeve," gasped Skeeter as he regained his breath. He dismounted and took a drink from his canteen. "That fella from the hardware store shot him off his horse. Can you believe it, an ordinary shopkeeper killed Troy Collis? He got him in the face."

"He ain't no ordinary shopkeeper," ranted 'The Butcher.' "He used to be a Texas Ranger. He came to the jail a couple of times to fix some locks on one of the cell doors, and Clem here recognized him from his time down on the border. He reckons that he was a dead shot when he rode with Captain Rip Ford."

Clem Johnson nodded in agreement, as he wrapped his bandanna around his left arm where a bullet had grazed him. "That's right. I remember seeing him with Rip Ford back in '49, when they were fighting Injuns. I heard that he was one of the Texas Rangers' best sharpshooters."

"Well, he was a dead shot back there in Tucson," agreed Skeeter. "He took Collis out with one shot to his head. I thought he was gonna shoot me next, so I hightailed it outa there."

"And where's that idiot, Gopher Spriggs?" said Shreeve Moor, looking down the trail. "The boy's a damn halfwit. He comes from a family of halfwits. I couldn't believe it when I saw him waiting outside the jail with the rest of you. Why the hell did you bring him along, Randy?"

Before Randy Moor could answer his brother, Waylon Coffey turned to the angry albino. "I reckon he's dead, Shreeve. I saw him fall off his horse back in town. He went galloping across the street when he saw something. I ain't sure what he was up to, but he looked dead after he hit the ground."

"Serves him right," said Shreeve Moor.

"I saw his pa, Keefer, get shot back there," said Waylon. He must have come looking for Gopher when he heard all the gunfire. Well, I reckon they're both dead now."

Shreeve Moor shrugged his thin, bony shoulders at the news of the Spriggs' family's demise and laughed insanely. "Well, that'll teach 'em to be more careful in future."

169

"I think that half-breed Injun, who was with Keefer never made it either," added Waylon Coffey as he looked back up the trail for his brother, Jeb.

Jeb Coffey was the last to ride in. His brother had been anxiously looking for him, thinking that maybe he had been shot in town as well. He came slowly trotting into the gully with the wounded Elvira Jones holding on behind him. Skeeter and Waylon helped get the badly wounded man off Jeb's horse, and they both laid him on the ground.

"Is he dead?" asked Randy Moor, walking over to Elvira and looking down at his still form. He wiped his snotty nose on the back of his sleeve, as he giggled inanely at the sight of Elvira Jones losing his lifeblood in the sandy ground.

"No, but I don't reckon that the poor bastard has got too long," said Jeb, kneeling to examine him.

"Well, we can't hang around here all day waiting for him to croak, and we ain't taking him with us. He'll slow us down," said Shreeve Moor, standing over the dying outlaw. He nodded over to one of the Comanches, the oldest brave, named Wild Coyote. The Indian acknowledged Shreeve Moor's silent command and quickly knelt down at the side of Elvira Jones, took out his knife and slit the man's throat, and he was dead within seconds. As the Comanche made to scalp Elvira, Jeb Coffey quickly pushed him off the dead outlaw.

"I ain't gonna let you scalp him, you damn savage, he was a friend of ours. Now get away from him."

Wild Coyote stood up, glaring at Jeb Coffey, waving the still bloody knife at him threateningly, but before he could reach him, he stopped as a rifle was cocked behind him. He turned and saw Waylon Coffey pointing his rifle at him.

"Back away from my brother, you damn heathen, there'll be no more killing," Waylon said as Wild Coyote hesitated, shrugged his shoulders, and bent down and wiped his knife on the dead man's shirt.

"Now then, boys, let's not get falling out," said Shreeve Moor, motioning for the Comanche to move away. "We ain't got time to bury Elvira now, 'cause we sure stirred up a hornet's nest back in town, and they'll most likely be trying to get a posse together soon. Although with those two deputy's dead, and the Marshall with a bullet in him, I don't reckon they'll be sending any lawmen after us just yet. Anyways, I sure don't want to be back in that jailhouse any time soon, so let's move out."

Wild Coyote went back to the other three Comanches, talking in his own tongue, and gesticulating back to the Coffey brothers. There wasn't much love lost between the Indians and the two white men, and it would take only a small spark to start a prairie fire between them.

Jeb Coffey removed Elvira Jones' pistol from his holster and tucked it into his own gun belt. He took out Elvira's makings and tossed them over to Waylon. "It ain't no use wasting good tobacco. I'm sure that he wouldn't mind us having it." He looked at his brother, as they both prepared to mount and spoke softly to him. "This sure ain't turned out like I thought it would, Waylon. Now that we've lost Troy Collis, there's no one here with enough sense to lead us."

"You're not wrong there, Bro," answered his brother with a shrug of his shoulders. "I wish that we'd stayed south of the border, instead of coming along with that crazy Randy Moor when he offered us easy pickings at the bank. His brother Shreeve ain't right in the head either. They are both as mad as a sack full of frogs."

They both mounted up, and with a last look at their dead friend, followed the others down the trail. Letting the rest of the gang get out of earshot, Waylon leaned over to his brother, as they cantered along. "First chance that we get, Bro, we're getting away from this bunch. I don't trust Shreeve Moor and his brother, and I don't like those no-good murdering Comanches either."

His brother nodded in agreement, as they dug their spurs in to catch up with the others.

The gang rode south into the dry desert country—a land of tall cactus, rolling sagebrush, and mesquite bushes. Homesteads were few and far between, populated by poor white families, Mexicans, and the occasional German immigrants, and Shreeve Moor was hoping to find a poorly defended property to stock up on provisions, steal some fresh horses, and hopefully kill some innocent people. He had been incarcerated too long in the Tucson jail and wanted to get as far away as possible and get back into his butchering ways before long.

As he rode along, Shreeve Moor put his hand in his pocket and felt the pair of ears that he had cut off the old deputy, back in Tucson. They were still wet with the deputy's blood, and he brought one of them out of his pocket and waved it in the air. The feel of it made him laugh out loud at the thought of adding to his new collection. He would put them around his neck, on a piece of rawhide, after he had cleaned them.

Shreeve Moor's brother, Randy, who was riding at the side of him, saw him laughing and joined in, even though he didn't know what was amusing him. He was just happy that he had managed to free his brother from the jail, and that he now had someone to look after him, and do all his thinking for him. Too much thinking made his headache and he never seemed to make his mind up quickly enough about anything. He usually wet his pants before he could make up his mind if he needed to take a pee.

The Coffey brothers, riding not far behind, saw the Moor brothers laughing and looked at each other grim faced.

Chapter 23

Later the next afternoon, Joel came riding into Tucson with Tex and Young Billy. They had ridden hard all night after Young Billy had found them the previous evening and told them about the jail break, and they all looked like they we're in need of a good meal and some sleep. Joel's empty stomach was rumbling, and he knew that the others would be feeling the same.

They had stopped once in the early hours, long after midnight, to allow the horses to drink from a stream that the moon's reflection had led then to. While the horses had grazed for a short while, the three men had divided up the piece of meatloaf that Tom had made them take with them, and consumed it hungrily. The meager portion was hardly enough to stave off the hunger, and Tex took a quick drink of water from his canteen to wash it down and mounted up, eager to be on his way.

"Come on, Joel," he said. "Let's make trail. We've still got a lot more miles to cover."

Joel knew that his friend was worried about 'Donna the Slut,' even though Young Billy had told him that she hadn't been badly injured. He beckoned to Young Billy, who was still standing at the side of his horse, as it munched on the damp grass. He had looked half-asleep as he leaned with one arm resting on his saddle, not looking his usual chirpy self.

"Come on, boy, let's move out," said Joel, feeling a mite sorry for the young lad. He lit the remains of his cigarette and walked over to him and touched him gently on his shoulder, making his head jerk up in surprise. Joel realized that Young Billy had been dozing off while his horse grazed, and he looked into the young cowboy's bleary eyes, reflected in the moonlight.

"How are you feeling, Young Billy? You look dead on your feet. I'll bet that you've not slept since you left Tucson. Would you like to head back to Tom and the others and rest up for a while? You shouldn't have too much trouble finding their campfire."

Young Billy had stirred himself from his reverie at the sound of Joel's voice. He squeezed his forefinger and thumb between the bridge of his nose, pinching it sharply to clear the sleep from his eyes, and looked up at Joel. "I'm fine, Joel. Just feeling a mite tuckered out, that's all. A good meal and a rest and I'll be as good as new. I want to go on with you and Tex." He paused as he splashed some water, from his canteen, on his face and took a long drink and gave Joel a weary smile. "Why, Joel, if I don't go with you, then who is going to keep the wolves and bears away from you both?"

Joel patted him on his shoulder and laughed as he mounted up. "Come on then, Young Billy. Let's catch up with Tex before he gets clean away."

Young Billy slowly shook his head from side to side, to get rid of the stiffness in his neck and shoulders, and mounted his horse, smiling at Joel to reassure him, but more to reassure himself. Joel spurred his horse into a gallop to catch up with Tex, who was already disappearing into the darkness, with Young Billy following behind, the sharp breeze, as he rode, putting some spark back into his eyes.

******

Pat and Zach had wanted to ride back with Joel and Tex and help track down the outlaws, but Charlotte wouldn't allow her new husband to leave her, and Tom had been reluctant to let his son go. Joel and Tex had been against the idea as well, so they had both reluctantly agreed to remain. Young Billy had wanted to get back to Tucson, so Joel had agreed that he should ride with them.

Joel had wanted to set off the next morning, after a good night's rest, but Tex had been eager to get to Tucson as soon as possible, as the news of 'Donna The Slut' being wounded had made him impatient to see how she was. The others had stayed the night around the camp fire, and Tom was going to send Pat, Charlotte, and Zach back to the ranch the next morning and accompany Father Benito back to Tucson, but the old friar had insisted that he could take care of himself, and, after careful thought,

174

Tom had agreed that he was more than capable of finding his own way back, alone.

As the three men rode down the main street of Tucson, heading towards Billy-Bob Cannon's hardware store, Joel and Tex recognized the huge figure of Hootie Swenson lounging on the boardwalk outside, puffing away on his pipe. He looked up as they approached and gave a wave when Young Billy shouted his name. Hootie wasn't alone, and he had been engrossed in conversation with another man, clad in buckskins, like himself, and wearing a raccoon skin hat on his head.

"Well, I'll be darned," said Tex, recognizing Hootie's companion. "That looks like that old French Trapper, Banjo Lafarge with Hootie. What the hell is that old scoundrel doing here?"

"That must be the fella that Hootie came into town to meet when he rode in with me," Young Billy said as they dismounted. "He said that he was waiting for an old friend."

The three riders tied up their horses and walked up to Hootie and his friend. Tex extended his hand to greet Banjo Lafarge, and the old trapper got up and, with a smile, took it in his own hand and shook it. "Well, if it ain't old Banjo Lafarge," grinned Tex. "Are you still coming out with the 'silver plates' and the 'mercy buckets,' you old scoundrel?"

"It's 's'il vous plait' and 'merci beaucoup,' you ignorant southern bastard," answered Banjo in his still thick French accent, as he removed his hand from Tex's grip and looked at it closely.

"What's up with you?" Tex said, looking at Banjo examining his own hand.

"Well, mon amie, I heard that if a Texan offers to shake your hand then you should check afterwards to see how many fingers you have left."

Ignoring the remark, Tex introduced Joel to the old trapper.

Banjo Lafarge was a French fur trapper, from up north, who had traveled all over Canada, the West, and down in Mexico, where he had met Tex. He had ridden with Kit Carson in 1842 when they had both joined up with the legendary John C Freemont. The Pathfinder, looking for the overland route to the Pacific, up the Platte River. He was a renowned tracker and beaver trapper and always carried an old Sharps Buffalo rifle with him. Every so often, he would meet up with his old friend, Hootie, and they would both disappear into the backwoods for a few weeks, or even months, returning with a few trophies, some new wounds, and a lot of tall stories to tell.

Banjo's real name was Pierre Lafarge, but everyone called him Banjo, because when he said good morning in French, "Bonjour," the Americans thought it sounded like Banjo, to their untrained ears. So, much to Banjo's dismay, the name had stuck. He expressed his sorrow to Tex, on hearing of the death of his friend, Steve, who he had met a few times.

On hearing of the arrival of Joel and Tex, Billy-Bob Cannon came out of his store and discussed the jailbreak with them. He then took them down the street to the undertakers, where the bodies of the dead outlaws were on display outside. They were all propped up in their open coffins, Troy Collis still with the goofy, surprised expression on his porcine features, and Billy-Bob proudly showed the two cowboys where his bullet had gone through the outlaw's eye.

"That's damn fine shooting, Billy-Bob," said Joel, clapping the storekeeper on his back. Tex nodded in agreement as a few of the townsfolk crowded around to congratulate the ex-Texas Ranger. The three of them then walked over to the Marshall's office, where Marshall Tucker was sitting outside in a chair, his arm bandaged and in a sling, and wearing a pained expression on his face. He started to get up when he saw Joel and Tex approaching, but Joel waved him back down.

"You sit right there, Marshall. We heard about the jailbreak and the shooting, and we're sure sorry about old Snowy and Deputy Slade."

Milo Tucker sagged back into the chair and sighed as he looked up at Joel and Tex.

"I want you to organize a posse, Joel, and get after those murdering bastards and bring them back to hang."

Joel nodded in agreement to the Marshall, as he turned to Tex, for the Indian fighter's opinion.

"You can count on us, Milo," he agreed, "We've got some unfinished business with that murdering scum, Shreeve Moor. If we can get some of the others to join us, then we'll track the bastards down."

"Well, I'd like to go along with you boys," said Billy-Bob, seeing the opportunity, at last, to get away from his hardware store and back in the saddle. "I might be a little trail rusty and a mite older than you, Joel, but you can see that I can still shoot straight," he added, pointing back across the street where the dead outlaw, Troy Collis, was posing in his open coffin. The outlaw seemed to be staring back at them with his one glazed eye. Joel turned to Billy-Bob. "We'd be happy to let you ride with us, Billy-Bob. You've got more experience chasing outlaws than both of us, but would your wife, Julie let you come with us?"

"You let me worry about Julie," smiled Billy-Bob, feeling happy and excited that Joel and Tex were considering letting him join the posse. "I'll square it with my wife. She ain't the boss in our marriage," he added, pulling a cigarette out of his vest pocket and furtively looking back up the street to make sure that Julie wasn't watching him, as he struck a match and lit it, taking a long pull on his smoke and grinning.

"You deputize us, Marshall, and we'll try and get a posse together," said Joel as he shook the trail dust from his hat. "Just as soon as we've had some grub, a hot bath, and rested the horses, we'll get organized."

Marshall Tucker reached into his vest pocket and brought out three shiny deputies badges and handed them to Joel. "Consider yourselves deputized boys," he said as the three men took them. "Dead or alive, I don't care which, but make sure none of them get away."

Joel and Tex pinned the badges to their shirts, Billy-Bob clasped his in his hand, as Marshall Tucker picked up a small pile of wanted posters that he had brought out from his office. He had been looking through them as Joel, Tex, and Billy-Bob had arrived and had managed to recognize all the outlaws from their pictures on them with help from some of the townsfolk who had witnessed the jailbreak, and Jeanie Eagle Feather, who knew most of the law breakers in the territory, as most of them had passed through her establishment. He handed them to Joel, discarding the ones which had the men who had been shot on them.

"Take these with you, Joel. You should be able to recognize the bastards from their pictures, although some of these wanted posters are a bit out of date."

Joel took a quick look through the wanted posters, folded them up and tucked them in his belt.

Jeanie Eagle Feather was across the street, outside her establishment mending the broken glass pane in the front door, her two cats, Mickey and Mannie, asleep under her chair. On seeing Tex, she gave him a wave and beckoned him over. She was holding some nails between her lips and a small hammer in one hand. Tex waved back and turned to Marshall Tucker. "I hear that Jeanie Eagle Feather took down one of the outlaws with her knife. That sure is one hell of a woman, Marshall."

Joel nodded in agreement. "I'll bet it was the same knife that she took off one of old 'One-Eared Leroy's' ears with."

"I'd better go and see how 'Donna the Slut' is, Joel. I'll see you back at Billy-Bob's place," said Tex, as he walked over to Jeanie Eagle Feather's establishment.

"Well save all your energy for the long ride, Tex."

Joel walked back with Billy-Bob, to his store, where Hootie and Banjo were sitting outside, engrossed in earnest conversation with Young Billy standing near them listening intently to what they were both saying. Hootie was puffing away on his old, clay pipe and breaking wind strong enough to fill the sails of a three-masted schooner. He was sporting a clean bandage on his head after Julie Cannon had re-dressed the wound for him. Banjo was snorting snuff up his nose from a battered old snuff box. His nose was always running from the snuff that he took, and he tended to sniff loudly and frequently, which irritated most folk, but it was a habit that he enjoyed. With his beard stained with dribble from his nose, he looked like he was eating the remains of a dead tom cat, as the shaggy, unkempt growth moved in time with his sniffing. He put away his snuff box as Joel and Billy-Bob approached, his gnarled fingers showing the first signs of arthritis as he put it into one of the many pockets in his old buckskin coat.

Billy-Bob turned to Joel as he went into his store. "I'll just go and have a word with Julie," he said with a sigh, looking at the deputy's badge in his hand.

"OK, Billy-Bob, but if she says no, then I'll understand."

Billy-Bob took Young Billy inside the store to have a quick sleep in the stockroom while Joel and Tex organized a posse.

After Billy-Bob had gone inside, Joel got out his makings and rolled himself a smoke, while the others looked at the shiny, silver star pinned to his shirt. He told them that he and Tex had been deputized and were going to organize a posse to track the outlaws down.

178

"Well you can count me and Banjo in, Joel," Hootie said. "We were going to go hunting anyways, so we may as well go after bigger varmints, and I didn't like that little runt, Shreeve Moor. He called me a drunken bum. Banjo here is the best tracker in the southwest. He could follow a week-old trail in the dark, so we should be able to follow their trail."

Young Billy poked his head around the door. He had heard the talk of a posse and didn't want to be left out. "You can count me in, Joel. I can ride, and you know that I can shoot. Please Joel, let me ride with you."

"I'll think about it, Young Billy. You've got plenty of ambition but not enough aptitude. I need to go over to the bathhouse first and wash some of this trail dust off me. Now go and get some rest, and I'll talk to you later."

"I'm a good tracker," pleaded Young Billy. "I can follow a trail."

"Good tracker!" laughed Joel. "Why you couldn't find your own backside with both hands down the back of your pants."

Joel turned to Hootie, who had been standing too close to him. "I reckon a bath wouldn't do you no harm either, Hootie, so you can come along with me. I don't want to follow in your trail for long, you smell like a wet dog, and your breath smells like something crawled in your mouth and died. So if you want to join us, then you'd better get on the right side of clean and tidy, my friend."

Hootie reluctantly followed Joel down the street to the bathhouse, muttering to himself in Swedish and rubbing the back of his head. Joel paid the man for them both, and they both stripped off and soaked in separate tubs of steaming hot water.

The bathtub was hardly big enough to accommodate Hootie's large frame, and when he lowered himself in, most of the water spilled over the rim, but he lay there and enjoyed the warmth, trying to get a good lather out of the cheap bar of soap. Joel gave the bath man an extra dollar to give Hootie's underwear a good wash while he was bathing and return them to him later.

Joel and Hootie returned to Billy-Bob's store and went into the kitchen where Julie had prepared a hot meal for them both. Tex was already eating, having returned from seeing 'Donna the Slut,' and he looked up at them both.

"You two both look nice and clean, especially you, Hootie. Why you look as pink and shiny as a new born baby, and you smell of soap, instead of stale booze and sweat." He pushed his empty plate away and stood up. "I'll go and see to the horses, Joel, while you both eat. Donna is fine; she's just got a flesh wound." He smiled at Joel. "It never stopped her from keeping me happy though." He looked over to Billy-Bob, who sat drinking coffee with a smug expression on his face, and the deputy's badge pinned on his shirt. "It looks like Billy-Bob will be joining us Joel."

Billy-Bob was about to reply when Julie entered the kitchen. "If I don't let him go with you, Joel he'd be moping around the store in a sulk for days. Me and the girls don't want him to go, but if it gets it out of his system, he can go." She looked at Joel and Tex. "You two had better bring him back in one piece, or you will have me to answer to. And make sure that he takes plenty of tobacco with him, 'cause you both know how irritable he gets when he hasn't got a smoke. And I'm fed up with him sucking those boiled sweets. He must think they hide the smell of cigarettes from me."

Billy-Bob sat silently, drinking his coffee with an embarrassed look on his craggy face, but feeling pleased with himself that Julie had allowed him to join the posse. He knew that when he returned from hunting down the outlaws, if he returned, his wife would make him work harder in the store and not let him have any more ideas of leaving his family ever again. *But what the hell*, he thought to himself. *It'll sure be worth the aggravation. I'll show Joel and Tex what an old Texas Ranger can do.* He wanted to, once more, capture the sense of never feeling more alive than when facing death, a sensation that he had left behind when he had resigned from the Texas Rangers and settled down in Tucson and married Julie.

Joel pushed his chair back from the table, wiped his mouth with the back of his hand, and thanked Julie for the meal. He took out his makings and with a wink to Billy-Bob and a slight nod of his head he went outside.

"I'll go check on the horses and see you fellas outside, when you've finished your breakfast."

Billy-Bob followed Joel outside, not catching the exasperated look that Julie gave him as he left the room. Joel rolled himself a smoke and handed the makings over to Billy-Bob as he joined him on the boardwalk.

"I see she ain't the boss then, Billy-Bob," laughed Joel as he lit his cigarette and handed the match over. Billy-Bob took the match, lit his cigarette, and smiled.

"Well she's letting me go, ain't she?"

Chapter 24

Approaching the edge of Madera Canyon, Shreeve Moor saw the smoke rising from the distant cabin chimney when they were more than a couple of miles away, and the albino turned to the others with an evil grin on his pale face.

"It looks like there's a homestead up ahead, boys," he yelled. His hand went to the cut-throat razor in his pocket, which he had taken from the Marshall back in Tucson. "We should get us some grub there. And I reckon, we're well enough ahead of any posse for us to get some rest and maybe have us some fun."

His brother, Randy, cackled with glee. "Sounds good to me, Shreeve. Let's go get 'em."

The riders spurred their horses on, all eager to be the first to get there, checking their guns to make sure that they were fully loaded, the four Comanche renegade's way out in front on their small fast ponies. The Coffey brothers rode a little behind the others, and Waylon looked over to his brother with a negative look on his face. His brother nodded to him, understanding what he meant. They hadn't come along for all this mindless slaughter.

Shreeve Moor turned in his saddle and shouted back to the Coffey brothers. "Come on, you two, keep up. You're gonna miss all the fun."

* * * * * *

Outside in the front yard, young Bobby Stokes sat whittling on a piece of wood as the riders approached. He had been watching his sisters' three children play while he whittled, occasionally throwing a stone at one of the chickens, if they ventured near him. The four Comanche renegades were the first in the yard, and their sudden arrival made Bobby fall back off the upturned bucket that he had been perched on. The Indians ignored the fat, white man, preferring to chase after the young children, who were by now running away, screaming at the sight of the savages.

As young Bobby started to get up off the ground, his whittling knife still in one hand, Shreeve Moor and his brother turned into the yard and headed towards him. Thinking that the fat man was a threat, because of the knife, Shreeve Moor brought up his rifle and fired at him. Young Bobby Stokes let out a scream, as he was hit in the thigh, and fell backwards shouting for his pappy. He struggled to get up as Shreeve Moor quickly dismounted and took out his cut-throat razor, in a movement too quick for him to comprehend, and approached him. The razor glinted in the sunlight as 'The Butcher' took hold of young Bobby's hair and with two swift, well-practiced slashes removed both of the fat man's ears.

Laughing insanely, Shreeve Moor wiped the blood-stained razor on the front of Bobby Stokes' shirt, folded and pocketed it, and waved the severed ears at his brother, Randy, who had dismounted and proudly watched as his brother carried out his grisly task. Shreeve Moor got up and walked away from Bobby Stokes, gleefully examining his trophies.

The fat man sat on the ground screaming, his hands covering the place where his ears had recently resided, as Randy Moor approached him. The blood lust was upon him, from seeing his brother's recent gory handiwork, and as young Bobby carried on shouting for his pappy, he pulled out his pistol and shot him in the other leg. Randy was going to have some fun with this fat man and would let him die very slowly.

The Comanche, Wild Coyote, shouted to the other three Indians and dismounted in front of the rundown homestead. He had heard someone shouting from inside the shack and pulled out his knife, hoping to take a scalp from whoever was in there. He had been stopped, earlier, from taking Elvira Jones' scalp, by the Coffey brothers, and he wouldn't be thwarted this time.

The other three Indians carried on chasing the frightened children, as Wild Coyote kicked the flimsy front door in and went inside. He looked around the dingy room and saw that it was unoccupied, but he could hear a man's voice coming through the ill-fitted door opposite.

With a savage grin, Wild Coyote took the large axe that was hanging from the wall and walked over to the door, as the shouting from the other room continued.

It was nearly noon, the sun was high overhead, and old Bobby Stokes was still lying in his bed. A jar of corn liquor, nearly empty, lay on the filthy bedding next to him. The stopper had worked loose and the remains of the liquor was slowly dripping out, creating a large stain on the already dirty sheet, next to him, and soaking into the crap stained long johns that he wore. As he turned over, his hand went into the small puddle of booze, which was already soaking through the dirty sheet and disappearing into the old mattress, and it startled him into a befuddled state of near wakefulness. He let out a yell on discovering that his precious liquor had nearly gone, rubbed his fat, unshaven face, and attempted to get up, but failed, falling back on to the booze soaked bed.

"Where the hell are you? You lazy cow," he shouted. "Get your fat ass in here and clean this mess up, will you. I'm getting wet lying here. And go and find me some more damn booze."

He grabbed the liquor jar and threw it across the small bedroom, making it bounce of the far wall, shaking the timber boarding and showering the already grimy floor with dust and dregs of corn liquor. The effort had been too much for his large, obese body, and the rolls of fat on him shook and wobbled in a grotesque parody of the sea in a large swell.

In his younger days, Bobby Stokes had run a team of mules and an old stagecoach, transporting people to various destinations in the territory, and also delivering timber and grain to town. He had once made a decent living out of it, but his laziness, and the fact that nobody liked the man, had made his business slowly disappear. The locals, in the small town that he had lived in, had all banded together and ran him out of town, and he had ended up in the Badlands, miles from anywhere.

He had been married four times and used to beat each wife with a whip if they got out of line. His first wife had died from the severe beating that he had given her, and the next two had each run away in the night while he had been drunk out of his head. His latest wife, named Blair, who was a good 15 years younger than him—he was about 78 years old—he had bought from a passing muleskinner. He had traded her for a pair of his prize hawks, which he had bred himself. Breeding hawks was old Bobby Stokes' only passion in life, except for the booze, and he kept them in a large shed out the back of his shack, which was the only clean place on his small piece of land. He cared for his birds a lot more than his own family. And kept the birdhouse in better condition than his own house. His wife, Blair, did all the work around the place, tending the few livestock, cooking and cleaning (if you could call it cleaning), and doing the occasional delivery on their only remaining mule.

Old Bobby had a few children from his three first wives and most of them had left home. The only two of his offspring remaining were his fat son, Bobby—he had been too drunk to think of a name for him when he had been born, so he called him after himself—and a daughter named Sandy. The younger Bobby Stokes was even fatter than his pa and sat around all day throwing rocks at the chickens to pass the time, and brewing cheap liquor for his pa, in an old still in a small cave at the rear of the canyon.

His daughter, Sandy, was a no-good whore who took drugs, when she could acquire them, from a local Chinese merchant who sometimes passed by. She had three children by three different men. The youngest had been fathered by a passing Apache Indian, who had kidnapped her one dark night when she had been lying outside, half stoned. But on seeing how ugly she was in the light of the next morning, he had promptly abandoned her to find her own way home, but not before he had given her a sound beating to show his disgust with himself.

It was rumored that Sandy's eldest daughter had been sired by her own father, old Bobby Stokes, when she had been raped by him in one of his frequent drunken moments. Sandy, although only about 40 years old, had no teeth left in her mouth, from years of neglect and drug abuse, and her ugly appearance and lack of cleanliness meant that men had stopped calling on her long ago. The only time these days that she shared a bed with another man was when her own pa forced himself on her.

Old Bobby Stokes was getting mighty angry now, as nobody had come to answer his call and come and sort him out. "Where the hell is that lazy no good bitch?" he shouted. "I'm in a mess here. Help me get out of this bed and get me some breakfast. If you don't get in here soon, you're gonna be mighty sorry."

He heard noises outside his window and the sound of someone screaming, as he started to sit up, throwing his fat legs out of the bed, his feet landing on the floor as he perched on the side of his dirty mattress. He thought that he could hear his son, Young Bobby, shouting for him, and the sound of gunfire outside. As he stood up, leaning shakily against a bedpost, he heard the sound of the outside door being smashed in and began to panic. He looked around the bedroom for his old rifle just as the bedroom door was flung wide open, crashing against the wall, and he saw a mean looking Indian standing there with a large axe in his hand. Old Bobby Stokes recognized the axe as the one that he always kept hanging on the wall, near the outside door, in case of any trouble. Well, it looked like there was going to be trouble now, and it was heading straight for him in the shape of a large, wild-eyed savage.

The old man backed away from the Comanche, Wild Coyote, snagging his long-johns on a bedpost, as he tried to retreat into the corner of his bedroom. The trap door in the back of his dirty underwear caught on a splinter of wood, pulling it open and exposing his bare rear end, as he turned away from the Comanche.

"Don't hurt me," he sniveled as he cowered in the corner of the bedroom. "Take my wife and kids. Take my mule, but please let me go."

He could hear gunfire and wild shrieks outside, as the rest of his family were caught by the outlaws.

I hope they don't hurt my poor birds, Bobby Stokes thought to himself as he cowered in fear.

Wild Coyote approached old Bobby Stokes, who had now dropped on his knees, facing the wall in an act of supplication. The Comanche looked down in disgust at the fat old man, who was sobbing loudly, his fat neck and shoulders shaking with fear, and his fat, freshly soiled ass protruding from out of his tattered underwear. He wrinkled his nose at the stench and wanting to get away from the filthy old man as soon as possible, raised the large axe above his head and, with a loud yell, buried it deep into the top of old Bobby Stokes' fat head. The force nearly split the old man's skull in two and, after trying unsuccessfully to remove it,

Wild Coyote grunted and left the bedroom in a hurry, leaving the axe behind.

Old Bobby Stokes was dead as he slumped to the floor. The axe had fell out of his skull as his face collided with the wall, and his brains were oozing out from the deep cleft in his head. Thankfully, he was too late to hear the noise coming from the direction of his birdhouse, as two of the Comanche's went rampaging through it, knocking his prize hawks from their perches. Some of the birds quickly flew out of the way of the two Indians, but others were cut down where they stood, hacked to pieces by their sharp tomahawks.

Sandy Stokes ran screaming as a Comanche leapt off his horse and chased her up the rear yard. Her eyes were wild with fear, and she let out a strangled sob from her toothless mouth, as she looked over her shoulder and saw that the young Indian was closing the distance between her. He let out a triumphant whoop, as she ran around the back of a small, dilapidated shed which the Stokes family used as a latrine. It was positioned over a deep hole in the ground with a log across it, and as Sandy opened the door and disappeared inside, thinking that she would be safe from the savage's clutches, the smell emanating from the open door made the Comanche suddenly stop in his tracks.

He wrinkled his nose at the disgusting stench and tied a bandanna around his face, as he approached the door that the girl had slammed behind her. He wasn't going to stay long near this disgusting place, but he would make sure that the white woman inside would not get away from him. He pulled out a sharp knife from his belt and rapped on the old door with the edge of its blade, the noise causing the woman inside to let out a whimper of fear, the feeble sounds bubbling through her toothless gums. The Comanche grinned at the sound of the woman's sobbing, as he reached out and gripped the small piece of tattered old rope, which served as a door handle.

Chapter 25

Back in Tucson, Joel had managed to assemble a small posse to track down Shreeve Moor and his gang. Along with himself and Tex, there was Billy-Bob Cannon, sporting his shiny new deputy's badge, Young Billy Brand, who had managed to persuade Joel and Tex of his abilities, and Hootie Swenson and his friend, Banjo Lafarge. Two other local men had agreed to ride with them, Tyler Creed, who was the local blacksmith's son, and Brad Stillman, a cowboy from one of the nearby ranches. Tyler Creed had wanted to enlist to fight in the war, but his pa had persuaded him to join up with the posse, hoping that it was the lesser of two evils. He was about 24 years old, a big, powerful young man, just like his pa and a good shot with a rifle. Brad Stillman was a couple of years older than Tyler, a good horseman and a decent shot. He was also trying to avoid the war and hearing about the posse being put together figured that joining up to chase the outlaws would be less hazardous than being in a battle.

Tyler Creed and Brad Stillman were both young and untried and could be hot-headed at times, but Joel and Tex had agreed to take them both as they were short of volunteers to make up a decent posse. Tyler was a lot like his pa, who was likely to throw his sizable weight around to get his own way, so Joel decided to keep an eye on the big lad in case he caused trouble with others. None of the other men who lived in, and around, town wanted to get involved in chasing the dangerous bunch of outlaws.

The only other person who wanted to ride with them was Jeanie Eagle Feather, who, after killing Gopher Spriggs, was keen to add to her tally, but Tex had dissuaded her, telling her that her business would suffer without her to keep an eye on her girls. She had readily agreed knowing that without her firm hand the girls would get lazy and the customers would take advantage of her absence. Jeanie Eagle Feather puffed on her pipe, as she watched young Molly cleaning the new piece of glass that had been fitted in the front door. She sat in her chair, in front of her whorehouse, and watched as the posse prepared their equipment ready to leave, thinking that maybe she should have left Donna in charge and gone with them.

It was early the following morning when they rode south out of Tucson. By the time they had got organized, the evening before, it had been getting dark, so after a good night's sleep and a hearty breakfast, they had left to pick up the outlaw's trail, which by now would be nearly two days old. Banjo Lafarge was confident that he could track them. He said that he could follow a Beaver's trail in the wilderness with a blindfold over both of his eyes.

Billy-Bob's wife and daughters stood on the boardwalk in front of the hardware store to see them off. Julie had given her husband the rest of his 'secret' stash of tobacco to take with him. His daughters, Chloe and Molly, were more interested in the departure of Young Billy Brand, and they had both given the embarrassed young cowboy a kiss on his cheeks, and they both waved vigorously at him as he rode away.

Jeanie Eagle Feather and her girls all stood outside the whorehouse, as the posse passed by with 'Donna the Slut' smiling at Tex. She walked over to him, her arm in a sling, as he rode slowly past and handed him a, nearly full, bottle of Jeanie Eagle Feather's best whiskey. Jeanie Eagle Feather had let Donna give it to Tex for free, but she knew that the cost would be deducted from her earnings. Tex took the bottle and leaned down and kissed 'Donna the Slut.' She had promised to leave the whorehouse when he returned and maybe marry him but had not yet told Jeanie Eagle Feather of her intentions. Tex reached in his pocket and pulled out two silver dollars and dropped them into 'Donna the Slut's' hand. He knew that nothing was free from Jeanie Eagle Feather's whorehouse.

"Now you save yourself for me, 'til I get back, Donna," he said quietly to her. "I'm going to keep my promise and settle down with you once I get the bastards who gave you that bullet wound." He gave her a wink and rode after the others, tucking the bottle of whiskey into one of his saddlebags.

Donna smiled to herself as Tex rode away. "How the hell does he think I'm going to save myself for him?" She laughed quietly. "I work in a damn whorehouse for a living." She stood in the middle of the street, watching him as he caught up with Joel. "I sure hope he comes back safe. I'd be lost without the big fool."

The undertaker was busy nailing the coffin lids down on the dead outlaws as they passed, as the bodies were all beginning to smell a bit ripe and most folk had been to look at them and pay him for the privilege. He now had enough money to plant them in the local cemetery.

As they passed the bank, it was busy with two men removing the remains of the glass from the large broken window and preparing to temporary board it up. A new timber window frame complete with large panes of glass would take a while to arrive from back east, especially with the civil war in progress.

Marshall Milo Tucker sat outside his office with his woman, Conchita, standing behind him and raised his hat to the small posse as they passed by. He hoped that they would all be up to the assignment that he had asked them to carry out. He knew that Joel and Tex had both been in harm's way before and were both experienced gunfighters, and if Billy-Bob Cannon's reputation was half as good as he told everyone, then he should be up for it.

The rest of the posse were an unknown quantity to him. He knew that Hootie Swenson was a fighter, and his reputation as a sharpshooter was faultless, but he wasn't young. Neither was Hootie's old friend, Banjo Lafarge, but Marshall Tucker knew that their experience would count against Young Billy Brand and the other two young men. He was just a little worried that the posse was small but didn't let it show as they rode past him.

The posse was well-provisioned and had three spare horses with them, in case any of the others went lame or were injured. They also had a pack mule with them, which carried the food and spare ammunition and was pulled along behind a reluctant Tyler Creed. Joel and Tex had agreed that they would all take turns looking after the spare horses and mule, except Hootie and Banjo, who took turns riding ahead looking for the outlaw's trail.

Tex took a last look behind him, as they reached the empty cattle pens at the end of the last building, to see 'Donna the Slut' standing in the middle of the street. Seeing Tex turn around in his saddle, she waved her scarf at him and rubbed a tear from her eye.

"You ain't going soft on me now, are you?" said Joel, seeing his friend raise his hat to his girl.

"Not me," shrugged Tex. "I just would have liked to have spent a lazy day in bed with her, and a bottle of whiskey, instead of riding out with this unsavory lot. Anyways, Joel, talking about going soft, what about you and that pretty Joan, back at the wedding." He laughed. "Come on, Joel, let's make trail."

As they rode out of sight of the townsfolk, Billy-Bob got out his makings and rolled himself a smoke. He tossed the makings over to Joel and lit his cigarette and absently wondered how his wife had known, all along, where he had hidden his stash of tobacco. He laughed to himself, as Joel threw the makings back to him, thinking what a fine woman his Julie was, and hoping that she had done the right thing in letting him join the posse. He knew that she was worried about him but had tried not to let it show. Billy-Bob leaned down and put the makings back in his saddle bag and saw his spectacle case next to his pack of cards and a small parcel of food. He smiled to himself—his wife Julie had thought of everything.

After a day's ride, Banjo led the posse into the gully that the outlaws had stopped in and dismounted, and was joined by Hootie. After a short discussion with Banjo, Hootie turned to the others who had followed them in.

"It looks like they had four other riders waiting here for them," Hootie said. "And they were riding unshod horses, Indian ponies. Me and Banjo reckon that they are Comanches." He led them over to the body of Elvira Jones, who had already been picked at by the local vermin, and picked up a feather lying next to him on the ground.

"This belonged to a Comanche," he said, examining the feather which Wild Coyote had lost from his hair in the scuffle with Jeb Coffey.

"They must be some renegades who have joined up with Shreeve Moor's gang," Tex said. So, we'd better be careful from now on. I don't want my throat cut like this poor bastard."

The two newcomers, Tyler and Brad, looked at each other on hearing Tex's comments. They had joined the posse for a bit of excitement, but didn't fancy tangling with savage Indians as well as outlaws. Tyler muttered something to Brad, which none of the others could hear.

"I hope you two ain't getting cold feet?" Joel said on seeing the nervous looks between the pair, as they glanced down at the dead outlaw. "This is a manhunt, not a Sunday picnic, so make up your minds if you want to stay or go back to Tucson." The two men didn't answer Joel. They both silently walked away from the mutilated outlaw's body.

Joel and Tex tried to match the dead outlaw with one of the wanted posters but, because his face had been badly mutilated by vultures, they were finding it difficult, until Tex noticed that it said on the description below the sketch of Elvira Jones that he was missing three fingers on his left hand. He examined the left hand on the body and there were three fingers missing. "I reckon this fella is Elvira Jones," he said to Joel. Joel agreed and tore a corner from the outlaw's poster and put it back with the others. This was his method of keeping a check on which ones were left. He wouldn't rest until all the posters had a corner missing, it would mean that they had caught them all or killed them all and could return to Tucson.

They decided to move on out of the gully and leave Elvira Jones to the vultures that were gathering near them. Some of the large carrion were hopping about and squawking loudly at the men who had disturbed their chance of a meal. Others were silently perched in mesquite bushes and some were on the branches of a large saguaro cactus, their shoulders hunched ready for instant flight. The sound of Coyotes howling nearby, their acute sense of smell drawing them to the scent of decaying flesh, meant that the birds would be having competition for the unfortunate outlaw's remains.

"Come on, Tex," Joel said. "Let's find somewhere else to camp for the night and leave these varmints to fight over what's left of Mr. Elvira Jones here."

The posse moved on as the sun moved down towards the distant mountains, Banjo and Hootie leading the way, still following the outlaws trail, as they looked for a place to camp for the night. The others followed behind with Young Billy Brand, who was loudly retelling his stories about the grizzly bear attack and the fight with the wolves to Billy-Bob, who was riding with him, and anyone else who was within earshot. Joel turned to Tex with a smile. "That boy is getting to sound a lot like you with his bullshit, Tex," he said, glancing behind them at Young Billy.

"It's when he starts to believe all the bullshit that he comes out with, then he'll sound like me," answered Tex with a grin.

Tyler Creed, riding behind Young Billy and Billy-Bob, listened to Young Billy telling his tales and looked over to Brad Stillman with an angry look. Although the rest of the posse liked Young Billy's amusing stories and enjoyed the light-hearted diversion from the serious business of chasing the outlaws, Tyler resented the attention that the young cowboy was getting from them all.

"If that damn loudmouth kid doesn't shut up soon, I'll be tempted to shut him up myself. I'm getting fed up with all his damn bragging and bullshit."

Brad Stillman nodded to Tyler as if in agreement with his opinion of Young Billy. He didn't want to get on the wrong side of Tyler, who was a big, strong fellow with wide shoulders and powerful forearms, built up from working in his father's blacksmiths shop. He also knew that Tyler had got a short temper and would lash out at the slightest provocation, so he kept his mouth shut, thinking that maybe joining the posse wasn't such a good idea after all.

Brad rode along in silence, letting Tyler move slightly ahead of him, the big man still muttering to himself, as Young Billy could still be heard laughing loudly to the others, oblivious to the bitter resentment that Tyler Creed was carrying with him.

The posse rode along at a steady pace. They were a good two days behind the outlaws, but Joel and Tex didn't want to push men and horses to the limit and allowed Hootie and Banjo to scout about a half mile ahead looking for signs of the route they had taken. They didn't have too much difficulty following the trail taken by Shreeve Moor and his gang, as they had not bothered to hide their tracks, probably believing that nobody would be following them after they had wounded the Marshall and killed his two deputies back in Tucson. The trail led them towards Madera canyon and on towards the Santa Rita mountains, heading for the Mexican border, east of Nogales. With the light beginning to fade, Joel urged the others to catch up with Hootie and Banjo.

Before sundown, Hootie and Banjo found a place to camp for the night next to a small stream. Both of them circled around the area before dismounting, a routine that they had carried out many times in the past, when out hunting, to ensure that they both had the layout of the land in their minds in case of sudden danger, and also to flush out any varmints, two or four legged that may be lying in wait for them.

While Young Billy was tending the horses, unsaddling them and putting short rope hobbles between their back legs, Joel and Tex set about making a camp fire. Joel collected some dry brushwood and tumbleweed and placed it between a few small rocks he had found. Adding a few dry broken branches from a mesquite tree, he lit a cigarette and tossed the match on to the pile which started to burn. Tex brought some dry bark, which he had peeled from a nearby sycamore tree, and added it to the fire, as he pulled his saddle nearer and flopped down on it, taking a swallow from the whiskey bottle he had removed from his saddlebag. Billy-Bob and Banjo Lafarge brought some more wood over and squatted by the fire, as Tex passed them his bottle. Hootie Swenson walked away from the campfire to relieve himself behind some mesquite, his large bulk was barely hidden behind the small bushes as he turned away from the campfire and bent his head, shoulders hunched as he let out a sigh of relief.

Tyler Creed was removing the reins from his horse, as Brad Stillman stood nearby, listening to Young Billy telling him about his travels with Joel and Tex, as he looked after the horses.

"You are sure gonna enjoy this trip, Brad. I've learnt a lot from Joel and Tex while I've been with them." He paused, grinning at the other young cowboy, as he patted his horses' neck. "Did I ever tell you about the time I saved them from a pack of hungry wolves up in the high country?"

Before Brad could answer he was pushed to one side by Tyler Creed, who grabbed Young Billy by the front of his shirt, lifting him on his toes as his shirt collar ripped, making him choke for breath.

"I'm sick of listening to all the crap you keep talking," yelled the young blacksmith, as Young Billy gasped, his face changing color as he struggled in Tyler's strong grip, his feet hardly touching the ground. "The rest of these fools can believe all the bullshit you come out with, but I don't," he fumed, prodding Young Billy in the chest with his other hand. "I bet you've never ever fired that gun of yours."

"Leave him be Tyler," said Brad Stillman, trying to pull Tyler Creed off Young Billy. "He don't mean nothing. It's just talk."

Tyler pushed Brad away with his big forearm. "You keep out of this, Brad. I thought you were on my side? You're just like the rest of them."

Just as Young Billy was about to pass out through shortage of breath, Tyler Creed suddenly released his grip on him, and he dropped to the ground, gasping for air, as a large hand gripped the back of his neck, squeezing hard.

"Pick on somebody your own size, and leave the boy alone," said Hootie Swenson, in a quiet voice, releasing Tyler from his strong grip. Tyler Creed turned around to confront his unknown assailant, ready to fight. The young blacksmith, still in a wild mood, swung a punch at the big Swede, who was looming over him. Hootie caught the fist in his left hand and gripped it hard, as Tyler winced at the strength of the big man. Hootie then hit Tyler in the face with his right fist, sending him staggering backwards into the horses.

"You alright, boy?" Hootie said as he helped Young Billy to his feet and dusted him down.

"I'm fine, Hootie," croaked Young Billy as he recovered from the choking. "Thanks for the help, but next time can you pull up your pants before you start fighting."

Hootie looked down at the front of his pants. He had been in the middle of relieving himself when the trouble with Tyler Creed had started and the front of his pants was wet and his suspenders were hanging down at his sides. He started laughing at the sight of himself, more in embarrassment than anything else, and quickly tidied himself up.

"Mustn't leave the stable door open, Young Billy. You never know what might escape." He laughed again, this time in a more cheerful manner, as he adjusted his clothing.

Tyler got up from the ground, pulling himself up by the saddle girth on his horse, wiping the blood from his broken nose as he gripped the saddle horn with one hand. He spat some blood on the ground that had filled the back of his throat and cursed to himself. He grew angry again, as he heard Hootie laughing with Young Billy, thinking that they were both laughing at his expense, and his hand closed on the shaft of the heavy blacksmiths hammer that he carried in his saddlebag. He always liked to have his big hammer with him back in Tucson, when working in his father's blacksmiths forge and would use it as a club if any of the customers refused to pay, so he naturally brought it along in case he needed to use it.

Tyler turned around with the big hammer held firmly in his hand and raised it high above his head, as he looked angrily at the back of Hootie Swenson, murder in his eyes and vengeance on his mind. Using the bloody bandage on Hootie's head as a target he started to swing the heavy hammer in a downward arc, as Hootie concentrated on pulling his suspenders up around his shoulders, oblivious of the danger behind him.

Suddenly, a shot rang out and Tyler Creed clutched at his side as the hammer fell from his grip, landing harmlessly on the ground behind the startled Hootie. Hootie looked at Young Billy, who was holding a still smoking revolver in his hand then turned around to confront Tyler who was jumping about, holding his bleeding side and sobbing to himself.

"You shot me, you little bastard," cried Tyler as he looked down at his wound, blood dripping on the ground, mingling with the blood from his nose that had spilled there earlier.

"No more than you deserve, you big ox," Young Billy said, feeling more than a little pleased with himself for stopping Tyler Creed from smashing Hootie's skull. "You nearly choked me. And if I hadn't stopped you from hitting Hootie with that big hammer, I reckon you would have killed him. Anyway, now you can see that I've fired my gun."

Hootie looked down at the hammer, where it lay on the ground, its shiny metal head glinting in the reflected firelight, and back at Tyler Creed, and reached out and gripped him by his shoulder, a wicked looking skinning knife suddenly appearing in the big Swedes other hand.

196

"I outa stick this in your cowardly guts, you sniveling bastard," he said as Tyler squirmed in his strong grip.

Joel, Tex, and Billy-Bob quickly rushed over from the campfire. They had seen the altercation between Young Billy and Tyler Creed building up, but when it looked like Hootie had dealt with the situation, they had left them to it. However, when Young Billy fired his pistol at Tyler, they decided to defuse the situation. Banjo Lafarge remained by the campfire and smoked his pipe. He knew better than to interfere when his old friend, Hootie, was involved in a fight.

Tex was the first to reach Hootie, who was still holding the injured Tyler Creed by his shoulder, who by now had stopped struggling and was holding his side where Young Billy's bullet had hit him. His nose was a mess, and he kept sniffing as the blood blocked his nostrils.

"Put the knife away, Hootie," Tex said. "I think he's had enough."

"He would have smashed my skull in if Young Billy hadn't stopped him," said the big Swede, letting go of the young blacksmith and pushing him away from him. "Get him out of my sight, or he'll be missing his private parts." He swore in Swedish and put his knife away and led Young Billy over to the campfire, pausing to pick up Tyler Creed's discarded hammer and throwing it into the bushes.

"Come on, boy, let's go sit down and share my liquor jar. You deserve a drink for saving me from that big hammer. I've still got a big wound in the back of my head and I don't fancy another."

"That was a fine bit of shooting, Young Billy," Billy-Bob said as the young cowboy sat down on his saddle. Young Billy laughed. "Thanks, Billy-Bob, but I was aiming for the arm that was holding his hammer."

Billy-Bob laughed, remembering when he had made a similar comment after he had shot Troy Collis, back in Tucson. He reached into his vest pocket and brought out his spectacles, holding them out to Young Billy. "I think you'd better try these on for size," he said as Young Billy laughed.

Joel and Tex brought the injured Tyler Creed back to the campfire and sat him down while Banjo brought out his small medicine bag from among his belongings and proceeded to examine his injuries. Banjo cut back Tyler's shirt with his knife and cleaned the wound with a splash of corn liquor from the jug which Tex had reluctantly handed over to him.

"Don't waste it all on him, Banjo," Tex said. "That's my only jug, and I need it more than him."

"He's not going to have it all, *mon amie*," said Banjo, laughing as he took a long drink from the jug and handed it back to Tex. Banjo turned back to Tyler Creed, who was moaning at the way that the Frenchman was roughly treating him.

"Stop your wailing, will you. *Mon Dieu!* It's only a scratch. The bullet only grazed your side. I would worry more about the state that your nose is in." He looked at Tyler's nose which was squashed, in a flat, bloody mess, to one side of his face, then over at Hootie, who was lighting his pipe from a burning twig out of the campfire.

"What did you hit him with Hootie?"

Hootie sat puffing his pipe on the other side of the fire and held up his large, clenched fist, which had what looked like some of Tyler's blood still on the knuckles.

"Just my fist, Banjo. He's lucky that's all I hit him with. If Young Billy hadn't shot him, I would have had his hammer buried in my skull." He went back to puffing on his pipe, ignoring the swearing that Tyler Creed aimed in his direction.

Joel and Tex took Brad Stillman to one side and questioned him about the altercation between Young Billy and Tyler. He told them about the hostility Tyler had for Young Billy, and his resentment that he had for the way that everyone listened to his stories.

"Do you feel that way too, Brad?" asked Joel. "I know that Tyler is a friend of yours, so does Young Billy's bragging get you riled as well?"

"No, Mr. Shelby, I quite like Young Billy. And Tyler ain't no friend of mine, I see him sometimes when I'm in town, maybe have a beer with him in the saloon, but he's just a big bully. I don't mind admitting that he scares me sometimes, so I try and avoid him."

"Well there's no need to be frightened of him, Brad," Tex said. "I reckon we'll be sending him back home come the morning." He looked over to Joel, who nodded in agreement.

They went back to join the others at the fire. Hootie had finished dressing Tyler's wound, and the young blacksmith sat holding a bloody bandana to his busted nose, looking over at Hootie with hate in his eyes.

Joel stood over Tyler, who looked up at him; his squashed nose making Joel suppress a laugh.

"You can head back to town in the morning, Tyler. We made a big mistake bringing you along, you're too darn troublesome. Banjo said that you've only got a flesh wound, so you'll be able to ride without any problem."

Tyler didn't answer he just kept dabbing at his nose. He turned and looked over at Brad Stillman.

"Are you coming back with me Brad? I knew we made a mistake joining this posse. We'll be better off back in town." With his broken nose, he sounded like an old bull frog when he spoke, making Billy-Bob Cannon double up laughing and the others turn away smiling.

"No, Tyler, I'm staying with the posse," answered Brad, still a little wary of Tyler Creed. "I'm going to help them catch those outlaws."

"Well, damn you then, Brad. Damn the lot of you. You can all go to hell as far as I'm concerned," said Tyler, all agitated, trying to get on his feet.

"You can stop right there, Tyler," Joel said, pushing the young blacksmith back to the ground. "Any more trouble from you and we'll tie you up 'til morning." He bent down and picked up Tyler's rifle. "You can have this back in the morning," he said, putting the rifle down on the packs, well away from Tyler's reach.

With the campfire well-lit, Banjo rustled up a hot meal for everyone. Hootie had managed to kill a pair of wild fowl, and added them to the dried salt beef that Banjo had prepared for the pan, along with some wild garlic and corn. Billy-Bob took Tyler a plate of hot food but the young blacksmith knocked it out of his hand as he tried to hand it to him, sending his cigarette flying from his mouth as the plate of food hit him in his face.

"You can keep your damn food," yelled Tyler as Billy-Bob tried to salvage his smoke which had landed in the greasy remains of the meal on the ground. Billy-Bob picked up the soggy cigarette, which he had only just lit, sighed, and tossed it into the fire.

"I don't care if you eat or not," growled the angry ex-Texas ranger, as he wiped some bits of food from his chin. "But you ruined my smoke, you piece of horse shit." He reached over and gripped Tyler's damaged nose between his finger and thumb and squeezed it hard. Tyler let out a scream as Billy-Bob released his grip and walked back to his place by the campfire and wiped Tyler's blood from his hand. He rolled himself another cigarette, as Tyler carried on yelling, fresh blood running down his face and dripping from his chin.

"That was a mite harsh, Billy-Bob," Tex said as Billy-Bob leaned back on his saddle and blew smoke from his cigarette. "Now, he ain't gonna shut up that bawling all night."

"Harsh! I took him some grub, and he knocked my cigarette out of my mouth. I've managed to get away from my store and not have to sneak around for a quiet smoke, away from my Julie, and he gives me goddam grief. Well, he had better calm down, or he'll or get some more of the same."

Tyler Creed heard Billy-Bob's comments and decided to suffer in silence. He dabbed at his sore nose with his already bloodstained bandana and vowed to get even with the lot of them. The wound in his side was sore, he knew that it wasn't too bad, but his nose hurt like hell. He was feeling hungry now but thought that he had better not ask for any food, not after the way that he had refused to have the plate that Billy-Bob Cannon had offered him. It was getting dark now, so he lay back against a tree trunk and decided to try and get some sleep—he would think of some way to get his revenge in the morning.

Chapter 26

Early next morning, Tyler Creed got his gear together and saddled up. He wanted to leave before any of the others woke, but Joel and Tex were already up. They had both been keeping watch since before dawn, looking out for anyone who might sneak up on them and also making sure that Tyler didn't cause them any more trouble. Tyler could see them both watching him and quickly finished securing his saddle and packed his rifle in its scabbard. He wandered over to the bushes where he had the bother with Hootie Swenson, the night before, and started to look around, kicking up dead leaves and bracken.

Tex went over to Tyler holding the young blacksmiths large hammer in his left hand. "I reckon that this is what you are looking for, boy? Well, you can forget it," he said as Tyler reached out for it. "This thing's too darn dangerous in your hands. I'll let you have it back when we get back to Tucson, perhaps, then you might have learnt some sense."

Tyler Creed stared aggressively at Tex, who swung the hammer at his side. "Now, mount up and get out of here, before I let you feel the weight of this hammer," said Tex, taking a step towards him. Tyler turned away and walked towards his horse. He might be bigger than Tex, but he knew that he would be no match for the Indian fighter in a brawl. As he mounted up Banjo, who had watched the stand-off, walked over and handed him a small gunnysack and a water bottle.

"Here's some food and water for the journey back, Tyler," he said. "And be careful with that gunshot wound. I've put some bandage in there as well, in case it needs re-dressing."

Tyler took the sack and water from the old French trapper without a word of thanks and looked over at Young Billy, who was standing with Hootie and turned and rode away. All of them stood and watched as Tyler Creed rode off, his big shoulders hunched over, partly with the pain of his wound and partly with the humiliation of having to return to Tucson and explain to his pa why he had left the posse, and how he had acquired a bullet wound and a broken nose.

He was seething with anger and could feel the others watching him, but he didn't want to hurry but couldn't wait to get over the rise of the nearest hill and away from the pitying looks that they had given him. He would get even with them, he fumed to himself, especially with Billy Brand and the big Swede, Hootie Swenson. He didn't care much for that old French trapper either and didn't like the patronizing way that he had given him the sack of food. As he rode over the hill, and out of sight of the others, he tossed the small sack and the water into the nearest mesquite bush. "Damn you all," he muttered to himself, "You can keep you're goddam charity."

An hour later, with the morning getting a lot warmer, Tyler Creed's nose was still bleeding, and he kept spitting out the bloody contents of his mouth. He wished now that he hadn't thrown the canteen of water away and the sack with some food in it, which also contained some bandages. He was feeling mighty hungry, having missed his breakfast, and the wound in his side was beginning to throb. He would now have to look for a stream so that he could bathe his nose and quench his thirst. The decision to join the posse was turning out to be one that he regretted, and he silently renewed his resolve to get even with the lot of them. He put his hand down to where his big hammer was usually lying, in the top of his saddlebag, and cursed again when he remembered that it was back with the posse, in Tex's possession. "Damn it, this is turning out to be one hell of a crappy day."

He spat out a fresh gob of blood and cussed again, as it landed on the front of his pants.

* * * * * *

Back at the camp, the posse were saddling up after eating a good breakfast. Joel kicked out the remains of the fire and looked at Tex and Billy-Bob, who were standing nearby. Billy-Bob rolled himself his first smoke of the day and handed the makings to Joel.

"I'm mighty glad that we've got rid of that troublemaker, Tyler Creed," said Joel as he handed back the makings to Billy-Bob and lit his cigarette. "You're not wrong there," drawled Tex, wafting the smoke away with his hat. Billy-Bob nodded in agreement. "He was always going to be trouble, that one. He could have killed Hootie with that big hammer. It's a good thing you didn't let him have it back, Tex."

"I should have taken his firearms as well," Tex said. "But I didn't want him to be unarmed out there on his own."

"Well, I don't think we'll see him again until we get back to Tucson," Billy-Bob said.

"I hope you're right," Joel said as he swung into his saddle. "Come on, let's make trail after those damn jail breakers."

Later in the day, about midafternoon, the posse were having a short rest out of the saddle, allowing the horses to graze freely on what food they could find, while they all ate a cold meal. Joel pulled out a couple of his last stogies and handed one to Billy-Bob, who gratefully accepted it. As they all sat in the shade of a pair of saguaro cacti, a sudden gunshot interrupted their reverie. Joel looked around at the others to make sure there were no casualties as another gunshot sounded, and pieces of the tall cactus dropped down on to Hootie's wide brimmed hat.

Hootie cursed in Swedish and shook the debris from his hat and looked up at the mark where the bullet had struck the cactus. "Whoever is shooting at us ain't a very good shot," he remarked, "why I'd have to be over ten feet tall before the bullet even parted my hair."

"There's someone up there on that ridge," Joel said, pointing back the way that they had traveled. His eyesight was better than the others, except maybe for Young Billy's. The rest of them looked in the direction that Joel was indicating, taking care to keep low and out of sight, as a puff of smoke was seen from the far ridge, followed a second later by the sound of another gunshot and the noise of a bullet as it ricocheted off a large rock way off to one side of them.

"One of those jail breakers must have circled behind us to try and slow us down," added Joel as he calmed his horse down and pulled out his rifle from its scabbard. He spits out the rest of his cigar that he had nearly swallowed when the gunfire began.

"Well, whoever it is ain't much of a shot with a rifle," said Tex. "Why he ain't no better than Young Billy was when he was shooting at that pack of wolves up in the high country."

"That ain't fair, Tex. I did manage to hit a couple of them," said Young Billy, more than a little put out that Tex had brought that episode up—he hadn't bothered to mention that part of the story when re-telling it to Billy-Bob and the others.

Joel, Tex, and Billy-Bob began firing their rifles at the unknown shooter, as Hootie and Banjo mounted their horses to hunt down the man under cover of their, more accurate, shooting. As they rode for the ridge, Tex yelled after them. "Be careful, you two. There may be more than one of the varmints up there."

Banjo waved his long Sharps buffalo rifle in the air as he held his reins in his other hand. "Be careful? *Mon amie*, to quote Voltaire 'I don't know where I'm going but I'm on my way.'" And with a yell, he hurried to catch up with Hootie.

Tex shrugged his shoulders and turned to Joel. "Not another one with smart assed sayings? As if I don't hear enough from you with your old grandpappy's words of wisdom."

Joel laughed. "There ain't nothing like a bit of culture, my friend. But I've never heard of Voltaire. Is he one of Banjo's friends?"

They all watched as Hootie and Banjo circled the ridge and approached from different sides. As they reached the top, they both dismounted and made their way separately towards the source of the gunfire, which had started up again. They were both about one hundred yards away from the shooter, creeping silently, when Banjo disturbed a ground nesting wild fowl, and with a shriek and a flapping of wings, it took off and flew away. The gunman turned towards the source of the noise and raised his rifle ready to fire it as Banjo, quick for his age, raised his long rifle and shot the man in his chest. Hootie was a couple of seconds behind as he fired his buffalo rifle, hitting the man in his shoulder as he staggered back from the force of Banjo's shot. Banjo nodded over to Hootie as they both approached the fallen gunman, who was lying on his back fatally wounded.

Back down with the posse, Tex turned to the others as they all heard the sound of two rifle shots. "That sounded like old Banjo's long rifle,

204

and I reckon the other shot must have been Hootie," he said. Joel nodded in agreement, as he put down his rifle and pulled his makings out. "We'd better wait and see if they caught the bastard," he said as he rolled himself a smoke. "Maybe it's at least one less of those jail breakers."

A short while later, Hootie and Banjo could be seen riding slowly back, Hootie holding the reins of another horse with a body lying across the saddle. They all walked over to the body of the gunman and Billy-Bob grasped the man's hair in one hand and raised his head. "Well, I'll be darned," he said as they all looked at the big face of Tyler Creed, his broken nose still covered in dried blood.

"Now there's a man that holds a grudge," said Joel. "He sure wouldn't let it go, but see where it's got him. His pappy ain't going to be none too happy when we tell him about this."

"Well, I'll let him have his sons hammer back," said Tex. "But I reckon we'd better say that he died in a shoot-out with the jail breakers."

"Yep," agreed Joel. "I think he'll like that better than telling him that his son was a cowardly, bushwhacking bastard." The others all nodded in agreement.

They all scraped out a shallow grave in the dry, hard ground, and placed Tyler Creed's body in it, which they had wrapped in his own saddle blanket, and covered over with the dry sandy earth. Young Billy and Hootie spent some time gathering rocks to place over the grave, to keep away any scavengers. They felt more than a little responsible for the young blacksmiths fate and the hard toil served as a form of catharsis, although Hootie didn't give a damn, but it seemed to help Young Billy as he quietly struggled with some heavy rocks. Hootie noticed that Young Billy wasn't his usual talkative self that morning, but said nothing as he helped the young cowboy cover the mound with rocks

Before they left, Billy-Bob said a few words over the grave and asked the others if they should leave a marker on the pile of stones.

"I don't think we'll waste any more time," said Tex, retrieving Tyler's large blacksmith's hammer from his saddlebag and wedging the shaft between two rocks. He stood back and examined his handiwork. "There, that'll do fine. It even looks like a cross if you close one eye." He spat on his hands, replaced his gloves, and mounted up and followed the others. Hootie tied Tyler's horse behind his own—they didn't want to leave it behind to fend for itself, so now they had another spare mount.

Banjo and Hootie rode ahead to find the trail of Shreeve Moor and his gang, which wasn't difficult as they hadn't made any effort to hide their tracks, and they soon came across a dead horse, abandoned by the gang. A flock of vultures soon scattered when the two men approached the carcass, and Banjo dismounted and examined it.

"This horse ain't been dead more than a day, Hootie. Looks like they just left it to wander about and die on its own, by the look of the trail it's left. They couldn't be bothered to put it out of its misery."

Hootie nodded in agreement, as he joined his friend by the dead horse. "Looks like it must have stopped a bullet or two back in Tucson, during the jailbreak," he said, looking at the blood soaked remains. "I'm surprised it made it this far. Come on let's leave it to these vultures."

They mounted up as the large carrion hopped about in anticipation of their impending meal, glancing back at the others, who were about half a mile in the rear, and waved them on.

Chapter 27

Smoke in the distance alerted Hootie and Banjo to a possible situation ahead, and they both reined in and waved to the others. They both sat back in their saddles, and Hootie lit his pipe, and Banjo pulled out his snuff box, as they waited for the others to catch up with them.

"What you stopped for, boys. Is this traveling getting too much for you old-timers?" asked Joel as he reined in at the side of the two old trappers. Ignoring the remark, Banjo pointed with his rifle at the smoke rising above the distant canyon, as the others gathered around him.

"Could be trouble up ahead, *mon amie*. It looks like the trail leads that way into that small box canyon."

Tex rubbed the black stubble on his chin and considered the problem. "I reckon that if those outlaws are still in there then we're in for one hell of a fight."

"Then we'd better go in on foot," said Joel, looking at the others.

They rode for another half mile then dismounted in some thicket and tied the horses up. Joel wanted Young Billy to keep out of trouble and stay with the horses, but after much protesting by the young cowboy and the promise by Hootie that he would look after him, he relented.

"Alright, Young Billy," he said. "But don't go rushing in looking for trouble, like you did back in the high country. Those outlaws are meaner than a few hungry wolves."

Young Billy nodded meekly in agreement. He wished that Joel wouldn't keep reminding him of his exploits, not after his recent bragging had unintentionally caused the death of Tyler Creed. He would, he thought, keep quiet for a while—well for a day or two at least. He held his rifle ready and walked behind the large frame of Hootie Swenson.

Banjo led them to the narrow entrance to the canyon and paused to examine the ground. He beckoned Hootie over and they both walked around and talked quietly to each other. Joel and the others went over to the two men to see what the problem was.

"What have you stopped for?" asked Tex, looking at Banjo.

The old French trapper re-lit his pipe and pointed down at the ground. "We think that they've been in there, but it looks like they have all come out again, heading that way." He indicated towards the north east. "We thought they were heading for the Mexican border, but it looks like they have other ideas."

Hootie agreed. "We reckon that they are still a couple of days in front of us, but it looks like they don't think they are being followed, they ain't in too much of a hurry."

Joel considered the information then turned to Young Billy. "You and Brad go back and fetch the horses and meet us in the canyon." He looked at the young cowboy. "It's only because you and Brad are the youngest, Billy, we've walked far enough in our cowboy boots."

Joel turned to follow the others, as Tex led them towards the source of the smoke. As they reached the clearing, they were confronted by a body lying face down in the dirt, surrounded by a few mangy chickens pecking at the blood-soaked ground around it. Billy-Bob turned the body over with the heel of his boot, although it took some effort as the dead man was obviously overweight.

"It looks like Shreeve Moor was here, alright," Tex said looking at the man's ear-less head. "He's started taking trophies again."

Joel went into the partially burned shack, which was still smoldering, and after a couple of minutes came out with his bandanna tied around his mouth. He removed it, took out a half-smoked stogie from his vest pocket, and lit it. "There's another body in there," he said, blowing smoke out of his mouth and wiping his forehead with his bandanna. "It's an old fat man with his brains all over the floor, and it sure smells in there. I reckon the poor bastard must have filled his pants on his way to meet his maker."

"That'll be old man Stokes," said Billy-Bob. "And that must be his son, Bobby. I knew them when they lived near town. A pair of no good thieving bastards they were. I always knew they would end up like this.

He still owes me for some work that I did for him when I repaired his old wagon."

"Well, let's have a quick look around for any survivors, although if I know Shreeve Moor, there won't be any," said Joel. "Then we better make trail and try to catch up with them."

A shout from Hootie took them around the back of the shack where there was an old latrine with its door ripped off. As the others arrived, Hootie pointed inside at the deep hole taking up most of the space, with a pole across it on two stumps. Banjo sniffed some snuff up his nose to mask the smell and looked down the hole and saw a pair of legs sticking out of the stinking mess. "*Merde!*" he said, pulling back from the smell. "Somebody has sure ended up in the shit."

"Come on," said Tex. "We ain't got time to bury these bodies. It don't look like there are any survivors."

"There's a young kid's body over in the remains of that bird shed. Scalped and butchered, with some hawks pecking it," said Joel. "But best leave it to the birds."

Young Billy and Brad Stillman rode into the yard with the horses. They both looked around at the scene before them, noticing the body of young Bobby Stokes with his ears missing and bloody bullet wounds in his leg and chest. Brad turned away at the sight of the butchered man and threw up behind his horse.

"You'll see worse than that before this manhunt is over," said Tex. "And next time you bring your breakfast up make sure that you're well down wind of me."

Pausing just long enough for the horses to drink from the water trough, they mounted up and rode out of the canyon, away from the scene of death and destruction.

As the posse disappeared, Blair Stokes, old Bobby Stokes wife, emerged from her hiding place in some mesquite bushes, clutching the two surviving children by their hands. They were both sobbing and calling for their mother, who was still in the latrine with her legs in the air.

"It's alright," she said, trying to calm them down. "We'll see if we can find your ma." She sat down on the upturned bucket that young Bobby had vacated earlier and looked at his mutilated body. "I'll bet that Pappy of yours is inside in a similar state," she said to the dead man. "That'll teach the old bastard not to stay in bed all day." She felt a sense of relief that they were dead, maybe now she could start to pick up her life again. She wondered who the other men were, who had just left, and thought that it might have been the first bunch of raiders, returning to see if there had been anyone else left to kill, so had kept well-hidden until they had left.

The two young children stopped crying and began chasing the few chickens that had survived, around the yard, one of them tripping over young Bobby Stokes' fat carcass.

Old Bobby Stokes' wife went into the shack and quickly came out, retching at the smell from inside the building. She placed a small bundle of clothing on the ground and went back inside and retrieved a few more of her belongings. She then picked up an oil lamp, lit it, and tossed it through the door of the shack

There was a sound of breaking glass and the already smoking building caught fire, and was a raging inferno within minutes. Blair Stokes bundled everything up in an old blanket, called the two children over, and walked out of the canyon without a backward glance.

"Come on, kids. Let's go and start a better life."

Chapter 28

Shreeve Moor's original intention was to cross the border into Mexico and try and lose any posse that might be tracking them, but he and some of the others were wanted by the Mexican authorities for murder and rustling, so he decided to head north east towards Santa Fe, where he knew some people who might give them shelter. He had a cousin who lived near Glorieta Pass, who had once been on the wrong side of the law but was trying to live a quiet life on a small ranch. His cousin, Marty, owed him a few favors, and he was certain that they wouldn't be tracked that far from Tucson.

The others agreed to the change of plan, all except the Coffey brothers, who were getting more and more disillusioned with the way things were turning out. Although they had both killed their share of men in the past and weren't opposed to acts of violence when the need arose, they didn't like the way that Shreeve Moor carried out wanton acts of sadistic murder and cruelty just for the pleasure that it gave him. They hadn't joined in the savagery back at the canyon and had both rested their horses away from the others, much to the displeasure of the Moor brothers.

The last straw had been when, earlier that day, they had crossed the trail of some Mexicans herding a few horses, which they had bought. The horses were for the boss of a large hacienda just across the border in Mexico, to add to his stock of good quality livestock. There were four men with two women and three children, stopped by a stream, with about eight loose horses and a small wagon, pulled by a pair of mules. Shreeve moor sent Wild Coyote and his three Comanches in first to see if there would be any resistance.

As the Indians rode in, whooping and hollering, the women began screaming and the men started firing their rifles at the attackers, hitting one of the savages and sending him flying backwards off his horse. Shreeve Moor and the others watched from a safe distance, on a rocky bluff, as Wild Coyote and the two remaining Comanches quickly subdued the Mexicans. Two of the men were killed, but the other two were captured alive.

What followed was a brutal, cold-blooded and violent orgy of torture and killing carried out by Shreeve and Randy Moor, together with the three Comanches. Even Clem Johnson and Skeeter Hancock were sickened by the brutal disregard for human life and held back from taking part.

While the others were occupied, Jeb and Waylon Coffey decided to slip away and quietly rode their horses south. As soon as they were out of earshot of the screaming and yelling, they spurred their horses into a gallop to put some distance between them and Shreeve Moor's butchers.

It was only some time later, after all the prisoners were dead and Shreeve Moor was adding to his collection of ears, that he realized that the Coffey brothers were missing. Skeeter Hancock and Clem Johnson came in leading their horses down from the bluff, both feeling a little troubled by the carnage, as Shreeve moor looked up from his grisly deed, as he removed an ear from a dead Mexican with his cut-throat razor.

"What kept you two?" he yelled at Skeeter and Clem, a maniacal look on his face as he wiped his grisly trophy on the front of his victim's serape. "You both missed all the fun." He turned and laughed at his younger brother, who was trying to remove a pair of fancy boots from another dead Mexican. The three Comanches were busy scalping the two dead women after they had had their fun with them. Shreeve Moor turned back to the two men who were still taking in the scene before them.

"And where the hell are the Coffey brothers?" He yelled, standing up, still clutching a bloodstained ear, and looking back behind Skeeter and Clem. "I bet those bastards have hightailed it outa here. Never did have any back-bone, those two. If I'd have seen them go I would have put a bullet in both of their backs." He put his razor away and pointed over to the Mexican's horses, which had started to wander off in different directions.

"Do something useful, you two, and round up those horses before they scatter to the four winds. They look good horseflesh, and we'll travel faster with our own remuda."

The two men nodded to each other and mounted up—they were glad to be doing something to take their minds off the slaughter. When they were out of earshot of the others, Clem rode close to Skeeter and spoke quietly to him. "I never saw the Coffey brothers ride off, did you, Skeeter?"

"No, I didn't, but it don't surprise me none. They were never very happy riding with those Comanches. I've rode with Jeb and Waylon before, and they were always up for a fight. They always used to like it when Troy Collis was gang boss, but since he got killed and Shreeve Moor took charge, I reckon they've been looking for a chance to get away."

"I know what you mean," Clem said. "Those two Moor brothers ain't got much brain to share between them, but we might as well stick with them for now. I don't want to end up back in jail or at the end of a rope."

Skeeter Hancock nodded in agreement and spurred his horse after the loose horses.

When they had managed to round up all the horses and hobble them near the Mexicans campsite, Clem and Skeeter joined the others for some food, which Randy Moor had found in the old wagon. Shreeve Moor was eating some salt pork and moaning about the Coffey brother's departure, between mouthfuls. "I'll bet they've gone to one of those towns nearby," he said, spitting bits of food from his mouth and wiping grease from his chin with his sleeve. "Well, we ain't wasting time chasing after those no-good pair of cowards. They'll probably get recognized if they go into a town anyways, and end up sent back to Tucson, or swinging from the end of a rope."

Shreeve Moor intended to avoid towns and large homesteads on his way up to Santa Fe, as he and his gang were bound to be recognized, and the jailbreak from Tucson must have been sent out on the telegraph wires as soon as they had left town. He called for the three Comanches to stop hunting for the Mexican children who had disappeared into the surrounding hills, and that they should get moving to New Mexico Territory—he was worried that if the Coffey brothers were captured, they might tell the authorities where they were heading just to get back at him and maybe get themselves treated more favorably.

******

After a couple of hours of hard riding, the Coffey brothers came upon a small town north of the Dragoon Mountains and rode slowly down the only street, alert for any trouble.

"It looks like a one-horse town, Jeb," said his brother, looking around for any signs of trouble.

"There ain't even a bank to rob," agreed Waylon. "It'll do to rest up for a couple of days before we head south to the border."

The place was peaceful, not a soul around, the only noise was a dog barking in the distance and a staccato rhythm of a hammer from a building with a blacksmith sign over the door. The street didn't even have the luxury of a wooden boardwalk to keep the locals dry when it rained. Avoiding the small, run-down building with a dilapidated, hand painted, Sheriffs sign hanging above the small window, they reined in next to the stables and were met by an old timer, who must have heard them arrive.

"Can I help you fellas?" The old, gray-bearded man said to them, wiping the sleep from his eyes and picking bits of straw from his tattered dungarees. He looked like he'd been sleeping off the booze by the look of the, nearly empty, whiskey bottle in his hand. Waylon Coffey thrust a couple of dollars into the old timer's other hand, took off his hat, and wiped the sweat from his brow.

"Take care of our horses, old fella, and tell us where we can get us a bottle of decent whiskey."

"Sure, fellas," the old timer said, gleefully pocketing the money and quickly gulping down the remains of his whiskey bottle. "There's a small saloon down the end of the street that'll see to your needs. You can get some grub there if you're hungry." He spits on the ground and grinned a toothless smile at the two men, noticing their dusty, dirt covered clothes and the tired looking horses they had been riding. "You fellas traveled far? You look like you've had a hard ride." He took off his old hat and scratched at a boil on the back of his neck. "I ain't seen you two fellas around here before, where you from?"

Jeb Coffey looked at the old man, menacingly, and took a step towards him. "You ask too many questions, old timer. Just look after the horses and keep your mouth shut." He put another silver dollar into the old man's shaking hand and patted him on his bald head. "If anybody asks, you ain't seen us."

"Yes, sir," the old man said, closing his bony fingers around the money and recovering slightly from the outlaw's implied threat. "I'll take good care of your horses, make sure they are fed and watered, and not a word to anybody," he said, winking at the two men as he took hold of the horse's reins and led them inside the stable. Waylon looked at his brother and smiled. "I thought the old timer was going to fill his pants when you threatened him. Come on let's go and get us some booze."

"Good idea," laughed Jeb. "It's good to get away from that Albino bastard and his gang. Especially, those no-good Comanches." They both walked down the empty street, carrying their rifles, glad to be free from Shreeve Moor but still wary of trouble, as they were both still wanted men.

As they walked past the Sheriff's office, a door opened and a big man with a star pinned to his vest, and a double-barreled shotgun held in both hands, stood facing them. He looked like his best lawman's days were well behind him, and he was just marking time until his retirement, sitting in his office in a one-horse town, trying to avoid any confrontation, but he couldn't let his years as a sheriff be wasted. The name on the faded sign, above his head, read *'Preston Hibbs—Sheriff'*.

"Hold it right there, boys," he said in his best peace-keepers voice. "I saw you ride in and I reckon your faces look familiar to me. Now both of you drop your rifles and step inside my office, and no funny business. I've dealt with your sort before."

Jeb looked at his brother, who raised his eyebrows in silent agreement of his intentions, and suddenly grabbed the Sheriff's shotgun barrel in one hand, pushing it away from them. At the same time Waylon hit the Sheriff in his face with the barrel of his rifle, making him let go of his shotgun and sending him staggering back into his jailhouse, landing hard on the timber floor, on his back.

"After you, Sheriff," said Waylon as both men followed the old lawman into his office, as he lay sprawled on the floor. Jeb Coffey bent down and relieved the Sheriff of his pistol before he could think about using it. Preston Hibbs held his jaw where the rifle butt had hit him and spat out a loose tooth along with a mouthful of blood and sat up wondering what the two men would do next.

"Now, no funny business yourself, Sheriff," Jeb said. "We've dealt with your sort before as well."

He walked over to the single cell at the rear of the office and opened the metal door. "You're too old for this line of work, Sheriff. Now get inside here and keep quiet." He helped his brother push the Sheriff into the cell and locked the door behind him, then tossed the keys under the small table at the other end of the room.

Waylon picked up a bottle of whiskey from the table, noticing the wanted poster that it stood on, and pushed it through the bars to the sheriff, who took it without a word. "We ain't going to be in town too long, Sheriff. Just long enough to rest apiece and get some grub, so we would advise you to keep mighty quiet. If you alert anybody, we will be back, and it won't be just a busted mouth that you'll be worrying about. You get my meaning?"

The Sheriff nodded in silent agreement, already opening the bottle of whiskey to have himself a drink. He knew better than to try and rile these two mean-looking hombres, he would stay put until they had gone—he didn't get paid enough to go up against the likes of the Coffey brothers.

He had learnt of the jailbreak in Tucson on the telegraph, from the machine on his desk, as that was another of his many duties that the small town expected of him. Preston had been looking through his small pile of wanted posters when he had seen the Coffey brothers ride into town and decided to, unwisely, try and arrest them—the reward money would come in useful for his own needs, he had thought. *Well,* he thought, rubbing his sore mouth, and sitting back on the bunk in the cell, *I might as well enjoy this bottle of whiskey that they gave me.* He took another swallow and rinsed his mouth out—the liquor seemed to sooth the ache in his mouth—and lay back and closed his eyes.

The Coffey brothers walked out of the Sheriff's office, closing the door behind them, but not before Jeb had had ripped the telegraph wire from the wall and Waylon had put the *'Sheriff's Out'* sign in the window. The town was still quiet as they walked to the saloon, the noise from the blacksmiths had ceased, and the dog had stopped its barking, and not a soul was about.

"I've seen more life in a graveyard," Waylon said.

"You're not wrong there, Bro," agreed Jeb. "But that's just how I like it, we don't want to go looking for trouble. Let's keep our heads down 'til we get to the border." He looked at his brother with a scowl. "Did you see those wanted pictures of us on the Sheriff's desk? They made us look like a right pair of ugly bastards."

Waylon laughed. "Well our pa used to say that we must have fell out of the ugly tree when we were born, but it ain't stopped me from attracting the ladies."

"The only ladies that you attract, Bro, are the ones you have to pay for."

They both laughed as they walked down the street, passing a small store where the man inside pulled the blind down on the door, as they passed.

Jeb pulled out his makings and rolled himself a cigarette and passed the makings to his brother, as they both entered the saloon. The only other occupants were a man with a dirty apron tied around his middle, who was sweeping up some dirt from the floor, a badly dressed woman, showing all her cleavage, dealing cards to herself, and three young, out of work cowboys, sitting in the far corner, playing cards and sharing a cheap bottle of whiskey between them and trying to make it last them all day.

They all looked up as the two strangers entered, and the barman put down his broom and wiped his hands on his apron. "Howdy, boys. You look like you could do with a drink. What will you have?" he asked, scuttling behind the bar.

"Two whiskies," Jeb said, walking up to the bar. "And leave us the bottle."

The barman put two glasses down and reached under the bar for his best whiskey. He thought better than to give the usual bottle of cheap firewater to the two men, as they looked like they were ready for trouble at the slightest provocation, so he opened the bottle, filled the two glasses, and placed it on the bar. He decided not to engage the men in petty conversation and went back to his broom to finish his chores.

Jeb Coffey swallowed the contents of his whiskey glass with one gulp and poured himself another. He sighed with satisfaction as the alcohol hit the back of his throat, giving him a nice warm feeling in his chest. He couldn't remember the last time he'd had a drink of good whiskey, and he enjoyed it so much that he thought that maybe he would even pay the barman for it later. He lifted his leg and struck a match on the sole of his boot and lit his cigarette and leaned with both elbows on the bar. He turned to the barman. "Me and my brother are mighty hungry," he said as the barman stopped sweeping and looked up at him. "Any chance of a bite to eat."

The barman nodded, wiped his hands on his dirty apron, and went through a door at the rear of the bar. One of the young cowboys nudged the man next to him and whispered something in his ear. They both looked over at the Coffey brothers, trying not to stare as the third cowboy tried, unsuccessfully, to roll himself a cigarette, spilling the makings all over the table.

Jeb Coffey had his back to the room, but he could see the three, half-drunk, cowboys through the large glass mirror behind the bar, looking at him and his brother and smiled to himself. He had met their type before in saloons from El Paso to Laramie and most places between. They probably recognized him and Waylon or thought that they did. He noticed that they were all carrying pistols strapped to their waists and knew that it was an even money bet that they had never fired them in anger.

Jeb drank his whiskey and refilled the glass, keeping an eye on the three men. He wasn't too worried about them, they would either want to be friendly and buy them both a drink, or push their luck and try to make themselves a reputation by shooting them down. Either way, they didn't look much of a threat to him.

Waylon Coffey leaned with his back to the bar and looked at the woman, who smiled up at him. *I have seen better-looking women,* he thought, noticing the grey roots showing through her once dark hair, and the loose flesh hanging from her arms—*a lot better, but then, I've had a lot worse.* He picked up his glass, which the barman had filled, and went over to her and pulled up a chair and sat down, and placed his hat on the table. He had noticed the three young cowboys talking quietly and looking at him and his brother, but like Jeb he didn't think they were worth worrying about, even so he pulled out his pistol and placed it on the table in front of him.

"Fancy a game mister?" she asked, giving him her best seductive look and producing a match from her bosom and lighting his cigarette. "Any sort of game you like. As long as it doesn't involve that pistol you've got there," she added.

"I'm always up for a game, what would you like to play?" Waylon replied as his brother chuckled from the bar.

The barman returned with a plate of cold meat and some chilies and placed it on the bar. Jeb Coffey took off his gloves, took a handful of meat, and indicated to the barman to take the rest of the food over to his brother, who was engaging the saloon girl in some flirtatious small talk. He chewed on the meat and smiled to himself.

This town will suit us fine, for the next day or two, he thought to himself. *There ain't nobody here to give us much trouble, the sheriff's locked away, and I don't reckon that we are being followed.*

He picked up the whiskey bottle, drank the contents of his glass, and walked over to the three young cowboys, who all looked nervously up at him as he placed the bottle on their table. He pulled a chair over to the table and sat down, with a smile.

"Howdy, boys," Jeb said as one of the cowboys dropped the pack of cards that he was shuffling, spilling them over the table. "Is there room for me to play?"

The three cowboys relaxed a little and nodded to the stranger. He looked like a fugitive from the law, but he didn't look like he was looking for aggravation. The dealer picked up the cards, shuffled them, and dealt them all a hand.

Chapter 29

The posse reached the scene of Shreeve Moor's latest massacre just after sunup. They had ridden hard for part of the night to try and make up the time between them and the outlaws, just resting for a couple of hours to let the horses graze and stretch their legs out of the saddle. Hootie and Banjo had discovered the bodies first and wandered around looking at them for any signs of life, as the others rode up.

"It looks like Shreeve Moor has been busy taking ears again," said Hootie, turning over one of the dead Mexicans.

"They must have put up a fight," Banjo said, standing over a body. "There's one of the Injuns here with a couple of bullets in him."

Finding a couple of shovels in the old wagon, they quickly dug a shallow mass grave for the Mexicans and placed their bodies side by side in it. They untied the two mules and let them wander into the sagebrush.

Hootie and Banjo walked around looking for the direction that the outlaws had taken, then both pointing one way and then another. The others went over to them, as they were both in a heated discussion.

"Well?" queried Tex. "Which way did they go then?"

Banjo took out his snuff box—something he liked to do when he was trying to make a decision—and placed a pinch on the back of his hand. With a finger pressed to the side of one nostril, he snorted the powder up his nose. Repeating the process in the other nostril, he wiped his hands and sniffed, his mustache was now covered with the brown powder, as he looked up at Tex.

Tex looked at the old Frenchman in disgust. "That's a damn filthy habit, Banjo. You might just as well stuff horseshit up your nose as sniff that crap. What with Joel and Billy-Bob smoking cigarettes and Hootie here puffing his pipe or chewing tobacco, it's a wonder I don't get consumption, or something worse. Now, have you made up your minds on which way we are heading?"

Banjo put his snuff box in his coat pocket and scratched his face. "Well, Tex, me, and Hootie reckon that most of 'em have gone that way." He pointed towards the northeast. "But it looks like two riders went in that direction." He indicated the tracks heading east.

"Do you know which two riders went east?" asked Joel. "Could it be Shreeve Moor and his brother?"

Hootie laughed. "Me and Banjo are damn good trackers, Joel. The best. But there ain't no way of knowing who's on those two horses. I've been this way before, and I reckon that there's a small town the way that those two riders are heading."

Joel, Tex, and Billy-Bob chewed over the problem. "Why would they split up?" asked Billy-Bob, looking at the other two.

"Perhaps, they had a falling out with the others," said Tex.

"Well, I reckon that I'll go and chase those two, Tex," said Joel. "While you and the others follow the main bunch. I don't reckon that we are too far behind them. I'll take Hootie with me, so that he can pick up your trail when we are done."

"I don't think it's a good idea to split up, Joel. What if it's that Albino, Shreeve Moor, and his brother?" Billy-Bob said.

"Well, even more reason the get after them. I reckon me and Hootie can handle two outlaws, whoever they are," Joel said. "But I don't reckon it's the Moor brothers."

Tex reluctantly agreed. "I guess you're right, Joel. We don't want to let any of the varmints get away, but be careful and don't take too long about it. We'll take our time following the main bunch 'til you catch us up."

Joel and Hootie mounted up, eager to be after the two outlaws and were about to leave when Billy-Bob Cannon went over to Hootie, who was placing his rifle in its scabbard.

"Hold up, Hootie," he said removing the shiny deputy's star from his vest and handing it to the big Swede. "Pin this on, Hootie, it'll make you look more like a lawman when you get to that town. But look after it, 'cause I'd like it back in one piece."

"Thanks, Billy-Bob," said Hootie, happily accepting the badge and fastening it to his buckskin shirt and grinning. "I'll take good care of it."

"Come on, Hootie," said Joel, wheeling his horse in the direction they had to go. "Let's make trail and catch those wanted men."

The others watched them go and saddled up themselves, following Banjo Lafarge who had taken the lead, looking for the trail of the outlaws.

As they rode away, the three Mexican children crept out of their hiding place in some mesquite bushes, about a quarter of a mile away. The oldest child, an eleven-year-old boy named Manuelito, had managed to keep the other two quiet all the time that they were lying sheltering there. He had covered their ears to stop them hearing the screams of their parents and relatives as they were butchered. They had had one scary moment when a rattlesnake had decided to occupy the same clump of bushes that they were hiding in and fearful that the noise of its rattle would attract the attention of the killers, the boy had swiftly dispatched it with a lucky blow from a small rock.

They had hidden there for hours, only venturing out as the dawn began to break over the distant mountains but had only taken a few steps when Joel and the others rode in. Manuelito quickly shepherded the two smaller children back to their hiding place, making them keep quiet, as they started to cry again, not understanding why they were going back to the bushes again. He couldn't be sure if the second bunch of men were as bad as the first, so the boy kept his brother and sister quiet until they too rode away.

They walked over to the camp, noticing the large mound of earth and rocks, which the older boy realized was a mass grave and, he too began to cry at the horror of it all, making the two smaller children begin to wail. Deciding to take charge, once again, Manuelito quickly rounded up the two old mules and finding some blankets and scraps of food from the cart, he led his young brother and sister south, away from the slaughter and in the direction of the border, and home.

* * * * * *

Joel and Hootie made good time, as Hootie had managed to follow the trail without any problem, as the Coffey brothers hadn't bothered to hide their progress, thinking that there wouldn't be anyone in pursuit. They arrived at the small town just before noon, after a fast ride. The sun was high overhead and the town was quiet, as they rode down the main street. Hootie Swenson was disappointed that there was no one in the street, as he looked down at the shiny deputy's badge, pinned to his shirt, and proudly polished it with his gloved hand. He had wanted folk to see that he was a proper lawman and puffed his chest out as he rode at the side of Joel.

Joel looked over at the big Swede and smiled to himself. He had seen Hootie looking at the star on his chest at least a half a dozen times on the ride.

"It's still there, Hootie. You ain't lost it," laughed Joel. "You'll polish the damn thing away if you don't stop rubbing it."

Hootie grinned at Joel. "OK, Joel, I just wanted to keep it nice and clean for Billy-Bob for when we get back."

Joel led them towards the small sheriff's office and, as they passed the stables and livery building, a head popped round the door. It was the old timer who looked after the place and as soon as he saw the two riders wearing lawman's badges, he quickly ducked back.

"Did you see that old fella, Hootie?" said Joel. "He didn't look none too pleased to see us. We must have a word with him later and see what he's hiding in his stables."

Hootie nodded as they dismounted outside the small sheriff's office and tied their horses to the hitching rail.

Joel looked at the 'Sheriff's Out' sign hanging on the inside of the door and paused a moment, then tried the door handle, and opened the door. He shrugged and walked in with Hootie following behind him. The place smelled of stale sweat, booze, and some other odor that lingered in the room, making Joel and Hootie pause at the threshold. Joel pulled out a half-smoked stogie and lit it to mask the rank odors and looked around the small, untidy office. He was about to turn and walk out when he saw movement in the cell at the rear of the office.

"Who's there?" said the man in the cell, rising from the bunk bed and approaching the cell door.

Joel noticed the dried blood on the man's face and then saw that he was wearing a sheriff's badge on his vest. There was a half empty bottle of whiskey on the floor, near the bunk bed, and Joel noticed the damp stain on the front of the Sheriff's pants and realized that the other smell must have been pee, as the man had obviously been caught short and wet his pants.

"Howdy, Sheriff," said Joel, approaching the cell. "How did you get yourself locked in there?"

"A couple of no-good bushwhackers snuck up on me while I wasn't looking," said Sheriff Preston Hibbs, feeling a mite embarrassed at the state that he was in, locked in his own jail cell.

"The keys are over there," he said, pointing at a small bunch of keys on the floor below his desk. "Get me out of here, and I'll tell you what happened."

Hootie picked up the keys and handed them to Joel, who unlocked the cell door and let out the unhappy looking sheriff, who went over to his desk and picked up the wanted poster that was on it.

"I see that you are both lawmen," said the Sheriff, not noticing how Hootie looked down at his deputy's star at the sheriff's remark and puffed his chest out. "I'm Sheriff Preston Hibbs, and I was assaulted in my own jail-house," he said, rubbing his still aching jaw. "Are these the bastards that you are looking for?" he added, handing the wanted dodger to Joel. Joel looked at the picture on the poster and pulled out his own small bundle of wanted posters. He shuffled through them and compared his own with the sheriff's.

"That's them," he said. "The Coffey brothers. Jeb and Waylon. They helped Shreeve Moor break out of jail, in Tucson, and shot up the town. We've been after the gang, but these two must have split up from the main bunch so we followed them here. Are they still in town?"

I reckon they are," said Sheriff Hibbs. "They said they were going to rest up for a while. They're probably in the saloon, but I ain't tangling with those two, they were a couple of mean looking hombres. They threatened to come back and deal with me if I told anyone that they were in town, and they are both big men." He looked up at Hootie, who towered above him. "But I don't think they are as big as you, my friend. Why I ain't seen grizzly bears as big as you," he paused, smiling as he began to recover some of his composure after his ordeal with the Coffey brothers. "No offence intended, my friend," he added as Hootie pulled out his pipe and lit it.

"That's alright, Sheriff," said Hootie, looking down at Sheriff Hibbs, as he puffed away at his clay pipe, filling the small office with tobacco smoke. "No offence taken. I ain't that big. My father and two brothers back in Sweden, they are all bigger than me. My father said I shouldn't smoke, he reckoned it would stop me growing. I reckon I should have listened to him." He kept a straight face as he loomed over Sheriff Hibbs, whose forehead was level with the shiny star pinned to his shirt. Joel smiled to himself. It wasn't often that Hootie made a joke at someone else's expense. In fact, he couldn't remember when the big Swede had ever made a joke before.

Chapter 30

"Come on, Hootie, let's go find the Coffey brothers," Joel said. He turned to Sheriff Hibbs, "You stay here, Sheriff, we'll find 'em." He paused and put his hat on. "Dead or alive it said on their wanted poster, so they've got a choice."

"Be careful now, boys," said Sheriff Hibbs. "Don't let them get the better of you. There's two or three impressionable, young cowboys, who spend most of their time hanging around the saloon, and they can be easily influenced by the Coffey brothers' reputation."

"We'll look out for them, Sheriff," said Joel, picking up Sheriff Hibbs' shotgun, which was leaning against the wall. "We'll borrow your scatter gun, Sheriff." He handed it to Hootie. "Leave that old hunting rifle here, Hootie, and take this. You'll find it a lot more useful inside the saloon. But don't point it in my direction."

Hootie took the shotgun and checked that it was loaded, nodded, and headed for the door.

"Hold up, Hootie," Joel said as he sat on the tabletop and removed his spurs, and placed them on a hook on the wall, where the sheriff kept his keys. "We don't want them to hear me coming. These are my lucky spurs."

He followed Hootie into the street. The sun was high overhead and the wind had started to blow in their faces. As usual, there was no one about, and the only noise came from the blacksmith's place, down the street, a sharp noise of metal on metal, which seemed to keep time with Joel and Hootie's footsteps, as they walked to the saloon. Joel adjusted his hat to keep the dust out of his face, and as they neared the saloon, they could hear raucous laughter coming from inside it.

Joel stopped at the bat-wing doors and motioned Hootie to wait. He spoke quietly to the big Swede.

"They won't be expecting trouble, and they won't know who I am." He unpinned the deputy's star from his vest and put it in his pocket. "Give me a couple of minutes then follow me in."

Hootie nodded and reluctantly began to remove his own lawman's badge. "You can keep that on, Hootie," said Joel, smiling. "Let 'em see that the law has arrived in town."

Joel hesitated again, as he was about to enter the saloon, as he suddenly thought about what he was about to do and the unknown danger that was facing them both.

I'm just a cowboy, he thought to himself. *I'm more used to roping steers and riding herd than chasing outlaws. How the hell did I let Marshall Tucker talk me into this.* He looked around at Hootie, who smiled at him, full of confidence in his own ability, and the uncertainty left him.

What the hell, he thought. *Hootie is a good man to have with me. He knows how to fight.*

He nodded to Hootie, who held the shotgun at the ready. "Let's do it, Hootie," he said softly as he pushed the saloon doors back and stepped into the relative gloom of the place. He paused for a moment, letting his eyes adjust from the bright sunshine of the mid-day street and glanced around the place. Behind the bar was a balding man, wiping the copper top counter with a cloth that looked dirtier than the stained apron he wore. He had a world-weary expression on his face, and as he wiped the bar, the part that he had 'cleaned' was sprinkled with ash from the cigarette dangling from his lips.

The only other occupants were four men sitting at one of the far tables, playing a game of cards. The man facing him, with his back to the wall, Joel recognized as one of the Coffey brothers, from the wanted dodger he had in his saddlebag. He wasn't sure which one he was, and he couldn't see the other brother in the room, but the man had noticed Joel enter the saloon and watched him as he walked over to the bar with his rifle held in one hand.

"What'll you have, stranger?" The barman said, pausing from his polishing and walking down the bar to Joel, pausing to flick the cigarette ash off the bar counter with his dirty cloth.

"I'll have a whiskey, mister," Joel said, removing his hat and placing it on the bar and looking through the large mirror at the occupants of the table and noticing the pistol on the table in front of the outlaw. The other three, younger men, were busy laughing and drinking, playing cards. They must have decided that Coffey was a man to look up to and were enjoying his notoriety by plying him with drinks.

Just then, the bat-wing doors creaked as they were pushed wide open, and Hootie Swenson entered the saloon, his large frame blocking out most of the sun that was shining through. He took three paces into the room and stopped, looking around, holding the shotgun in his big right hand. He never looked at Joel, giving all his attention to the four men sitting around the table in the far corner.

The three young cowboys stopped laughing and looked over at Hootie, as the room went quiet. The only noise came from one of the rooms upstairs, as the faint laughter of a woman could be heard.

Joel raised his head at the sound from upstairs; he had found where the other Coffey brother was.

At the sight of the deputy's star on Hootie's chest, Jeb Coffey picked up his pistol, stood up, and pointed it at the big Swede.

"Are you looking for me, big fella?" he yelled, cocking his gun as the three others stood up, knocking their chairs back, and reaching for their own pistols. "Well, this ain't your lucky day, you big lug," said Jeb. "If all they can send after us is a big, old giant like you, then I ain't gonna lose any sleep when I put a bullet in that large head of yours."

Joel quickly turned around from the bar, rifle held in both hands. He had seen Hootie enter the saloon and Jeb Coffey reach for his gun and knew that he had to act fast. He fired quickly and put a bullet in Jeb Coffey's shoulder, making him stagger backwards, his pistol firing harmlessly into the ceiling, as another bullet hit him in his forehead.

The three young cowboys began shooting wildly at Hootie, as they saw Jeb Coffey go down. Hootie was hit in his leg, and his hat was knocked off his head with a bullet through it, as he fired the shotgun at them, discharging both barrels simultaneously. He yelled, "Remember the Alamo," and stood with both arms raised in triumph, letting out a piercing owl hoot, as the three men lay on the bar room floor, groaning, with blood everywhere.

"Are you hit, Hootie?" asked Joel, seeing the tear in Hootie's pants, and the blood-staining the material.

"I'm fine," Hootie said, examining the wound. "It's nothing, just a graze. Thanks for that, Joel. You saved me from a bullet from that bastard." He bent down and retrieved his hat, looked at the bullet hole in it, and put it back on his head, swearing to himself in Swedish.

Joel drew his pistol and walked over to the four men that he and Hootie had shot down. Jeb Coffey was dead, slumped against the back wall, blood smearing the wall where he had slid down, but two of the young cowboys that Hootie had shot were still alive. The other man who had been standing in front of his friends, was dead—his face and chest peppered with buckshot. He had taken the full force of the heavy gauge shotgun that Hootie had fired.

A sudden commotion on the stairs made Joel turn around and look up. Waylon Coffey was halfway down the stairs with a pistol in his hand, dressed only in his underwear and boots and a gun belt strapped around his waist. He paused, one hand on the handrail, and took in the scene in the bar room below him. Seeing his brother lying dead on the floor, Waylon let out a yell and fired his pistol at Joel. "You've killed my brother, you bastards. Well you ain't going to get me that easy."

The bullet missed Joel, and Waylon Coffey attempted to fire again, but the hammer fell on an empty chamber. Cursing, he turned back up the stairs, re-loading as he went, as Joel shot at him and missed, as he disappeared onto the landing. There was a sound of a door slamming and a woman yelling, as Joel ran up the stairs, two at a time, pointing his pistol in front of him.

Joel reached the door that Waylon Coffey had gone through and kicked it open, just in time to see the outlaw jumping out of the window to the street below. Waylon's recent companion, the mature whore, stood the other side of the bed, holding her dress in front of her naked body and screamed again, as Joel went over to the window.

Waylon Coffey landed in the dusty street, and for a big man, he landed lightly, coming quickly to his feet, still holding his pistol, which he had re-loaded before leaving the bedroom. He stood up and raised his head to see Joel looking down at him from the window above. He quickly cocked his pistol and, with a sneer on his face, pointed it up at Joel.

As Joel looked out of the window at Waylon Coffey, he saw him pointing his pistol at him, preparing to shoot, when he suddenly saw Hootie Swenson appear from out of the saloon door. Hootie took two steps, with his big, long legs, towards the outlaw and holding the empty shotgun in both hands by the barrel, took a swing at the man.

Hootie had heard the commotion upstairs and, realizing that Waylon Coffey had jumped out of the bedroom window, he went out into the street, still carrying the shotgun. He knew that he had fired both barrels of the shotgun earlier, and seeing the outlaw point his pistol up at Joel, he quickly reversed the weapon and gripped it by the barrel.

As Waylon was about to fire his pistol up at Joel, he hesitated, for a moment, as he saw Hootie appear in the street and rush towards him. He was suddenly knocked to the ground as the hard, wooden shotgun stock connected with his face, with all the force that the big Swede could muster.

"Take that, you no good bastard," Hootie yelled as he stood over the unfortunate Waylon Coffey, waving the shotgun in the air, ready to strike again if he moved. The shotgun stock had nearly parted company with the rest of the weapon, such was the force that Hootie had put into the blow.

"The law has finally caught up with you, mister," Hootie added, looking proudly down at the deputy's star pinned to his chest. "And you don't mess with this lawman." He shouted, another owl hoot making a dog start its barking again, somewhere close.

Joel smiled to himself at Hootie's words. He had seen him knock down the outlaw, to save him from being shot, and heard Hootie's proud boast, and was glad that he had brought the big man along.

As Joel turned away from the window to leave the bedroom, the woman rushed at him screaming.

"Who's gonna pay me now?" she yelled, as Joel fended her off. "He owes me for the time that I spent with him. I don't work for nothing you know."

"Take it easy, will you," Joel said, pushing her back on the bed. He noticed the outlaw's clothes hanging on the bedpost. "See what money he's got in his pants, and you can have some of that."

She sat on the bed, with the dress that she had been holding to hide her modesty, slipping out of her hands, exposing her flabby breasts. Joel looked away in disgust at the sight of the whore and headed for the door, glad to get out of there.

"Anyways," Joel said, over his shoulder as he closed the door behind him. "Maybe your last customer didn't get his money's worth. As my old grandpappy used to say, 'If the goods look cheap, then don't expect good quality.'"

He heard her shout and something hard hit the other side of the door, as he went down the stairs.

As Joel reached the bottom of the stairs, the barman's head bobbed up from his place of safety behind the bar. Joel looked over to him, as he headed for the door to the street.

"You can come out now, it's all over, and if there's a doctor in town, then you'd better go and find him quick. There's a couple of those men could do with some medical attention." He removed the deputies' star from his pocket and pinned it back on his vest.

Out in the street, Hootie stood over Waylon Coffey, who lay unmoving on the ground. The usually deserted street had attracted a few of the locals, who, on hearing the gunfire and Hootie's noisy disturbance, had ventured out of the few buildings in the town.

The blacksmith, who had been doing all the hammering earlier, was now standing at his door, holding a pair of heavy metal pincers in one hand and a large hammer in the other. Across the street, outside another establishment that displayed a sign that read, *'Barbering and Shaving,'* above the door, stood two men. One man's face was half covered in shaving soap, and the other man held a cut-throat razor in one hand and a towel in the other. Two other men were peering around a half-opened door, down the street, one with a rifle in his hand, and a small boy started to wander, inquisitively, up the street towards them, until he was dragged away, screaming, by a woman.

From out of the sheriff's office came Sheriff Preston Hibbs, walking slowly towards the saloon. He had heard the gunfire and was holding a rifle, unsure of the outcome between the outlaws and the deputies, but because he had just finished the contents of the whiskey bottle, he had regained some of his old courage and had decided to try and stand up for himself.

"Need any help?" he said, looking up at Hootie as he reached the prone figure of Waylon Coffey.

"I don't reckon we do, Sheriff," Hootie said. "This one's dead. I reckon I must have hit him too hard, his neck is broken." He handed the damaged shotgun over to the sheriff, who took it and looked at the broken stock.

"Sorry about that, Sheriff, it wasn't very strong. They don't make guns like my old long rifle anymore."

Joel glanced down at the body of Waylon Coffey and turned to Sheriff Hibbs.

"His brother's inside, Sheriff. He's as dead as this one here. There's also one of your local hot-heads dead, and two of his friends wounded. They decided to throw in with the Coffey's but picked the wrong side. They shot at my friend here, but he gave them both barrels of your shotgun."

Joel holstered his pistol, pulled out his makings, quickly made himself a cigarette, and lit it. He inhaled some smoke and sighed, as a feeling of relief from the excitement of the recent events swept over him, as the barman came running up the street, trailing an older man with a small bag in one hand behind him.

"I've got the Doctor, Mister," he said to Joel, leading the man into the saloon. "And the Undertaker is on his way, but I reckon they'll both want payment for their services."

Joel followed them into the saloon, walked up to the bar, and drank the remains of his whiskey from the glass. He re-filled it and drank that as well, allowing the warm liquor to hit the back of his throat, and filled another glass and handed it to Hootie, who had followed him in.

"You'll probably find some money in the dead man's pockets, that might help, and his brother has left his pants upstairs. There could be some money in those, unless that whore has taken it all," Joel said to the barman. He turned to the Sheriff Hibbs. "There should be a decent reward for the Coffey brothers. You can have that, Sheriff. And their horses must be around somewhere, and they won't need them anymore."

Joel turned to Hootie, who was enjoying the rest of the whiskey. "No more of that, Hootie. We've got to make trail after we've had some food. We've got a hard ride ahead of us to catch up with Tex and the others, and I want you sober for the journey. Young Billy told me about the last time you drank too much, back in Tucson."

Hootie shrugged and quickly emptied his glass. "That weren't all my fault, Joel."

Joel pushed the whiskey bottle down the bar, out of Hootie's reach, and tossed a few dollars on the bar.

"A hot meal would be appreciated," he said to the barman. "And be quick about it. My large friend here is mighty hungry, and if he doesn't get something inside him, pretty soon, then he might have to chew on one of your legs."

The barman looked up at Hootie, who smiled down at him, benevolently, then turned around and rushed into the kitchen behind the bar. "Ham and eggs coming right up, boys," he said as he disappeared through the door and started clattering his kitchen utensils.

Hootie turned to Joel and chuckled. "You ain't wrong there, Joel. I sure am hungry after all that excitement. But I don't reckon there's much meat on that barkeep. He looks a bit of a runt." He pulled his clay pipe out of his front pocket and lit it, resting one elbow on the bar.

Joel and Hootie leaned against the bar, as they waited for the food to arrive, and watched as the doctor examined the wounded men. The sheriff, with the help of some of the locals, carried out the bodies of Jeb Coffey and the unfortunate young cowboy.

In no time at all, the barman had rustled up two large plates of ham and eggs with some thick slices of cornbread on the side and placed them on the nearest table for Joel and Hootie to consume. He went back in the kitchen and brought a pot of hot coffee and two mugs.

"Much obliged, mister," Joel said. "That's just what my friend needs to sober him up. He's drank too much of that fine whiskey of yours."

As the barman picked up the part used whiskey bottle from the bar, to return it to the shelf below, Joel stopped eating and raised his hand to get the man's attention.

"Hold fast with that whiskey bottle, mister. I've got a Texan friend who'd appreciate that fine liquor. Just put the stopper on it, and I'll take it with me."

The barman brought the bottle to the table and placed it in front of Joel, as he looked in his pocket for some money to pay the man.

"No charge, mister," said the barman, holding up both hands. "It's on the house."

Chapter 31

After a good meal, Joel and Hootie took their leave of the town. Sheriff Preston Hibbs thanked them both for getting him out of jail and dealing with the Coffey brothers. He promised to let Marshall Tucker, in Tucson, know that they had both been killed, as soon as he had repaired the telegraph, and that they were still on the trail of Shreeve Moor and the rest of his gang. He also wished them luck in catching the rest of the outlaws.

Joel had changed his mind and decided to take the two horses belonging to the dead Coffey brothers, as spare mounts for the fast ride to catch up with the others. The old stable man had protested, at first, but after Joel had allowed him to keep the outlaw's fancy saddles and saddlebags, and Hootie had backed him into a corner, he had relented. He had, earlier, seen the way that Hootie had quickly dispatched Waylon Coffey, as he had watched from the door, and was more than a little wary of the big man.

There was still a lot of daylight left, so they both rode north east, Hootie leading the way, hoping to cross the rest of the posse's trail before nightfall. Hootie found horse tracks towards evening, and they followed them for a few miles until it got too dark to see them clearly, deciding to rest up until dawn and catch up with the others after a good rest.

They knew that they were on the right track, as earlier, Hootie had discovered an empty whiskey jar, suspended in a tree, tied from a branch with some buckskin twine. The setting sun's rays were shining through the branches and reflecting off the brown glass, as it slowly revolved in the breeze, at head height above the ground. Joel had cut the jar down, with his knife, and smiled at Hootie.

"This sure looks like Tex's whiskey jar," Joel had said. "He must have left it there for us to see."

Hootie had taken the jar from Joel and shook it, smiling as he removed the stopper and quickly swallowed some of the contents. "He must have left us a drink, as well," the big Swede had said, handing the jar to Joel, who finished off the remains of the liquor.

"We must thank him for that kind thought when we meet up. But it ain't like him to waste whiskey, he must be going soft," Joel had said, tossing the empty jar into a mesquite bush. "He'll be mighty happy when he sees this bottle of good whiskey that we've brought him."

They made a fire and roasted a Porcupine that Hootie had caught, after he had startled it when taking a leak in the bushes. Joel had been unsure about eating the animal, but after Hootie had removed all its quills, skinned it, and removed its innards, and spit roasted it, he had changed his mind.

"This ain't at all bad, Hootie," said Joel, chewing a mouthful of the animal's tender flesh and washing it down with a cup of hot coffee. "I never knew that Porcupine could taste this good."

"The Injuns treat Porcupine as a delicacy," Hootie said, laughing. "Among the southern tribes, it is considered an honor if you are offered some at a meal." He paused as he finished chewing on the remains of the carcass. "Once, up on the Platte River, me and Banjo were so hungry that we killed a skunk and ate it. It tasted fine once we had skinned and roasted it. You'd eat anything if you were starving."

"That must be why your breath always smells like the back end of a buffalo," said Joel, laughing.

Hootie sat back and belched, reached for his pipe, and lit it with a burning stick from the fire.

"I shall save these," he said, picking up one of the Porcupine's sharp quills, and examining it. "They are good to trade with some of the friendly tribes."

Joel nodded and flicked his cigarette into the fire. He lay back on his blanket and pulled his hat down over his eyes. "Let's get some sleep, Hootie. We'll try and catch up with the others tomorrow."

Joel and Hootie were well into New Mexico Territory, the next day, when they both heard gunfire in the distance, up ahead.

"Sounds like they found trouble, Hootie," said Joel, pulling his rifle from out of its scabbard. "Or maybe trouble has found them."

Hootie nodded and drew his pistol. His long rifle was too unwieldy to use when mounted.

* * * * * *

Shreeve Moor had thought he was being followed, or rather he had been told by the Comanche, Wild Coyote, that there were riders on their trail. The Indian had suspected for a few days that there was some sort of posse behind them, He had seen smoke in the distance and thought it must be from a campfire, so he kept sending one of his braves to back trail to determine if he was right.

On hearing the news, the Albino had told Wild Coyote to take his two remaining warriors and find out who was following them.

"Maybe it's Jeb and Waylon Coffey," he said. "Perhaps, they've had second thoughts and want to rejoin us." He laughed and looked at Wild Coyote. "Well, if it is them, then you can kill the yellow bastards. I never did like them much anyways, they were always whispering to each other. And if you do kill them, don't forget to bring me their ears for my collection." He stroked the grisly necklace of ears that was hung around his neck and gazed at them fondly, like a father to a favorite child, and cackled with glee.

Wild Coyote nodded and turned to his two braves and spoke to them in their own tongue. He hated the Coffey brothers and owed them for stopping him from scalping Elvira Jones, after the jailbreak. They all yelled and whooped as they mounted their ponies, looking forward to some killing.

Shreeve and Randy Moor, along with Skeeter Hancock and Clem Johnson, carried on towards Glorieta Pass. He turned to his brother, as they rode away, the three Comanches traveling in the opposite direction.

"Let those Injuns deal with whoever is following us, Randy. And if they don't make it to Glorieta, well, I don't give a damn. I never did trust Injuns, anyways. Let them fight it out with the Coffey brothers, or whoever else is following us."

"Sure thing, Shreeve. We don't need them Comanches anymore. They're just no-good heathens."

Skeeter and Clem urged their mounts on and followed the Moor brothers, hoping to get safely away from any law that might be following them. They were both getting a little tired from being on the run and wished that they had both gone with Jeb and Waylon Coffey when they had the chance. They had both seen how Shreeve Moor was getting a little crazier as the days passed and wondered what sort of butchery he would find to do next.

******

Wild Coyote and his two Comanches stopped back-tracking down the trail after a few hours, and he sent the youngest and more agile, brave, called Dark Moon, to climb a small rocky hill and look for signs of who was following them. After a while, the young Comanche returned and reported that he could see some white men resting in amongst a few trees. He told Wild Coyote that he couldn't be sure, at that distance, how many there were, and if it was the two white men called Coffey.

Wild Coyote sat on his haunches in the dust, for a moment, thinking what to do next. He was an experienced warrior and wasn't going to rush headlong into anything without first finding out what the three of them were up against. They were all equipped with latest repeating rifles, which Randy Moor had supplied them with before the jailbreak in Tucson, so along with their traditional bows and arrows and tomahawks, he thought that they were a match for any white men. He stood up, stretched the stiffness from his back and legs, and called over the other Comanche—a thickset warrior called Winter Rain—who had fought many times alongside Wild Coyote and carried the scars of battle on his arms and body.

Wild Coyote explained to Winter Rain his strategy. He wanted him to creep up to where the white men were resting and determine how many were there, and how well-armed they were. If he thought that they could defeat the white men, he should let out a yell, or fire his rifle, and Wild Coyote would ride in with Dark Moon, and they would kill them all. But if he thought that they were outnumbered, then Winter Rain should quietly return.

Wild Coyote realized that his small band of renegade Comanches had diminished in size since leaving the main tribe. There had been twelve warriors at first, but after a couple of skirmishes with wagon trains, the jailbreak in Tucson, and the encounter with the group of Mexicans, a few days ago, his band had been reduced to three, including himself, and he decided that they must be more careful in future. The young half-breed, Farlow Rainwater, who had been killed back in Tucson, had been one of his brother's sons, a product of his brother's union with a white woman, who had been a prisoner of the tribe.

* * * * * *

Tex had decided to rest for a while to give Joel and Hootie time to catch up with them. He wished now that he had kept the last of his whiskey for himself, instead of leaving the jar, with a couple of swallows in it, hanging from a tree for them to see. He cussed to himself. *Maybe*, he thought, *they hadn't seen it, or maybe they had both been shot by the two outlaws that they had been chasing. No*, he mused, *Joel and Hootie would have been a match for any two, no-good varmints that they came up against. But it was still a waste of damn good liquor*, he thought.

Although there was still plenty of daylight left, he had called a halt among some trees, by a small stream, to give them all a break from hours in the saddle, and they had lit a fire hoping the smoke would help Joel and Hootie to find them.

Billy-Bob Cannon and Young Billy Brand were both sitting on their saddle blankets, playing cards, although Billy-Bob was doing most of the playing, and winning, and Young Billy was trying to get his head round the difficult game of poker. Tex had played with Billy-Bob during most of their time out of the saddle, as he always thought that he was skilled at the game, but after losing nearly every game with the ex-Texas Ranger, he had become frustrated and stopped playing. One evening, Tex had pulled out his gun on Billy-Bob, accusing him of cheating, and it was only after Banjo and Young Billy had calmed him down did he apologize, but he never played again.

Brad Stillman had been sent up the trail, by Tex, to keep a lookout in case they were surprised by anyone, and told to keep alert as they would be moving out in a couple of hours. Tex was squatting down against a tree, lost in thought as he rubbed his finger on the abscess in his gum, which had returned. He thought again about the whiskey jar that he had left, and how the contents might have helped relieve the ache in his mouth, and also about Father Benito's remedy which had relieved the pain before.

Banjo Lafarge was standing next to Tex, leaning against the same tree, as he pulled out his snuff box. Tex looked up at him, feeling a mite irritable with his tooth hurting him.

"Are you still stuffing that filthy crap up your nose, Banjo?"

Hootie laughed. "To quote Rousseau, *mon amie*, 'There is nothing better than the encouragement of a good friend.'" He opened his snuff box and looked down at Tex. "What with your bad tooth and losing at poker, you are getting to be a miserable bastard."

Tex grunted something in reply, as Banjo carried on talking and sprinkling snuff on the back of his hand. "Rousseau also said that gambling is only the resource of those who do not know what to do with themselves,"

"Will you stop spouting that philosophy crap," Tex said. "What with Joel always quoting his old grandpappy, and you telling us what some long dead, boring, Frenchman had to say, it's getting to be mighty wearisome these days. And will you stop shoving that damn shit up your nose. If you need to do it, go somewhere else."

Tex growled and settled back against the tree, pulling his hat down over his forehead, as Banjo ignored him and carried on tapping snuff out of his box, onto the back of his hand.

Just then, a shadow moved in front of them, and the Comanche, Winter Rain, stood silently looking at them both from only a few feet away. He carried a rifle in one hand and in the other hand he clutched a wicked looking tomahawk that glistened with fresh looking blood on the blade. He smiled in triumph, eyes glinting with fury, as he closed the short distance between himself and the two white men, raising the tomahawk high above his head to deliver a killing blow to the sitting Tex. He ignored the small, old Frenchman, deciding that the man squatting down would be the more dangerous. He would deal with the older man after killing the other one, as he didn't look like much of a threat.

Winter Rain had disregarded the orders of his leader, Wild Coyote, deciding to kill all the white men himself and gain all the glory that it would bring. He would show the other two how a Comanche should behave and not creep around, cautiously, as Wild Coyote had told him to. He let out a blood curdling war cry, as he prepared to bury his tomahawk in the head of the unsuspecting white man.

Chapter 32

Banjo, surprised at the sudden appearance of the savage looking Indian, carried on sprinkling snuff on the back of his hand, as Winter Rain closed the gap between them with the intention of burying his tomahawk in the top of Tex's head.

The Frenchman suddenly recovered from his shock, at seeing the Indian appear before them, and stopped absent-mindedly sprinkling the snuff from his box, which had formed a small heap on the back of his hand. Quick as a flash, and with all his breath, Banjo blew the pile of snuff into the Comanche's face making him drop both his weapons and clutch his face, which was covered in the brown powder. Winter Rain's loud coughing shook Tex from his daydreaming, and he was suddenly aware of the savage looming above him.

A shot rang out as Tex put a bullet in the savage's chest, and he quickly got to his feet, his toothache now forgotten. Banjo dropped his snuff box and pulled out his knife, but Winter Rain fell to the ground, already dead, his spirit had gone to the happy hunting ground, taking his foolish recklessness with him.

Billy-Bob and Young Billy came running over, their poker game abandoned, both with their pistols in their hands, as Banjo Lafarge rooted around on the dusty ground, trying to salvage the remains of his snuff.

"Where the hell did he come from?" said Billy-Bob, looking down at the dead Comanche whose face was covered in brown powder, masking the war-paint that he had applied that morning.

"I ain't sure," said Tex. "But if Banjo hadn't blown snuff in his face, I reckon that tomahawk of his would be resting in the top of my head." He looked down at Banjo, who was searching around on the ground, next to the dead Comanche. "What the hell are you looking for, Banjo?"

"I'm looking for the rest of my snuff," Banjo said, picking up his snuff box from the ground and examining the contents.

Tex clapped a hand on the back of the kneeling Frenchman, nearly knocking the snuff box from his hand. "Thanks for that, Banjo," he said. "You saved my life. I shall buy you a fresh supply of the stuff next time we are in a town, and I shan't call it a filthy habit again. Just don't sniff it around me." He looked up the trail and turned to Banjo. "And what's happened to young Brad? He was supposed to be keeping a lookout. I hope he ain't asleep."

The sound of horses approaching alerted the four men, and they all reached for their rifles at the sound of gunfire.

Wild Coyote had been losing patience waiting for Winter Rain, when the sudden sound of a gunshot made him leap on his pony, and he shouted Dark Moon to ride with him. He assumed that Winter Rain had fired his rifle and wanted them to come and help him defeat the white men, so with a loud yell, and firing his rifle into the air, he led Dark Moon towards the few trees and bushes.

Billy-Bob and Young Billy were the first to see the two Comanches, as they burst through the thicket, both firing their rifles in their direction.

"Take cover, Young Billy," Billy-Bob shouted as a bullet buried itself in the tree next to them both.

Ignoring Billy-Bobs command, Young Billy cocked his rifle and levelled it at one of the Comanches, as he closed the distance between them. He shot the savage from his horse, and with a yell of satisfaction, turned to see the other Comanche, Wild Coyote, riding towards them. Before Young Billy could fire his rifle again, Billy-Bob fired twice as the Indian shot at them, his wild shot hitting the branch above them, as he toppled backwards off his horse.

"Good shooting, Billy-Bob," Tex said, looking warily in the direction that the two Comanches had come from. "You too, Young Billy. But keep your damn fool head down, there could be more of them out there. It ain't just a pack of wolves attacking us."

Tex went over to where the two Indians had fallen from their horses, followed by Billy-Bob and Young Billy, who was grinning from ear to ear, feeling more than a little pleased with himself. Banjo Lafarge was still rooting on the ground for the remains of his snuff, hoping to salvage some of the contents of his precious box that had been spilled. He was cursing to himself in French, occasionally chuckling as he found a small pinch of the brown powder and carefully replaced it in his box.

Feeling that he had picked up all of the snuff that he could see on the dusty ground, his eyesight was not as good as it used to be, Banjo pocketed his snuff box and went over to see what had happened to Brad Stillman, who was supposed to be acting as lookout at the edge of the trees.

Perhaps, he fell asleep, thought Banjo. *I hope the young fella is alright.*

Wild Coyote was dead, but the other Comanche, Dark Moon, who Young Billy had shot, was still alive and bleeding from a wound in his side.

"Next time, shoot to kill, Young Billy," Tex said as the wounded Comanche tried to reach his fallen rifle, which Tex kicked out of his reach. "We ain't taking any prisoners on this trip."

Dark Moon groaned as Tex grabbed him by the hair and pulled him into a sitting position, the Indian Fighter's knife appearing in his hand, leveled at the savage's throat.

Tex spoke to the Comanche in his own tongue, demanding to know if there were any more Indians with him. Dark Moon kept silent, determining to show his cold face to the white man, even though he was in pain and losing a lot of blood. Tex repeated his question, still holding Dark Moon by his hair, and when he failed to get an answer, he drew the sharp blade of his skinning knife along the Comanche's left cheek, making him yell in pain as blood ran down his face and dripped off his chin.

After asking the same question for the third time, and bringing his wicked looking blade close to the Indians other cheek, Tex got an answer from the frightened Comanche, who could see his chief, Wild Coyote, lying a few yards away, face down in the dirt. He told Tex that there had been only three of them, and that one of them had come down earlier to see how many they were up against. Tex informed Dark Moon that the other Comanche was dead, as well as his chief, who he could see lying not too far away.

As Tex was interrogating the Comanche further, Banjo Lafarge came over looking very angry and holding his pistol in one hand. He stood looking down at Dark Moon, as he answered Tex's questions.

"Has he told you all that you want to know, Tex?" he asked, speaking quietly in his thick French accent.

Tex nodded to Banjo, and was just about to tell the others what the Indian had said to him when Banjo cocked his pistol and shot the Comanche through his heart, making Tex let go of his hair in surprise, as the Indian dropped to the ground, dead.

"What the hell did you do that for, Banjo? You're not still mad 'cause you lost all of your snuff, are you?" asked Tex, wiping his bloody knife on the dead Comanche's pants.

"No, Tex. I just found Brad up there with his throat cut. One of these bastards must have done it. I'm sorry, *mon amie*, but he had it coming." He holstered his pistol and sniffed up his nose.

Just then there was a sound of horses behind them, and as they turned around, expecting more of the attackers, Joel and Hootie came riding in, holding their guns at the ready.

"Is everything alright?" asked Joel as he looked around, noticing the dead Comanches lying on the ground. "We heard shooting and thought you were in trouble."

"We're fine now," answered Tex. "Well, young Brad got bushwhacked by these bastards, but the rest of us are OK."

Joel and Hootie dismounted and Tex told them what the Comanche had said to him before Banjo had shot him.

"He told me that Shreeve Moor had sent the Indians back to see who was following them, and to make sure that we were all killed." He paused as Billy-Bob and Young Billy carried the body of Brad Stillman into the clearing. They were going to give him a decent burial before they moved on.

"The Comanche also said that Shreeve Moor and the rest of his bunch were heading up near Santa Fe, to a ranch near Glorieta Pass, where he said he knew someone, and that they would be safe."

"Well, we can't be too far behind them, and there's a few less of them now, what with these three Indians dead, and we left the Coffey brothers at the undertakers, in the town, back there," Joel said, shaking the trail dust from his hat. "We've rode hard to catch up with you, so a quick rest and some food, and we'll get back in the saddle. We've brought the Coffey brother's horses along as spare mounts."

"Well, take the load off first, Joel, and tell us what happened back in that town," Billy-Bob said, leaving Brad's body for the moment and coming over with Young Billy, to greet Joel and Hootie, as he lit a cigarette.

They all gathered around Joel and Hootie, as Joel got out his makings and rolled himself a cigarette and told them how they had caught Jeb and Waylon Coffey in the town saloon, and they all laughed as Joel told them how Hootie had killed Waylon Coffey with the butt of a shotgun.

"He caught him with his pants down," explained Joel. "Out in the street in just his underwear."

"Well, if it hadn't have been for Banjo, here, and that shit that he sniffs up his nose, I would have been wearing a Comanche tomahawk in the top of my skull," Tex said, telling Joel and Hootie about the Indian attack.

Banjo held his arms apart and shrugged his shoulders at Tex's comment, pocketing his snuff box with the small amount of brown powder left in it. "*C'est la vie*," he said, smiling at Tex.

"We saw your whiskey jar that you left hanging up," said Joel. "And you left a couple of swallows in it for me and Hootie to drink."

"Yes," said Hootie. "It was much appreciated."

"Well, I wish that I had kept it," Tex said, rubbing his jaw. "This damn toothache has come back, and a mouthful of liquor would have eased the pain."

Joel walked over to his horse and brought out the bottle of whiskey from his saddlebag. "Here, Tex," he said, tossing the bottle over to his friend, who caught it with both hands. "We brought you this from the saloon back in that town. Its good whiskey, Hootie will vouch for that, so don't waste it."

Tex pulled the stopper off the bottle and took a long drink, swilling the contents around his gums, and sighed with satisfaction as the liquor warmed his throat and numbed his aching gum. He replaced the stopper and smiled at Joel and Hootie.

"Thanks, fellas, it's much appreciated." He was about to put the bottle in his own saddlebag, when he saw the look on Banjo and Billy-Bobs faces. He handed the bottle to Banjo and smiled. "Here, Banjo, you deserve a drink for saving me. But don't drink too much, pass it over to Billy-Bob." He looked at Young Billy, who was standing with a look of anticipation on his face.

"Give Young Billy a drink, Billy-Bob. He did shoot that Comanche off his horse. But not too much now, Young Billy," Tex said. "You know you can't hold your liquor. We don't want it all over the camp fire."

Billy-Bob handed the bottle over to the young cowboy, who gratefully accepted it. He took a drink, just a small one, smiled at Tex, and handed the bottle back to Billy-Bob.

Hootie Swenson unpinned the deputy's badge from his buckskin shirt, polished it on his sleeve, and gave it back to Billy-Bob.

"Thanks for the loan, Billy-Bob. It sure felt good walking into the saloon, back in that town, wearing a lawman's badge and facing the Coffey Brothers."

"That's OK, Hootie, anytime," said Billy-Bob.

After a short break, they buried Brad Stillman in a shallow grave, with just his hat, weighed down with a rock, resting on it. Banjo said a few words over the grave, and they all saddled up, with Hootie and Banjo, taking the lead looking for signs of the outlaw's trail.

Chapter 33

With the Civil War in its second year, and after beating the Union forces, under Colonel Edward Canby, at Valverde, Brigadier General Sibley pushed on up the Rio Grande, determined to capitalize on his victory

After making his headquarters at Albuquerque, Brigadier Sibley's Confederate force occupied Santa Fe on March 10th. His goal was to occupy the Santa Fe Trail as far north as Colorado, intending to join with forces from California.

Sergeant Peticolas and a few of his sharpshooters had engaged the enemy along the Rio Grande river making them retreat in confusion, as they shot at them from the high ground and quickly returned to their own lines. His two young recruits from Arizona, Ross and Jamie, had excelled themselves in combat, both showing courage under fire. Jamie had been wounded in the left arm but had quickly returned from the field hospital to take his place at his cousin's side.

They had both sent letters back home, to their folks in Arizona, telling them that they were both with the Confederate forces, but because of the fast pace that the army was moving, had not yet received a reply.

A few of the younger recruits, some hardly into their teens, had become disillusioned by the war. They had joined for the excitement and freedom, but after their first taste of battle, and seeing the dead and dying, and men with limbs missing, had deserted at the first opportunity. Only a few had left but it took Captain Hampton, along with Sergeant Peticolas, all their efforts to keep the morale of their 4th Texas Mounted in good shape.

Sibley sent an advance force of between 200 and 300 Texans, under Major Charles L Pyron, over the Glorieta Pass, at the southern end of the Sangre de Cristo Mountains. The capture of the pass would allow

Sibley to advance and capture Fort Union, a key base along the Santa Fe Trail. The Confederate and Union forces were, unbeknown to each other camped on opposite sides of Glorieta Pass, where the Santa Fe Trail narrows, as it winds through a low point in the Sangre de Cristo Mountains. Troops were sent ahead by both sides to detect enemy forces.

******

Shreeve and Randy Moor along with Skeeter Hancock and Clem Johnson had avoided Albuquerque. They didn't want to be seen in a town, in case they were recognized, and they had also heard sounds of gunfire and heavy artillery in that direction.

"I don't like the sound of that," Skeeter said to Shreeve Moor. "I hope we ain't getting caught up in that damn fool civil war."

Shreeve Moor stopped his horse and looked around, looking more than a little worried. He tugged at his top lip which was beginning to swell up, one of the first signs of him getting overstressed.

"I didn't know that the war was this far south," he said, looking back down the trail and scratching his chin. He paused for a minute, deep in thought, "I wonder what happened to those Comanches that I sent back to ambush the posse, who were trailing us?" he added. "They ain't caught up with us yet."

"Perhaps, they killed them all, and scalped them," said his brother, Randy, trying to cheer him up but feeling a mite nervous himself, as his horse pricked up its ears, and wheeled around, at the distant sound of gunfire

"Yeah! And perhaps they all got themselves killed. They should have been here by now, if they had managed to beat them. I wonder who was in that posse? They must have been on our trail since we left Tucson," replied Shreeve Moor.

"Well, I reckon we should get out of here," Clem Johnson said as he heard some more gunfire in the distance, sounding like rolling thunder as it echoed off the distant mountains. "Skeeter's right, we never should have come this far. Maybe we should head east away from all this trouble. If we don't get caught by that posse, then we could end up in the middle of a battle."

"You two ain't thinking of pulling out, are you?" Shreeve Moor said, looking at Skeeter and Clem as they both sat their horses, nervously glancing in the direction of the gunfire. He dropped his hand to his pistol and gave them both a menacing look.

"We ain't come this far to give up now. We gotta stick together," said the Albino, glowering at the two men. "I told you, I've got kin on the other side of the mesa, who'll look after us and give us shelter. Nobody will find us there, and I can't see any soldiers going that way, there ain't nothing to fight over towards Glorieta." He moved his hand away from his holstered pistol and gave them both a reassuring smile, which looked more like a vicious leer in his evil looking face.

Clem Johnson relaxed a little and nodded to Skeeter Hancock. He turned back to Shreeve Moor, still with a hard look on his face.

"OK, Shreeve, we're still with you. We got out of jail, and we got this far, so we may as well keep going."

"Come on then, let's get across this mesa, there can't be much further to go." Said Shreeve Moor, urging his horse into a gallop, as the others followed him, heading north across Glorieta Mesa.

Skeeter and Clem followed the Moor brothers, both trying to think of a better way to get out of their present predicament.

They all rode in silence across the mesa, listening to the sporadic sound of gunfire, Shreeve Moor taking the lead as he tried to remember the way to his cousin Marty's place. It was a few years since he had been this way, and he wasn't even sure that his cousin still lived there, *but, what the hell*, he thought, *anywhere is better than rotting in the jail in Tucson.*

******

Banjo and Hootie arrived at the edge of Glorieta Mesa the following morning, after an early start, pausing for the others to catch up, and also because they could hear sporadic rifle fire in the distance.

"I don't like the sound of that," Hootie said as the rest of the posse came riding over. He dismounted and filled his pipe, while Banjo tapped a tiny amount of his precious snuff onto the back of his hand, and sniffed it up his nose, causing him to sneeze loudly. He swore in French and wiped his nose on the back of his sleeve.

"I think I've got too much sand and dirt in this damn snuff box, Hootie, from when I dropped it on the ground. Maybe even some gopher shit, by the smell of it. That's what you get for helping someone out of a tight spot. I think I'll stick to my pipe for now." He put his snuff box away and knelt down with Hootie to see the tracks, made by horses, more clearly. They both briefly discussed the situation and Banjo stood up and pulled out his old clay pipe, as Joel reined in at the side of them.

"Which way are they headed, Banjo?" he said, hearing the noise of gunfire himself for the first time. "And what's all that shooting about?"

Hootie was crouched down, examining the tracks on the ground. He looked up and nodded to Joel.

"Well," said Banjo, lighting his pipe and pausing as he took a lungful of smoke. He blew out the smoke, in a bluish/grey cloud, and pointed into the distance with his pipe. "Shreeve Moor, and his gang, have headed that way, across that mesa. Me and Hootie reckon that there's only four of them left now." He paused again, as he reached for his water canteen and took a swallow and replaced the stopper. "There's tracks of seven horses, but we reckon that only four of them have got riders on them. The other three must be spare mounts, and they must have been pushing the horses hard, because some of them have thrown a horseshoe."

Banjo took another long puff of his pipe and sighed with satisfaction, as Hootie stood up and joined them both.

"We reckon that there must be some sort of battle going on over there," said the big Swede, pointing in the direction of Glorieta Pass.

"Well, let's get after those murderers," said Tex. "They can't be too far ahead. The sooner we catch them, the sooner we can get back down south, away from this damn war. I can't wait to get back to my Donna and a warm bed."

"That's right," agreed Billy-Bob. "Julie and the girls must be missing me, and I sure miss the comforts of home."

Joel nodded in agreement. It had been a long, hard ride, he thought, and he too would be glad to get it over with. His thoughts went back to the Travis ranch and Joan, the young school teacher that he had met. *Now that lady is worth the long ride back*, he thought. He smiled to himself as he tightened his horses cinch, and Clover turned her head to him and blew steam from its nostrils. He stroked Clover's long mane, adjusted his gun belt, and mounted up.

"Come on then," Joel said, looking at the others. "Let's get it done."

They all mounted up and rode across the mesa, with Joel and Tex in the lead. There was no need for Hootie or Banjo to find the trail, as the recent deep marks of seven horses, some with a shoe missing, was easy enough to follow in the damp ground, covered with mist and early morning dew.

Billy-Bob steered his horse alongside Hootie Swenson and shouted to him. "Here, Hootie, catch this," as he threw something shiny towards the big man. Hootie grabbed the object in his big hand and looked down to see what it was. It was the deputy's badge, and he looked quizzically at Billy-Bob.

"Keep it, Hootie," said Billy-Bob. "You earned the right to wear it." He reached down into his saddlebag and brought out his old Texas Rangers badge. "I've still got this," he said laughing as he pinned it on his vest. Hootie let out a loud yell and pinned the deputy's badge on his shirt, catching up with Banjo to proudly show him what he was wearing.

Chapter 34

On the morning of March 28th, 1862, the third and final day of the Battle of Glorieta, Confederate and Union forces moved towards each other. Confederate Lt. Col. William Scurry, with about 900 men, left Johnson's Ranch and traveled east along the Santa Fe Trail.

Scurry led his men down the gullies in the sloping field with a center assault column of approximately 500 Texans to attack the Union forces at Pigeon's Ranch. His cavalry dismounted and joined the Fourth Texas foot soldiers, advancing eastwards along the trail.

Colonel John P Slough, leader of the First Regiment of the Colorado volunteers, brought up the Union's artillery and formed a battle line across the Santa Fe Trail, to face the advancing Confederate force, waiting for them to get within range of his big guns.

Shreeve and Randy Moor, along with Clem Johnson and Skeeter Hancock had crossed the mesa and were heading for Pigeon's Ranch, along the Santa Fe Trail, when Union Captain John Ritter's four 12-pounders and field howitzers, along with Claflin's three mountain howitzers opened up on the Confederate lines. Without warning, the peaceful morning suddenly became a cacophony of deafening sound. The thunderous noise made a flock of birds take flight, and a herd of mule deer panicked and scattered in different directions, trying to flee from the uproar.

Suddenly, realizing that they were caught up in the middle of the battle, Shreeve Moor shouted for the others to turn back, as shells flew overhead, but in a panic, Clem and Skeeter, their horses terrified by the noise, carried on down the trail, into the middle of the barrage, and both men and horses were hit by stray artillery fire. Clem Johnson was blown to bits, as he and his horse, took a direct hit from a howitzer shell. Skeeter Hancock was hit in the back and leg by shrapnel from an exploding shell above him, and he was flung to the ground as his horse collapsed from the .58 caliber Minie balls embedded in its flank, fired by Union sharpshooters positioned just behind the heavy artillery.

Skeeter Hancock, badly wounded, pulled himself along through the long grass, as there was a lull in the artillery barrage. He could see Clem Johnson—or what was left of him, lying a few yards away, partially hidden by a dip in the ground—and dragged himself towards him, thinking that, perhaps, he was just wounded. "Clem! Are you alright? Have you been hit?" he croaked, his slow progress marked by a trail of blood in the damp grass, as he dragged himself along with both hands.

Skeeter reached Clem Johnson, who was lying face down, and, thinking that his friend was still alive, he tugged at his shoulder to turn him over. It was only then, when he looked at Clem, did he realize that the lower half of his body was missing and his right arm had been blown off, and he quickly let go of the dead outlaw's shirt and threw up in the grass. In pain from his wounds, he pulled himself up on his elbows to look for Shreeve Moor and his brother, wondering if they had been caught by the artillery fire.

Catching sight of the Moor brothers, who were about one hundred yards away and still on their horses, both trying to decide the safest way out of the conflagration around them, Skeeter took a big breath and yelled at them.

"Shreeve," he gasped. "Help me, will you? Clem's dead and I've been hit. Get me outa here."

Shreeve and Randy Moor ignored Skeeter's pleading, both gazing at the bloody remains of Clem Johnson and his horse, transfixed at the sight of the mangled bodies, with steam emanating from the horse's exposed, warm intestines that lay on the ground.

Not getting an answer, Skeeter yelled again, wincing as the effort made him grimace with pain.

"Shreeve, Randy. Get me out of here. I helped get you out of that jail, back in Tucson, didn't I?"

Skeeter collapsed on his back, the effort of shouting taking its toll, making him cough up blood, as he gasped for breath, lying there waiting, in vain, for help from the other two outlaws.

Suddenly, Shreeve Moor pulled himself together, Skeeter's shouting bringing him out of his trance. He turned to his brother, who looked at him for guidance.

"He's a goner, Randy. Leave him. Let's find somewhere safe before all that shooting starts up again. I sure don't want to be around when it does."

"Yeah! But which way is safe, Shreeve," Randy Moor said, looking back at Skeeter Hancock, who lay there dying, too far gone to shout anymore.

Terrified, and unsure which direction would be the safest, the Moor brothers dismounted and led their horses away from battle field, away from the trail, and back onto the mesa, and took cover in a deep arroyo. They sat down on the grass, both exhausted by the recent events, and Shreeve Moor pulled out a small bottle of cheap liquor from his pocket, took a drink, and passed it over to his brother.

"Phew! That was close, Randy," Shreeve said, wiping the sweat from his brow. "We were damn lucky to get out of that in one piece. A damn sight luckier than those other two."

Randy Moor took a long drink and handed the bottle back to his older brother and nodded. He was still shaking and there were fresh wet stains on the front of his pants, around his crotch.

"Do you think that we should go and see if Skeeter Hancock is alright," Randy said, nervously looking back the way that they had come. Maybe we could help him."

"No way, Randy. I ain't going back there. He's probably dead by now." The Albino chuckled nervously to his brother. "I did think about going and collecting Clem and Skeeter's ears for my collection but thought better of it. Anyway, we had better think about getting out of here, before things start hotting up again."

Shreeve Moor put the bottle back in his pocket and scratched the sparse, white hair on his head, while he thought about what to do.

"I guess Pigeon's Ranch is out of the question now. If cousin Marty is still there, then he must be in worse trouble than we are. We might as well head back down south and find somewhere quiet to rest up for a while. I don't reckon that there's a posse after us anymore, either Wild

Coyote and his Comanches have killed them, or they've heard all this ruckus and hightailed it back to Tucson."

Shreeve Moor led his brother out of the arroyo, both quietly leading their horses back along the mesa, as sporadic gunfire and the occasional artillery fire sounded, not too far behind them.

Less than half a mile away, Joel Shelby and the posse had dismounted and took cover in a few trees on the mesa. They had had heard the artillery barrage that the outlaws had been caught up in and had decided to wait to see if it was safe to progress any further.

"Sounds like one helluva battle going on over there," said Billy-Bob, leaning against a tree and lighting a cigarette.

"I ain't heard nothing like that since I was with General Sam Houston at San Jacinto," agreed Hootie, as he gazed across the mesa.

"We'd better wait here and see if it calms down," Joel said. "If those outlaws got caught up in that battle, then I don't give much for their chances."

Tex nodded in agreement. "Maybe it will save us the bother of having to shoot them down." He reached in his saddlebag and took out the bottle of good whiskey, took a drink, and handed it to Banjo. "Here, Banjo, have a drink of this and keep that filthy snuff in your pocket."

The sound of riders heading in their direction alerted the posse, and Joel saw the two men first, as he reached for his rifle.

"It's that bastard Shreeve Moor and his brother," said Joel, cocking his rifle and walking towards them.

As they rode towards the trees, Shreeve Moor looked up and saw a man, holding a rifle, walking towards them with some other men following close behind. He slowed his horse down and his brother, Randy, noticing the men, let out a groan.

"It's that damn posse, Shreeve. You said they wouldn't be following us." He looked over to his brother for inspiration and guidance. "What are we gonna do now?"

"Shut your sniveling, Randy," said the Albino. "They ain't taking me back to that damn jail."

He pulled out his pistol and fired at Joel, his shot missing the target, as his brother pulled out his rifle and began firing at the others.

"Give yourself up, Moor," shouted Joel as another bullet flew past him, this time a lot closer than the first.

Shots rang out behind Joel, and he saw Randy Moor, hit more than once, fly back off his horse, one of his boots trapped in his stirrup, as he was dragged along the rough ground.

Before Shreeve Moor could fire again, Joel fired twice, in rapid succession, both shots hitting the outlaw in his chest. "I gave you fair warning," said Joel as Shreeve Moor slumped forward in the saddle and fell off his horse.

The others came walking over, Tex, Billy-Bob, and Banjo all holding smoking rifles, as Joel turned Shreeve Moor over with the toe of his boot.

"Is he dead, Joel?" Tex said, looking down at the body of Shreeve Moor. "Well, that looks like we got most of them. I reckon those other two must have been killed in that battle up yonder, but I ain't going over there to check."

Hootie Swenson went over to Randy Moor's horse, which had come to a halt, still with the outlaw's body hanging from the stirrup, and looked down at him. He pulled the dead man's boot free of the stirrup and walked back to the others, leaving the horse to carry on eating the grass.

As they were all standing around, discussing what to do about the two dead outlaws, there was a thunder of hooves as a troop of blue-coated soldiers came riding towards them, and the six men stood still as they were surrounded by the cavalrymen.

"Easy now, boys," Tex said. "No sudden moves. This lot look like they're ready for trouble."

The leader of the troop, a young Lieutenant, holding a pistol in one hand, looked down at the posse, and the two dead men lying on the ground.

"What's all this about then?" he said, "Did you lot bushwhack these two?" He pointed to the Moor brothers, both with fresh bullet holes in their bodies.

"We ain't bushwhacked nobody," Tex said in his unmistakable Texas drawl. "We've been hunting down these men. We are all deputies."

"The only law around here mister is the Union army, and you sound like a damn rebel to me," the Lieutenant said. He turned to his sergeant, an older, mean looking man, with a scar down his left cheek. "Sergeant Willis, put these men under arrest and remove their weapons. We're taking them back with us."

The Sergeant, and some of his men dismounted, while the rest of the troop remained on horseback, keeping the posse covered with their rifles.

"You ain't taking my weapons," said Tex as two young troopers approached him.

"You'll do as you're told mister, or suffer the consequences," bellowed Sergeant Willis, pushing his face up close to Tex, who stared coldly back at the man. Tex shrugged his shoulders and raised his hands to allow one of the soldiers to remove is pistol and take his rifle—the long skinning knife in his boot remained undiscovered.

The others handed over their weapons, all but Hootie Swenson, as the big Swede, offended by the way one of the privates had manhandled him, seized the man by the throat and lifted him off the ground.

Seeing the plight of his unfortunate soldier, Sergeant Willis went over and raised his pistol to Hootie.

"Put that man down," yelled the Sergeant, cocking his pistol and pointing it at Hootie. "Do as you're told, old man, or I'll put a bullet in you."

Hootie flung the still struggling private into Sergeant Willis, knocking them both to the ground.

"Don't call me an old man," Hootie yelled. He then raised both hands and quietly stood there while a soldier removed his pistol. The Sergeant dusted himself down and glowered at Hootie. The man wasn't injured, just his pride was hurt, and he faced the big Swede, who was still holding his hands up, and reached out and ripped the deputy's badge from his buckskin shirt, and tossed it onto the ground. "You won't be needing this, old man," he said accentuating the last two words as he walked away.

The Lieutenant, who was still mounted, and had quietly watched the altercation, called Sergeant Willis over.

"Sergeant, take three men with you and escort the prisoners back to Artillery Hill, at Glorieta Pass. I shall join you, with the rest of the troop, as soon as I have completed a sweep of this part of the mesa." He looked down at the Sergeant, who stood rigidly to attention, and continued. "Treat them as prisoners of war, and treat them with respect, I shall question them on my return."

The Lieutenant raised his hand and waved his men forward, as he wheeled his horse around and led the troop across the mesa, leaving Sergeant Willis, red faced, as they rode away. He turned to the three troopers, who were covering Joel and the posse with their rifles.

"Get them on their horses and tie their hands together." He glowered at Hootie, as he produced some rope from his saddlebag, and gave it to his men.

They gathered all the weapons and tied them to the posse's spare horses and took the prisoners across the mesa, towards the Santa Fe Trail.

Chapter 35

Sergeant Willis and his three troopers dismounted at the base of Artillery Hill, in a small wooded area, to wait for the rest of the troop. He made the prisoners sit in a group, watched over by his men, while he sat and had a smoke and took a drink from his water bottle, which was filled with whiskey. He was still fuming at the way that the young Lieutenant had spoken to him in front of his men and thought that if he didn't return soon, then he would deal with the prisoners in his own way, especially the big, buckskin clad mountain man. He could say that they were killed trying to get away.

Joel looked at the others and spoke quietly to them. "We sure are in a tight spot here, boys," he said, trying to make light of the situation. "As my old grandpappy would say, 'it looks like we're between a rock and a hard place.'" He looked over at the Sergeant and wondered if he would let him have a smoke, as he had used up all of his makings earlier.

"I've been in worse situations," said Tex, looking over at Young Billy, who sat with a worried look on his face. "Cheer up, Young Billy. Let's turn that frown upside down. At least we ain't surrounded by wolves, or a grizzly bear."

Young Billy smiled back at Tex, hoping that the others would find a way to get them free.

Tex leaned over to Joel, and whispered to him. "I've still got my skinning knife tucked in my boot." He looked over at the troopers who were guarding him, but they hadn't heard him. "If I get the chance, I'm gonna cut these damn ropes off, then we'll take care of these bastards."

Joel nodded to Tex. He figured that their chances were either slim or worse, but better than no chance at all. He sat on the ground, keeping an eye on the Union Sergeant, who was still drinking the contents of his water bottle. The craggy Sergeant sat with his eyes closed and, even from the short distance between them, Joel could smell the liquor on his breath, as shots rang out, not too far away along the top of the hill.

At the far end of Artillery Hill Sergeant Alfred B Peticolas became separated from the Texans sent to attack the southern flank of Artillery Hill. C Company were somewhere to his rear and he had only his two young sharpshooters, Ross Phillips and Jamie Heald, at his side. He turned to the young lads, knowing that he could rely on them both in a tight situation, as they had both proved themselves in the recent skirmishes with the enemy.

"Stay here, boys," he said, looking at Ross and Jamie. "I'm just going to have a scout along this ridge. I won't be long, so keep your eyes open for me coming back and shoot at anything that moves, unless it's me."

Sergeant Peticolas grinned at the two young soldiers, tapped them both on the top of their caps, and walked leisurely along the top of the hill, through a gap in the Federal lines, firing at every opportunity down at the enemy. Ross and Jamie lay on top of the hill, one of them covering one side of the ridge in turn and picked off any Union soldiers who tried to ambush Sergeant Peticolas, as he made his way along the top of Artillery Hill. They both lay there talking to each other, watching as their Sergeant disappeared from view, his tall figure stooped over as he reloaded his rifle.

Joel and the others, heard the gunfire along the top of Artillery Hill, and waited for a chance to try and escape, but the soldiers guarding them were alerted by the shooting and stood over them, not taking their eyes off the prisoners. The only man who seemed unconcerned was Sergeant Willis—a hardened veteran of the army's battles in the Indian campaigns—who was still finishing the contents of his water bottle and making himself another cigarette, spilling most of the makings in his lap.

Joel looked up the hill, as a movement caught his attention, and he saw a tall, bearded soldier in a grey Confederate uniform, with sergeant's stripes on the sleeves, sliding down the hill on his heels. A sudden shout from one of the soldiers guarding them made the others look up and, before he could raise his rifle the Sergeant fired twice, hitting two of the young troopers.

Tex, who had pulled the knife from his boot at the sudden diversion, jumped to his feet as Sergeant Willis, now fully awake, pulled out his pistol and leveled it at the Confederate Sergeant, who was still making his way down the hill. With his hands still tied together, Tex took three steps towards Sergeant Willis and plunged the sharp knife into the man's chest, below his raised arm. Sergeant Willis gasped in pain, turned his head towards Tex, his eyes turned upwards as the long knife penetrated his heart, and he dropped the pistol and collapsed to the ground.

The remaining Union trooper guarding them, raised his rifle as Hootie Swenson caught him in a bear hug from behind, his tied hands dropping over the man's head and gripping his chest, making him drop the rifle. As the young soldier struggled in the big Swede's grip Billy-Bob hit him hard with both bunched fists together on his chin, and he slumped to the ground as Hootie released him.

Sergeant Peticolas reached the bottom of the hill, looked down at the body of the Union Sergeant, and then at Tex, who was still holding his knife with his hands tied together.

"I'm obliged for that, mister," he said, taking the knife from Tex and cutting the rope that bound his hands. "That blue-belly was fixing to shoot me." He handed the knife back to Tex who cut the bonds holding Joel's wrists together, as he came over to join him.

Sergeant Peticolas looked down at Joel's boots as his spurs jingled, rubbed his beard, and smiled at him.

"I'd recognize those fancy spurs anywhere, my friend. Didn't we meet, last year, on the Gila River? Aren't you Joel Shelby? And what the hell are you doing here in the middle of a battle?"

Joel smiled in amazement, as he recognized the man, although his beard had grown longer since their last meeting, and shook Sergeant Peticolas by the hand. "You're damn right there. It's Sergeant Peticolas, ain't it? Fancy meeting you again and thanks for getting us away from these soldiers."

Joel briefly explained to Sergeant Peticolas about the jailbreak, and chasing the outlaws with the posse, and how they had ended up at Glorieta Pass, not realizing that a battle was in progress.

"Well, you better get the hell out of here, my friend," Sergeant Peticolas said. "If any Union soldiers come back and find you with these dead soldiers, they gonna shoot first and ask questions later. I'm behind the enemy lines myself, and I ain't hanging around much longer."

Sergeant Peticolas turned to go, he paused and looked back at Joel, and pulled something out of his pocket, and handed it to him.

"You gave me that, last year, when I was out of tobacco, and I've kept it all this time. It's about time I gave it back; it's far too fancy for a lowly Sergeant like me. Although it did save my life a few days ago. Thanks for the loan."

Joel looked at the finely engraved leather tobacco pouch that the Sergeant had given to him and smiled. He had run out of tobacco and was gasping for a smoke.

"Take care, Alfred, our paths may cross again sometime. You never know,"

Sergeant Peticolas nodded and walked away, pausing to pick up Sergeant Willis' Federal overcoat, which was lying on the ground, near the man's pack, and putting it on.

"This should help me get back through the lines. It looks about my size," he said. "Take care, Joel." He ran up the hill, in a crouch, and was out of site within minutes, as the sound of gunfire came closer.

"Come on, boys," said Tex, getting his pistol and rifle from one of the spare horses, as the others did the same. "Let's make trail outa here. I ain't being taken prisoner again, and as that Sergeant friend of yours said, Joel, those Union soldiers ain't gonna be too happy when they see these bodies."

"Yep!" agreed Joel. "Let's ride. Time ain't our friend right now."

Without another word, they all mounted up and rode away from Artillery Hill, back up and across Glorieta Mesa. They left the Union soldier, who Billy-Bob had knocked out, bound and gagged, not wanting to kill the frightened young man.

As Sergeant Alfred B Peticolas reached the top of Artillery Hill, he walked into a line of Union soldiers, but with the stolen Federal greatcoat on, he looked like a Union soldier. A Federal officer, Lt. Colonel Samuel Tappan, thinking that Peticolas was one of his own troops, allowed the young Texas Sergeant to continue along the top of Artillery Hill and back to the safety of the Confederate lines.

The two young Confederate soldiers, Ross and Jamie, were still patiently waiting for the return of their Sergeant when a figure in a Union overcoat came along the hill towards them. The two young soldiers raised their rifles, ready to shoot the enemy soldier, when the man removed the greatcoat to reveal his Confederate uniform.

"Take it easy, boys," shouted Sergeant Peticolas, as he waved to Ross and Jamie. "It's only me. You can put down your rifles, I'm coming in."

He reached the two soldiers and sat down on the grass, to catch his breath, and told them about his escapade along Artillery Hill, and how he had helped an old friend to escape. He reached into his pocket and cursed at the realization that he had given the tobacco pouch back to Joel.

"I don't suppose you young fellas smoke, do you?" he said, looking at Ross and Jamie.

They both nodded negatively at Sergeant Peticolas, who shrugged his shoulders and stood up.

"Come on then, lads. I've had enough excitement for one day, let's get back to the others."

After encountering Sergeant Peticolas, Federal Lt. Colonel Tappan abandoned Artillery Hill and led his men along the logging road used earlier by Claflin's artillery battery. The Confederates, on the top of the hill, fired at the Colorado volunteers as they rapidly withdrew down the narrow road towards its junction with the Santa Fe Trail, east of Pigeon's Ranch. One group of retreating Federals stopped at Pigeon's Ranch to return the Texans' fire.

Chapter 36

The posse had left the bottom of Artillery Hill, where they had been held prisoner, when less than half an hour later, the Union Lieutenant returned with his troop, and discovered the bodies of Sergeant Willis and the two troopers, along with the trussed-up soldier.

"What happened here, soldier," asked the Lieutenant, looking grim faced at the private, as he was freed from his bonds.

The private stood up and dusted himself down, and wiped some blood from his mouth with the back of his hand. He must have bit into his own lip when Billy-Bob Cannon struck him earlier. He looked at the Lieutenant with embarrassment, and stood there while he explained what had happened.

"The rebel Sergeant went back up the hill, sir," said the Private, after telling his officer about the rescue. "The prisoners rode off back up the mesa. They ain't been gone too long."

"At ease, Private," said the Lieutenant, showing some compassion for the young soldier's predicament and handing him his water bottle. "Think yourself lucky that they didn't kill you too." He looked at his men, who had gathered round to hear what the Private had to say.

"Come on, men," he said, walking towards his horse. "Let's catch those murdering bastards. We can't let them get away with this." He mounted up and the others did the same, as he spurred his horse up onto the mesa. They had with them an Indian scout, who had no trouble in following the tracks left by the fleeing men.

Joel and the posse rode steadily south along Glorieta Mesa, away from the sound of battle. It was the final day of the Battle of Glorieta Pass and the noise of exploding ammunition made them look back as thick smoke rose up in the distance.

Union Major John Chivington had sent his men down a steep bank from the mesa to burn the Confederate supply wagons and run off the mules and horses. Eighty Confederate wagons, and the supplies they contained, were destroyed, and most of the mules and horses were stampeded up a narrow canyon. Only a few Confederate guards and teamsters managed to escape towards Santa Fe. The loss of so much supplies and ammunition were a decisive turning point in the battle.

Tex turned to Joel, as they all slowed down to look at the conflagration that was happening back at Glorieta Pass.

"I think we got away just in time, by the sound of all that. I reckon that they'll be too busy to follow us now. "

"You're probably right, Tex," replied Joel. "But we still need to be careful. If any Union soldiers find us, they ain't gonna be too happy about us killing their own men."

They slowed their horses down to a steady trot, not wanting to tire out their mounts, dividing the small amount of food that they had saved, and eating as they rode across the mesa. After a hurried discussion with Hootie and Banjo, they decided to head south-east towards the Pecos River and try and put the river between themselves and anyone who may be following them.

That afternoon, a late winter snowstorm fell in the area of the pass and the posse were caught up on the fringe of it, and as they were resting their horses, they came under fire from the Union cavalry who were chasing them. As they quickly mounted up Banjo and Tex were hit by a fusillade of rifle fire from their pursuers. Banjo was only slightly wounded in the arm, but Tex fell off his horse, hit by three deadly .58 caliber Minie balls, fired by Union sharpshooters. They were in an area of large rocks and boulders, and the fall compounded Tex's injuries, as he fell to the ground, badly wounded.

They all dismounted and took cover behind some boulders, and returned the fire, while Joel bent over his friend, who was lying on his back, bleeding heavily from his wounds.

"Are you hurt bad, Tex? Can you ride?" Joel said, looking down at him, already knowing the answer to his questions.

"It sure feels bad, Joel," Tex said, in a quiet voice, coughing as he spoke, staining Joel's coat with flecks of blood. "I don't reckon I'll be able to ride any time soon, so you'll just have to carry on without me, my friend."

"We ain't leaving without you, Tex," said Joel as bullets ricocheted off the nearby boulders, the others firing back at the Union soldiers, the sound of Banjo's old hunting rifle booming out nearby.

"Don't be foolish, Joel," said Tex, as Joel helped him into a sitting position. "I've been hit in the back and my leg's shattered. I'm done for, and you know it, and don't you be giving me any of your old grandpappy's crap. Leave me here and go, I'll cover you as best I can."

Joel was joined by Billy-Bob, who knelt down and squeezed Tex lightly on his shoulder. He had heard the exchange between Joel and Tex and could see that Tex was dying.

"Tell him, Billy-Bob," said Tex, a bubble of blood forming in the corner of his mouth as he spoke. "It's best this way. I don't want to die an old man lying in bed surrounded by a lot of folk I don't even remember." He paused for a moment, as he took a breath. "I can buy the rest of you some time. Prop me up between those two boulders, and leave me a spare rifle and some ammunition, and I'll keep those blue-bellies busy for the rest of the day." He sagged back, exhausted by the long speech that he had made.

Billy-Bob looked at Joel and nodded. He could see that he was close to tears at the state of his old friend.

"He's right," said Billy-Bob. "He'll be lucky to last more than an hour or two, the state that he's in. It could be our chance to get away."

"Okay," Joel said, reluctantly. "I'll get him a spare rifle and a blanket."

They propped up Tex between two large boulders, facing the Union soldiers, wrapped in a blanket and with a spare rifle and ammunition resting on a rock. He looked up at Joel and smiled, as the others prepared to leave, and reached out to take Joel's hand.

"Look after Young Billy, Joel," he said, looking over at the young cowboy, who was grief-stricken at the sight of his mentor's tragic situation and smiling weakly up at him. "He's still wet behind the ears, but he'll be fine once he's grown a bit more." He suddenly took a shot at one of the Union soldiers, who had crept forward during a lull in the shooting. The man went down and Tex smiled to himself.

"Now get outa here, Joel." Tex paused to take a breath. "One more thing, before you go, tell my Donna that I loved her and that I should have married her." As Joel turned to go, Tex grabbed him by his sleeve. "Leave me the rest of that good whiskey, Joel, and take my horse with you. And cheer up, I'll soon be sharing a camp fire with my old friend, Steve, again."

Joel fetched the whiskey and wedged the bottle between a crack in a nearby boulder, removing the stopper for him, and nodded to his friend and walked, sadly, away. The others were returning fire as they left, leading their horses behind them, and keeping as low as possible. They weaved their way through the tall boulders and, once out of sight, mounted up and rode quietly away, the sound of Tex's rifle fire echoing behind them.

Tex smiled to himself as he saw an Indian scout creeping towards him. He took a long swallow of whiskey, placed the bottle carefully down, and cocked his rifle and shot the man in the head. He picked up the bottle and had another satisfying drink and spit out the blood in his mouth.

I'd better be careful with this whiskey, he thought to himself. *There ain't much left, but it sure eases the pain.* He shot at two more soldiers, wounding them both and making them limp back to the others, keeping them pinned down, unable to chase after the rest of the posse. A bullet took out a piece of rock just above his head, and he ducked back and blinked the dust from his eyes.

Slipping in and out of delirium, mainly from the pain but also from the effects of the whiskey, Tex saw his old friend, Steve, at his side, helping him shoot at the soldiers.

"Come on, Tex old friend, we can beat these damn northerners. Let's give 'em hell," said Steve."

Tex perked up at the sight of Steve and carried on shooting at the soldiers, hitting another one who was foolish enough to stand up in plain sight. He took another sip of whiskey and looked around to offer Steve a drink, but his friend had gone. He shrugged and reached for some more ammunition for his rifle, and the effort made his wounds bleed. As he reloaded his rifle, he looked around and Steve was at his side again, firing the spare rifle.

"I told you I was a better shot than you," he laughs.

"Oh, yeah?" yelled Tex with a fresh energy, emptying his rifle, spitting on his hands, and picking up his pistol. "We'll see about that."

"Did I tell you how good I was with a bow and arrow, back at Painted Rocks?"

"Yes, you did, old friend," Tex said, slurring his words and forcing a smile at Steve.

The Union soldiers were getting closer, and Tex reached for the bottle of whiskey again, but he didn't have the energy left to pick it up. He tried to raise his pistol but sagged back as he began to slip away.

"Come on, Tex," Steve quietly said. "Let it go now, it's time we got outa here. Let's make trail."

"I'm right behind you, pardner, but I don't think I can walk. I'm badly wounded."

"Course you can, Tex, "Steve said as the sound of battle begins to fade around them.

"I'm mighty glad you came back for me, old friend," Tex said, following Steve. "I never wanted to die alone."

"Well, you got that bastard Sheep's Head for me. I'm just returning the favor. After all, there's no greater gift than friendship, old buddy."

Tex smiled and fired his pistol at the approaching soldiers. He suddenly felt a quiet calmness creep over him, as he laid back and died, the smile still on his face.

After not receiving any more return fire from Tex's position for a while, the Lieutenant urged his men forward, and they all move stealthily towards the large boulders. When they reached Tex, the soldiers were surprised to see only one man lying there.

"I thought that there was more than one man shooting at us, by the ferocity of the gunfire that was coming at us," remarked the Lieutenant, as he looked down at the body slumped behind the rocks. He noticed another rifle resting across a boulder, still smoking. "There must have been someone else with this man," he added. "But it looks like he's gone. They sure put up one helluva fight."

The Lieutenant decided, with the evening closing in, to make camp there and try to catch the other men at first light. Out of respect for Tex's courage, in the way that he had held his men at bay, they gave him an honorable burial, wrapping his body with a blanket, and covering him with stones, and wedging his rifle on top, with his hat atop it. The bugler played the last post and the men saluted as the sun went down.

The troop had lost six soldiers, including the Indian scout, with three of the troopers wounded. Two of the soldiers had been killed by Joel and the others before they had left Tex behind.

Chapter 37

Joel and the others had heard the shooting as they rode away, and it seemed to carry on for quite some time, until, probably because of the distance, they couldn't hear it anymore. Pausing to listen, Billy-Bob nodded his head negatively.

"I can't hear anymore gunfire, Joel. I reckon it must be all over."

Young Billy Brand, whose hearing were a lot keener than the others, cupped a hand over one ear and listened, as he sat in the saddle. He sat there for a while as the others looked at him.

"I could still hear gunfire a moment ago," he said. "But it's stopped now. I think Billy-Bob is right, they must have got Tex." He removed his hat and wiped his eyes with the back of a gloved hand. He could hardly speak as he looked at the others, his eyes red. "I sure liked Tex, he was good to me."

"Come on now, Young Billy," Joel said. "He was too badly injured to move. He knew what he was doing. I'll miss him more than you, but that's the way he chose to die." He tapped Young Billy on his shoulder. "Just remember him how he was, and the stories that he used to tell you. You'll have a few tall tales of your own if we get back to Tucson in one piece."

Young Billy nodded, sniffed up his nose, and urged his horse forward. He didn't want the others to see the tears running down his cheeks, and rode ahead of them in silence.

Hootie started to catch up with Young Billy, but Billy-Bob signaled him to leave the young cowboy alone.

They arrived at the banks of the Pecos River as the sun was beginning to set. With the late snows and heavy rain from the mountains, the river was running fast, and they decided to try and find a way to cross in the morning. Young Billy made a fire, and while Hootie and

271

Billy-Bob kept a look out for any soldiers who might be still chasing them, Joel dug the bullet out of Banjo's arm. He bandaged the old French trapper's wound, the best he could, and fashioned him a sling with a spare belt from one of the saddlebags.

"How's that, Banjo? It should hold 'til we get back. You could do with a couple of stitches in the wound, but, as Tex would tell you, my sewing ain't up to much."

Banjo grunted something, which Joel assumed was an expression of gratitude, and reached for his snuff box with his good hand and handed it to Joel.

"Would you put some snuff on the back of my hand, *mon amie*? I cannot do it myself with my arm strapped up."

Joel duly obliged, and Banjo sniffed up the brown powder, replaced the box in his pocket, and wiped his beard with his sleeve.

"I'm afraid that Tex didn't like me using snuff. He always made a fuss if I took it near him." The Frenchman sighed. "But I would give the habit up if he was still here."

"I know, Banjo," said Tex, lighting a cigarette from the fire. "It's been one hell of a day. Let's get some shuteye. Perhaps, it'll be a better day in the morning."

They were up before first light. Joel and Young Billy had relieved Billy-Bob and Hootie in the night and kept watch until the morning, although Joel had seen that Young Billy had been asleep a couple of times but hadn't the heart to wake him. They all sat drinking coffee and looking down at the fast-flowing river.

"I ain't seen the Pecos as bad as this before," Hootie said, watching as a large tree swept past.

"Well, I figure that we've got two choices," said Joel. "Stand and fight, or swim with the horses across the river." He paused to light his first cigarette of the day, and passed his fancy tobacco pouch to Billy-Bob, as he looked across at the far bank. "I sure don't fancy the river much, I had a belly full of swimming in the Salt River, last year, but we don't know how many soldiers are chasing us."

"I'm for chancing the river, Joel," said Billy-Bob. "If we can get that stretch of water between us and those Union soldiers, then I reckon they'll give up the chase.

The others nodded in agreement to Billy-Bob and began to saddle up their horses.

They found a way down to the riverbank, a few yards further upstream, and Billy-Bob urged his horse into the water, Young Billy just behind him. Billy-Bob looked round at Young Billy, who was looking at the fast-flowing water with fear in his eyes.

"Come on, Young Billy. Did I tell you about the time I crossed the Rio Grande with Captain Rip Ford and the Texas Rangers? It was in the middle of a storm in the night. This is just a little stream compared to that."

He heard Young Billy urging his horse forward to catch up with him and smiled. He knew the young cowboy was a sucker for a good story, and hoped it would take his mind off the roaring river.

"Keep up, boy," Billy-Bob yelled, above the sound of the roaring waters. "Let's get to the other side, and I'll tell you some more, about Rip Ford."

Hootie followed next, keeping an eye on Banjo, who was using one hand on his reins, the other arm still in a sling. He had tethered Tex's horse to the cinch of Banjo's mount to help prevent him from falling off, and positioned himself on the other side. He turned to Joel as he entered the river.

"It doesn't look too bad, Joel. Are you coming?"

"Doesn't look too bad? You must be joking. I'll just finish my smoke, Hootie, then I'll be right behind you I want to see how you four get across first."

Joel sat on his horse, its hooves in the shallows, watching the other four men's progress in the river. He hadn't been lying when he had said that he didn't like the idea of crossing the river, and the memory of his time spent drifting, naked, down the Salt River, in the middle of a storm, in the night, chased by apaches, brought all his latent fears to the front of his mind.

His horse, Clover, moved nervously about in the shallows, sensing the anxiety in its rider, as Joel waited to see how the others fared in the fast-flowing river. Billy-Bob and Young Billy had reached the middle of the river, and the other two were close behind them, their horses swimming in the deep water, as they drifted downstream. The horses were frantically kicking their legs, as their riders urged them towards the far bank.

For every couple of feet that they gained across the river, the horses were pulled another foot downstream, and suddenly as Billy-Bob's horse hit a deep undercurrent, it was spun around and it reared up in the water, unseating its rider. Billy-Bob yelled as he fell backwards into the cold water, and he tried to swim against the current, weighed down by his clothing and boots. He came to the surface, coughing and spitting out water, as he tried to grab his horse's mane and missed. As he was pulled by the current, Young Billy leaned over in the saddle and grabbed him by his collar, keeping a tight grip, and urging his horse towards the riverbank. Billy-Bob's horse, now free of its rider, swam quickly towards the bank, and as its hooves found the gravelly riverbed, it reached the shallows and made its way out, snorting and stamping at it stood on dry land.

Young Billy dug his heels into his horse's flanks, and the young, strong mare found the shallows, and followed Billy-Bob's horse up the shallow bank. The young cowboy, his arm aching from holding on to Billy-Bob, released him and the ex-Texas Ranger was dumped unceremoniously in the shallows. Still holding on to his hat, Billy-Bob staggered to his feet and, as Hootie and Banjo came up beside him, he grabbed hold of Hootie's stirrup and was pulled out of the river.

They all dismounted and looked back across the river to where Joel was still sitting astride his horse, trying to summon up the courage to follow them. Hootie yelled something to Joel, but with the sound of the river and the distance, his voice was lost to him. Billy-Bob was busy trying to light a fire, to get himself dry, as Young Billy joined Hootie in shouting and waving.

Joel shrugged, wondering what they were yelling for. He wasn't in a hurry to get wet, so reached into his pocket for his makings, to have another smoke before he followed the others, and he suddenly remembered that he had given his fancy tobacco pouch to Billy-Bob.

Damn, he thought. *I hope Billy-Bob has kept my tobacco dry. I suppose I'd better get over there if I want another smoke.* He sighed, not looking forward to the trip across the river.

As he urged Clover forward into the river, he suddenly understood why Hootie and Young Billy were yelling at him, as he heard the sound of hooves, heading towards him, and he touched the horse's flanks with his spurs to move it on into the flowing river.

Reaching the deep water his horse began to swim, and Joel looked behind him to see a troop of blue-coated soldiers, standing on the riverbank, pointing their rifles in his direction.

Joel heard shots as he reached the deep fast-flowing torrent, and bullets hit the water to one side of him. Cursing, he slid off his horse and grabbed the mare's tail, as he went low in the water to make himself less of a target, allowing Clover to pull him through the torrent.

On the far bank, Billy-Bob and Young Billy fired their rifles at the soldiers, but the distance was too far to cause them any problems, and they just stood and laughed as they carried on shooting at Joel, who was bobbing about in the current.

There was a loud shot from the far bank, as Hootie fired his old long rifle at the soldiers. He had cradled his buffalo gun in a low branch of a tree, to steady his aim, and he let out a loud owl hoot has his bullet found its mark, knocking one of the soldiers to the ground. Banjo handed his own Sharps long rifle to Hootie, as he wasn't able to fire it with his arm in a sling, and Hootie took steady aim and pulled the trigger, hitting another Union soldier in his leg and making the others fall back behind some trees.

Joel lost his grip on his horse's tail, his wet gloves slipping, and he tried to swim for the far bank, as Clover was pulled downstream in the fast current. Gasping for breath in the cold water, he kicked out but couldn't make any headway and realized that he was going to follow his horse down the river but was suddenly caught in a current that pulled him back to the bank that he had just left. He drifted to the shallows and paused in the water, on his hands and knees, as two Union soldiers came walking towards him, and dragged him roughly out of the river.

Billy-Bob and the others watched impotently, from across the river, as Joel was pulled out of the water and taken prisoner.

"We've got to help him," said Young Billy, watching as Joel was surrounded by the soldiers.

"He should have crossed when we did," Billy-Bob said to Young Billy, standing near the fire holding his pants to dry. "There's no way that we can get back across that river and try to rescue him."

He cussed to himself and picked up some tobacco that he had managed to dry by the fire and rolled himself a cigarette, and looked at the fancy leather tobacco pouch that was on the blanket next to his wet clothing.

"I've still got Joel's makings. He's going to be in need of a smoke where they're taking him."

"That's unless they just go and shoot him," commented Banjo, gazing across the wide river.

They all rested for most of the day but kept watch across the river, in case they were surprised by any more Federal troops. Hootie had managed to kill a small deer and they had ate their fill while their clothing, and equipment dried.

While keeping watch, Young Billy heard a sound in the bushes and alerted the others. Something—a man, or large animal—was approaching from down river, and they all leveled their rifles towards the noise, in case a Union soldier had managed to cross the river. Billy-Bob let out a shout as he recognized Joel's horse, Clover, and he whistled her over to him. She looked wet and caked with mud, her front leg bleeding from a graze on its fetlock, but she let out a snort as Billy-Bob approached her and nuzzled him with her nose.

"Good girl," said Billy-Bob, pleased to see Joel's horse. "I thought we'd seen the last of you."

Billy-Bob led the horse over to the fire, removed the saddle and saddle bags, and rubbed it down with some damp grass. The wound on its leg was superficial, so he let the horse wander off, and it rolled in the grass, nickering as it got to its feet.

"At least, they didn't get Joel's horse," said Banjo, watching Clover grazing. "We'll have to take it back with us to Tucson. Just in case Joel gets back."

Young Billy stood looking sadly across the river. In the course of two days he had lost both of the men that he had looked up to, Tex had died and Joel was a prisoner of the Union army.

They headed south the following morning and found a shallow ford in the Pecos River, about 20 miles downstream, which allowed them to cross without getting too wet. The journey back to Tucson was a somber affair, as although they had killed all the jailbreakers, they were returning with some of their posse killed, and Joel a prisoner of the Union army.

Billy-Bob led them back, with Hootie and Banjo retracing the route that they had taken on the way up from Tucson. They traveled at a slower pace than when they had been chasing Shreeve Moor and his band of outlaws, although Billy-Bob couldn't wait to get back to Julie and the twins. He had decided that he was finished with the hard riding, fast shooting, and sleeping outdoors, although to cheer up Young Billy, he still told his stories, somewhat exaggerated, about his time in the border country, fighting Indians and outlaws, with Captain 'Rip' Ford and the Texas Rangers.

One evening, sitting around a warm fire, Hootie and Banjo smoking their pipes, and Billy-Bob finishing off the last of Joel's tobacco, Young Billy asked him why he was called 'Rip.'

"Well," said Billy-Bob. "His real name is John Salmon Ford and when he was in the Mexican War with the Texas Mounted Rifles, he got the nickname 'Rip' for sending out official death notices with the citation 'Rest in Peace' written at the top."

Young Billy cheered up, a little, as he listened, and Hootie agreed that he had heard the story before, and it was true.

"I heard that Rip Ford has got a commission in the Confederate army and is off to fight in the war. I did think about joining him, but my Julie wouldn't let me go. She only let me ride with this posse 'cause she thought it would be easy, but it wasn't that easy. I sure hope we get to see Joel again."

The others nodded in agreement, as Hootie turned to Young Billy.

"That man has got more luck than most, Young Billy. He'll be back."

Chapter 38

Tied to a horse, Joel was taken back to Glorieta Pass and handed over to Major John Chivington's unit and put with a group of Confederate prisoners who were marched to the rail head in Colorado, where a stockade had been erected to accommodate the prisoners.

The walk was long and hard, stragglers were beaten, and two soldiers were shot as they tried to escape. One of the cavalry officers, in charge of the escort, took a liking for Joel's fancy spurs and with great reluctance, and the persuasion of a guard's rifle butt, he unbuckled them and handed them over. He was sure going to miss those spurs.

On arrival at the stockade, the prisoners were herded into an old adobe building, adjacent to the guard's quarters, before they were interrogated and processed.

Joel sat with his back to the damp, dirty wall, the better to keep his eyes on the other occupants of the crowded, dark room. Although the prisoners were all on the same side, they would cut someone's throat for a morsel of food, as they hadn't been properly fed since leaving Glorieta—a still warm body was testament to the ruthlessness of this. The poor sod had taken a small piece of weevil infested biscuit from his pocket, thinking that he wouldn't be seen in the gloomy surroundings, and one of the men, who hadn't been properly searched, had killed him with a small, lethal skinning knife and ate his biscuit.

It must have been daylight outside, as the sun shone in a narrow beam through the only small window high up near the ceiling, the dust motes reflecting in its narrow beam, disturbed by the movement of the inmates, as they moved about, trying to find a place to sit in the crowded room.

Joel kept to himself, no one spoke to him, although a few kept looking his way, wondering why he wasn't wearing the grey uniform of the Confederate army, and he wasn't in a hurry for conversation, as he sat thinking about his old friend, Tex.

I've got to get outa here, this ain't my damn war, he thought. *And I must see Donna, and tell her that Tex died bravely.*

He thought of the schoolteacher, Joan, who he had met at Pat's wedding and vowed to get back and see her again. *I could sure do with a smoke,* he thought, feeling in his empty pockets. *I never should have given my makings to Billy-Bob Cannon.*

After a while, he was taken out, under guard, and led to the camp commander's office, where he was pushed roughly through the door and stood with an armed soldier either side of him, in front of a man with a Majors insignia on his uniform. The Major was busy with his head under a towel, over a bowl of steaming water with something soaking in it.

Standing either side of the Major were two sergeants, both craggy looking, older men, with mean looking expressions on their faces. They both looked at Joel, sizing him up, and stepped a pace forward. One carried a short length of thick knotted rope, and the other a heavy army belt with a heavy metal buckle swinging from one end.

One of the guards stamped his feet to attention, and the Major removed his towel and raised his head, and looked at Joel through bleary eyes.

"Who have we got here, then?" the Major asked, talking thickly with the effects of a bad cold. "What rank are you, what brigade were you with?"

"I'm not in any army," said Joel. "I just happened to get caught up in the battle." He was about to tell the Major that he was a deputy Sheriff and remembered that he had removed his badge and tossed it away on the long march after getting a lot of strange looks from the other prisoners.

"Look, I ain't even wearing a uniform," he added, looking down at the Major.

The sergeant with the length of rope suddenly hit Joel across the face with it.

"Don't answer back, you no good piece of southern shit," the sergeant yelled as Joel held his cheek, which had started to bleed. The other sergeant grinned, swinging the belt that was wrapped around his hand, his hands visibly shaking.

"That's no excuse," the Major said, standing up and looking Joel in the eye as he blew his nose on a dirty bandanna. "A lot of you damn rebels haven't got uniforms. You'll rot in here until we've won the war." He nodded to the guards to take Joel away.

As Joel turned to leave, the sergeant who had hit him with the rope, barred his way. He put the rope over his shoulder and reached for the silk scarf that was tied around Joel's neck, showing under his bandanna.

"That's a fine piece of silk you've got there," he said, pulling it from around Joel's neck. "I'll bet you stole it from someone." As the sergeant put the scarf, in his top pocket and pushed him towards the door, Joel saw that the man was missing one of his hands.

As the guard opened the door to take Joel out, the Major spoke again.

"Just be careful in here, boy, and make sure that you behave yourself. This prison is full of psychos and killers, and that's just the guards, especially my two sergeants here, as you can see." He laughed at his joke as the door closed behind Joel.

Joel was led out to the large compound where the prisoners were lining up for a meal, and he went and stood at the back of the line, his stomach rumbling. He couldn't remember the last time that he'd had had a decent meal, and as a prisoner passed him, carrying a plate of slops, he knew that he wouldn't be getting a decent one today.

Men were pushing and jostling each other, as Joel reached the front of the queue, and he was handed a tin plate filled with some greasy stew, and a cup of strong coffee. He looked at the meal and decided that, if he was going to stay alive then he must try and eat it.

He took his food over to the edge of the compound, past a group of men who were fighting each other; the guards seemed to ignore the fracas, letting the prisoners sort out their own grievances. Joel didn't want to get involved in their petty squabbles and found a reasonably quiet place, near the fence, and put his tin plate and cup on the ground, and was about to sit down when a commotion nearby made him look round.

A buckskin clad man, a few years older than Joel, was squatting down against the fence, with two men, in Confederate uniforms, standing over him. One of the men was waving a small knife at the man, and the other soldier was waving his fist in the man's face.

"Give us that plate of food mister." The man with the knife said. "We need it more than you. You don't look like a soldier, and I'll bet you were never in any battle."

His colleague kicked the man in his thigh, making him wince, but he kept hold of his tin plate, as he fell back against the fence, the two men still looming over him.

Joel, sighed and walked over and came up behind the men and punched the man with the knife, hard, in his kidneys. The man groaned and dropped the knife, and stumbled, as the other man turned around to face Joel, bringing his fists up, ready to fight him. He suddenly fell to his knees, kicked in the back of his legs by the man in buckskins, who had got to his feet and joined in the fight. He punched the man in the face, as Joel prepared to hit the other man again, but the fight had gone out of him, and he skulked away, bending down to retrieve his knife from the ground.

Joel put his boot on the knife and looked the man in the eye.

"Don't even think about it," he said, standing a good few inches taller than the weasely-looking prisoner. "Now clear off and leave us alone."

The man moved away, followed by his friend, who had got to his feet holding his bloody nose. They both glared at Joel, as they shuffled back to the other side of the prison compound, and Joel handed the knife to the man who had been threatened.

"Thanks for that, my friend," the buckskin clad man said, holding his other hand out to Joel. "I can eat my food in piece now. Sit down and join me. The name's Harley White."

Joel went back to fetch his tin of food and cup of coffee, and discovered that they were gone. He shrugged his shoulders and went and sat down with his new friend.

"Some bastard has taken my food," he said, returning to Harley White, and sitting on the ground next to him. "And I ain't even got me a cigarette to smoke."

"Well you're welcome to share my grub, although it ain't that appetizing," said Harley, reaching into his large fringed coat and taking out his makings. "I've got plenty of tobacco though," he added, passing Joel his pouch.

Joel declined the food, but gratefully accepted the makings and rolled himself a cigarette. He sat smoking and looked at the other man.

"The name's Joel Shelby," he said, handing the makings back to Harley, and blowing smoke down his nostrils. He told Harley how he had been in a posse, chasing outlaws, and was captured at Glorieta after they had killed the last of the outlaws.

"If I hadn't been too cautious about crossing the Pecos River, I wouldn't have been taken prisoner, and I'd have been on my way back to Tucson by now."

"Well," said Harley White, rubbing the scar that ran down from his left ear, disappearing into his ragged beard. "I had similar bad luck." He put the last lump of food into his mouth, chewed a couple of times, and turned his head and spit it out through the fence. "Just be grateful that you had your slop stolen, Joel. It's like chewing a Buffalo's private parts."

"I'll have to take your word for that," laughed Joel. "But I'm so hungry I could eat the soles of my boots."

"As I was saying," said Harley, "I happened to be at Glorieta Pass, delivering some fresh horses to Kozlowski's Stage Stop, when the battle started. I tried to get away from the fighting but was stopped by some Union soldiers." He paused to make a cigarette, and handed the makings to Joel again. "Because I hail from Texas they thought I was with the Confederate force. They took all the money I had made from the sale of the horses, and brought me here. I've been here for about three days."

"Well, I ain't going to rot in this place," Joel said. "There must be a way out of here?"

"If you can find a way out, then I'm right with you," said Harley, pushing the small knife that his attacker had dropped down his boot. "But this fence is patrolled day and night, by armed guards, and there's a watchtower at each corner of the stockade," he added, pointing at one of the towers. "There's also one at the main gate, and that's manned day and night."

Harley looked at the fresh cut on Joel's cheek, which he was lightly rubbing with his bandanna. "I see that you've met the two sergeants, then?"

He told Joel that they were named Bob Summers and Eric Foley, known throughout the prison as Bob the Sod, and Eric the Trembler. They were army veterans and had both been wounded in one of the first battles of the civil war, and had been taken out of active service to help set up prison stockades, and look after captured soldiers; although their notion of looking after prisoners was hard discipline and starvation.

Bob the Sod had only one hand, the other removed by a confederate cavalryman's sword, and Eric the Trembler suffered with the effects of being caught in an enemy artillery barrage, and had the permanent shakes, hence the nickname Eric the Trembler.

"Well," said Joel. "That bastard with one hand took my silk scarf that a lady friend of mine gave me."

Just before evening, the main gates were opened and a steam locomotive slowly chugged in, stopping at the end of the line against the buffers, near the guard's quarters. There were three old freight wagons behind it, which were carrying some more Confederate prisoners, and fresh supplies of food and ammunition. The prisoners were ordered out and taken to be interrogated by the Major and his two sergeants.

Joel and Harley watched the proceedings from the fence, and Joel turned to Harley with a smile.

"I've got me an idea, Harley. Perhaps, we could hide under one of those freight wagons when they are taken back out. If we hid between the wheels and the floor of the wagon, then we wouldn't be seen."

"I think they are called bogies, Joel, but we'd never make it. The train usually leaves after dark, and you could easily hang on to the gaps in the floorboards, and not be seen, but they search under the wagons before they leave. A prisoner tried it before I came here, and I was told that he was killed for his troubles. I'll show you what happens when it leaves, later on."

Joel and Harley moved away from the train, to a place where they could watch without raising suspicion.

As night was falling, and the guards lit torches around the fence, and the perimeter guards were doubled, the locomotive driver and his mate fired up the boiler ready to leave. The driver tooted his whistle, and the guards opened the gates that straddled the railway line, and there was a sudden barking and growling as a soldier walked down each side of the train, holding a large, fierce dog on a long chain. There was a hush amongst the prisoners, who watched in anticipation of what might happen, as the dog sniffed near the dark underside of the wagons, straining against the taut chain, as the guard held it in check.

As the dog reached the last freight wagon, it began to growl louder, lips drawn back to expose its vicious teeth, as it pulled against the chain restraining it. The guard smiled to himself, and bent down to remove the chain from the dog's collar, and stood back as it ran under the wagon. There was a scream from below the wagon as the large dog dragged a man out of his hiding place. The guard pulled the dog away from the prisoner, who was bleeding badly from a wound in his thigh, and a sudden shot rang out as Bob the Sod shot the man in his other leg.

"That'll teach you," the sergeant said as the prisoner lay wailing in pain. He looked around at the group of prisoners, who were standing watching, holding his still smoking pistol. "I've told you before, there's only one way out of here, and that's in a wooden box. Now take him to the hospital, and get away from here, before I shoot another one of you damn rebels."

The prisoners quickly dispersed, two of them carrying the unfortunate man away, but not before they had thoroughly searched him for any food or other useful items he may be carrying.

Harley White turned to Joel. "See what I mean, Joel. It would be foolish to try and get out that way," They walked back to the fence and sat down, and Harley passed the makings over to Joel, who gratefully accepted them and rolled himself a cigarette.

"I'll pay you back for your kindness when we get out of this damn place," Joel said, handing the tobacco pouch back to Harley.

"There's no need for that, Joel. You helped me when those two thieves tried to take my food. And you sure need a friend in this damn place," he paused to strike a match. "And I should forget any ideas about escaping on that train. It's far too risky,"

Joel nodded, lost in thought, as he sat looking at the train as it moved away from the prison, fire from its smokestack silhouetting the guard in the tower, as the other guards locked the gates.

"We'll see," he said, smoking his cigarette in the darkness, and scratching his ear. "As my old grandpappy used to say, 'A quitter never wins, and a winner never quits.'"

Joel heard later, from another prisoner, that the train came to the prison about once a week, to bring supplies, and sometimes fresh prisoners, and he was also informed by one of the guards that all the prisoners would be moving up north very soon, to a larger, more secure, prison camp, so he decided that he would have to make plans to escape as soon as possible.

After a lot of thought, and walking around near the rail head and kitchens, for a couple of days, Joel had decided on his plan of escape and sat outside one morning in the prison compound, and asked Harley what he thought about it. When Joel had finished quietly explaining the details to Harley, he sat and waited while his new friend pondered over the problem. Suddenly Harley burst into laughter, tears running down his cheeks, as some of the inmates, who were close by stared at him.

"What's so funny, Harley? Don't you think it will work?"

"I'm sorry, Joel," Harley said, wiping his eyes with the back of his hand. "It's just plain suicide what you figure on doing. And I ain't sure that it will work. But we don't have any other options, and as you said before, 'a winner never quits,' and I want to get back to my wife and kids, down south, so yes, I'll give it a go."

"Well, as my old grandpappy used to say, 'You've got to know how to put the extra into ordinary,'" Joel said, pleased that Harley had agreed to his plan. "It'll be easy, trust me."

Harley patted his boot. "If that dog gets anywhere near me, I'll cut its damn throat with this knife before it gets a chance to sink its teeth into my legs."

Harley had come up from El Paso, where he lived with his wife and two sons. He bred horses and supplied the stagecoach stops with fresh horses every few months. His last delivery had been at Kozlowski's stage stop, at Glorieta Pass, and not realizing that the civil war was active in those parts, he had spent the night there and was captured on the first day of the battle.

Joel's plan was for them both to hide under the freight wagon nearest to the locomotive, as it got dark, and hang below the floor, above one of the bogies. First, they would cover themselves in mud to throw off their scent from the dog that came sniffing below the wagons, and secondly, they would get a dead mule deer from the nearby kitchen, and put it below the last wagon—Joel had seen a couple of mule deer hanging outside the kitchen, ready for the guard's meals. When the dog pulled the deer out from under the wagon, the guard would think it had been trapped there, on route down the line and, hopefully, not bother to look any further under the wagons.

Joel and Harley were kept busy over the next couple of days, collecting small lengths of fence wire, while no one was looking, and wrapping them around their waists. The wire would help support them under the freight wagon. They also found a few large nails, which they thought may be useful in their escape. Joel had suggested that they should save some food for the journey, if they were lucky enough to get out of the prison camp without being seen, but Harley rejected the idea as he thought that the dog's strong sense of smell would detect any food they carried, and they would be discovered.

Three days later, an hour before nightfall, the locomotive slowly steamed into the compound, with the usual three freight wagons attached, and a few bedraggled looking confederate soldiers were herded out, and escorted to the Major's office. Joel and Harley looked at each other in anticipation and positioned themselves nearby, out of sight of the guards, and waited for it to get fully dark.

They had one scary moment when the guard with the big dog walked around the train, and the dog suddenly stopped and went into a barking frenzy. Joel and Harley froze when the guard let his dog off the chain, both preparing to run if it chased them, but it ran in the opposite direction, chasing after something that had gone to ground in the large pile of logs that was for the locomotives fuel. They both breathed a sigh of relief when the guard shouted his dog and took it back inside, attached to its chain, and they settled down, waiting for things to go quiet again.

"Are you ready for this? Harley," whispered Joel as night began to fall.

"I was born ready," answered Harley, preparing himself for Joel's crazy escape plan.

They both watched as the two sadistic sergeants patrolled around the train, looking for any prisoners who were still hanging around. Bob the Sod was swinging his piece of thick, knotted rope with his good hand, and Eric the Trembler had a pistol in one hand and a flaming torch in the other. It was obvious to any onlooker which one of the sergeants was carrying the torch, as the light it cast, moved and flickered as they walked about.

The light from Eric the Trembler's torch exposed a prisoner hanging around the freight wagons, and Bob the Sod caught the man with his ropes end, sending him scurrying back to one of the prisoner's huts.

The two sergeants laughed, finished their patrol, and headed for the warmth of their quarters, as Joel and Hartley watched them go from their dark hiding place.

Chapter 39

Joel and Harley waited until the guards, who were patrolling around the train, were both on the other side, talking to the driver and his mate, in the steam locomotive. They quickly pushed the dead mule deer, which Joel had stolen from outside the kitchen, below the last freight wagon and quietly positioned themselves below the first wagon, above the bogie, but not before they had covered themselves in mud. They attached the lengths of fence wire through the boards and hung there, waiting for the driver and his mate to fire up the locomotive and the guard with the dog to start his patrol. This would be the riskiest part of the escape and, even though there was a chill in the night air, they both began to sweat.

Suddenly, the night sky turned even darker, as it began to rain, not normal rain but a heavy downpour, the likes of which Joel hadn't witnessed since he had been tied up on the banks of the Salt River, the year before. Joel shuddered at the memory and looked at Harley, who he could barely see in the dark, just his eyes reflected in the sudden light as a flash of lightning lit up his muddy face.

They heard one of the guards yelling above the noise, to the driver and his mate, trying to persuade them to come back with them to the guard's quarters.

"Come on, boys," yelled one of the guards. "You won't be leaving here tonight. Not in this weather. There's a hot meal and a warm bunk waiting inside the barracks."

Joel and Harley heard running feet nearby, as the four men dashed past in the storm, splashing through the mud at the side of the track.

"What about getting the dog out to search under the wagons," yelled one of the guards, as he paused at the end of the train.

"It'll wait," shouted the other guard. "If there's anyone still hiding under there come the morning, they'll be in a right sorry state. Come on, let's get out of this storm, we'll look in the morning."

They ran to the guard's quarters and slammed the door behind them, leaving Joel and Harley suspended below the freight wagon, rain dripping on them through holes in the floorboards, streaking their mud coated faces, and making them shiver as the cold wind gusted under the wagons.

Harley, his arms aching from hanging below the wagon, let go his hold and dropped the short distance to the railway sleepers.

"We can't stop here all night, Joel," he said, rubbing the feeling back into his hands. "I remember you saying it would be easy. We might as well give it up and try and sneak back inside."

"No, I think that I said it's not going to be easy, but I ain't giving up yet, Harley, I've got another idea," Joel said, landing at the side of Harley.

"Well I hope it's a darn sight better idea than the last one."

"I didn't know it was going to rain, did I? Come on, follow me, I'll get us out of this prison if it kills me."

"It probably will," yelled Harley above the noise of the storm, as he followed Joel from under the wagon.

"Watch out for the guard in that watchtower," Joel said, turning to Harley. "Although I don't reckon that he'll be able to see much in this storm."

Joel waited for a flash of lightning, and as it went dark again he quickly climbed up to the footplate of the locomotive, and as Harley prepared to follow Joel, there was a sudden movement behind him.

"Where the hell do you think you're going? Johnny Reb," said Bob the Sod, a pistol held in his good right hand. "Thinking of leaving us, are you? Well, you'll hang for this in the morning. But only after I've beaten the shit out of you first, come on."

As Bob the Sod turned Harley around, prodding him with his pistol, Joel leapt from the locomotive, landing on the sergeant's back, and stabbed him between his shoulder blades with the long nail that he gripped in his right hand.

Bob the Sod grunted as the nail went through his thick great-coat, and pierced his flesh. He shrugged Joel from his back, more surprised than hurt, and started to turn around to see who had attacked him. Harley quickly pulled the small knife from his boot and thrust it between the sergeant's ribs, making him drop his pistol as he fell to the ground wounded.

Before Bob the Sod could shout for help, Harley cut the man's throat and stood over him, looking at Joel.

"What are we gonna do with him? We can't stuff him under the train, they'll find him in the morning and then search for us."

Joel looked down at the body of the sergeant, as a lightning flash lit up the scene, and thunder sounded overhead, the heavy rain washing the man's blood under the tracks. He pointed to the nearby large heap of logs.

"We'll hide him under that lot. Come on, let's hope the other sergeant isn't still around."

They picked up the body of the sergeant and struggled over to the log pile with him, which luckily was shielded from the watchtower by the freight wagons, and carefully removed some logs and placed him in the hole, and replaced the logs. Before they covered the sergeant's body, Joel reached into the man's top pocket and retrieved his silk scarf, smiled to himself, and put it in his own pocket.

They waited for the next flash of lightning, to make sure that Bob the Sod was hidden from view, and ran back to the locomotive, quickly climbing the metal steps to the footplate.

Joel stood on the footplate dripping water, looking around at the various levers and handles that were displayed in the short interval of another lightning flash.

"Don't tell me that you're thinking about getting this engine going, and getting us out of here?" Harley said, wiping the rain from his eyes with the back of his wet sleeve.

"No, I ain't Harley. I don't know the first thing about steam engines. I can't see these noisy contraptions replacing the horse. I don't think they'll catch on at all." He put his face close to Harley's ear, so that he could be heard above the noise of the rain on the locomotive's metal roof, and the howling of the wind as it blew through. He pointed to the tender behind the cab, which held the logs and coal for the firebox.

"We're gonna hide ourselves amongst all that fuel back there, Harley. Bury ourselves, well-hidden below it, just like Bob the Sod back there but not too deep, just deep enough so we won't be seen when morning comes."

Harley smiled to himself in the darkness, and clapped Joel on his back.

"I like it, Joel. It's better than hanging below that freight wagon, waiting for that vicious dog to find us; and find us it would. Come on let's get on with it before this storm finishes, and the guards start patrolling again."

They both climbed into the tender and moved to the rear, pulling coal and logs to one side and forming a hole in the pile of fuel, stopping every time there was a flash of lightning in case they were seen. After deciding that they had formed a deep enough hole, Harley and Joel climbed into the depression that they had made, and pulled the coal and wood over themselves, until they were, hopefully, hidden from view by anyone who happened to look inside the tender.

They both settled themselves down for an uncomfortable night in the fuel tender, lying on sharp lumps of coal, and wood, wet from the rain and covered in coal dust, as the storm raged around them.

* * * * * *

Joel was suddenly woken up, from his fitful slumber, by voices and noises nearby. He touched Harley on his shoulder, and put a finger to his lips, as he opened his eyes. Harley nodded that he understood, and they lay there not moving, both suddenly realizing that it was morning, as daylight filtered through the coal and wood, above them. The storm had abated, but it was still raining hard, and they could hear someone shoveling fuel from the front of the tender, presumably to feed the fire that would heat the boiler up for the steam to power the engine.

As the stoker shoveled fuel into the firebox, it caused a sudden movement in the mass of coal and logs, which Joel and Harley were lying in, making them both slide forward, nearly exposing their hiding place. The movement of fuel stopped as the stoker decided that he had put enough into the firebox, and there was a clanging noise has he closed the door.

Joel and Harley breathed a sigh of relief, as they lay there, still covered by coal and logs, but not as deep as before, as they heard shouting, and a dog barking nearby.

The guard was patrolling along the side of the wagons, allowing his dog to sniff below them, when it starting to growl and pull on the long chain attached to its collar. He released the chain and the dog scrambled below the last wagon, snarling and barking as it dragged something out from between the wheels. The guard ran forward to see if his dog had found a prisoner, who had been hiding below the wagon, and laughed when he realized what it was. Eric the Trembler came to join him, and they both looked down at the body of a mule deer.

"It must have been caught under the wagon down the line somewhere." The sergeant said, pulling the dog away from the carcass. "There's nothing else under there."

The other guard waved to the soldiers at the main gates, and they began to open them, as the engine driver leaned out of his cab and spoke to one of the guards. He tooted his whistle and reversed the steam engine slowly out of the compound, making the tender, with its load of fuel, shake and shudder as its buffers connected with the wagons. Joel and Harley lay there partly exposed by the train's movement, as it passed through the gates, and below the guard's tower. They remained perfectly still, trying to blend in with the coal and logs, hoping that the man in the watchtower wouldn't see them, but he was too busy trying to keep out of the rain, and quickly ducked back as the locomotive belched thick grey smoke from its smokestack, shrouding him in a dense cloud of vapor and soot.

The gates were closed as the train moved away from the prison, picking up speed as it rolled through the open country, heading west, with Joel and Harley lying uncomfortably in the wet fuel, rain soaking their already wet clothing, but both grinning at each other, knowing that they had made it.

* * * * * *

Back at the Union prison, the guards were examining the remains of the dead mule deer, and one of them called over the camp cook to see if he wanted to use it in his kitchen.

"I'm already missing one of the deer that I left hanging outside the cookhouse," the cook said, pulling on a coat to keep off the rain. "And I reckon this is it." He pointed to the deer's legs which were still tied together. "Look, it's still got the rope on its legs that I hung it up with."

Sergeant Foley turned to the guard. "One of the prisoners must have put it there to distract us, while he got away. We'd better have a head count before the Major hears about this. Get all the prisoners out in the yard."

The guards assembled the prisoners, who all stood out in the rain, grumbling, and wondering why they had all been brought outside. After four head counts, each one different to the last one, and a few beatings to keep the men in orderly lines, it was decided the two of the prisoners were missing. The sergeant checked the list and called the guard, who was the dog handler, over to him.

"How did you let them get away?" yelled Eric the Trembler at the guard, who stood there trembling but not trembling as much as the sergeant was. "Now, let that dog off its lead to see if it can find anything."

The guard did as he was ordered and the dog ran around the track where the train had stood, sniffing at the wet ground. It suddenly stopped at the side of the rails, pawing at the ground, and the sergeant went over to see what it had found. It was a pistol, an army service revolver, and Eric the Trembler recognized it.

"That's Bob Summers' pistol, I'd recognize it anywhere. I ain't seen him around this morning. Where the hell can he be?"

The dog was sniffing at the woodpile, and the guard let out a shout.

"Over here Sergeant Foley, I think I've found Sergeant Summers."

Eric the Trembler looked down at the body of his old friend sergeant Bob Summers, a long nail sticking out of his back, and began to tremble and shake with anger.

"They've killed him," he yelled, as some of the prisoners stood watching, pleased that one of the bullies had got his just deserts at last.

"I want six men, armed and mounted in five minutes. They must be on that train. They can't have gone far."

******

A few miles down the track, the fireman, a young black man, started to shovel more fuel from the tender, to feed the firebox, making Joel and Harley slide down the heap towards the footplate. He jumped back in surprise as the two men suddenly leapt onto the footplate, bringing logs and coal down with them, making the driver turn around as he yelled. The driver saw Joel and Harley and reached for the rifle which he kept hanging near the throttle, but Joel was ready for him. He had seen the rifle hanging there the night before, when they had climbed aboard the engine, in the split second when the lightning had flashed.

As the driver put his hand on the rifle, Joel put one arm around the man's neck, and his other hand behind his head, both arms locked together.

"Leave it there, mister. Don't give us any trouble, and we won't give you any."

The fireman still held his shovel in both hands, and he swung it at Joel as Harley seized his wrists, making him drop it as it clanged to the footplate. Joel released the driver and took the rifle as Harley brandished his knife at the two men.

"Where the hell did you two come from? Have you escaped from that Union prison back there?" the engine driver growled, rubbing his throat where Joel's forearm had nearly choked him.

"Yes, we have," Joel said, cocking the rifle to make sure it was loaded and pointing it at the driver and his mate, who had got to his feet and was leaning against the side rail. "Now, just keep this thing moving 'til we tell you otherwise, and we'll get along fine."

Harley picked up the shovel and gave it back to the fireman, and indicated for him to carry on stoking up the fire, which he did, reluctantly, then he went and leant against the rear of the engine with Joel. Grinning at Joel, Harley pulled out his makings, which he had managed to keep dry, and rolled a cigarette, and passed it to Joel.

"I think this calls for a smoke, my friend," he said, making himself a cigarette, and trying to light it with his damp matches. The fireman saw his predicament and opened the door to the firebox and brought out a hot coal on his shovel, and offered it to Harley and Joel. They both lit their cigarettes, keeping an eye on the man in case he turned the situation to his own advantage, but he just tossed the coal back into the fire and closed the door. Harley nodded to the fireman and offered him the makings which he accepted, and then he offered them to the driver. The driver held his hand up and nodded his head in a negative gesture and pulled out a pipe from his pocket and filled it with tobacco. As they all smoked, in silence, the tension seemed to leave the situation, and the rain stopped, as the engine chugged along, leaving the Union prison way behind.

Joel and Harley explained their situation to the two railroad men, and how they had both come to be in the Union prison, and had escaped to get back home. The driver looked at them both, standing on the footplate, soaking wet and filthy with coal dust, and sympathized with their predicament. He picked up an oily rag and opened the firebox door, letting the heat spill out into the draughty cab.

"Dry yourselves near there, boys. You both look like you could do with a good bath, but I can't help you there." He picked up a coffee pot and placed it on a metal shelf near the firebox door. "We'll soon have a hot coffee for you both."

Joel thanked the driver and handed him his rifle back, who nodded and put it back in its usual place.

"Where are you heading?" Joel asked.

"There's a large Union camp towards Durango. We have to get supplies and maybe some more prisoners for the prison back there, so you'd better get off before then. I ain't got any sympathies either way, in this damn war, we just work for the railroad."

"We'll leave you soon, just in case we were missed, and they send some soldiers after us," said Joel, turning around and warming his backside near the firebox.

"They'll be after us as soon as they find that sergeant's body in the woodpile back there," Harley said. "And they'll hang us, for sure, if they catch us. So we'd better think about getting away from this train any time soon."

The driver leant out of the cab and looked back down the track, the way that they had traveled, then turned to look the way that they were heading.

"We should be getting towards a slight upward incline in the rails, pretty soon, and that will slow this old engine down to a walking pace, for a few miles. If there's anybody coming after us on horseback, that's where they'll catch up with us, so you both outa get off before then."

Joel and Harley nodded to the driver and adjusted their ragged clothes, which were now dry, ripped and dirty, but nice and dry from the heat of the firebox.

Chapter 40

Towards noon, the driver slowed the engine down to a walking pace in a valley of green rolling hills, and Joel and Harley jumped to the ground. As the train rolled past them, the driver shouted and they both looked up as he threw his rifle to Joel.

"You may need this more than me. Take care now, and I shan't tell them I saw you when they ask me."

Joel and Harley stood at the side of the track, and they both waved at the two railroad men, who were leaning out of their cab.

Harley looked up at the weak sun, trying to shine through the clouds, and back at the nearby hills. "Come on, Joel, let's get outa here and head south. My wife and kids must wonder why I'm late home."

"I'm right with you," laughed Joel, glad to be free, as they left the railroad tracks behind them.

"Do you know something, Joel?" asked Harley, stopping and looking back at the smoke from the locomotive, as it rose above the trees around a bend. "I gotta admit that I never thought we'd make it back there."

"Well," laughed Joel, clapping Harley on his back. "To tell you the truth, neither did I."

They both laughed as they walked through the long grass, glad to be out of the prison, and heading south for the long trek home.

They walked all day, only stopping towards evening near a stream, fed by a small waterfall gushing from a rock face. Joel managed to shoot a buck rabbit, which Harley skinned and gutted with his knife. Cooking it was a problem as it took them an age to find dry kindling, and nearly another hour to get the fire lit, but once they had it going, they soon roasted the animal with a sharp stick through its body.

Having the pleasure of a full stomach for the first time in over a week, they heaped some wood on the fire and sat back and enjoyed a smoke with some of Harley's last tobacco.

"A mug of coffee would go down a treat, after that rabbit, but we'll have to make do with water from the stream," said Joel, sitting with his back against a tree, hands clasped behind his head. "Now, didn't I tell you that we'd get out of that Union prison?"

"Yes, you did, Joel. But we had a lot of luck on our side back there. As I said before, if we'd have stopped under that freight wagon, I reckon that we would be both be carrying some nasty bites from that dog's teeth."

The next morning, it was a fine sunny day, so Joel and Harley stripped naked and had a good wash under the waterfall, using the juice from a cactus plant as soap. They also washed their dirty clothes and ate the remains of the rabbit for breakfast. They then set off at a fast pace, hoping to put some distance between themselves and the railroad in case they were being followed.

Towards midday, they saw a troop of confederate soldiers riding north but decided to avoid them and hid in a thicket until they had passed by. Sometime later, they came across a ragged bunch of Union soldiers camped in a wooded area, and crept near them, hoping to steal two horses, and maybe some food, as they were both feeling hungry.

Joel checked the rifle that the railroad man had gave him, and saw that there were only three bullets left, so with that, and Harley's knife, they weren't well armed enough for a fight. They lay in the undergrowth, watching the soldiers who were sitting around a fire passing a bottle of whiskey around, and getting louder as the drink took a hold.

There were five soldiers, and from their loud conversation Joel and Harley could tell that they were deserters, and not from the Union prison, and an ill-disciplined bunch, who hadn't even bothered to post a guard, or unsaddle their horses, which were tethered nearby.

As it got dark the soldiers, after finishing one bottle of whiskey and starting another, began to fall asleep, and Joel and Harley decided to make a move. They circled the sleeping soldiers and crawled towards the horses, trying not to startle them as they approached. Joel took off his gloves and rubbed his hand across the nearest horse's muzzle, speaking softly to it, as Harley did the same with another horse. They both silently mounted, as the other horses started to nicker and stamp their hooves, waking one of the deserters who shouted for the others to wake up.

"Something is at the horses," yelled the soldier in the darkness, as the others began to stir.

"Come on, Joel, let's get outa here," said Hartley as he leaned over in the saddle and cut the other horses loose with his knife. Joel let out a yell, scattering the loose horses before them, as a shot rang out, hitting a tree near them. As they rode away through the trees, which was a problem in the dark, another shot was fired and a loose horse in front of Joel was hit, and he swerved his horse to avoid it as it fell.

Harley rode into a low branch which sprung back and hit Joel, who was following behind him, catching him in his chest and nearly unseating him as he struggled to see in the dark. Luckily, it was a bright moonlit night, and as they cleared the woods, they urged their horses into a canter, across a grassy, starlit plain, the two remaining loose horses keeping pace with them.

They could hear shouting and gunfire behind them, back in the woods, but by now they were well out of range, so kept the horses to a slow trot, hoping to avoid any hidden obstacles. Harley seemed to know the way south, as he kept looking up at the night sky and occasionally altering their route.

Reaching a rocky area, they decided to walk the horses and walked side by side, with the two loose horses, which had still been following them, tethered behind them. Harley laughed and tossed his makings to Joel.

"Well, it looks like your luck is still holding out, Joel,"

"It nearly run out, back there," Joel said, making himself a cigarette. "I nearly came off my horse when you swung that tree branch into me."

"Sorry about that but let's ride. It's getting towards dawn and we need to put some miles between us and those soldiers."

"I don't reckon that they'll be moving fast. They shot one of their own horses, and we've got the rest."

They rode hard for most of the morning only stopping when they decided to rest for a while, and check out the saddlebags which were on all the horses. Two of the horses carried rifles and ammunition, and canteens of water were on some of them. There was also salt beef in one of the saddlebags and a small number of Federal banknotes in another.

"It looks like we struck lucky again," Joel said as he pulled out a full bottle of whiskey from one of the saddlebags and tossed it over to Harley.

"Yep, but no tobacco. I reckon I've just enough left for later."

The following day, they reached the Little Colorado River and, much to Joel's delight, found a shallow crossing that hardly wet the horse's fetlocks, and rested for a while on the south side. Harley got out his makings and looked inside his tobacco pouch.

"I reckon, if we're careful, there'll be enough for a couple of smokes before we part company." He passed the makings over to Joel, and looked up at the clear blue sky, and pointed to the distant hills. I'll be heading that way, towards Texas, and El Paso. It's a long ride, but I'll be glad to get back." He lit his cigarette and pulled out the bottle of whiskey. "Here's to us, Joel," he said, taking a long drink and handing the bottle to Joel. "It's been a pleasure to meet you. If you're ever down near El Paso look me up, I've got a place about twenty miles north of the town."

"Well, be careful with those army horses, Harley. If the Union army catches you, they'll think that you've stolen them, which you have. You don't want to see the inside of another Union prison, or get hung for being a horse thief."

Joel tossed his cigarette butt into the shallows and took the reins of his horse, which had been drinking in the river, and handed the whiskey bottle to Harley.

"You'll probably need this on the long ride ahead of you. I'm heading for a friend's place on the Gila River. It's quicker than going to Tucson, and there's a lady who lives near there, who I'd sure like to see again." He handed the reins of his spare horse to Harley. "You might as well take this. I don't need a spare mount. These army horses are okay, but I sure miss my old horse, Clover. I don't reckon I'll see her again."

They shook hands and went their separate ways, and it was with some sadness that Joel rode to Tom Travis' ranch, the death of his good friend, Tex, still fresh in his mind. He pulled out the silk scarf and tied it loosely around his neck and tucked it under his bandanna.

The End

Author's Notes

This book is a work of fiction, and the characters, places, and events are a product of the author's over active imagination. However, some of the people and events, woven into the story, are factual.

Billy-Bob Cannon was often telling the others about the time that he spent in the Texas Rangers under the command of 'Rip' Ford.

John Salmon Ford, known as Rip, served as a Captain in the Texas Rangers in 1849. He also commanded the Confederate forces as a Colonel that won the Battle of Palmito Ranch, the last engagement of the Civil War in 1865.

Alfred Brown Peticolas served as a Sergeant in the 4th Texas Mounted and fought at the Battle of Glorieta Pass—which Joel and the others were unfortunate enough to get involved in. He did walk through the Union lines along Artillery Ridge and carried out his exploits, before returning to the Confederate lines, wearing a stolen enemy greatcoat.

For further information on Sergeant Alfred B Peticolas, the author recommends *Rebels on The Rio Grande: The Civil War Journal of AB Peticolas* by Dr. Don E. Alberts.